To Find You Again

To Find You Again

Maureen McKade

BERKLEY SENSATION, NEW YORK

TO FIND YOU AGAIN

A Berkley Sensation Book / published by arrangement with
the author

PRINTING HISTORY
Berkley Sensation edition

ISBN: 0-7394-4441-7

BERKLEY SENSATION™
Berkley Sensation Books are published by The Berkley Publishing
Group, a division of Penguin Group (USA) Inc.,
375 Hudson Street, New York, New York 10014.
BERKLEY SENSATION and the "B" design
are trademarks belonging to Penguin Group (USA) Inc.

PRINTED IN THE UNITED STATES OF AMERICA

Alan, for your faith and love.

Natasha, for your support and confidence.

And much thanks to Deb Stover, Kathleen Crow, Von Jocks, and Susan Wickberg for your suggestions, critiques, and margaritas.

ONE

"A MAZING grace! How sweet the sound . . ."
The voices of the Sunset Methodist Church members blended with wheezy organ notes to circle Emma Louise Hartwell with its rhythm. Emma's lips moved with the remembered words, but no sound came forth. Although she held her head high, and, aimed at the front of the church, her gaze followed dust motes, which drifted aimlessly through sunlight slanting in between boards covering one of the windows. Next week the shutters would be removed, heralding the church's official recognition of spring.

Emma shuddered as the four walls closed in on her, and her heart pounded like a war drum. She should've waited until next Sunday to make her first public appearance. At least, then, she would have the illusion of freedom as she looked through the glass panes. Now there was only warped wood and shadowed corners, so unlike . . .

No! She didn't dare think about that, not while surrounded by those who had judged and sentenced her even though they didn't know the truth. Of course, if they knew everything, her total condemnation would be assured.

Her attention wandered across the congregation, and

she recognized many people from her childhood. Biddie Little, the organist, who still hit the wrong key at the most inopportune time. Thomas Lyndon, the owner of the Sunset Bank and Trust, who had his nose so high in the air that Emma wondered how he could walk without tripping. Sally Warner, a childhood friend, who was now married to George Orton, another of Emma's classmates, and already with two children—another reminder of the time she'd lost.

A hushed scuffle between the Morrison children caught Emma's attention. The boy and girl were tugging and punching at one another as their parents ignored them.

A Lakota child would never be so disobedient during a religious ceremony. They were taught from infancy to remain quiet and to honor their elders, as well as to revere their traditions and rituals. But then, the Lakota children wouldn't have had to sit on hard benches surrounded by four walls for two hours either. Emma, who'd grown up attending Sunday service, found herself anxious to escape the confinement. However, the intervening years had taught her to remain still and silent, like a mouse when a hawk passed overhead.

The final hymn ended with a concluding groan of the organ, and Emma herself nearly groaned in relief. She wished she could forego decorum and run outside like the children, but this was the first time she'd attended service with her family since her return five months ago. Her mother said they had wanted to spare her the pitying looks. Emma believed her parents wanted to spare *themselves* the town's censure. However, enough time had passed that they hoped for a parcel of acceptance.

Familiar townsfolk greeted John and Martha Hartwell, as well as their fair-haired daughter Sarah, but only a few acknowledged Emma's presence. Even Sally and George, whom she'd known for years, didn't stop to visit with her, but only sent her guarded nods, as if she had a catching disease. Still, Emma could understand their wariness. They had all grown up with the same stories she had heard about the "red devils."

But they hadn't lived in a Lakota village for almost seven years.

Emma followed her family to the doorway where the minister stood, shaking hands with the members of his flock.

"Fine job, Reverend," Emma's father said. He'd spoken those same words to the minister every Sunday that Emma could remember. It was another one of those oddly disconcerting reminders that some things hadn't changed.

"How is Emma doing?" the reverend asked.

Emma bristled inwardly, but kept her outward expression composed and her eyes downcast. They talked about her as if she wasn't standing right beside them. She hated that, but had promised her parents to remain as inconspicuous as possible.

"She's fine, Reverend," Martha Hartwell replied.

Emma risked sneaking a look at her mother and recognized the strain in her forced smile.

"We're thinking of sending her to visit her aunt back in St. Paul," her father interjected.

Emma gasped and opened her mouth to protest, but his warning look silenced her. Her cheeks burned with humiliation and anger. Her parents were going to rid themselves of their embarrassment one way or another. And they hadn't even deemed her important enough to discuss their plans for *her* future. Bitterness filled her and the air suddenly seemed too heavy.

"Excuse me," Emma whispered and stumbled past her sister, her parents, and the minister.

Her face burned from all the looks—pitying, accusing, and morbidly curious—directed toward her, as if she were a wolf caught in barbed wire. Her eyes stung, but she lifted her head high and held the tears at bay with the same stubbornness that didn't let her despair overcome her. She had lived a life that few white women could even imagine. Nobody had a right to judge her.

Nobody.

Although her long skirt and petticoats encumbered her

movements, Emma continued marching down the road, away from the church and the townspeople who now seemed like strangers. She knew her father would be angry and her mother disappointed in her behavior, but they had no right to treat her like a simpleton. She was twenty-two years old and perfectly capable of taking care of herself. Her parents, however, didn't see it that way. They saw a daughter who'd become a blemish on the oh-so-respectable Hartwell name, and it was their responsibility to remove the rot.

The sun's rays were warm, but the breeze chilly as it struck Emma's face and cut through her long cape like it wasn't even there. Her hair, done up in a proper bun beneath her bonnet, escaped its confines and tendrils whipped about her cheeks.

She rounded a bend and her gaze blurred as the tears finally defeated her control. Now that she was out of sight, she surrendered to the anguish twisting in her belly, making her gasp for air. But she didn't slow her pace. She prayed to God and Wakan Tanka, the Great Mystery, to escape the suffocating life that was now hers.

Nobody knew what she had left behind when she was returned—not even her family.

Pain arrowed through her breast and Emma stumbled. A firm hand caught her arm, steadying and shocking her.

"Easy, ma'am."

She whirled around and the stranger released her. The man hastily removed his hat and fidgeted with the brim. He wore brown trousers with a tan buckskin jacket and a red scarf around his neck. Thick, wavy brown hair hung to his shoulders and his dark blue eyes were steady, but guarded. The man's black-and-white pony stood patiently on the road, its reins hanging to the ground.

"I'm sorry if I startled you, ma'am. It's just that I saw you stumbling-like and thought you might be sick."

The man's voice was quiet and husky, as if he didn't use it very often.

Emma's cheeks warmed and she dashed a hand across

them to erase the telltale tear tracks. "No, that's all right. I didn't hear you."

A cool spring breeze soughed through the tree's bare branches and Emma shuddered from the chill beneath the too-light cape.

The man removed his jacket, revealing tan suspenders over a deep blue shirt, and awkwardly placed it over her shoulders. "You shouldn't be out here, ma'am. You'll catch your death dressed like that."

Emma's fingers curled into the soft material and the scent of cured deerhide tickled her nose with memories of another life. She caught herself and tried to hand the jacket back to him. "No. I can't—"

"I'm fine. You're the one who's shivering like a plucked sage hen."

She almost missed his shy, hesitant smile.

Trembling from the cold and from her thoughts, Emma snuggled back into the coat, grateful for the warmth. "Thank you," she said softly. Besides the leather, she could smell woodsmoke, horses, and the faint scent of male sweat in the well-worn jacket. "You're right. It was stupid of me to run off like that."

The man dipped his head in acknowledgment, and his long hair brushed across his shoulders. His gaze dropped to the hat he turned around and around between work-roughened hands. His reticence was oddly comforting.

"Are you from around here?" Emma asked.

"Yes'm. About four miles northwest."

That would make him a neighbor.

The steady clop-clop of hooves directed Emma's gaze to the road. A man dressed in a cavalry hat and pants and a sheepskin coat rode into view. He drew his black horse to a halt.

"I was wondering what happened to you, Ridge," the man said, eyeing Emma like she was a piece of prime rib.

She shivered anew, but this time it wasn't from the cool wind.

"Ease off, Colt," the man called Ridge said without force. "The lady needed some help is all."

"She all right?" the man asked.

"The lady is fine," Emma replied curtly. She'd had enough of people talking about her like she was invisible to last a lifetime.

The clatter of an approaching buckboard put an end to their stilted conversation and Emma's heart plummeted into her stomach when she spotted her father's stormy expression.

The soldier backed his horse off the road as the wagon slowed to a stop beside them.

"Get in, Emma," her father ordered in a steely voice.

Words of refusal climbed up her throat and she swallowed them back. She wouldn't humiliate herself or her family in front of two strangers. With tense muscles, she returned her Good Samaritan's jacket. "Thank you."

She kept her chin raised and her backbone straight as she climbed into the wagon's backseat, which was covered by a thick blanket. Ridge's hand on her arm aided and steadied her until she sat beside her sister.

"Stay the hell away from my daughter, Madoc. She doesn't need the likes of you," her father ordered.

Shocked, Emma only had a moment to give Ridge a nod of thanks before her father whipped the team of horses into motion.

She knew she was in big trouble by the fearful looks her sister kept casting her. Her mother, too, was pale. There would be little mercy from her father for embarrassing the family with her abrupt departure from church, and for her improper actions with the man called Madoc.

A man her father thought wasn't good enough even for her.

RIDGE Madoc kept his anger blunted as he placed his hat on his head and shrugged into his jacket. He caught the lingering scent of the woman's flowery perfume, and his belly coiled with heat. Frowning at his body's instinctive, but unwelcome reaction, Ridge accepted his horse's reins from his friend.

"Did you recognize her?" Colt asked as Ridge vaulted into the saddle without the use of his stirrups.

"Not 'til Hartwell showed up." Ridge shifted, the leather creaking beneath him. "She was the one rescued from the Lakota a few months ago."

"The one everyone's calling a squaw woman," Colt said as they rode toward Ridge's place.

Ridge glanced sharply at his friend, seeing beyond the coolness to the anguish below. Colt's wife had been killed by a band of renegades in Texas four years ago when they'd been stationed down there.

"Might've been better off if she was killed or never rescued at all," Colt added quietly.

Ridge mulled over his friend's words, seeing some truth in them. Miss Hartwell was carrying more than her share of shadowed ghosts. He'd seen them in her pretty brown eyes. But he'd also seen strength and determination in her pint-sized body. Miss Hartwell was a fighter. "Don't you think that's her decision?"

"Would you want her back if she'd been your wife?"

Uncharacteristic impatience made Ridge snap back, "If she was, I'd just be happy she was alive."

"Even if other men'd had her?" Colt's voice was soft, almost gentle.

Ridge ground his teeth together at the thought of Miss Hartwell being forced to submit to such indignity. "It wasn't her fault."

"There's a lot of folks who figure a white woman should kill herself before letting an Indian touch her."

"And there's a lot of Indians who think the same about the *wasicu*."

Colt only grunted a response.

Ridge took a deep breath then let it out slowly, calming

his mind and body the way he'd learned from the People when he was a young man, before he met Colt in the War. Although the two men had been to hell and back together, they disagreed on the Indians' place on the ever-decreasing wilderness. Both had their reasons.

Ridge had spent time with various tribes. He'd even fancied himself in love with a Sioux maiden one time, but he had no horses to gift her parents. In the long run, it had been for the best. Ridge respected most of the Indians he'd encountered, but his path didn't lie with them.

Ridge and Colt rode in silence, which grew more comfortable as they neared Ridge's place. Coming around a rocky bend, Ridge beheld his one-room cabin, which looked small and insignificant in the shadows of the Bighorn Mountains. He'd grown up here, although the rundown building he'd lived in had been burned to the ground by his own hand when he'd returned. Too many memories had been locked in that shack, and most all of them were bad.

"Looks good, Ridge. You must've been working some on it since I been here last," Colt commented, breaking the late morning's hush.

"Added the lean-to at the end for wood and fixed up the barn some so Paint had a dry place out of the weather." Ridge angled a look at his friend. "It's been what, two months?"

Colt shrugged. "I reckon. Army keeps me pretty busy with the growing Indian troubles."

Ridge understood too well. That was one of the reasons he'd quit his job as a scout. The other was this place—it was his now, free and clear. His stepfather had finally died a little over a year ago—Ridge figured meanness had kept him alive when he should've been dead and buried a long time ago. Ridge had only been six years old when his ma married Harry Piner, and twelve when she'd died. Three years later, Ridge'd had enough of his stepfather's violent temper. He had run away and never looked back. Until now.

"So, you gonna put me to work before you feed me?" Colt asked.

"Damned right. You gotta earn your grub," Ridge shot back with an easy grin.

"Tell me why I came here to work on my only day off in three weeks."

"Because I make the best venison stew this side of the mountains."

Colt chuckled and slapped Ridge's back in easy camaraderie. Then the two men took care of their horses before starting to repair the sagging corral fence.

EMMA endured the awful silence all the way home by thinking about the man who'd been so kind to her. Madoc. The name sounded vaguely familiar, but she couldn't place it. The other man, his friend, was in the cavalry. She'd seen enough of those uniforms that early morning when her peaceful existence had been shattered. She shut down the nightmarish memories before they carried her back into oblivion, where she'd lived for so long after she'd been returned seriously injured to her family's ranch.

The wagon rattled into the yard and her father halted the horses in front of the house. He hopped down and helped Emma's mother, then her sister. Emma didn't wait, but clambered down herself, earning a disapproving scowl from him.

"Wait in the study, Emma," he ordered. Then he exchanged a brusque look with her mother.

Gritting her teeth, Emma nodded curtly and followed her sister up the steps to the wide veranda. Sarah opened the arched door and they entered the spacious house. As Emma started upstairs to her room, her younger sister grabbed her arm.

"You're supposed to wait for Father in the study," Sarah said.

"I'm going to change out of my church clothes first."

Sighing, Sarah trailed after her, right into Emma's bedroom, and perched on a dainty spindle-footed chair.

"Father's not at all happy with you, Emma. Running away was bad enough, but talking with Ridge Madoc . . ." Sarah shivered. "Father says his mother was a tramp, and the apple doesn't fall far from the tree."

"Father says a lot of things." Emma reached up to undo the tiny pearl buttons at the back of her dress. "Who's his mother?"

Sarah shrugged. "All I know is she was married to Harry Piner."

Emma struggled to place the name. "The mean old man who lives in that shack just north of town?"

"Yes, but he died last summer. Then, right before you came home, Mr. Madoc claimed the place. Father was angry because he wanted the rest of the land, but since the rightful heir showed up, he couldn't get it."

Emma paused to look at her sister. "What do you mean, 'the rest of the land'?"

"Father's been buying pieces of Mr. Piner's land over the past few years. Whenever the old man needed money for whiskey, he'd come to Father and sell some more."

"But Mr. Madoc won't sell what's left?"

Sarah shook her head. "He plans on settling there."

No wonder her father didn't want Madoc anywhere near her. Besides having bad blood, he had also thwarted her father's plans for the land. Still, Mr. Madoc had been kind to her, and Emma had found little kindness since she'd returned.

She moved to stand in front of her sister, her back toward the younger woman. After a moment, she felt Sarah's fingers undoing the remaining buttons.

"Thanks." Emma couldn't get the confining dress off fast enough. She hung it in her armoire, and removed two of her four petticoats, placing those in the closet, too. She rummaged past the dresses the seamstress in town had made for her over the last few months, and picked out one of her past favorites, a somewhat faded green-and-blue paisley smock.

"You're going to wear that?" Sarah asked, staring at the old dress like it was a dead snake.

"I like it."

"Father hates it."

"He doesn't have to wear it." With the buttons up the front, Emma didn't need Sarah's help. The fabric stretched taut, threatening to undo the button between her breasts. The first time she'd worn the old dress upon her return, she noticed she'd gained an inch or two in her bosom, although the rest of the dress was loose.

"So why does this Ridge Madoc have a different last name?" she asked, oddly curious about him.

"I heard Father and Mother talking about him one time. I guess his mother was married to Mr. Madoc's real father who owned the place first, but that was before we moved here," Sarah replied.

"Emma Louise! Get down here!" Her father's bellow thundered from the foot of the stairs.

Sarah's eyes widened. "Now he's even angrier with you."

Emma shrugged, almost surprised by her unconcern. "What can he do to me that hasn't already been done?"

Her sister gasped.

Emma strolled out of her room and down the stairs where her red-faced father stood. Martha Hartwell stood a few feet behind her husband, her lips set in a grim line.

"I thought I told you to throw out that rag," he said, motioning to her dress with a slicing motion.

Emma began to cross her arms, felt the fabric tug across her chest, and instead, clasped her hands in front of her. "It's *my* dress. I can do with it what I please."

Her father's eyes sparked with anger, and a muscle clenched in his jaw. "The study."

Still wrapped in indifference, Emma walked into the dark paneled room with heavy, navy-blue velvet curtains on the two large windows behind his desk. She glanced longingly at the overflowing bookshelves. Without the books, she wouldn't have survived her confinement over the past several months.

Emma settled into a wingback chair in front of the desk, sitting with her feet flat on the floor and her hands resting in her lap like a proper young lady. She would've preferred to sit with her legs folded beneath her, but she figured she'd provoked her father enough for one day.

Her mother perched on the twin of Emma's chair, her face pinched with worry. Her father, however, didn't appear the least bit anxious. No, he was spitting mad.

"What do you have to say for yourself, young lady?" he demanded.

She met his glowering eyes without flinching. "You and Mother have no right making decisions which affect my life without talking to me first."

Her father blinked, apparently startled by her forthrightness. "You're our daughter and you live under our roof. That gives us the right."

"Would you ship Sarah off without talking to her about it?"

"Sarah is not you."

Boiling anger and hurt engulfed Emma as she gripped the armrests. "What you mean is that Sarah is still clean and pure, but poor Emma is used and soiled." Her nostrils flared and her fingernails dug into the armrests. Long-held silence exploded in defiance. "I am not a *thing* you can cast aside and forget about. I have a life. I have hopes and dreams."

"Which will never be realized around here," Emma's mother interjected almost gently. "No respectable man will have you."

Emma's stomach caved and she stared down at her fisted hands, which had somehow ended up in her lap again. She absorbed the pain of her mother's words, praying her expression didn't reveal her anguish. Once upon a time when she was a young girl, Emma had dreamed of meeting a handsome, dashing young man and living happily ever after. A part of her still yearned for that happy ending, but fate had stolen that wish, leaving no hope of ever realizing it. She raised her head and turned to the older version of herself. "Thank you for sharing that with me, Mother."

Her mother flinched, and even Emma was shocked by the depth of her own bitterness.

"That's enough, Emma Louise," her father ordered. He stood and paced behind the desk, his body silhouetted against the windows. He'd taken the time to remove his jacket, but still wore one of his white church shirts with a string tie and vest.

The regulator clock ticked loudly in the muffled silence. Emma concentrated on its steady rhythm—tick-tock, tick-tock—to block out the other sounds swirling through her head, but the memories were too powerful to be denied any longer.

Pounding hooves.

Gunshots.

Screams.

Blood.

Her heart hammering, Emma stared at her hands, almost surprised to find they weren't scarlet stained. Instead, she noticed how they'd finally lost their dried parchment texture, but weren't nearly as smooth as they'd been seven years ago.

Her father stopped pacing, but remained standing behind his desk. The silence was so intense that when he rubbed his jaw, Emma heard the rasp of his short whisker stubble against his hand. "Maybe it was wrong of your mother and I to make plans behind your back, but we were only thinking of your best interests."

Emma bit her tongue.

"As you know, your aunt Alice is a widow with no children. Your uncle left her very comfortable financially, and we doubt she'll ever marry again. She's willing to let you move in with her and begin a new life."

It wasn't that Emma didn't like Aunt Alice. She did. She

admired her aunt's independence and used to enjoy watching her put her brother—Emma's father—in his place. There were few people who could tangle horns with John Hartwell and come out unscathed and victorious. His older sister was one of them.

Emma took a deep, steadying breath. "I'm fond of Aunt Alice, but I want to stay here. This is my home, where I was raised. I don't want to leave."

Her father's stern expression faltered and Emma caught his helpless look directed toward her mother. Emma had no doubt he loved her—still loved her after everything that had happened, but didn't know how to show it. The only time she'd seen him truly emotional was when he'd come to the infirmary at the fort after the cavalry had brought her in, wounded and weak from blood loss and shock. For the first time in her life, Emma had seen tears in his eyes. Since then, though, he'd gone back to his characteristic detachment.

Her mother leaned forward to lay a hand on Emma's. "Believe it or not, we don't want you to leave either. Your father and I discussed this for weeks before we contacted Alice. But surely you must see it's for the best. In St. Paul, no one knows of your time with the . . . Indians." Martha Hartwell's voice quavered. "Although you won't talk about what happened while you were with them, we can imagine how you must've suffered."

"I was treated well." That was true. Emma hadn't told them much about her years with the Lakota tribe. At first, it had been because she hovered on death's door for a week after coming home. In the days that followed, her body healed but her mind had shut down after the horrific visions and sounds she'd experienced the morning the soldiers attacked the village. And now it was too late to tell them. Everyone seemed to think they already knew, and anything Emma said would invariably be seen as the ravings of a madwoman.

"They're a lot like us," she finally said. "The children play, the women cook and clean, and the men hunt and protect the women and children. Parents love their children and want them to grow up to be good and responsible adults, too."

"They're heathens," her father said curtly. "They murder women and children."

Emma smiled, but there was no warmth behind it. "Then I guess the whites and Indians have more in common than most folks think, don't they?"

Her mother gasped. "You sound like you're defending them."

"They stole you away from us, away from your home," her father added, his husky voice revealing both anger and distress.

"They saved my life," Emma corrected.

"And God knows what they made you do while you were with them," he continued as if she hadn't even spoken.

"They didn't make me to do anything I didn't want to."

Her mother squeezed her hands. "Thank God. We prayed that you wouldn't be forced to—" She broke off.

But Emma knew exactly what she meant. She had lived with that fear for weeks after she was carried into their camp, not realizing she wasn't a captive. She was treated decently and her adoptive parents had cared for her and protected her. And when the time came, Emma hadn't been scared. Nervous, yes, but not frightened.

Not of Enapay.

She'd chosen to hide that fact from her parents and Sarah. They wouldn't understand. Nobody would understand unless they had walked her path.

"We're relieved," her father broke the stillness. "That way, when you do find a man to marry, he won't know."

"Know what?" Emma asked.

"Of your circumstances."

Dare she tell them? Did it matter?

"Please let me stay," Emma pleaded, ready to put an end to the conversation.

Again, the mute exchange between her mother and father. Emma was beginning to hate those secret looks.

"In two weeks you will go on an extended visit to your aunt's," her father proclaimed. "That'll give you some time to prepare."

Emma wanted to kick and scream, to throw a tantrum unpleasant enough that her parents would change their minds. But she wasn't five years old, and John and Martha Hartwell truly believed they were doing the right thing for their eldest daughter.

There would be no changing their minds about this.

Emma nodded even as every muscle in her body rebelled against the simple motion. "Two weeks."

"Two weeks," her father repeated.

"It's for the best," her mother reiterated, as if trying to convince herself.

Emma stood and walked out of the room. Her legs moved as if someone other than herself was controlling them. Keeping her mind and expression blank, she climbed the stairs and entered her room, locking the door behind her. Once there, she opened a dresser drawer and dug beneath her underclothing to find what she sought. Her fingers recognized the soft leather and they closed around a small moccasin.

Slowly she brought it out and hugged it to her chest.

Two

DUSK was falling as Ridge and Colt sat in companionable silence in the cabin. They had turned two chairs toward the stove and were drinking coffee after finishing the pot of venison stew Ridge had made.

"How're Pres and Sarge doing?" Ridge asked.

Colt stretched out his long legs and crossed his ankles. "They're getting tired. They would've come with me, but the colonel's got them going out again, looking for those Indians that hightailed it off the reservation."

Ridge scowled. "From what I heard, most of 'em were women and kids. They ain't going to hurt anyone."

"Maybe, maybe not. But I guess there were a few young bucks with them—the kind that got something to prove."

Ridge stood, plucked a rag from a nail on the wall, and used it to pick up the hot coffeepot on the stove. He raised the pot to Colt, who nodded and held out his cup. Ridge topped it off, then refilled his own. After returning it to the stove, he sat down and tipped his chair back so that the two front legs were off the floor.

This was Ridge's favorite time, when he could sit back and enjoy some peace and quiet after a day's work. When he'd been with Colt and the others in the army, evenings were spent in easy camaraderie, usually playing poker for matchsticks and drinking coffee.

Ridge had left those days behind. His last order had been to find an Arapaho village. After he found it, the peaceful camp had been destroyed by soldiers drunk on glory and vengeance. It wasn't a battle as much as it had been a massacre. Even now, Ridge could see and hear the carnage. It made him sick to remember.

"You should've stayed on," Colt said in a low voice.

A cold fist wrapped around Ridge's spine. "No. I couldn't."

"Maybe if you had, they wouldn't a done the same thing to that Lakota village."

"They didn't listen to me before." Ridge sipped his coffee, his stomach churning with guilt and bitterness. "Why would the next time be any different?"

Colt continued as if his friend hadn't spoken. "The Hartwell woman almost got herself killed." His lips turned downward in disgust. "She was dressed just like one of them, acted just like 'em, too, from what I heard."

Reining in his anger at Colt's disapproval, Ridge pictured the woman with the fawn-colored eyes as she thanked him for his coat. It was a damned shame her life was ruined. No white man wanted a "squaw woman."

He became aware of Colt's scrutiny.

"You ain't thinking of ignoring Hartwell's warning, are you?" Colt asked.

Ridge shook his head. "Nope. Miz Hartwell's got enough problems."

"Damned shame she's ruined," Colt said, unknowingly echoing Ridge's thoughts. "She's a pretty filly, but no man in his right mind's going to want to get hitched to her."

Ridge's hand tightened around his cup. He recognized the truth in his friend's words, but that didn't mean he had to like it.

Colt finished his coffee and glanced out into the disappearing daylight. "I'd better get back to the fort. Colonel

Nyes wants us to check on those folks settling along the river tomorrow so we'll have to leave early. Wants to make sure they haven't had any Indian troubles."

"My guess is they haven't. Too far west."

Colt nodded. "Yep, that's what I figure, but what the old man says goes."

"Nyes must be running out of Indians to kill if he's looking for more." Sarcasm sharpened Ridge's words.

"I don't like the colonel, but I can understand his position. The man has his orders, just like the rest of us," Colt said with a hint of defensiveness.

"A man like him can hide a whole lot of hate behind orders."

Colt's jaw muscle clenched. "Maybe it is a good thing you quit."

The two men parried sharp looks until Colt turned away to retrieve his hat and jacket. Ridge sighed and donned his, also. They'd been friends too long to let a difference of opinion get between them.

"I reckon it was," Ridge said quietly.

Colt dipped his head in acknowledgment. They walked out to the stable where Colt's horse was penned next to Paint. While the cavalry captain saddled his gelding, Ridge leaned a shoulder against a post.

"I appreciate you coming out to help me, Colt," Ridge said.

Colt paused long enough to give him a crooked grin. "You'd do the same for me."

Ridge smiled. "I reckon, even though your venison stew tastes like chewed-up leather."

"And how the hell do you know what chewed-up leather tastes like?"

"I've eaten your stew."

The two men chuckled as Colt led his horse outside. Ridge extended his hand, and Colt clasped his forearm as Ridge did the same.

"You take care, soldier," Ridge drawled.

"You, too, pard."

Colt mounted in one fluid motion, lifted a hand in farewell, and urged his horse into a trot.

Ridge folded his arms on the top corral pole and watched his friend swallowed up by the dusky shadows. He took a deep breath and let his gaze wander across his land.

His land. That sounded good, even if instead of five hundred acres, only one hundred remained. Damn Harry Piner for selling off what was rightfully his.

Ridge didn't remember much about his real pa, but what he could recollect filled him with both warmth and soul-deep loneliness. He recalled his pa lifting him onto the saddle in front of him and the two of them riding around the yard as his ma had watched with a gentle smile; helping clean the tack and the smell of oil and leather and his pa's wool shirt; carrying in two pieces of wood because he was too small to handle anymore and his pa's big hand patting his shoulder to thank him for helping fill the woodbox.

Then his pa had died and his ma married Piner. It hadn't been bad the first year. Harry had seemed like he cared for them, and had tried to make the ranch profitable. However, the harsh winter and falling market prices had seemed to conspire against him. He started drinking, and his temper grew shorter, especially with his stepson and later with Ridge's ma. His violent outbursts often left both mother and son with painful bruises.

In the end, Ridge's ma gave up, and twelve-year-old Ridge was left with his stepfather's mean temper and painful lessons learned with a leather belt or a fist. When Ridge turned fifteen, he ran away and never looked back.

Until now.

His father's ranch was almost lost by Harry Piner. It was up to Ridge to make things right. He planned on rebuilding, which meant finding a way to buy back the land Piner had sold to Hartwell for a pittance. Then Ridge would find a respectable woman to marry and raise more Madocs who'd make his ma and pa proud.

The major obstacle in getting started was money. He needed more than he had to buy the blooded bull he had his eye on down in Cheyenne. The rancher who owned the bull said he'd give Ridge until June to come up with the cash. After that time, he'd put it up at auction.

He knew Colonel Nyes would hire him back in a heartbeat—experienced scouts were hard to come by. But Ridge didn't want anything to do with the army and Nyes's solution to the "Indian problem." With spring coming, the big ranches were going to need more help. He'd find a job at one of those and save his money.

The wife and children would have to wait.

EMMA dropped her needlework to her lap, pressed her head back against the settee, and closed her eyes. She'd slept little the previous night after a vivid dream about wolves and mountain lions, and through it all, the sound of a crying wolf cub. The nightmare had left her shaken and anxious, and Emma had learned not to ignore such omens. Although she wasn't certain what the vision meant, she knew she couldn't go to St. Paul. Her journey lay in a different direction, one she had ignored for too long—at first by blaming the winter, then by trying to forget. But not a day passed that she didn't draw out the child's moccasin and imagine how much he'd grown.

Although that path held numerous perils, she had no choice. The plan to leave was dangerous to contemplate, even alone in the front room when her mother and sister were in town shopping, and her father in his study with the door closed.

A tap-tap on the front door startled her and she waited a moment, expecting her father to answer it. When he didn't come out of his office, she realized he probably hadn't heard the quiet knock. She debated whether to get the door herself or to inform her father of the visitor.

A month ago, there wouldn't have been any hesitation—she would've disappeared into her room while her father saw to their caller. But Emma'd had enough of cowering in corners. All it had gained her was a one-way trip to her aunt's. It was time she started making her own decisions and facing her fears. No longer would she shame her husband's memory, or hide from her son's fate.

She laid her needlework aside and went to the front door. Taking a deep breath, she swung it open and her eyes widened at the sight of the man on the porch.

"Mr. Madoc," Emma greeted, trying to hide her startled pleasure at seeing him again.

Ridge Madoc appeared equally surprised and he quickly removed his wide-brimmed hat. Obviously, he hadn't expected her to answer the door. "Ma'am. I, uh, came to see Mr. Hartwell about a job." He shifted his weight from one moccasined foot to the other, like a schoolboy called up in front of the class.

Emma caught her frown before it could form. "Did he ask you here?"

Ridge shook his head, then brushed his longish brown hair back from his brow. "No, ma'am. I wanted to see if he was doing any hiring."

Emma glanced over her shoulder, grateful to see that the study door remained closed. "He doesn't handle the hiring. Our foreman, Bob Tucker, does that."

"Do you know where I might find him?"

"He told my father he'd be staying around the yard this morning, keeping an eye on the mares that are due to foal." Emma looked past Madoc, shading her eyes against the bright sun. She couldn't spot the foreman, but had an idea he'd be in the far barn. Emma made a quick decision. "I'll take you to him."

"You don't have to."

She smiled at his flustered expression. "It's all right. I need to get out of the house before I go crazy anyway. Just give me a minute to get my coat."

Giving him a nod of apology, she closed the door. Although she'd lived outside the strictures of civilization for years, Emma didn't dare invite him into the house without a chaperone nearby. Of course, she could've gotten her father, but he would have a fit if he knew Madoc was here.

The only chance Ridge had of getting a job was to talk to Mr. Tucker directly.

She donned her coat, remembering to wind a wool muffler around her head and neck. After finding her gloves, she tugged them on and slipped outside, bumping into Madoc's solid body.

He caught her shoulders and steadied her.

A shiver passed through her at his strong, yet gentle grip. "You catching me is becoming a habit," she said, keeping her voice light.

He released her and stepped back, his expression anxious. "Sorry, ma'am. I didn't mean any disrespect."

Emma risked placing a gloved hand on his sleeve. "That wasn't what I meant. I'm grateful for your assistance." She smiled behind her scarf, and hoped he could see the sincerity in her eyes.

Ridge studied her a moment, then a slow smile stole across his lips. "My pleasure, ma'am."

Although Emma knew he was only being polite, she liked his diffident smile and the sound of his husky voice. She started down the porch steps and heard Ridge follow. As they walked across the yard, he kept half a step behind her, which made conversing difficult. She slowed her pace so he could catch up, but he slowed accordingly and continued following her.

At least he didn't mind being seen with her. Most respectable people did.

"Were you in the army, too?" she asked, turning her head to glance back at him.

"Yes, ma'am."

"When did you get out?"

"Last year."

She'd slowed even more while they'd talked, and Ridge finally ended up walking beside her.

"Why did you get out?" she asked.

"You sure ask a lot questions, ma'am."

Chagrined, Emma risked a glance at him and instead of irritation or anger, she spotted a twinkle of amusement in his eyes. It made her feel only marginally less guilty about asking such personal questions. "I'm sorry. It's really none of my business."

His humor disappeared. "It's all right, ma'am. I'm just not used to talking about myself."

"I can understand that." Emma had found the less said about her life with the People, the better.

She increased her pace, but Ridge remained beside her instead of fading back again.

"I fought in the War Between the States," he finally said in his husky timbre. "After my enlistment was up, I signed back on as an army scout and stuck with that until—" He angled a look at the blue-capped sky, then settled on the buttes in the distance. "Until it didn't seem right anymore."

Emma's stomach knotted. "Were you the one who led them—" The knot moved up and threatened to strangle her.

"No." His answer was immediate, telling Emma he knew what she was trying to ask. "I quit last fall."

Relief flowed through Emma like a swift-running river. It was important to her, knowing he hadn't been involved in the butchery; her instincts weren't wrong about the soft-spoken man. They arrived at the barn and Emma said, "Mr. Tucker's probably in here."

"Thank you, ma'am." Without another word, Ridge slipped inside the building.

Emma was tempted to follow, but her upbringing stopped her. Proper young ladies did not get involved in men's discussions. She laughed without humor. Nobody saw her as proper any longer, although her father insisted on continuing the charade for appearance's sake.

She trudged back to the house, hoping her father hadn't noticed her absence, but if he had, did it matter? Passing by Ridge's horse tied to the hitching post in front of the house, Emma paused to pat the horse's neck. She slipped off a glove and ran her palm over his velvety nose.

She tipped back her head to gaze at the blueness unbroken by clouds, and to breathe in the fresh scent of the awakening earth. It was the Moon of the Greening Grass

and soon the countryside would be filled with infant wild-
flowers and leafing trees.

And what of her son? Was Chayton playing with the
rest of the children? Was he scampering after butterflies
among the blooming flowers and laughing in delight?

Or had Chayton been struck down like so many others
the night the soldiers had come to the village? The pain
struck her then, like a knife twisting in her belly and she
breathed in short pants to stem the tears.

She had refused to think about the possibility of her
son's death, unwilling to open her heart to the overwhelming grief. But now, she could no longer bury the soul-deep
anguish. Her arms ached to hold her son and her ears kept
searching for the sound of his voice. He'd been such a
happy child, eager to explore, his pudgy legs propelling
him from one adventure to another.

Burning tears stung her eyes and she swiped her arm
across her face. Crying wouldn't help her—she'd done
enough of it the past five months and it had achieved nothing but a one-way trip away from everything she held dear,
especially Chayton. Her baby . . .

Emma sensed someone approaching and glanced back
to see Ridge Madoc returning. The stiff set of his shoulders
and the tight lines in his face told her the outcome of his
talk with the foreman hadn't been favorable.

She stepped away from his horse, pulled her glove back
on, and waited until he drew even with her. "He didn't hire
you," she stated.

"That's right." The clipped words were a sharp contrast
to his usual drawl.

He jumped onto his horse's back and fitted his toes into
the stirrups.

Emma grabbed the reins before he could escape and
placed a hand against the horse's neck as she gazed up at
Ridge. "I'm sorry."

He stared down at her and his eyes softened beneath his
hat brim. "I'll find a job."

"Couldn't you go back to scouting for the army?"

His mouth twisted up again. "No, ma'am. I've had a bellyful of killing."

Emma released his horse's bridle and crossed her arms, hoping to hide her sudden trembling. "I'm glad," she said softly. "Goodbye, Mr. Madoc."

Ridge touched the brim of his hat with two fingers and nodded. "Ma'am."

Emma watched the former scout ride away. *He* would know how to find the remnants of her tribe, but convincing him to help her would be difficult. It would entail her having to tell him about her son and late husband, and she wasn't strong enough for that.

Although the sun was warm, the ever-present wind was cutting and she reluctantly returned to the house. To her stupid needlework and her useless existence.

EMMA stood in a shadowed corner of the town hall, trying to remain inconspicuous. She had fought a long battle with her parents to allow her to attend this dance, and won only because they believed she'd be leaving for St. Paul in a few days. If they suspected she only wanted an opportunity to speak to Ridge Madoc, their permission would've never been granted.

She closed her eyes to block out the expected, but still hurtful, snubs and listened to the music, which was overlaid by children's laughter and the buzz of conversation. The sounds carried her back, to before her life with the People. She used to love attending socials, pretending she was the belle of the ball. She'd slip outside and, in the shadows, dance with an imaginary beau. In her pretend world, she'd been graceful and coquettish, knowing the right words and expressions to charm a man.

No matter how hard she tried, Emma couldn't return to her make-believe world. It, like so many other things, had been lost to her.

At least her sister Sarah still had her dreams and the possibility of them coming true. She'd danced twice with

William Lyndon, the banker's son; Sarah had confessed her pining for him to Emma.

"Marybeth told me he was an army scout."

Startled, Emma's eyes flew open. Two women stood about six feet away, their heads close together as they conversed behind their palms.

"His name is Pony Cullen," the other woman said to her companion, as if imparting a deep dark secret. "Colonel Nyes says he's his finest scout."

Emma followed their gazes to a tall, rail-thin man wearing a well-worn pair of uniform trousers and a brown shirt. When he turned to refill his cup from the men's punch bowl, she saw his face was pockmarked and sharply angled.

Suddenly, he lifted his head and stared straight at her, as if he knew she was studying him. Emma should've dropped her gaze, but his caught her, held her, like a cat toying with a baby bird.

Out of the corner of her eye, she saw the two gossiping women now had their sights on her. Idly, she wondered what the scandalmongers could come up with which hadn't already been whispered behind her back.

Cullen finally turned away, freeing Emma. She searched the room, hoping Mr. Madoc had shown up, but she couldn't spot him. The women had said Pony Cullen was a scout—would he work for her? Or should she stick to her original plan of asking Ridge Madoc?

Before she could decide, Cullen ambled out the back door. Emma figured he had to answer the call of nature after drinking so much "punch." Now would be an ideal chance to talk to him in private.

Ignoring the two gossiping women, Emma followed after the scout. The evening air nipped at her cheeks and she shivered from both the chill and nervousness.

After waiting a few minutes in the cool darkness, she spotted Cullen returning from behind the building. Before her courage escaped her, Emma strode purposefully toward him, hoping to intersect his path in the relative privacy beside an ancient oak tree.

"Mr. Cullen," she called.

He stopped and raised his head. From her distance, Emma couldn't read his expression. As she neared him, a knot began to form in her belly. "My name's Emma Hart—"

"I know who you are," Cullen interrupted.

Emma's cheeks burned. Of course, everyone knew her. "I heard you were a scout."

She was close enough to see Cullen's gaze rake over her, and the knot expanded.

"You heard right," he said.

"I'd like to hire your services," Emma stated, imitating her father's no-nonsense business voice.

"What kind of services ya lookin' for?" He licked his thin, dry lips.

Emma's fingernails bit into her palms. "I'd like to hire you to find some Indians."

Startled surprise was followed closely by cruel chuckles. "Got so you liked them bucks, huh?"

"What?"

Cullen stepped closer, leaving less than a foot between their bodies. "You don't need to go lookin' for one of them. I can give you what you need right here."

Emma recoiled, bile rising in her throat as his meaning became clear. "That's not why—"

Cullen grabbed her wrist and yanked her against his chest. The stink of tobacco and sweat made Emma's stomach roll. "You're no better'n a whore now, Miz Hartwell." He deliberately slurred her name.

Emma struggled to escape his grip. "Let me go!"

"Go ahead and yell. Ain't nobody gonna help a squaw woman." He tangled his fingers in the hair bun at the nape of her neck and jerked downward, forcing her head back.

Emma opened her mouth to scream but Cullen's lips smashed down upon hers. Her cry died in her throat as terror and disgust gave her added strength. She shoved at him, but he only tightened his hold on her hair. Her scalp burned and tears of pain trickled down her cheeks.

She hadn't survived a near drowning and seven years
with the People only to be beaten, or worse, in the town she
grew up in—a place she should've been safe. Anger replaced her fear and she stomped down on his foot with her
heel. He muttered an oath and his grip loosened. She
pulled away, only to have her arm grabbed. His fingers dug
into the tender flesh and Emma had no doubt there'd be
bruises.

"So, you like it rough?" Cullen grinned down at her, exposing yellowish-brown stained teeth. "I do, too."

Tendrils of panic snaked around Emma's chest as she
struggled to escape. Although the two busybodies had
seen her leave, Emma doubted they'd say anything if she
didn't return. And even if they did, who would lift a hand
to help her?

Emma Hartwell had committed an unforgivable sin
seven years ago—she'd chosen to live.

$\mathcal{T}$HREE

ORIGINALLY, Ridge'd had no intention of attending the dance in town that Saturday night. What little he knew of dancing was associated with Indian ceremonies and he didn't figure that type of dance would be looked upon too kindly.

But although he hated politics, he knew how it worked. If he was to become a respectable member of the community which had shunned him as a child, he had to rub elbows with the local folks, even those he didn't like.

He rode down Sunset's main street as his gaze wandered across the numerous buggies, wagons, and saddle horses lined up and down the road. It looked like everyone from a twenty-mile radius had come in for the dance.

A block from the meeting hall, he dismounted and tossed the reins loosely around a post. Even this far from the dance, he could hear voices and the occasional rise of fiddles above the hum of conversation. The sound reminded Ridge of a disturbed beehive.

He tried to swallow, grimaced, and stuck a finger between the paper collar and his neck, and tugged. If the dance didn't kill him, the shirt damned sure would.

Ridge adjusted his hat and trudged across the street like he was headed to a ladies' tea party. Against his better judgment, he sidled into the crowded hall. Removing his hat, he ran a hand over his head, ensuring the leather tie still held his long hair back. He searched the many faces and nodded to those who met his gaze. Many of them returned his nod of greeting.

Howard Freeman, owner of the hardware store, crossed through the mess of people to greet him. Freeman grinned broadly and extended his hand. "Must be some special occasion to get you into town."

Ridge shook his hand and smiled with genuine warmth. "Seeing you dressed up like a Thanksgiving turkey is more than reason enough."

Freeman chuckled, his fleshy chins resembling a turkey's wattle. "Look at you! I almost didn't recognize you wearin' a store-bought suit."

Ridge smoothed a hand over his vest self-consciously and resisted the urge to tug at his collar again. "I reckon you won't see me wearing it very often. Damn thing's gonna choke me."

Freeman laid a fatherly hand on Ridge's shoulder. "I always said it ain't the clothes, but the man wearin' them that counts."

Ridge noticed Hartwell and his wife chatting with Thomas Lyndon, the mayor as well as the bank president. Hartwell caught his eye, scowled, and turned away. Ridge frowned—the two men were probably scheming to force some small farmer into selling out to the mighty rancher.

"Maybe not, but men like Lyndon and Hartwell don't see it that way," Ridge said, his lips curled in distaste.

"They ain't bad men, Ridge, just used to things bein' a certain way." Freeman clapped him on the back. "You shouldn't be standin' around jawin' with me. In fact, I think Grace is just waitin' for some fella with two left feet to ask her to dance."

Ridge followed Freeman's pointing finger to the man's daughter, a red-haired gal with freckles dusting her nose and cheeks. She was standing by the refreshment table, watching the dancers as she swayed to the music. "I don't know anyone with two left feet, but I reckon I could handle her."

"Just don't be handlin' too much. Even though you're a friend, you're still a man and she's my daughter," Freeman warned, his eyes narrowed.

Ridge held up his hands, palms out. "I'll behave."

"See that you do." Freeman winked and moved away to greet someone else.

As Ridge wandered through the crowd, he spotted Hartwell's youngest daughter dancing with a boy he recognized as the banker's son. At least they'd be able to marry off one daughter well.

He swept his narrowed gaze across the room, looking for the elder Hartwell girl. Not that he expected to find her—the merciful thing would be to leave her at home, safe from the narrow-minded folks. But Miss Hartwell didn't strike him as one to back down. He admired her for that.

Strangely disappointed when he didn't see her, he continued to ease his way through the crowd, bumping and jostling and mumbling apologies as he made his way toward Grace Freeman.

Suddenly his path was blocked by a man wearing a dark blue double-breasted coat with the insignia of a cavalry officer. Silver eagles with spread wings decorated his shoulders.

"How've you been, Madoc?" Colonel Nyes asked, his voice politician-smooth.

"Busy." The word came out tersely.

"I heard you were working for the Circle C, getting a hired hand's wages." Nyes took a sip from his punch glass, which had more than punch in it by the smell of the officer's whiskey-scented breath.

"You heard right."

"I thought you'd be working on your own place." The colonel smoothed his pale blond mustache with his thumb and forefinger over and over, a smug habit Ridge hated.

"I'm doing both."

"We both know you could be earning twice as much working for me."

Ridge laughed without a trace of humor. "Blood money. No thanks, Colonel."

Anger glittered in Nyes's narrowed eyes. "Since when do you care about that? I've heard rumors about what you did before you joined the army. This isn't much different."

Ridge stiffened. "Anybody ever teach you not to listen to rumors?"

"Rumors are often reliable fonts of knowledge. Surely you should know that, Madoc." Nyes eyed him closely. "I can use someone with your talents. We've got murdering redskins on the loose and you can help us find them."

"So we can be the murderers instead?"

Nyes stared at him with something akin to disgust. "I never figured you'd go soft, seeing as how you never had any trouble killing undesirables before."

Ridge fought the urge to smash his fist into the colonel's aristocratic nose. "Go to hell, Nyes."

The pompous bastard smiled. "That's your destination, Madoc."

Ridge spun away before his tenuous control broke, and nearly plowed down a couple dancing at the fringe of the swirling bodies. The room was suddenly too damned hot and he fought his way to the nearest door, forgetting about Grace Freeman and everything else in his need to escape. Stumbling into the cool night air, he breathed deeply to exorcise the sleeping demons Nyes had stirred.

Raised voices caught his attention and he searched the shadows for the source. A man and a woman stood close to one another about thirty feet away, beneath the outspread limbs of an oak tree, telling Ridge he was an uninvited witness to a lover's spat. He clapped his hat back on his head, intent on going home where he heard only the wind and the coyotes.

"Let me go," the woman cried out.

Ridge recognized the voice and the desperation in the

tone. Even before he made a conscious decision, he was striding toward Miss Hartwell. The man was gripping her arms and had pinned her against the tree as he nuzzled her neck. She was struggling to escape.

Ridge grabbed the taller man and jerked him away from her. The man flexed his hands at his sides as he stared down at him. Ridge balanced on the balls of his feet and his hands closed into fists. "Come on, Cullen. Or is it only ladies you can beat up?"

"She ain't no lady, Madoc." The scout Nyes had hired to replace Ridge motioned toward Miss Hartwell. "She spread her legs for them; I figger she'd spread 'em for anybody."

Rage poured through Ridge's veins and he swung, catching Cullen on the jaw and spinning him around. With a roar, Cullen charged and Ridge tried to sidestep him, but the man managed to knock him off-balance. Cullen followed with a blow that snapped Ridge's head back. Although Cullen was rail thin, he had deceptive strength. Ridge staggered and ducked, barely escaping a second fist aimed at his face. He kicked Cullen in the groin and the scout dropped to the ground, clutching his privates.

Ridge leaned over the fallen man. "Keep your filthy mouth shut and your goddamned hands off Miss Hartwell." Ridge grabbed a handful of Cullen's greasy hair and jerked his head back so they were eye-to-eye. "You understand?"

Cullen stared at Ridge, his narrow-set eyes flat and filled with pain and hatred.

Ridge tightened his hold and felt a measure of satisfaction when Cullen grunted. "I said, you understand?"

"I understand," Cullen said through clenched teeth.

"Good. 'Cause if I hear about you bothering her again, I won't be so forgiving."

Ridge released him and backed away. He watched while the sorry son of a bitch pushed himself to his feet and stumbled away. Only after Cullen was gone did Ridge give his attention to Miss Hartwell. Her face was silvery-white in the moonlight and one sleeve had been tugged down, leaving a pale shoulder bared. Ridge had to restrain himself from going after Cullen. "Are you all right, Miss Hartwell?"

Wrapping her arms around herself, she managed a small nod, but her voice was surprisingly steady. "Yes, thank you, Mr. Madoc."

The woman had grit, but she was shy of brains coming out here with Cullen.

"You should get back inside."

She glanced in the direction Cullen had gone, then looked back at Ridge. "It's not what you're thinking."

"You don't know what I'm thinking, ma'am."

Her lips thinned. "I didn't lure him out here and I didn't invite his attentions."

Ridge, starting to feel the ache from the scuffle, shifted restlessly. "Then what were you doing?" The question came out more accusing than he'd intended.

The woman straightened her backbone and raised her chin. "I offered him a job. I want him to track down the Indians I used to live with."

Ridge cussed inwardly and reined in his temper. "I'd sooner trust a rattlesnake than Cullen."

"I realize that now. I made a mistake."

"Why do you want to find them?"

She glanced away and her spine stiffened even further. "That's none of your concern."

"Fine. I suggest you get back inside now." Ridge leaned over to pick up his hat and slapped it against his thigh before settling it on his head. "Evening, ma'am."

He turned to leave but she caught his coat sleeve.

"I *have* to find them," she said with quiet intensity.

He met her scrutiny with his own and read the sincerity and desperation in her eyes. His gaze flickered across her shoulder and he spotted bruising on her milky white skin. Rage burned through him anew at the evidence of Cullen's violence. Gently, he reached out and pulled the dress back into place, hiding the signs of Cullen's attack.

Miss Hartwell's eyes widened, and he heard her soft inhalation of surprise and saw the delicate flare of her nostrils. Ridge forced himself to release the cloth and stepped back.

"The best thing you can do is forget about 'em and move on with your life, ma'am," he said quietly. He touched the brim of his hat and strode away.

All the way across the street he could feel Emma Hartwell's sharp gaze drilling into his back. She was a fool to want to go back to the Lakota. There'd be some hot-headed braves who'd blame her for what had happened to them and vengeance wouldn't be pretty or swift. Although her life wasn't the best here, at least she was alive and safe.

He tightened his saddle cinch and mounted up, but before riding out, he took one last look. Miss Hartwell was walking back into the hall, her proud carriage bowed. He shrugged aside the whisper of guilt and deliberately turned away.

A full moon lit the night and a breeze stirred the leafless branches to create fluid shadows on the forest floor. A baby animal yipped, cracking the brittle silence, and an owl's hoot immediately followed. Moments later a wolf pup emerged from the scanty brush. He raised his head and let loose a pitiful howl that wavered and waned in the silvery darkness.

A mountain lion's roar answered the forlorn call and the young wolf whimpered. The pup rose but immediately collapsed onto the dead leaves blanketing the earth. He whined, calling for his mother but only the owl, perched on an overhanging branch, heard the cry.

The owl tipped its head, and its bright, round eyes focused on the weak animal. "The fearsome beast comes, little one," the owl spoke to the pup.

The small wolf shuddered with both fear and exhaustion.

The mountain lion stalked into the clearing, his eyes glittering in the moonlight. His nostrils flared and he swung his head unerringly toward his prey.

The pup laid there silently, as if knowing there was no

hope. The lion padded over and batted his shoulder with his massive paw. The wolf pup whimpered as he rolled over and over to finally rest on his side. The mountain lion bared his teeth as if smiling, and picked up the pup by his scruff and tossed the young animal into the air.

The pup dropped to the ground and yowled in pain. The cat stalked back and continued its cruel game with his helpless prey.

A full-grown wolf jumped into the clearing, startling the mountain lion away from his toy. The wolf laid back her ears and growled at the larger animal. The mountain lion snapped at the wolf, angered by the interruption, but the interloper refused to desert the pup.

The cat roared and leaped toward the wolf, who jumped at the same moment. The two animals met in a clash of sharp teeth and razor-like claws. The wolf drew first blood and the shrill screams of the mountain lion filled the forest. The cat sprang at the wolf and buried his teeth in the side of her neck. The night echoed with the cries of a battle that would be fought to the death.

And the pup lay unmoving on the cold, barren ground. . . .

"No!" Emma screamed, her eyes flashing open as she jerked up in bed. The dream held her in its talons for a brief moment longer before releasing her and fading away, leaving an aching emptiness in its wake.

Sweat covered her brow and rolled down the scar between her breasts. Her hands shook as she drew them across her face.

The bedroom door flew open and her sister ran into the room, her robe flapping behind her. "Emma, are you all right?"

Emma nodded and clasped her sister's hand, pulling her down to perch on the bed beside her. "I-I had a dream."

"More like a nightmare," Sarah guessed.

"No. A vision. I saw—" Emma closed her eyes, knowing to continue would only make her sister think she was crazy. She met Sarah's puzzled gaze. "You're right. It was only a nightmare." She gave her younger sister's hand a final squeeze and released it. "I'm all right. You can go back to bed."

"Would you like to talk about it? I know I always feel better after I talk to someone." Sarah brushed a strand of hair back from Emma's damp forehead and kept stroking her brow gently, like their mother used to do when they were children. "I had nightmares for weeks after you disappeared. I kept hearing you cry for help, but I could never find you." A tear slid down her wan cheek.

Emma's own eyes filled with moisture and she wrapped her arms around her little sister. Sarah's shoulders shook as she cried soundlessly against Emma's neck. Emma hadn't even considered how her absence might affect her sister, who'd just turned thirteen when she'd disappeared. Her memories of Sarah were those of a brat, throwing a tantrum when she didn't get her way. Their father had spoiled her, giving her gewgaws and making allowances for her, something he'd never done for his eldest daughter.

Emma remembered her resentment at the unfairness, and the deep-seated bitterness flared briefly. But the past was gone; in fact, it seemed a lifetime ago. There was no doubt her sister had been changed, too, by Emma's disappearance.

"At first I was scared," Emma said softly as she continued to rock the younger woman. "After I was brought to the village, I was taken care of and adopted by Talutah and her husband Fast Elk, the brave who found me. They'd had a daughter who would've been my age but had died only a month earlier." Emma easily remembered the fondness and patience her adopted parents had shown her as they taught her their language and customs. "They live in a harsher world, which is why their ways seem so barbaric to us. But deep down, they're a lot like us."

Startled, Sarah drew back to look at Emma. "You can say that after what they did to you?"

Emma cupped her sister's tear-dampened face and peered into her eyes. "They saved my life, Sarah. I know people around here say I was their captive, but I was free to leave if I'd wanted to. But where would I have gone? I was miles from any town. I lived with them and didn't allow my fear to turn into hatred, and I became friends with them. After a while, I learned to enjoy my new life."

She wished she could confess everything—her marriage, her child, how she came to love her adoptive parents—but fear kept her from doing so. Sarah might understand or she might not. Emma couldn't take that chance, especially now that she knew what must be done.

Sarah clasped her hands. "I'm glad, Emma. I'm glad they saved your life and I'm glad you're home."

Emma's throat tightened and she hugged her sister one last time. "Thank you for coming to check on me."

Sarah rose and smiled tremulously. "You used to do it for me when we were little. Goodnight, Emma."

"Goodnight."

After Emma heard her sister's bed frame creak in the room next to hers, she threw back her covers and rose to sit in the window seat. Pushing aside the curtain, she gazed into the darkness, lit only by a slivered moon. In two weeks the moon would be full, just as in her vision.

And Emma was certain it was a vision, sent to her by Owl, the messenger. For the past week, he'd been trying to tell her something. Now she understood. She had to find Chayton, the wolf pup in her vision, before he was killed by the lion.

Who was the mountain lion? Or had the large cat only been the symbol of approaching death? The unease she'd been experiencing throughout the past days bloomed to full-grown dread.

She'd been preparing to escape before she was forced to travel to St. Paul, but she'd wanted to find a guide. Her aborted attempt to hire Cullen had been a desperate measure.

Even now, in the security of her own room, Cullen's dirty words retained their power to humiliate her. Emma drew up her knees, laid a burning cheek on their coolness, and wrapped her arms around her legs.

She closed her eyes, remembering how grateful she'd been when Ridge Madoc had come to her assistance. But then she'd seen the look in his eyes. He thought little better of her for being alone with a man in the darkness. Maybe he figured she deserved what Cullen had done. But, no, if he thought that, he wouldn't have interfered. He'd heard her cry out and had acted like a gentleman to help her. But as much as she wanted to make Ridge the hero, he, too, couldn't look past her being a "squaw woman."

However, for a moment, when he'd so carefully fixed her dress over her shoulder, Emma couldn't deny the empty yearning in her chest. After Enapay had died, she'd buried her needs and found solace in caring for her child. But sometimes, in the middle of the night, she remembered how her husband had touched her and made her body writhe until he filled her and quenched the fire in her belly. When those memories became too powerful, Emma would touch herself under the curtain of darkness and find the release her body so desperately craved. But it was never enough. Ridge's touch reminded her of dark nights and shared pleasures.

A breeze jangled the shutters and Emma ached with fear for her son. How could she have left him behind? It didn't matter that a soldier's saber had wounded her or that terrible screams and horrific sights had paralyzed her. She should have searched until she found Chayton or died trying. But that choice had been taken from her when a soldier had recognized her white features and whisked her away from the decimated village.

Emma tried to quash the torment rising in her breast, but a tiny sob broke free. She had a choice now, and she chose to search for her son. Dear God, she prayed he was still alive.

She would leave tonight under the cover of darkness. There was no time left to secure a guide, but at least she knew where to begin her journey.

* * *

DAWN colored the sky coral, pink, and orange as Emma rode into the main encampment on the reservation. Exhausted, she kept her horse to a plodding walk as it wove in and out of the haphazard tipis. A skinny yellow dog yipped once, then slunk away. Emma's nose wrinkled under the barrage of rank sweat and both human and animal excrement. The smell was nothing like the village where she'd lived—the people there had kept themselves and their camp tidy and clean.

She recognized hopelessness as the culprit here, where the Indians had given up and surrendered in exchange for handouts from their captors. Some of the Lakota on the reservation no longer even tried to retain and practice the old ways, which were frowned upon by the Bureau of Indian Affairs agents.

Moisture filled Emma's eyes, and she blinked back the tears. She couldn't help them and to feel pity would only insult the proud people. Women and men wrapped in blankets crept out of their lodges and stared at her. Emma searched the impassive bronze faces, hoping to find someone she recognized, but nobody looked familiar.

By the time Emma reached the end of the village, she was trembling so much she could hardly draw her horse to a stop. She slid off her mount and her legs wobbled. Her feet were numb in the snug riding boots, which she hadn't worn since she was fifteen, and her thighs beneath the split riding skirt were irritated and chafed. She would've gladly exchanged her civilized garb for moccasins, a deerskin dress, and leggings.

An elderly Indian stepped forward, his shoulders hunched, but his eyes keen.

She faced the old man and bowed her head. *"Tunkasila."*

Although she couldn't see him, she could feel his surprise at her use of the Sioux word for grandfather.

"Táku eniciyapi hwo?" he asked.

"I am called Winona by the Lakota," she replied, continuing to speak in the language she'd learned. She risked lifting her head and when the old Indian didn't give her a disapproving look, she grew bolder. "I seek my son. Five moons ago my village was attacked by horse soldiers." Emma couldn't control the shudder of horror at the memory of that night.

The elderly man studied her for a long moment, then turned and motioned for her to follow. A young boy materialized beside her and took her horse's reins. Emma gave him a brief smile and allowed the boy to lead the animal away.

Keeping her gaze aimed downward, she followed the old man to his tipi.

"Timá hiyúwo," he said and disappeared inside.

Emma loosened her chinstrap and allowed her hat to slide down her back, to rest between her shoulder blades. Taking a deep breath, she accepted his invitation to enter and ducked under the deerskin flap, praying he could give her the information she sought.

$\mathcal{F}$OUR

RIDGE herded nine cattle into the canyon to join the other fourteen head he'd found that morning. He halted his horse under the miserly shade of a scrub oak growing next to a small stream. He dismounted and allowed Paint to drink.

Although it was early April, the midday sun was comfortably warm on his head and shoulders. Most of the snow had melted, but a few pockets remained, hidden in enclaves steeped in cool shadows.

He hunkered down beside a riffling brook and cupped his hands to drink the icy cold water. After wiping his mouth with his sleeve, he rose. His stomach growled, reminding him he hadn't eaten since dawn. As he unwrapped some dried venison from the cloth in his saddlebag, he caught a plume of dust to the east. As he chewed the jerky, he squinted at the dust cloud and the horse creating it. The rider rode unerringly toward him and Ridge tensed.

He narrowed his eyes until he could make out the nearing figure. John Hartwell. What the hell was he doing here?

Ridge kept his arms hanging loosely at his sides, but his muscles coiled. Did Emma tell her father about the fight between him and Cullen the night before last? And, if so, was Hartwell planning to thank him or shoot him?

Hartwell halted his horse on the other side of the four-foot wide stream. He didn't wear his usual suit, but typical range gear, although his wool trousers and waistcoat were newer and of better quality than a hired hand's. Hartwell's cheeks were flushed, and sweat mixed with dust streaked his face. He remained in the saddle. Ridge figured the man enjoyed looking down on folks.

Ridge nodded a mute greeting.

"Madoc." There was more hospitality in a rattlesnake's reception. "I've got a job for you."

Anger came directly on the heels of surprise, and Ridge laughed, a cold, harsh sound. "I wasn't good enough to work on your ranch, so what makes me good enough for this job?"

"You were a scout," Hartwell said tersely. "I need you to find my daughter. Emma ran away Saturday night."

The night Ridge had found her alone with Cullen. He ground his teeth and felt the tug of his jaw muscle. "Maybe she ran off with some fella."

Hartwell shook his head impatiently. "My other daughter said she had a nightmare. It upset her but she wouldn't tell Sarah about it." He looked away, embarrassment and a hint of humiliation in his expression. "Sarah thinks she went back to the savages that kidnapped her."

After Emma's confession about trying to hire Cullen to find her adopted tribe, Ridge wasn't surprised. But he wasn't about to confess that to Hartwell. He shrugged. "They're probably scattered seven ways to Sunday."

"I'll give you a hundred dollars to find her and bring her back home," Hartwell offered.

A hundred dollars. That was more than he would make in three months working as a ranch hand, and the balance he needed to purchase the bull. But what about his land—the land Hartwell had practically stolen from Harry Piner.

"On one condition," Ridge said flatly. "You sell me my land back at the same price you paid for it—fifty cents an acre."

Hartwell's mouth gaped and his face reddened, but this time it was with antagonism instead of embarrassment. "That's extortion."

"That's business," Ridge shot back. He lowered his voice and smiled without an ounce of warmth. "You know all about business."

Hartwell's knuckles were white as he gripped his saddle horn and a vein in his forehead pulsed angrily as he glared at Ridge.

"Your daughter for my land. Your choice, Hartwell." An eagle's cry sliced through the tension and Ridge glanced up to spot the mighty bird soaring high above them—a favorable sign.

He looked back at Hartwell to find the man still mulling over his offer. Ridge's lips curled in disdain. A man who had to consider a choice between his daughter and some land was a miserable excuse for a human being.

The rancher's eyes blazed. "All right."

"I want it in writing." Men like Hartwell respected words on paper.

"Damn you, Madoc. My word's good."

Ridge merely stared at him.

Hartwell capitulated with a snarl. "Come to the house and I'll have a contract ready to sign."

Ridge relaxed. "Why didn't you get me yesterday? She's got a day and a half lead now."

Hartwell glanced away and rubbed at a patch of dust on his cheek. "I tried to find her myself, then I went to Colonel Nyes. The son of a bitch said they'd keep an eye out for her during their patrols, but didn't want to expend the manpower to find a—" He clamped his mouth shut, but Ridge knew what he was going to say.

It looked like he and Hartwell had something in common after all: a mutual dislike for Nyes.

"She's not in her right mind, Madoc," Hartwell confessed in a low voice. "But she's still my daughter."

In the few instances Ridge had talked to Emma Hartwell, she hadn't seemed crazy. He also had a feeling the woman had reasons no one but herself knew for wanting to find those she'd lived with. But a hundred dollars and the chance to recover his land at a dirt cheap price was more than reason enough to take the job. Bringing Emma Hartwell back to her own folks was the right thing to do, too, even if Ridge didn't care much for her father.

Ridge mounted his horse. "I have to tell the foreman I'm leaving; then I'll meet you at your house in an hour."

Hartwell nodded, relief in his haggard expression.

EMMA patted her mare's neck soothingly as she tracked the progress of a black bear and her cub a hundred yards away. Although she knew a sow with her young could be dangerous, Emma also knew that as long as she didn't make any threatening moves or try to get close to them, the bear would ignore her.

The sow stopped and lifted her nose to scent the air. Fortunately, Emma was downwind. She watched the cub rollick in the clearing, oblivious to the dangers surrounding it. He had his mother—she would take care of him.

Unlike Chayton, whose mother had abandoned him.

No! She hadn't. Not voluntarily. When she'd finally recovered physically, her mind had remained sick from the horrible memories of that night. And even if she'd had the strength to look for Chayton, the winter weather would've denied her the opportunity.

But now, with the arrival of spring and the information she'd gained at the reservation, Emma knew the general location of her people. Or at least those who weren't killed the night of the attack, she thought with a bitter tang.

She'd asked about her son, but the old man hadn't known anything about him. If Chayton were still alive, he'd be with the group which was now headed northeast.

Sunlight sprinkled through the trees, dappling the meadow. A droplet on a spider's web captured the sun and wove it into a tiny colorful rainbow. A gift for those who truly saw. The tribe's shaman had taught her that, and Emma had listened.

As she stared at the water drop, the colors swirled, then coalesced into the image of a brown eagle riding the wind high in the sky. The eagle soared closer and closer until Emma found its keen eyes staring directly into hers.

She gasped and blinked. The image disappeared and only the droplet remained. Someone was searching for her. It shouldn't have surprised her.

Five days had passed since she'd left the reservation. She knew her father would send somebody to find her and bring her back. Shivering despite the warm air, Emma hoped she wasn't leading the army straight to the reservation runaways, only to have the soldiers finish what they started.

The bear and its cub disappeared into the brush, and Emma urged Clementine, her horse, through the meadow. The mare danced nervously, tossing her head at the fresh bear scent, but Emma handled her with a firm hand.

Emma trusted the intuition she'd gained while living with the People. The shaman had said she possessed a second sight, a rarity among the *wasicu* who did not understand. But Emma embraced her fledgling gift. Now she prayed it would lead her safely to her son.

RIDGE knew he was close. After four days of trailing the surprisingly trail-savvy woman, he had come to admire and respect her skills. Few white men, let alone a woman, could travel such distance in such a short amount of time and manage to cover their tracks so well. There'd been times when he'd followed a blind trail, only to have to backtrack and find the real one.

The sun had set two hours ago, but Ridge knew he was near his quarry and had chosen to continue on, hoping to find her that night. He was rewarded for his persistence when he smelled faint woodsmoke on the breeze. Following it led him directly to her.

Ridge surveyed the small camp and spotted her bedroll a few feet from the glowing embers. Her horse was fifteen feet away, hobbled and grazing contentedly. Ridge dismounted and ground-tied Paint. Moving on soundless moccasins, he entered her camp. Her horse raised its head and snorted, but was too accustomed to being around people to raise an alarm.

Miss Hartwell slept on her side, facing the fire's remains, and her blanket was tugged up to her chin. The orange glow of the embers reflected reddish-gold strands in her honey-brown hair and illuminated her winged brows and slightly upturned nose. Her lips were pressed together, with the lower one slightly fuller than the upper, giving the impression she was pouting.

Suddenly, Ridge wanted to discover if her lips were as soft and sweet-tasting as they appeared. Before his mind could offer an argument, he was drawing nearer to her.

The woman threw off her blanket and charged upward. Orange glinted off silver metal and Ridge felt a blow, followed by a sharp burn across his forearm. He reacted without thought, grabbing the wrist of the hand that held the knife and wrapping his other arm around her waist. He squeezed her wrist until the knife thudded dully on the ground.

She fought in his arms, flailing arms and legs, and they rolled across the dirt, ending up with Ridge straddling Emma's waist. He locked his ankles down on her lower legs and imprisoned her hands on the ground above her head. Lying atop her, Ridge could feel her breasts rising and falling against his chest and his body reacted instinctively to her feminine curves.

Ridge gnashed his teeth and willed his blood to cool. "Settle down, Miss Hartwell. It's Ridge Madoc."

The moment he said his name, she ceased struggling.

"Mr. Madoc?" she asked.

"Yeah," he answered curtly, sitting up so she wouldn't feel him so intimately against her belly. "You gonna behave?"

Her stiff muscles relaxed beneath him. "Yes."

Releasing her hands, he shifted off her, kneeling to her side. With the fight drained from both of them, Ridge could now feel the blood soaking his sleeve and dripping onto the ground. The throbbing in the gash told him it wasn't a mere flesh wound.

Damn.

"I'm surprised it was you," she said quietly as she sat up.

"What?"

"I knew my father would send someone. I didn't think it would be you."

Ridge shrugged, then hissed when the movement sent an arrow of pain through his wounded arm.

Miss Hartwell scrambled to her knees and gazed down at his injury. "Your arm. How bad is it?"

"Could be better."

Her annoyance disappeared, replaced by concern. "I'll build up the fire so I can take care of it."

Ridge didn't argue, knowing it needed to be cleaned and maybe sewn, too. She completed her tasks quickly without speaking. Although Ridge wasn't accustomed to being around a woman, he felt little awkwardness with Miss Hartwell. She didn't prattle on and on about this and that, but worked efficiently with a minimum of commotion.

"Move closer to the fire, Mr. Madoc," she ordered.

Ridge did so and worked to remove his jacket and shirt so she wouldn't have to cut the sleeves off. The woman assisted him, easing the two pieces of clothing off the wounded arm.

Without any sign of embarrassment, she ripped a camisole dug out of her saddlebag into three pieces. Upending her canteen, she wet one and began to clean away the blood around the wound.

Although Ridge usually preferred silence, he found he wanted to hear Miss Hartwell's voice. "Where'd you learn to use a knife?" he asked.

"Fast Elk, the husband of Talutah. I lived with them." Her brow furrowed, but she didn't look up. "There were a handful of young Indian men who felt the same way as Cullen, only it was because I had white skin."

Ridge wasn't shocked by her matter-of-fact statement. It didn't matter what color a man was, there were always some who enjoyed hurting folks. "You must've been a good student."

She glanced up. "Fear is a good motivator." She returned her attention to the wound.

The night's silence surrounded them with only the fire's crackling and the occasional coyote's yipping disturbing the serenity. Ridge kept his gaze on Miss Hartwell's bowed head as she cared for the injury with surprising expertise. He had an idea this was another thing she'd learned when she was with the People.

"I'm going to have to stitch it," she announced.

"Figured."

"It's going to hurt."

"I've been cut before," Ridge said. "I've got a bottle of whiskey in my saddlebags. You can use that to soak the needle and thread in."

She nodded and rose gracefully to disappear into the darkness. It wasn't long before she reappeared leading Paint. After tying his reins to a low-slung branch, she retrieved the bottle.

Kneeling by the fire, Miss Hartwell dribbled some of the liquor across the needle and thread. She recapped the bottle and was about to set it to the side.

Ridge reached for it with his good hand. "I could use some before you start."

She eyed him mutely as he took three long swallows and shut his eyes to enjoy the burn and growing numbness that followed. A small hand took the bottle from him and set it aside.

"Do you often drink whiskey?" she asked.

Ridge opened his eyes to find the lips he'd been admiring earlier thinned with irritation. "Only when a crazy woman attacks me with a knife."

She bent over his arm and pushed the needle through a

flap of skin on one side of the gash and tugged the thread through the bead of blood welling from the tiny hole. Ridge averted his gaze and ground his teeth.

"I'm sorry," she finally said when she was half done. "I didn't know it was you."

"Who'd you think it was?"

"I didn't think. I only reacted."

"That'll get you killed," Ridge said, studying the fiery hues of red and gold in her hair as she stitched the wound.

"Or the person who's foolish enough to try sneaking up on me when I'm sleeping."

In spite of the situation, Ridge grinned. "Yes, ma'am. That, too."

He felt rather than saw her reluctant smile.

Long, graceful fingers moved the needle cleanly through skin. There was no hesitation in her movements, only a steady economy of motion. He wondered if she'd been so calm and quiet before she'd been taken, or if she'd learned patience with the Lakota, just as he had.

She finished and tied off the thread. As she reached for a piece of the torn-up camisole, he looked down at the neat black stitches that held the cut together.

"You do good work, ma'am," he said.

"The wound or the stitching?"

He spotted a hint of amusement in her eyes. "Both."

She wrapped the cloth around his arm, smoothing the material with an experienced hand. It'd been a long time since Ridge had been near enough to a woman to smell her and he savored Miss Hartwell's musky feminine scent, overlaid by trail dust and sweat.

"I'm going to make some tea that will help with the pain," she announced as she tied off the makeshift bandage.

"You don't have to—"

"I know, but I feel bad enough that I was the one who injured you."

While she poured water into a battered pan, Ridge stood to care for Paint.

Miss Hartwell rose and halted him with a touch on his wrist. "What're you doing?"

"Gotta unsaddle my horse."

"I can do it."

"No, ma'am. A man takes care of his own horse unless he's dead or dying."

She glared at him. "Fine. But don't be surprised when your wound starts bleeding again."

"I'll be careful," Ridge groused.

Miss Hartwell didn't say anything more but settled down to ready the tea leaves to steep once the water was hot. Using his uninjured left hand, Ridge took three times as long to unsaddle and rub down Paint. By the time he finished, he was exhausted and the tea was ready.

Miss Hartwell handed him a steaming cup as he lowered himself to his saddle, which lay on the ground by the fire. "Thank you, ma'am." Although he wasn't a tea drinker, he took a sip and swallowed, enjoying the warmth and slight bitterness as it flowed down his throat.

"I'm not going back, Mr. Madoc," she said quietly, but with an edge of steel.

"Your family wants you home."

Anguish flashed in her eyes. "I miss them, but I can't go back. Not yet."

"Why?" Ridge finished his tea.

She stared into the flames. "I have something I have to do first."

"What's so important that you'd abandon your own family?"

She laughed, but it was a raw, hurtful sound. "Abandoning family. That's what this is all about, Mr. Madoc."

"I don't understand, Miss Hartwell." Ridge peered· at the woman and her figure blurred. He squinted and managed to clear up the picture for only a second. His eyelids flickered downward and he fought to keep them open.

"You should get some rest, Mr. Madoc. You lost a lot of blood."

"Home. In the morning," Ridge slurred.

"Yes, Mr. Madoc. In the morning you can go home."

He felt a gentle pressure on his arm, guiding him to lie down. A blanket settled over him, and small, competent hands tucked the material around him. "Thank you, ma'am," he murmured.

His last memory before dropping off was that of a woman's tender touch feathering across his brow.

When Ridge awakened the next morning, groggy and confused, the sun was high above the horizon. And Emma Hartwell was gone.

$\mathcal{F}$IVE

ADJUSTING the canteen and bedroll straps crisscrossing his chest, Ridge followed the suspiciously distinct trail Emma had left behind. He knew her skill at hiding her tracks firsthand, yet she wasn't making any effort to hide the two sets of hoofprints now. Why?

He should've been more wary of her willingness to help after she'd knifed him, but he hadn't expected someone like Miss Hartwell to be so treacherous. The woman he'd found stumbling near town nearly two weeks ago wouldn't have attacked him. Nor would she have drugged his tea.

Even as young as he'd been, he remembered his pa's strict lesson on treating women with respect and courtesy. He'd always said it didn't matter if the woman was a lady or a whore, Ridge always tipped his hat and opened doors for her. Emma Hartwell was no whore, despite what many of the townsfolk thought. Yet she hadn't acted like a lady either.

So how should he treat her?

Like a bounty.

Ridge cringed inwardly. She wasn't anything like those men he'd hunted for the price on their heads. Most of them had been more like animals, and when he'd defended himself, it was more like putting down a rabid creature than shooting a man.

After he joined the army, he swore he'd never return to bounty hunting, although he'd been tempted over the last month. The money was a whole lot better than chasing cattle around all day, but tracking down murderers and thieves was a dangerous job. Too dangerous for someone who had a reason to live.

Ridge stumbled over an exposed tree root, jarred his injured arm, and bit back a curse at his uncharacteristic clumsiness. He'd been walking steadily for over three hours, feeding off anger and humiliation. However, his emotions were starting to drain and he couldn't ignore his arm's throbbing or the stinging blisters on his feet.

The ground was littered with boulders jutting out of the earth and Ridge lowered himself to one with a groan. His feet nearly groaned in relief.

He was getting soft. A year ago a little cut wouldn't have taken so much out of him. A year ago he wouldn't have been wounded and left afoot by a gal, either. At least she'd left his saddlebags, canteen, and rifle so he wouldn't starve or be helpless against a wild animal.

He tucked the canteen between his injured arm and his side, then used his other hand to remove the stopper. Raising the canteen to his lips, he took a few sips of the cool liquid. The water helped clear his foggy head, but he didn't dare drink too much. He wasn't certain how far he'd have to walk, but he *would* find Miss Hartwell, even if he had to track the woman halfway to hell. Then he'd haul her crafty little backside back to her daddy's ranch—tied belly down across her horse's saddle, if he had to—and collect the one hundred dollars.

A wolf's bay sounded from nearby and Ridge jerked his head up, searching for the wild animal. The sun slid behind a gunmetal gray cloud and another howl ripped through the stillness. A shiver skidded down Ridge's spine as he rose. It was uncommon for a wolf to howl during the day. He turned slowly, making a full circle, as he sniffed the air and squinted to see around the surrounding rocks and trees.

Nothing.

Clutching the rifle more tightly in his good hand, Ridge slung his canteen and saddlebag over a shoulder. Puzzling over the wolf, he continued following the trail, which had grown fainter across the rocky ground.

The horses' tracks became clearer as reddish soil replaced the rough land. Ridge increased his stride. Clouds continued to blot out the blue skies, urging him faster. If it rained, he'd lose the tracks completely, as well as his chance to find Miss Hartwell.

Half an hour later, Ridge rounded a corner and nearly stumbled into Paint. The horse, his reins wrapped loosely around a bush, raised his head as he munched a mouthful of grass.

Ridge grinned and laid a gloved hand on Paint's neck. "You're a sight for sorry eyes, fella."

Paint snorted and tossed his head, then lowered his muzzle to tear up some tender spears of grass. As the animal ate contentedly, Ridge examined him, sliding a hand along his flanks and down his legs, but didn't find anything amiss. It appeared the woman wasn't completely heartless. She probably only wanted to slow Ridge down to make good her escape.

He spotted a piece of paper caught between his saddle and the blanket, and tugged it out. He recognized his name written on the folded sheet, opened the paper, and stared at the letters for a long moment. Swallowing hard, he crumpled the note and tossed it away.

After tightening Paint's cinch and ensuring the bridle was fitted correctly, he shoved his toe into the stirrup and hauled himself up carefully. The stitches in his arm pulled and he clenched his jaw. It was merely another reminder of why he wouldn't return without Emma Hartwell.

The woman owed him.

*   *   *

THE Lakota elder had told Emma to ride north and east if she wished to find her adopted people. Although they'd had only a six-day head start and most of the survivors were women and children on foot, Emma wasn't surprised she'd been unable to catch up to them.

Generations of nomadic living had given the Lakota the skills and tools to disassemble their homes and be ready to journey in less than an hour. The first time Emma had witnessed the entire village preparing to abandon a site, she'd been terrified that the Indians would kill her and leave her body behind. After being reassured she wouldn't be harmed nor abandoned, Emma had resolved to do her share rather than to be a hindrance. It had been the beginning of her acceptance, and she had grown to have an abiding respect for their ways.

Emma halted her horse with a slight draw on the reins and gazed out across the vast expanse of land. North and east covered a wide swath of territory. Would she ever find them in the sprawling wilderness?

If only she'd been able to convince Ridge Madoc to help her. However, that option was lost to her, especially after what she'd done to him. Wounding him with her knife and then putting sleeping herbs in his tea hadn't been enough. She'd also taken his horse. He wouldn't be happy, but she hoped her note convinced him she wasn't going back until she attained her goal.

A chill slipped inside her jacket and goose bumps danced across her arms. She glanced up at the clouds, dark and swollen with rain, and worry sent another shiver through her. What if Ridge didn't find shelter? He was already injured. What if the wound became infected? She had cleaned it well, but infection was common even with minor cuts.

She turned in the saddle, resting one hand on her horse's rump as she studied her back trail in the fading light, and was pleased to see no evidence of her passage. She'd left a trail a child could follow when she'd taken his horse because of her guilt-stricken conscience. Surely he had found the animal by now, read her note, and headed home.

After she left his horse, she'd circled around and re-sorted to covering her tracks once more in case he was pig-headed enough to follow her. She suspected he wasn't a man to give up easily, which would've been an admirable quality under different circumstances.

Clementine snorted and stamped her front hooves. It was time to quit woolgathering and continue her search. She urged her mare northeast and prayed she was moving closer to her son.

A cold drizzle started at dusk, forcing Ridge to push Paint harder. Rain would wash away the faint signs of Emma's trail. She'd returned to covering her tracks, which told him she meant for him to find Paint. He didn't know whether to be grateful for her thoughtfulness, or annoyed for giving him cause to feel guilty for taking her back home.

After hours of following the almost-nonexistent trail, he caught sight of a small flickering fire. He was too far away to tell if the body moving around it was Emma's, but he suspected it was.

He dismounted and tied Paint in some sparse shelter. Stepping carefully onto the wet ground, he drew closer to the flames until he recognized the figure. He'd found his prey. Again.

His attention on Emma, he accidentally kicked a stone and it skittered across the hard ground. As quiet as the sound was, the woman must've heard it. She froze and lifted her head to peer into the darkness.

His heart pounding, Ridge remained still, ignoring the light rain that continued to fall. Her wary gaze skipped across him and she finally gave her attention back to what-ever she was preparing over the tiny fire. He'd do well to remember her keen senses in the future, as well as her un-canny vigilance.

Letting out his pent-up breath, he sidled closer until he stood only ten feet away, hidden by a tree trunk. With no intention of taking a chance this time, he withdrew his revolver, but didn't cock it. As furious as he was, he recoiled at the thought of even shooting a warning shot if she tried to escape. He only hoped she didn't know that.

He stepped into the slight clearing.

Emma froze.

"Miss Hartwell," Ridge said, his voice a cool parody of politeness.

Emma stared at him, her expression revealing nothing. Then she leaned over and deliberately stirred the contents of a small kettle hanging over the fire. "Mr. Madoc. Would you like some stew?"

Ridge caught his smile before it could grow. The woman definitely had spunk. "What'd you put in it?"

She glanced up at him and her eyes held the hint of a twinkle. "I didn't know I'd be having company."

"Then I reckon you'd best step away from the food until I'm done eating." He motioned with the barrel of his gun. "Move back."

"What're you going to do?"

"Something I should've done last night. It would've saved me a mess of trouble." He motioned with his chin. "Back."

Her eyes flickered to his revolver. "Are you going to shoot me if I don't?"

This time he did smile, but it was without warmth or amusement. "Don't worry. I'd just graze you, ma'am."

Her lips thinned, her humor fleeing. "I doubt my father would appreciate you bringing me back with a bullet wound."

Ridge snorted. "Your father could barely choose between his precious land and you."

Emma flinched and her gaze fell, but not before Ridge spotted her humiliation at the plainspoken truth. It was as if she'd suspected all along, and his words confirmed her father's opinion of her. Suddenly he felt like the lowest vermin for hurting her with his rash words.

"Step back, ma'am," he said, gentling his voice slightly.

She left her improvised spoon, a stripped twig as thick as her thumb, in the kettle and did as he ordered.

"That's good enough," Ridge said when she was some feet from the fire. "Now put your hands on your head and leave 'em there."

She glared at him, her eyes sparking with fury and helplessness, and Ridge was relieved to see the bleak anguish had vanished. He could handle an angry woman, but a teary-eyed one scared the hell out of him.

With her damp hair straggling in clumps about her face and her clothes limp from moisture, Emma should've looked like a drowned rat. However, the rain made her long skirt cling to the curve of her legs, and her jacket hugged the fullness of her breasts. Her wrath only made her more breathtaking.

Clearing his throat and mind, Ridge concentrated on the task at hand. He retrieved the pieces of rope he'd brought with him and approached her warily. Her narrowed gaze followed him and he was reminded of a trapped animal.

"Sit down, but keep your hands on your head," he ordered.

Emma remained mute as she lowered herself to the ground. Without the use of her hands, she plopped clumsily onto the wet, unforgiving ground.

"Now roll over onto your belly and put your hands behind you," he said.

Her mouth fell open with indignation.

"Just do it, ma'am," Ridge said before she could speak. After his lousy day, he wasn't up to any verbal sparring.

Pressing her lips together, Emma laid flat on the ground. After a moment's hesitation, she placed her hands at the small of her back.

Ridge closed in behind her and squatted down. "Easy, ma'am. I'm not going to hurt you unless you force me to."

She lifted her head and glared at him over her shoulder. "But only a flesh wound."

Ridge smiled, knowing full well she could see him. "That's right, ma'am."

Despite his injured arm, he made quick work of tying

her wrists. He could feel the tension in her shoulders and arms, and wished he didn't have to resort to old bounty-hunting methods. But she'd already proven herself untrustworthy, and he couldn't chance losing her again. Her return meant a prized bull and the beginning of a cattle herd.

He shifted around to straddle her hips and grasped her ankles, pulling them upward like he was tying a calf. She twisted like an eel, trying to dislodge him or make him lose his grip on her.

"Damn it, woman, stop fighting or I'm gonna hurt you," he warned.

Emma struggled even more.

Ridge leaned back, placing more of his weight on her hips, and wrapped his good arm around her calves. Her dress draped down to reveal heavy stockings with black lace-up boots beneath the single petticoat. The boots weren't made for hard riding, and the kid leather was almost worn through where the stirrups had rubbed. He suspected she had her share of blisters, too, but also figured she'd chew glass before admitting it.

Because of his injured arm and her resistance, it took longer to truss her. Once done, he released her legs and pushed himself upright, barely containing a groan. "I'm going to get my horse and bring him on into the camp."

"You can't leave me like this." Emma rolled onto her side to stare up at him accusingly.

"Yes, ma'am, I can. I'm tired, sore, and hungry, and I don't want to have to be watching out for your tricks."

"Fine." Her tone said just the opposite.

Ridge adjusted his hat. Every fiber in his body rebelled against leaving a woman tied up and on the wet ground, but she'd brought the situation on herself. If she'd agreed to go back with him without any fuss, they could be sharing a meal instead of acting like two cats fighting over the same piece of dirt.

He spun around and strode off to retrieve Paint. Returning five minutes later, he noticed the woman had managed to wriggle over to a tree and sat crookedly against the bole. Her clothes were smudged with dirt and mud, as was her face.

"That doesn't look too comfortable," he commented, working the saddle's girth loose.

"It's better than lying facedown in the mud," she retorted, her grimy chin out-thrust.

Ridge laid the saddle on a rock. "You do look a mite dirty there, ma'am."

If her eyes could shoot bullets, he'd be six feet under. He turned his attention to removing Paint's bridle. "What's so dang important about finding them?"

Emma remained mute. Ridge figured he'd have an easier time coaxing a rattler off a warm rock than getting Emma to talk. Not that it mattered to him why she wanted to go gallivanting around the country looking for people who didn't want to be found.

Ridge hobbled Paint and then concentrated on rubbing down the horse with the saddle blanket. Once that chore was done, he stepped over to the small fire and added branches from the pile Emma had gathered to feed the hungry flames. He leaned over to sniff the kettle's contents, and everything blurred. Dizziness swirled through him and he nearly pitched forward into the fire. Bracing his legs, he waited for the light-headedness to disappear. His wound's blood loss and his long trek were catching up to him.

"Are you all right?" Emma asked.

"Yeah," Ridge lied. He wasn't about to admit to Miss Hartwell any weakness. "What's in the kettle?"

"Rattlesnake."

"Kin of yours?"

An unladylike snort met his ears. Miss Hartwell had more than her share of starch in her ladylike backbone. "More likely yours."

"At least you haven't lost your sense of humor," Ridge said dryly. "I'm going to have some stew, then I'll feed you."

"I can feed myself if you untie me."

"That's not going to happen, ma'am. I don't take kindly to folks who knife me, then drug me." He dug out a tin plate and spoon from his saddlebag. "Makes me mad and when I get mad I get stubborn."

"Ornery," Emma corrected.

Ridge shrugged. "I reckon that, too, but you gave me reason enough." He returned to the cookfire and spooned some stew onto his plate, always keeping one eye on the woman. He sat on the ground as he shoveled a bite of food into his mouth. It was better than anything he could've thrown together. "It's good, ma'am."

"I'm glad you find it to your liking." Emma's voice could've frozen water. "I hope you're going to leave some for me, or is that part of your plan—starve me so I'm too weak to cause any trouble."

Ridge pretended to consider her suggestion while inwardly amused at her tart words. "That ain't a bad idea."

"My father would probably appreciate it."

Ridge glanced sharply at the woman and found her lips curled into a cynical scowl. "I told you I'd feed you."

"And I'm supposed to take your word for that?"

"My word's good."

He glared at her when she looked like she was going to continue arguing, and she lapsed into silence.

Ridge finished eating though he hardly tasted it. How had he ever thought Emma demure and retiring? She had the uncanny ability to both fluster and anger him in the same breath. It was at least a four-day ride back to Hartwell's ranch. If he had to, he'd gag her for the entire trip.

He straightened to refill the plate for Emma, and barely stifled a groan. Between the knife wound and his achy muscles, he wanted nothing more than to lie down and sleep.

After carrying the food to Emma, he sat cross-legged beside her. "Hungry?"

"No."

"Eat anyhow. I don't want you swooning."

"I've never swooned in my life."

Ridge rested his hands on his knees and held the plate between them. "Not even when the Indians got you?"

"Not even then," she replied quietly.

"Most women would've."

"So I've heard." She paused. "I also heard most women would've killed themselves rather than stay with them."

Ridge met Emma's amber eyes. "I never could understand that. I figure living is the important thing."

"Then you're not like most white people."

He shifted uncomfortably. "Better eat afore it gets cold." He raised a spoonful of stew.

Emma, her gaze never wavering from Ridge, opened her mouth and he stuck the spoon inside. He watched as her lips closed around it, and he drew the spoon out. The full lips remained together and she chewed almost daintily.

Suddenly realizing he was staring, he looked back at the plate as he refilled the spoon. He kept a tight rein on his thoughts, concentrating on his injured arm's ache instead of Emma's tantalizing lips. He lifted his gaze to her eyes once, only to find her cheeks flushed beneath the grime, and he glanced downward again.

Some minutes later he scraped the plate clean. "More?"

She shook her head. "But I would appreciate some water."

Nodding, he found her canteen and held it up so she could drink. When she was done, he placed it back on her saddle, which rested on the ground not far from the fire, along with her bedroll.

Night cloaked them in darkness except for the glow of the fire. All Ridge wanted to do was curl up and go to sleep, but he had to clean up the camp, change the dressing on his arm, and decide what to do with Emma.

"If you let me loose, I'll wash the dishes," Emma volunteered, and added with an accusatory tone, "Besides, I'd like to clean up and change my clothes."

"A little dirt never killed anyone."

"I give you my word I won't try anything."

"Why should I believe you?"

"Because my word's good," she threw his earlier declaration back at him.

"I got no reason to trust you, ma'am."

"I never gave you my word last night." Then she added quietly, "If I had, I wouldn't have run out on you."

Despite his previous objections, he considered her request. He didn't like the idea of her sleeping in damp, muddy clothes. She could catch a cough or worse. He'd seen it happen too often.

As if reading his mind, Emma sneezed once, then a second time.

He knelt behind her. "Don't give me any grief, Emma. I'm not in the mood," he said, leaning close to her ear.

"I won't," she replied, her voice husky.

He untied her wrists, but had her release her own ankles. Standing, he leaned a shoulder against the tree she'd been sitting against. "No dallying."

Emma nodded, but didn't meet his gaze.

She cleaned the kettle, plate, and spoon with practiced ease, and Ridge knew she hadn't learned that living in Hartwell's fancy house either. Once the kettle was spotless, she refilled it with water to heat over the fire.

"I'm going to change my clothes," she said.

Ridge's first impulse was to turn around and give her privacy. But he suspected if he did that, he wouldn't see her again. He kept his stance relaxed, but his breath came in shorter bursts as he resisted the images that invaded his thoughts. "Go ahead."

"That's hardly proper, Mr. Madoc."

Ridge barked a sharp laugh. "If you haven't noticed, ma'am, nothing about this is proper."

"You can't expect me to undress in front of you."

"That's exactly what I expect." He could see evidence of Emma's inner battle in her frown and wrinkled brow. "We don't have all night."

Although her actions were of surrender, her clenched teeth and blazing eyes told Ridge another story.

Keeping his face blank, he watched her remove her jacket. Her fingers shook as she unbuttoned her blouse and slipped the soiled shirt from her smooth shoulders. The firelight cast flickering shadows across her slender neck and the slope of her breasts, disappearing beneath her white camisole. When her hands went to her skirt, Ridge's heart stepped up its pace even more. Once she'd undone the hooks, she skimmed the skirt down her slender hips and legs. She gracefully lifted one dainty foot, then the other as she stepped out of the pool of cloth.

His breathing grew rougher. It'd been a long time since he'd been with a woman and his body wasn't shy about reminding him.

Emma glanced up and her gaze ensnared his. The black circles in her eyes nearly covered all of the light brown, inviting him to dive into their depths and never come out. Her lips parted as if she too were having a hard time finding air.

Ridge's blood pounded sluggishly in his ears, drowning out everything else. The night faded until only Emma remained. Emma, lit by firelight and resembling a beautiful wild creature with her full lips parted and her breasts straining against the thin-clothed camisole.

A soft whimper escaped her, startling Ridge back to cold reality. He dropped his gaze and tried to ignore the throbbing in his groin, which far surpassed the discomfort of his arm.

He listened to Emma as she donned clean, dry clothes and when he thought she was done, he finally raised his head. Emma was kneeling by the fire, her back to him. She dunked a cloth into the warm water, wrung it out, and wiped her face.

Ridge joined her and removed his jacket.

Emma's eyes widened and although she tried to hide her fear, he found it in her white-knuckled grip of the damp rag.

"I'm only going to change the dressing on my arm," Ridge reassured her, annoyed that she thought so little of him.

Her fingers eased their pressure on the wet rag. "I'll do it."

He tilted his head in question.

"I won't try anything." For the first time since he'd caught her, her smile was genuine. "I promise."

Ridge unbuttoned his shirt and slipped the injured limb from his sleeve. He extended his arm to her.

Emma unwound the dressing, which had dried blood on the inner layers. "You broke open the wound," she scolded.

"It happened while I was walking."

Emma darted a glance at him as her cheeks reddened, but she didn't apologize. They both knew she wouldn't have meant it.

"Some of the skin around it feels hot," Emma said. "It doesn't look like it's infected, but I'd like to put something on it that'll draw out the bad blood."

"It won't knock me out?" he asked warily.

"No."

He nodded. "Go ahead."

Emma retrieved a buckskin bag from her saddlebags and opened it to dig out some dried plants. Cupping the herbs in one hand, she dribbled some water over them with the other. Once the mixture held together, she daubed it on the stitched gash.

Ridge sucked in his breath at the stinging sensation.

"It only hurts for a minute or so, then it'll start to tingle," Emma explained.

By the time Emma finished rebandaging his forearm, even the tingle was nearly gone.

"I could make you some tea for the fever."

"No tea."

"Suit yourself."

Ridge redonned his shirt and jacket. The camp was in order and Emma was dressed in dry clothes. He moved Emma's bedroll and saddle to the other side of the fire, then picked up the two lengths of rope he'd used to bind her. "Come here," he ordered Emma.

"What?"

"You heard me."

She didn't move. "What if I promise not to try to escape overnight?"

Ridge smiled. "My faith only goes so far, ma'am."

She continued to stare at him. "So does mine. How do I know you're not planning to—to use me?"

Ridge scowled. He didn't like her thinking he was the same as Cullen. "Because if I planned on using you, I would've done it by now."

She crossed her arms. "But maybe you've thought about it."

"Don't be calling the kettle black, Emma," Ridge said, his patience fast disappearing. "I wasn't the only one thinking."

Emma attempted to hold his stare, but surrendered with a barely discernible murmur. She walked over to her bedroll and lowered herself like a lady sitting down to afternoon tea. Her spine ramrod straight, she placed her hands at the base of her spine.

"In front," Ridge corrected. "Or you'll never get any sleep."

Puzzled, she held out her hands. Ridge forced himself to tie her wrists, tight enough that she couldn't wriggle free, but loose enough that they wouldn't cut into her tender skin.

"Take off your boots," Ridge said.

Using her tied hands, she removed her boots awkwardly. He set them beside his bedroll.

He plucked his lariat from his saddle and wove one end around the rope binding her wrists. Stringing out the rope, he tied it to the tree Emma had been sitting against.

"What're you doing?" Emma demanded.

"Making sure you don't go anywhere."

Once he had her secured, Ridge returned to his own blanket and saddle on the far side of the fire. "This way you can't reach me or any of the supplies. You can't even get close enough to the fire to burn the rope off." He laid down on his side, facing Emma. "Go to sleep."

She remained sitting up, her shoulders stiff.

Ridge closed his eyes, but kept his hearing focused on

Emma. It was a long time before she finally settled into her bedroll amidst some muttered Lakota curses.

Only when he heard her breathing even out did he allow himself to find sleep.

$\mathcal{S}$ix

CORAL and red filaments twined through the eastern sky, announcing the sun's return. Winona allowed herself a few moments to enjoy the gentle flow of life beginning to circulate around her. An owl hooted quietly, as if recognizing the reverence of a new day, and wings rustled as the creature left its perch.

A child whimpered and Winona cocked her head toward her own shelter, but a mother's hush came from a tipi twenty feet away. It wasn't Winona's son; he remained sleeping soundly.

She picked up a basket from beside her tipi and walked the path leading to the river. Her toes struck a soft object and she bent down to pick up a small moccasin. Smiling, Winona realized it was the one her son had been missing last night. Chayton hated to have his feet covered, and always tugged his moccasins off and left them on the ground. She tucked the tiny leather shoe into the belt where she carried her healing herbs.

Following the narrow game trail to the river, Winona enjoyed the freedom of this life. She still remembered her old home and the girl she'd been, but it was like someone else's *past, no longer hers. Her clearest memories were those of her husband and the child they'd created. Winona's footsteps faltered. She missed Enapay and had mourned her husband's death nearly two years past, but she had Chayton to care for and love. Although she'd received marriage offers after she became a widow, she'd declined them. Perhaps later, but for now she lived for her son and the joy he brought her.*

The vibration of the earth startled Winona and she froze. The tremors grew more distinct until they became thunder—the thunder of horses' hooves. Gunshots rang out in quick succession, followed by horrific cries and screams of terror. The colorful woven basket slipped from Winona's fingers and bounced lightly on the ground, forgotten.

"Chayton!" Winona raced toward the village, oblivious to the thorns that scratched her arms and legs, leaving tiny blood trails in their wake. Breaking through the brush, she barely noticed the horse soldiers with their guns and sharp sabers. Pushing through panicked people and horses, Winona didn't see the blade arc toward her. Nor did she feel the blow or the blood that immediately welled from the wound between her breasts.

She had to find Chayton!

Struggling to her feet, Winona couldn't figure out why her legs wouldn't obey her or why her eyes became blurry. A horse's foreleg struck her shoulder and she lifted her head to gaze into a white man's shocked face.

He leaned down, grasped her wrist, and dragged her up onto the saddle in front of him. She cried out, struck at him with her fists but the iron band wrapped around her waist didn't loosen. Her chest burned and it hurt to breathe. Her limbs grew heavy.

No! She had to stay awake. Had to find Chayton.

As consciousness receded, a mountain lion's scream rent the air. . . .

Emma jerked upright, but something tugged at her wrists, sending her back to the ground. Did her captor tie her onto his horse? No, she wasn't riding. She lay panting, struggling to separate dream from reality. Opening her eyes, she focused on the dim form of a sleeping man on the other side of orange embers.

Ridge Madoc.

Emma bit her lip to keep from crying out her despair. Despite the night's coolness, perspiration rolled down her neck, adding more moisture to her sweat-drenched collar. Her heart beat so hard she thought it might jump out of her chest.

The dream-memories faded, but the terror lingered. Her stomach cramped with remembered helplessness. She didn't know if Chayton was alive or dead, and the not knowing tore a hole in her heart.

A tear escaped and slid across her temple and into her hair. When Chayton was learning how to walk, she'd forced herself not to hover like an overprotective mother. Children had to learn from their mistakes or they would never gain wisdom. Harsh lessons, perhaps, but Emma respected the Lakota way and tried not to dishonor her husband's memory. But every bruise Chayton had gained, Emma felt tenfold.

What if Chayton no longer walked on this earth? What if he had been murdered by the soldiers?

Emma's throat thickened and she fought to breathe without weeping. She had survived because she hadn't given in to useless tears. But no matter how hard she fought to hold back the agonized grief, she lost the battle.

Tears flowed and her shoulders shook with long-hidden sorrow. She cried for the fifteen-year-old who had her girlhood stolen. She cried for the young woman who struggled to be accepted and loved in an alien culture. She cried for the wife who lost her husband, and the mother who lost her son.

"Emma?"

Ridge's tentative voice startled her. She'd forgotten she wasn't alone in the night's darkness. She could barely make out his prone figure on the other side of the fire's remains. He was partially upright with his elbows braced on the ground, his head turned toward her.

"Is everything all right, ma'am?" he asked.

She bent over to wipe her tear-streaked face on the coarse blanket, then cleared her throat. "Yes."

Emma held her breath, hoping he would lie back down and leave her alone to grieve. She felt his searching gaze on her and remained still.

"Might help to talk about it," he finally said.

"There's nothing to talk about."

Ridge sat up and crossed his legs beneath him. "My ma always said, 'Ridge, there isn't any shame in having nightmares. It's only your heart telling you to share your problems.' "

Emma tried desperately to keep her emotions bottled inside, but Ridge's compassionate words defeated her. Her breathing hitched, sounding like a strangled sob, but she would allow no more tears.

She heard a faint "damn" from Ridge and then her hands were enfolded. The rope was unwound from her wrists and callused fingers rubbed them. "It's okay, Emma. Everything's gonna be all right."

Nothing would be all right until she learned of Chayton's fate.

She struggled to escape when Ridge awkwardly patted her back. "Leave me alone." Much to her shame, her voice was as weak as her resolve.

He didn't speak but firm hands settled her against his chest, his legs outstretched with her cradled between them. He wrapped one strong arm around her shoulders and the other around her waist as he held her close. Resting his chin on her crown, he rocked her gently. He crooned words in a language Emma didn't recognize, but the tone was soothing and comforting. She borrowed his strength as she rebuilt the shattered wall around her memories.

For five months she'd kept her secrets, harboring them within her heart. Not even her family—*especially* not her family—would understand how she could've loved an Indian. A white woman wasn't supposed to submit to heathens, but Emma hadn't submitted—she'd embraced the

Lakota way, which was even a greater sin in most people's eyes.

She wouldn't—couldn't—tell Ridge. He might be more open-minded than most folks, but to see pity in his face would be just as humiliating as seeing disgust. However, she was more determined than ever to find those she'd lived with for over six years.

Giving in to temptation, Emma remained in Ridge's capable arms a few moments longer. She relished his warmth and security after months of feeling isolated, despite living with her parents and sister. The steady rhythm of his heart beneath her ear helped her relax muscles she hadn't realized were tight with tension. It would be so easy to fall asleep in his arms.

Emma forcibly roused herself and sat up. Ridge immediately released her, but not before she heard his sharp intake of breath. His wound. She'd forgotten about it while she'd wallowed in self-pity.

"Did I hurt you?" she asked, her breath misting in the cold air.

"It's nothing, ma'am."

Although Emma couldn't make out his expression, she sensed the ache was more than "nothing."

"Let me make sure it didn't start bleeding again," she said.

He shook his head, tucking his injured arm close to his side. "It didn't."

Emma knelt in front of him, her backside resting on her heels. She tugged her jacket tighter around her and crossed her arms, placing her hands in her armpits. "Thank you."

Ridge glanced away, as if embarrassed. "Wasn't nothing, ma'am."

Emma smiled. "Maybe not to you." Her smile disappeared. "I have to find them, Ridge." It seemed ridiculous to call him Mr. Madoc after she'd spent the last ten minutes within his capable arms.

"You don't know where they are," he stated.

"I know the general direction. With your tracking skills, you might be able to find them."

Ridge allowed a tight grin. "Seems to me you have more than enough savvy to find them yourself, with you knowing how to hide your tracks and all, ma'am."

"Hiding a trail and following a trail aren't the same. You see things I don't." *And I see things* you *don't,* she thought, remembering her visions of the wolf, the lion, the eagle, and the owl.

"Your father hired me to bring you home."

"He didn't give you a time limit."

"Don't go playing with words, Emma. We both know what he meant."

"It means you'll get paid whether you bring me back before or after I find them," she insisted.

"I don't have time to be running around the country after you," he argued. "I got work to do back at my place."

"How much is he paying you?"

"One hundred dollars," Ridge replied after a moment's hesitation.

"How would you like to double that?"

He narrowed his eyes. "How?"

"You find my—" She broke off, shocked she'd almost given away her secret. "My people and I'll pay you another hundred dollars."

"And where're you gonna get a hundred dollars?"

"Do you think I'm lying?"

"Ma'am, I think you'd say or do damn near anything to get what you want."

His words cut deep, especially knowing he was right. "Maybe. But you will get the extra money. I swear it."

He didn't refuse her outright, which gave Emma hope. She pressed her advantage. "Think of how much more two hundred dollars will help you and your ranch than one hundred."

He scowled, but didn't reject her offer. Emma remained silent, intuitively knowing she'd pushed him as far as he would go.

"How long do you plan on visiting with the People once you find 'em?" Ridge asked.

Emma squelched a smile of victory and considered his question. "Long enough to make sure they're all right and to say my goodbyes."

"A day? Two days? Five?"

Irritation quashed her growing sense of relief. "Five, maybe more."

"How much more?"

"I don't know."

"One week, Emma."

She opened her mouth to argue, but clamped it shut. Ridge had a stubborn set to his grizzled jaw. "One week," she repeated, but didn't promise.

"Then we go back to your ranch, and you and your pa'll pay me."

"That's right." Emma's own jaw ached with tension. Her plans were dependent upon whether or not she found Chayton. If he wasn't with the first group they stumbled across, she planned on continuing her search. And if he was there, she wasn't certain whether she'd stay at the village or bring Chayton to the ranch.

Ridge stood, his movements more graceful than Emma would've expected for an injured man. "You'd best get back to sleep. We'll have a long day tomorrow, ma'am."

"Do you have any idea where they might be?"

"Maybe."

"Where?" Emma demanded, coming up on her knees.

Ridge squatted beside the coals and coaxed them back to life with some small twigs. Then he added a handful of larger pieces until the fire illuminated his face, which possessed a calmness Emma didn't share.

"Where?" she repeated with more impatience.

"Places I remember from when I lived with them."

Emma's mouth gaped. "You lived with the Lakota?"

"Long time ago. Things were different then."

"Were you a captive?"

"No."

"Then—"

Ridge held up his hand. "Go to sleep, Emma."

She studied his expression, which gave away nothing. "That's why you were such a good scout." She didn't intend for it to come out accusingly.

He merely stared at her, until she looked away. She smoothed her bedroll, anxious to have something to do.

"Are you going to tie me up again?" she asked quietly.

"Do I need to?"

"No."

Ridge tilted his head, but didn't speak.

Self-conscious, Emma settled in her makeshift bed and pulled the blanket up to her chin. Her cheeks felt stiff from dried tears, and her body ached, but it was a good ache, like she'd spent the day scraping buffalo hides with the other women after a successful hunt.

"Goodnight, ma'am," came Ridge's soft drawl.

After a moment, she whispered back, "Goodnight."

ACCUSTOMED to waking at dawn, Ridge opened his eyes to find the first streaks of light appearing in the dark blue sky. He turned his head and spotted Emma's head peeking out of her bedroll. He hadn't expected her to run off again, but she had a habit of doing things he didn't expect.

The fire had died down, but embers remained because of the late night addition of wood. He stifled a sigh and rose to answer nature's call. When he returned to the camp, he recoiled the rope which he'd used to tie Emma to the tree, and set it beside his saddle.

Fifteen minutes later, he leaned over, intending to awaken Emma by touching her shoulder. His bandaged arm reminded him that wasn't a good idea and he drew back. "Wake up, Emma," he said in a low, firm voice.

She immediately stirred and lowered the blanket from her face, revealing eyes more alert than Ridge expected. Glancing up at the lightening sky, she levered herself to a sitting position. "You shouldn't have let me sleep so late."

Ridge allowed a slight smile. "Sun's just coming up. Most folks would call this early."

Emma wrapped her arms around her drawn-up knees, keeping the blanket over her lower body. Her lips tilted upward. "True. Mother and Sarah think dawn is the middle of the night."

"What about your father?"

Emma's smile disappeared and she pulled her knees closer to her chest, as if protecting what lay within it. "He'd be eating breakfast now."

Ridge cursed himself for bringing John Hartwell's specter between them. "Coffee?"

"When I get back," Emma said, throwing her blankets off.

"Where're you going?"

Emma stood and gazed down at him, amusement in her twitching lips. "Where did *you* go when you first woke up?"

Ridge's face heated and she laughed lightly.

"You heard me?" Ridge asked.

Emma shrugged. "I'm a light sleeper, remember?" She leaned down and patted his shoulder. "Don't worry. I didn't peek."

Ridge kept his attention on the tin cup he clutched in his hands as she walked into the brush. He wasn't used to women teasing him about such personal matters. Hell, he wasn't used to being around a woman, teasing or not. It was going to take some getting used to.

A few minutes later Emma returned and Ridge handed her a steaming cup of coffee.

"Thank you." She eased down on the ground and sipped the hot bitter liquid.

Ridge expected her to talk, to ask him about the time he'd lived with the Lakota, but she remained silent. He had his own questions for her, but it didn't seem right badgering her when she seemed content to let him keep his secrets.

It wasn't until they'd saddled their horses that Emma spoke.

"I know this wasn't what you signed on for when you agreed to find me, but I'm grateful for your help," Emma said, meeting his gaze squarely.

Ridge shifted under her direct look, feeling exposed and vulnerable. He adjusted the brim of his hat and eyed the fat fluffy clouds. "Like you said, ma'am, two hundred dollars'll do more than a hundred."

Her eyes flickered downward, to where the reins were threaded through her gloved hands. When she looked up again, her expression was neutral. "They're headed northeast."

Ridge nodded. "Figured so by the direction you'd been riding."

"Do you think we'll find them in the next day or two?"

"Maybe, but might be closer to two or three." He felt a twinge of irrational annoyance. "I promised you we wouldn't go back until we found them, and I aim to keep that promise."

"I trust you."

Although Ridge's chest tightened with her soft declaration, he couldn't fully believe her. As sure as he knew the mountains wouldn't fall down overnight, he knew Emma Hartwell was hiding something.

He only hoped her secret wouldn't get them both killed.

THE spring day warmed as the sun rose higher in the endless blue sky. Emma opened her jacket and loosened the wool scarf from her head so that it draped around her neck. Before they'd hit the trail that morning, she'd pinned her hair into a bun at her nape to keep the strands out of her face.

Content to bask in the uncommonly warm rays, she didn't attempt to speak with her former captor. She also suspected Ridge was a man who didn't tolerate empty conversation, which suited her fine. However, her gaze often strayed to his easy rocking motion, which belied the thin slash of his lips and clenched jaw. She wondered if his memories of this area were pleasant or something he preferred to forget. She opened her mouth to ask, but abruptly chose silence. It would be discourteous—in both white and Indian societies—to ask such a personal question.

"They aren't there," Ridge announced in the late morning.

Startled by his voice's intrusion after hours of silence, Emma glanced at him. "What?"

A minute shift of the reins and Ridge halted his pinto pony. Emma drew up beside him, their stirrups brushing.

"One of the places I thought they might be holed up." He pointed to a line of trees a mile or two away. "If they were there, I'd've seen some sign by now."

Disappointment weighed heavily on Emma as she slumped. She knew it was unrealistic to think finding them would be so simple after just a week of searching, but she'd hoped that with Ridge's knowledge it would be easier. However, the people she'd lived with were desperate and wouldn't settle for a traditional camp location. Food wouldn't even be their major consideration—concealment and security would be until they found a larger group to join.

Ridge's gloved hand settled on hers as it rested on the pommel.

"We'll find them, Emma," he assured.

The weight of his hand was comforting and something else—something that dipped into her belly and lay there warm and tingly. She lifted her gaze to meet sincere midnight blue eyes and managed a smile. "I know you'll do your best."

Ridge searched her face and Emma's cheeks heated. He abruptly removed his hand and his attention drifted forward again. Emma's mare followed without urging.

While she'd lived with the People, they'd ranged for miles in the wilderness, following the food supply. She kept hoping to spy something that looked familiar. Instead, her attention kept wandering to Ridge and the way he set the saddle and the keen eyes that saw so much more than even her own. It was obvious he was comfortable in the untamed land. Perhaps even more so than so-called civilized towns. He was a man she could admire and respect, but it saddened her to think his thoughts weren't nearly as charitable of her.

Emma took a deep breath and let it out slowly, then inhaled again, filling her lungs with fresh air. Clearing her thoughts like the shaman had taught her, she pictured the bright, pure air swirling through her body, illuminating the dark, stale places. She imagined the life pulsing around her, from the most insignificant ant to the greatest buffalo. All were connected as one through Mother Earth, each an integral part of the cycle of life and death; of rebirth and transformation.

An increasingly familiar scent intruded—Ridge's unique blend of deerhide, woodsmoke, and honest labor. His masculine essence triggered a new awareness to her body that she tacitly ignored.

Emma placed her unwelcome attraction to Ridge into the far recesses of her thoughts. She couldn't afford to be sidetracked from her mission by long-denied needs, especially with a decent man like Ridge Madoc. But then, it was his very decency that attracted her even more powerfully than his muscular body, smooth-shaven features, and clean scent.

Ridge slowed and Emma's horse came abreast so they rode side-by-side.

"I've missed this," Emma said quietly. At Ridge's questioning glance, she waved her hand outward. "This. The land. Quiet. Peace." A magpie flew past and the sunlight turned drab feathers to shiny blue. "Freedom."

Ridge remained mute, but Emma knew he'd heard her.

"Do you miss it?" she asked curiously.

"Sleeping on the ground, eating cold biscuits and tough jerky, not being able to take a long, hot bath?" He flashed her a wry smile. "Yeah, sometimes I miss it."

Emma laughed softly. "Yes, bathing in a mountain-fed stream isn't one of my favorite things either." She sobered and her gaze wandered across the wilderness. "But it wasn't a bad life. The People, they care for one another, watch out for each other's children." Her breath hitched in her throat. "They share their bounty with the rest of the tribe. When one suffers, everyone does. Not exactly how the whites see things, is it?"

"Two different kinds of people, Emma," Ridge began. "For one, the world is there for the taking and folks want the biggest piece they can get their hands on. It's like a grown-up marbles game—whoever has the most wins. For the People, they look at things different. Respect for the land and honor of one another and those who came before them are their beliefs. Without them, they don't have anything."

Although surprised by his relatively long speech, she nodded, her gaze turning inward, to the reservation camp she'd visited before starting her search. "But that's changing."

"It's the way of life, Emma. Things're always going to change."

"But that doesn't make it right."

"I never said it did," he said patiently. "But you and me can't stop it, so it doesn't do any good to get all riled up about it."

Emma's thoughts turned to her son, a child of both worlds, but embraced by the Lakota. If she took him back to her parents' home, what kind of life would he have? But if she and Chayton stayed with the Indians, how much longer would her adopted people remain free? And she didn't want to raise her child on a reservation, unable to walk freely on the same plains as his father's ancestors.

"Maybe if enough people got riled up about it, we *could* change things," Emma said.

"Maybe." Ridge didn't sound hopeful.

Emma leveled her gaze at him. "Would you?"

Ridge rubbed a wind-weathered cheek with a gloved hand. "I'm a simple man, Emma. All I want is a piece of land I can call my own, some cattle to run on it, and a good woman to share my life and raise my children."

"What if someone stole your land, scattered your cattle, and hurt or killed your wife and children?"

He met her gaze. "Your pa already stole my land."

Emma flinched. From what she'd heard, her father hadn't exactly stolen the land, but what he paid for it was equivalent to cheap beads and cheaper blankets. She didn't know how to respond to Ridge's bitter statement so she chose silence.

Her thoughts returned to the People and where they might be headed. She knew there were a number of Sioux further southeast, in the Black Hills of the Dakota Territory. However, many of the Tetons preferred the Powder River basin. Was that where her adopted people were going? Or was it Canada where the U.S. government couldn't touch them?

"What about Canada?" she asked.

"I already thought of that, but figured they'd more'n likely stay on land they know. The next camp I'm checking is about fifteen miles from here," he said, keeping his gaze aimed forward. "I should know if they're there once we get within a few miles of it."

It would be a long fifteen miles.

$\mathcal{S}$EVEN

BY nightfall, Ridge was certain the Indians were nowhere near the second possible camp. His next guess was some fifty miles away and it would take the better part of a day to get there, provided the weather cooperated. As he unsaddled his horse, Ridge raised his head and sniffed the cool air. There was a change coming. He suspected winter was going to make another appearance.

He and Emma prepared their camp, moving around one another in companionable silence. Emma volunteered to make their supper, which consisted of rabbit, biscuits, and gravy. A jackrabbit had jumped out of a patch of brush in front of them that afternoon, and Ridge's shot had been true.

By the time the meal was ready, Ridge's stomach was grumbling. He accepted a tin plate with three biscuits slathered with gravy and a large portion of the roasted rabbit. Emma had used some of her dried plants to spice up the meat, giving it a rich flavor.

"That was real good, ma'am," Ridge commented after he mopped off his plate with the last biscuit.

He volunteered to clean their plates; Emma didn't argue. When he returned from the stream, she was sitting near the fire, her legs to one side and a blanket wrapped around her shoulders. If not for her light skin and honey-brown hair, Ridge would've thought she was an Indian.

As he approached her, he noticed an open book held in her hands.

"Thank you," Emma said quietly as she looked up. The fire's glow glossed her face with warm tints. "I hope you don't mind if I read for a little while."

Ridge shook his head. "You don't need my approval, ma'am."

She tucked a finger in the book to hold her place and closed it, then rested her chin on her fist to simply look at him. Ridge tried to ignore her steady gaze, but his body felt it all the way down to his marrow. He lowered himself to a nearby log and opened his saddlebags to slide the clean plates and forks back into them.

"I know I don't need it," she said. "But it would be rude of me to ignore you all evening."

Ridge barked a short laugh. "We aren't at some ice-cream social, Emma, so there's no need for you to be so polite-like." He finished fastening the saddlebags' straps. "You don't owe me anything but one hundred dollars once I get you home."

Her mouth pursed, like she just bit into a rotten apple. "You'll get your money."

"I know."

The fire crackled between them, occasionally snapping and shooting sparks into the air.

"Would you like me to read aloud?" Emma asked quietly.

He kept his gaze aimed downward, afraid she'd see how much her simple offer touched him. He cleared his throat. "If you'd like. It won't bother me."

"I hope you like humorous stories." She smiled and mischief glittered in her eyes, along with the firelight. She dipped her head and began. "*The Celebrated Jumping Frog of Calaveras County* by Mark Twain."

Ridge watched the movement of her bow-shaped lips as

she formed the words effortlessly. The sight mesmerized him, and tempted him to run a gentle finger along the full lower lip. He could imagine the softness, like a wild rose petal.

He closed his eyes, afraid temptation would overwhelm his common sense, and merely listened. He liked Emma's mellow voice as it rose and fell in a pleasant cadence. The only other woman who'd read to him had been his mother, and her voice hadn't been as easy on the ears. Emma had a way of making the story sound like something special and magical.

The story was about some gambler who trained a frog named Daniel Webster to jump. To Ridge, training a frog to jump seemed a useless thing to do, but the Twain fella had written it in such a way that it made Ridge chuckle and shake his head.

Of course, Ridge wasn't certain it was the story or Emma's way of reading it that made it so amusing.

Some minutes later Emma stopped and rubbed her eyes. "I thought I could finish it this evening, but I'm afraid it'll have to wait for another time."

Although disappointed, Ridge shrugged.

A breeze kicked up, stirring the fire and sending sparks swirling upward. Emma shivered and closed the book. "Winter's reminding us it's still here."

"Feels like it," Ridge murmured.

"Did my reading aloud bother you?"

He jerked his head up. "No. You've got a pretty voice." He suddenly realized what he'd said and snapped his mouth shut.

Emma smiled and laid her hand on his coat sleeve. Despite the clothing between them, Ridge fancied he could feel the warmth of her delicate fingers. "Thank you. I've always enjoyed reading. It's one of the things I missed most when I was with the People." Her eyes focused inward. "Sometimes when Enapay returned from a raid, he would bring me back a book."

"Enapay?"

Emma's eyes widened and he heard a catch in her breath. "He was a friend."

Suspicion followed closely on the heels of unexpected jealousy. "Sounds like more'n a friend."

"If he was, that's my business," Emma said without meeting his gaze.

Ridge eyed her warily. Was Enapay the reason Emma needed to find the tribe she'd lived with? And if he was, was it any of Ridge's concern?

"We'd best turn in," Ridge said.

Emma placed her book in her saddlebags as if it were gold bullion. But, then, maybe books were Emma Hartwell's treasure.

Without exchanging another word, Ridge and Emma slid into their respective bedrolls.

Ridge pondered Emma's slip and his own reaction to it. It was only natural for a man to want to protect a woman, even when the woman didn't want protecting. A lot of folks already suspected Emma had been sullied by the Indians, but if she'd chosen an Indian lover, her life would be made more hellish by neighbors and so-called friends.

What if she *was* trying to return to an Indian lover?

Unsettled, he turned on his side so his back was to the woman.

THE temperature fell rapidly overnight, and the following morning Emma and Ridge moved through their morning tasks quickly, eating jerky and leftover biscuits, and drinking icy water for breakfast. They readied their horses to head out just after sunrise.

Few words were exchanged between Emma and Ridge, and unwieldy silence hung between them. The horses tugged at their bits and danced nervously at skittering leaves as if sensing the tension. Emma kept a snug hold on the reins and tried not to think about the previous night's blunder. She'd been so careful for months. Why had she slipped up last night?

Because Ridge Madoc makes me feel too comfortable.

He could've continued questioning her about Enapay, but he hadn't. He also hadn't looked at her any differently this morning, although she had expected him to renege on their deal. However, he'd surprised her again. Any other man wouldn't have been so tolerant. Especially her own father.

The day remained cool as Emma and Ridge traveled through terrain which became more barren with every mile. The mountains were over their left shoulder, and the winds that swirled down from the snow-capped peaks battered at Emma, despite her warm coat, muffler, and scarf. During a short rest in the late morning, Emma added a blanket to her shoulders. Ridge cocked an eyebrow at her, but nodded when an especially vicious wind swept through, the bitter cold cutting to the bone.

Midafternoon brought an unholy scream that made the hair stand up on Emma's arms. The blood drained from her face as she cast about fearfully for the source of the inhuman sound. Or was this a vision reminding her of the danger ahead?

"Mountain lion," Ridge said, his breath misting through the scarf covering the lower half of his face.

Relief flowed through Emma. Ridge had heard it, too, which meant it wasn't part of her dreams. However, it still unnerved her.

"It's all right, Emma," he added. "It's half, maybe three-quarters of a mile away."

He obviously thought she was frightened of the animal, and Emma wasn't about to disabuse him of that notion. How could she explain her dreams without making him think she was crazy?

"Springtime. He's probably looking for companionship." Emma forced lightness into her tone.

"Not likely. They would've mated by now and the female would be carrying the young."

"Don't they mate for life, like wolves?" she asked, intrigued despite herself.

Ridge shook his head and his eyes twinkled above his wind-ruddy cheeks. "They're just like alley cats."

Emma recalled the hideous howls in the early spring from the feral cats, and her cheeks heated beneath her wool muffler. "Oh."

Ridge chuffed a quiet laugh.

Emma couldn't help but smile and her tension eased.

Half an hour later, they arrived at a river swollen with spring melt from the mountains. Chunks of ice streamed by occasionally, carried down from higher elevations.

"We'll have to find a better place to cross," Ridge said.

Emma's heart thumped loudly, and she fought the panic rising in her breast. "Good idea. This doesn't look safe," she agreed, raising her voice to be heard above the river's raging current.

Ridge turned his horse downstream and Emma followed, hunching her shoulders. They rode for nearly a mile before the river widened and the current slowed.

"How deep is it?" Emma tried to keep her gaze averted, but her attention kept returning to the streaming torrent.

A crease formed between Ridge's eyebrows. "If I remember right, not more'n two or three feet. The horses shouldn't even have to swim."

Emma studied the meandering expanse. Although it wasn't nearly as fast-flowing as upriver, fear clawed at her throat. Ever since she'd nearly drowned that fateful day seven years ago, she'd had an irrational fear of water. She hated crossing anything larger than a stream, but living with the Lakota, she'd been forced to do so or be left behind in the wilderness.

"Are you all right, Emma?" Ridge's concerned voice broke through her heart-pounding fear.

"Fine," she answered too quickly.

"If you're scared, we might be able to find a better place farther downstream or—" He paused deliberately. "We can go back."

"I'm not scared," she snapped.

Ridge scrutinized her and Emma held his gaze, unwilling to let him use her fear as an excuse to abandon her quest.

"All right," he said grudgingly. "Take off your boots and stockings, and carry them around your neck so they don't get wet."

Emma didn't want to expose her feet to the cold air and colder water, but recognized the wisdom in Ridge's suggestion. She dismounted and removed her boots. She glanced at Ridge to find his back to her and she quickly rolled down her heavy black stockings. Bunching the stockings, she placed them in her shoes. She tied the laces together and placed them behind her neck.

Before she could return to the saddle, Ridge joined her and cupped his hands. After a moment's surprise, Emma smiled gratefully and placed her bare foot in his warm palms. He raised her up and she gracefully swung her right leg over the saddle. As she fitted her right foot in the stirrup, Ridge gently guided her left foot into the other one, but didn't immediately release her.

Emma gazed down at him, but could only see the top of his hat and his wide, competent hands covering her bare foot. His thumb brushed across the sensitive instep and her toes curled as pleasure raced through her veins.

Ridge abruptly released her and mounted his horse. He, too, had tied his moccasins together and draped them over his neck. After one quick look at Emma, Ridge kneed his horse down the sloped bank and toward the water. The animal balked and Ridge kicked the gelding's flanks. With a snort and toss of his head, Paint entered the cold mountain water.

Emma's hands trembled and her body tensed tighter than a bowstring. If she wanted to discover her son's fate, she had no choice but to follow. Emma used the end of her leather reins to lightly slap Clementine's rump and the mare leapt forward, only to stop sharply at the edge of the river.

Emma sailed over the mare's neck to splash into the river. The icy cold water shocked the air from her lungs, and she frantically scrambled to her hands and knees in the shallows. She gulped in air as her body trembled.

"Emma, you all right?"

She blinked the droplets from her eyelashes and focused on Ridge, who'd ridden back across the river. Her heart racing and her lungs screaming, she could only nod.

He dismounted, getting his own feet wet in the shallow water. "What happened?"

"Uh, Clementine balked. Stupid of me. Flew over her head," Emma managed to gasp out.

Ridge frowned as if he didn't believe her, but only held out his hand. She accepted it gratefully and he tugged her to her feet.

"Your shoes are gone," Ridge said.

Emma's hand went to her neck but there was nothing there. They were the only shoes she had. "They can't be far." She frantically searched for the boots, but couldn't spot them.

Ridge scowled. "The current must've caught them. C'mon." He helped her up the steep bank, to where Clementine stood calmly, as if she'd done nothing wrong.

The cold breeze struck Emma, ripping away more heat from her chilled body. She wrapped her arms around herself and shivered.

Ridge released her and retrieved the blanket from her saddle. He wrapped it around her shoulders and picked her up.

"What're you doing?" Emma asked, struggling weakly to escape his arms.

"You might cut open your foot." Ridge carried her to a large rock where he eased her down. "I'll be right back."

When he rejoined her, he carried a second pair of moccasins. He knelt down and, with an economy of emotion, tugged the first deerskin boot, then the second, on her nearly numb feet.

"Thank you," she murmured.

"They're a mite big on you, but better than nothing. And since the river's not any deeper'n a couple feet, you won't get them wet."

"Are you sure?"

Ridge nodded. "I was all the way across when I looked back and seen you in the water."

"Sorry," she mumbled.

"It's all right," he said gently.

Emma's nerves jangled, but the terror she'd felt only minutes earlier loosened its stranglehold with Ridge's soft-spoken words. She leaned forward and rested her forehead against his chest. "I-I thought I was g-going to drown," she stammered.

"The water wasn't deep enough to drown in, but you did get soaked." He rubbed her back. "There's a shack only a mile or two from here where we can spend the night."

Emma nodded as she felt the first snowflake land on her cheek.

"Can you ride?" he asked.

"Yes."

Ridge helped her to her horse, then gave her a boost into the saddle. She settled uncomfortably on the cold seat, her wet clothes bunching around her legs and thighs.

"Here." Ridge held the reins up to her.

She accepted them and watched Ridge mount his black and white horse. He nudged the animal closer to her.

"Stay right behind me, Emma," Ridge said. "We'll cross slow and easy-like."

She closed her eyes momentarily against the renewed fear, but nodded gamely.

"Remember what I said. Stay close," he repeated.

Keeping her gaze on Ridge's back instead of the churning water, Emma followed him. Her heart sounded louder than the rushing water as she clung to the saddle-horn, her knuckles white. Her mare moved farther into the river. Goose bumps covered her skin and her teeth chattered, although Emma wasn't certain if it was from dread or the cold.

Ridge's horse scrambled up the opposite bank and out of the river. Clementine followed without prodding and Emma was once again on solid ground.

"Are you doing all right?" Ridge asked, his brow furrowed in concern.

She nodded, lightheaded with relief to have the crossing behind them. "Just c-cold."

"We'll be at the shack in five or ten minutes."

"Thank heavens," she murmured.

By the time they arrived at the small cabin, Emma's teeth were chattering uncontrollably and she had little feeling in her fingers and toes. Although her mind was sluggish, she knew she had to get out of the wet clothes and into something dry.

She started to dismount, then felt herself lifted from her horse. Blissful warmth radiated from Ridge and she snuggled against his chest. Closing her eyes, Emma imagined she was back in her tipi wrapped in heavy buffalo robes.

Ridge lifted the latch and the door swung open, the force of the wind causing it to crash against the wall.

He carried Emma inside, and the near silence was eerie after the dull roar of the blizzard. As his eyes adjusted to the darkness, he spotted a rough frame bed. Although it was bare and narrow, it was better than the dirt floor. He checked for mouse nests, found none, and lowered Emma to the thin mattress.

"Stay here. I'm going to get a fire going," he said to her.

She rolled onto her side and pulled her knees up to her chest. "So cold."

"I know. Just give me a few minutes and I'll have the place warmed up."

He went outside and moved the horses around to the lee side of the building, where he found a stack of firewood. He quickly hobbled the horses and loosened their girths. Promising to return to remove the tack, Ridge tossed Emma's saddlebags over his shoulder, then loaded his arms with wood and carried it into the cabin. He glanced at Emma who was still lying curled up on the bed—she appeared to have fallen asleep. He knelt beside the iron stove in the center of the single room. Five minutes later a fire blazed in the stove's belly.

Certain the fire had caught, he closed the stove door and rocked himself to his feet. Finding a lantern with some kerosene left in it, he lit the wick and pale yellow light filled the small cabin.

Now that he could see the room, he searched Emma's saddlebags for dry clothing. He found a skirt and blouse, but no undergarments. After a quick search of the cabin, he unearthed two old woolen blankets in a crate and laid them on the end of the bed, along with her clothing.

He debated whether to touch Emma while she was asleep, but decided it would be safe since he'd seen her knife in a saddlebag. Besides, she needed to change into dry clothing.

He shook her shoulder and she blinked blearily at him.

"You have to take off your wet clothes, Emma."

She nodded and her hands went to the buttons on her coat, but she only fumbled with them, as if she couldn't get her fingers to do what she wanted.

"Let me, Emma."

After a moment, she nodded in surrender and remained pliant as he removed her jacket, then the soaked blouse beneath it. Her damp camisole lay against her skin, so translucent Ridge could see the tan circling her peaked nipples through the cloth. He swallowed hard and ignored the undeniable charge of lust through his veins. Keeping his gaze averted, he skimmed the undergarment off and tossed it aside. He covered her naked breasts, glancing at them only once as he buttoned her blouse. Steeling his reaction to her feminine body, he removed her skirt and petticoat with the same impersonal motions and slipped on the dry skirt.

His gaze traveled to her face where he met half-lidded eyes. "Thank you," she whispered, her expression as trusting as a child's.

"You're welcome," he said, an odd lump in his throat.

He eased her back down on the bed, her eyes already closing, and covered her with the dry blankets. Fighting the urge to kiss her brow, Ridge dragged a shaking hand across his forehead. Although he was tired, he was glad he still had the horses to take care of. He needed the distance from Emma to cool his hot blood.

Half an hour later, Ridge finished laying out Emma's wet clothing around the tiny cabin. He'd changed out of his damp buckskins into some men's clothes he'd found in the same box as the blankets. Although the pants were a little snug and the shirt hugged his chest, he was glad for the dry clothing.

Ridge added more wood to the fire and stretched, popping his spine in two places. Outside, the light gave way to darkness. The wind continued to blast, and the cabin creaked from the assault. Spring blizzards weren't uncommon but this one had caught him unprepared. They wouldn't be continuing their journey for a day or two, maybe longer.

Ridge considered making something to eat, but exhaustion won out. The bed looked inviting, even without Emma in it. But she was there and it wasn't proper to be lying beside a woman who wasn't your wife or a whore, even if he had seen her in her full glory.

Sighing, he laid down on the floor close to the stove and crossed his arms over his chest. He'd slept in a lot worse conditions.

BEING on his own since the age of fifteen, Ridge was a light sleeper. Even the absence of sound often awakened him because of its peculiarity. This time, however, it was Emma's restlessness that woke him.

Ridge rolled to his knees beside the bed. Emma's face was damp and he rested his palm lightly on her brow. She had a slight fever.

He massaged her blanket-covered arm. "Easy, Emma."

She turned toward him, but her eyes remained closed.

Her agitation eased and Ridge breathed a sigh of relief. He rose and added more wood to the fire, then laid back down on the floor.

Emma grew restive again, and Ridge debated for only a few seconds before climbing onto the narrow bed beside her. Leaving the blankets between their bodies, he lay on his back, his side touching hers.

She snuffled and rolled halfway on top of him, hiding her face in the crook of his shoulder. It was sweet torture to hold her softness and feel her breasts against his chest. He was sorely tempted to skim his hands below her blouse and cup them in his palms. The cold had pebbled her nipples earlier. Would his touch do the same?

Ridge's eyes shot open. This was Emma Hartwell, a woman who trusted him with both her life and her virtue. *But what if there was no virtue to protect?*

Ridge shoved his doubts aside. It didn't make any difference. He wouldn't take advantage of a good woman who'd already had a world of hurt in her life. He rested his chin on Emma's crown and focused on the blowing wind.

Within moments, he was asleep.

$\mathcal{E}$IGHT

EMMA shifted in the warm cocoon as she was lured toward waking. She ignored the pull and snuggled deeper into the arms that embraced her. In fact, there was an entire wall of solid heat behind her. She smiled to herself.

An erection lay nestled against her buttocks and, caught between wakefulness and slumber, Emma pressed against familiar hardness. Desire meandered through her veins and settled in her belly. She knew it had been a long time since she'd lain with her husband. He must have been riding with a raiding party and returned last night while she'd been asleep. Unlike many warriors who were gone for days, her husband didn't awaken her to spill his seed in his wife immediately after his return. He was a considerate lover, concerned with her pleasure, too.

Through the lazy haze of passion, Emma felt the thrill of hands stroking her bare stomach and moving higher to her breasts. She tingled with need, knowing the pleasure that awaited her by joining with her husband. Rolling onto her back, Emma reached for the hem of her deerskin dress . . . only to encounter cotton.

Bewildered, she opened her eyes to see not Enapay, but

a stranger looking down at her. She rolled away and was caught by a strong arm.

"Easy, Emma. You'll fall off the bed," the man said in a husky voice.

Memories returned. *Ridge Madoc. Traveling. The river. Icy water.*

She searched the dim room, not recognizing anything, except the man lying in bed with her. "Wha—how'd we get here?"

He leaned back, placing more space between their bodies. "We rode here, remember?"

She had to think a moment. "My horse threw me into the river. You came back and then you led the way across." She shifted so she wasn't in danger of falling off the bed. "You said you knew where there was a cabin."

Ridge smiled, his teeth uncommonly white against his dark growth of whiskers. "This is it. It ain't much, but it's out of the weather."

"I'm just glad it's warm. Thank you." She glanced down, noticing her blouse was mis-buttoned and it was different than the one she'd been wearing. So was the skirt, and she wasn't wearing any undergarments. She pressed her thighs together. "Did you—?" She motioned to her clothing.

He glanced down and murmured, "You were asleep, so I dressed you in dry clothes."

Ridge levered himself off the crowded bed and Emma couldn't help but notice how snug his clothing was, especially the trousers. The material outlined his hard length. Her cheeks warm, she raised her gaze. "It seems I owe you another thank you."

Ridge knelt in front of the stove, his back to her, and opened the stove door. The fabric of his shirt threatened to split across his shoulders and hugged his firm torso down to where it was tucked into his trousers. Her body pulsed with unfulfilled passion and she wished she were brave enough to kneel behind him and wrap her arms around his lean body.

"You don't owe me anything, ma'am. It's part of the job." He added the last piece of wood.

Although his words were true, they hurt, and erased her desire completely. "I'm still indebted to you," she said lamely.

He turned to look at her over his shoulder. His gaze was steady with no sign of the hunger she'd glimpsed moments earlier. "One hundred dollars worth."

Humiliation made her cheeks burn, and she silently scolded herself. Lying so close in the narrow bed had made Ridge's maleness react as nature intended. Any other woman would have produced the same response. Ridge had made no secret of the fact that he was leading her to the Indians only for the money. So why did his businesslike manner disturb her?

"Are you hungry?" he asked.

"Yes," she simply replied.

"There's some cans on a shelf. We can open one of those."

Emma watched as he looked at each can, then set one filled with tomatoes on a tiny rickety table. "Tomatoes for breakfast?" she asked, frowning at his choice.

Ridge shrugged. "Why don't you pick what you'd like while I check the horses?"

Emma stood and had to wait a moment for a wave of dizziness to pass. She was aware of Ridge's scrutiny and waved a hand at him. "I'm fine."

He didn't say anything, but donned his moccasins and coat. He paused by the door. "There's an empty can under the bed you can use while I'm gone." He left the cabin and cold wind shimmied across the floor.

Emma quickly found the can and did her business, then placed it outside the door. Before checking out the tin goods, she found her only remaining pair of black stockings in her saddlebag. Flushing slightly, she drew them on, along with the now-dry undergarments Ridge had removed and hung up to dry. She also tugged on Ridge's oversize moccasins to keep her feet warm.

Emma brushed her hair and tied it in a ponytail that fell halfway down her back. Now that she was dressed decently, she padded to the corner of the cabin. She picked up the cans and read each label, then picked out two—peaches and hominy—and placed the tomatoes back on the wall shelf. Although she liked tomatoes, she couldn't fathom eating them in the morning.

By the time Ridge returned bearing an armload of wood, Emma had opened the tin cans and had the hominy heating on the stove. She also used water from the canteens to make a pot of coffee.

"Smells good," Ridge commented. "I seen a kettle that I'll use to bring some snow in."

"Does it look like the storm will be ending soon?" Emma asked.

He shook his head, his expression grim. "Not likely, ma'am. Maybe tomorrow."

Emma turned back to the stove so he wouldn't see her disappointment, and began to mash the hominy.

"They won't be able to travel, either," Ridge said, guessing her thoughts.

"I know, but I've been looking for so long."

"Everything will work out the way it's supposed to, Emma."

She knew Ridge couldn't offer her any more reassurances, and was glad he didn't insult her by trying. She wouldn't despair, not after coming all this way.

After Ridge brought in a snow-filled kettle and put it on the stove, they ate the simple meal at the small table. Emma had the only chair, and Ridge sat on an empty cracker keg that had been beside the bed.

As the blizzard continued unabated through the long morning, Emma busied herself by exploring the shack. But there was little to find except for two pairs of wool socks. She donned a pair over her stockings, which made the moccasins fit a tiny bit better.

Ridge finally changed into his own clothes, which relieved Emma. She had found herself eyeing him far too often in the too-small shirt and trousers.

Ridge kept the potbelly stove full of wood. The heat kept the cabin comfortable, but the fierce winds drove through the cracks in the walls. He plugged some of the worst ones with mud he made from melted snow and dirt from the floor, but the room remained drafty.

Near noon, Ridge opened the door to bring in more wood, and a four-foot snowdrift greeted him. They were lucky it didn't cover the door. He hauled in five armloads of wood and Emma carried them from the door to the stove, where she made a neat pile. It gave her something to do, as well as assuaged some of her guilt for being so useless yesterday.

With the last armload, Ridge stomped the snow off his boots and removed them by the door. Emma handed him the other pair of wool socks she'd discovered.

"Thanks," he murmured.

"You're welcome." She crossed to the stove and stirred the contents of a small kettle. "I made some lunch, if you're hungry."

Ridge's stomach growled, eliciting a wry smile from him. "Guess I am, ma'am."

Emma had combined some of her seasonings with the tomatoes to make a decent soup, and had mixed up sourdough biscuits to go with it. It wasn't a feast, but it filled them.

After their lunch, Ridge brought out a folded map and opened it on the table. Emma joined him, leaning close to see the squiggles and lines.

"Where are we?" she asked, pointing at the map.

Ridge stabbed a point. "Here. About fifty miles southwest of the Yellowstone River."

"So that crooked line is the Yellowstone River?"

He nodded. "And this one here is the Tongue and this one the Powder." He dragged his finger upward. "I'm thinking the Lakota group went this way."

Emma nodded, hoping he was right. She leaned closer. "Where's the fort?"

"Fort Fetterman, where we came from, is back here." He pointed to a square south of their location, and then motioned to another square almost due west. "That's Fort Logan."

She straightened. "Why don't you write the names on the map? It'd be easier to follow."

Ridge refolded the map. "I know where everything is."

"But—"

"It's my map, Emma, and I like it the way it is," he said curtly.

He collected his revolver and rifle, along with his cleaning supplies and brought them to the table.

Sighing, Emma went in search of something to do and retrieved her book. She sat at the table across from Ridge.

"You can read out loud, if you'd like," he offered.

"It won't bother you?"

He shook his head. "It's better than listening to the wind howling." He grinned boyishly. "Besides, I want to find out what happened to Daniel Webster."

She smiled, inordinately pleased. "So you *were* listening."

His eyes twinkled. "I told you I was. Go on."

Amused by his eagerness, she began to read. As she did, the blizzard disappeared from her thoughts and only Ridge's occasional snort of laughter drew her out of the imaginary world of Jim Smiley, Daniel Webster, and Simon Wheeler. Half an hour later, she closed the book.

"That Twain fella sure knows how to spin a yarn," Ridge remarked. He'd finished cleaning his weapons while she read, and had leaned back in his chair for the remainder of the tale.

Emma gazed into his twinkling eyes and nodded. "Last month I read his first book that related his journey to Nevada to look for gold. I enjoy his humorous slant on his fellow human beings."

Ridge eyed her with something akin to awe. "You sound like you've read a lot of books."

She shrugged, embarrassed. "I suppose I have. Before I lived with the Indians, I used to read all the time." She gazed unseeingly at the stove, her mind going back to the day her life was irrevocably changed.

"Why'd you fall off your horse, Emma?" Ridge asked curiously.

She blinked at the unexpected question. "She stopped fast and I went over her head."

Ridge's eyes were somber. "You're a good rider. What's the real reason?"

Emma stared down at her book, debating whether to tell him or not. She took a deep breath and raised her head. "I'm terrified of crossing rivers."

"Why?"

"I was fifteen years old. I'd ridden to my secret place so I could read without Mother or Sarah bothering me. There was this huge oak tree beside a river. We'd gotten a lot of rain and the water was higher than usual and it was moving fast, just like the river we crossed yesterday. I was walking along the bank when the ground gave way under my feet. I fell in."

She shuddered, remembering too well how the fast-flowing water bore her downstream, and how exhausted she became trying to break away and swim to shore.

"My dress was so heavy, it kept dragging me down. It took everything I had to keep my head above the water. I don't know how far the current carried me until it began to slow and I managed to crawl out. The next thing I remember is waking up to find an Indian standing over me." In her mind's eye, she pictured the savage warrior who became her adopted father.

"I'm sorry." Ridge laid his hand on hers.

She gazed down at the veins that textured the back of his hand and the long slender fingers more fitting of an artist than an army scout. "Don't be," she said softly. "He and his wife treated me like their own child." She traced one of the narrow white scars that crisscrossed his knuckles. "How'd you get these?" she asked.

He shrugged. "Got them when I was a kid."

Her fingers found another scar on his palm. "How about this one?"

A corner of his lips quirked upward. "Made the mistake of sticking my nose in where it didn't belong. The man who did it ended up teaching a stupid boy how to survive in the wilderness. Tracking, hunting, trapping, and anything else involved in staying alive."

"How old were you?"

"Fifteen." He drew his hand out from between hers. "Are you going to read some more?"

"I need to give my voice a rest." Grinning, she pushed the book toward him. "But I wouldn't mind listening to your voice."

Ridge shook his head and rose so abruptly his chair almost tipped over. "No, ma'am. You don't want to listen to this croaky voice."

Emma rested her cheek on her propped up hand. "You have a beautiful voice, Ridge."

His face reddened. "A man's voice can't be beautiful, Emma."

"Yours is," she insisted. "Read the next story. Please?"

He turned away, shaking his head. "I've got to check the fire."

Emma frowned, not understanding his reticence. He obviously enjoyed stories, yet he didn't want to read. Her gaze caught the canned goods on the shelf and recalled how Ridge had chosen tomatoes for breakfast. She thought of his map and how well it was marked, yet no names were written on it.

"Do you know how to read, Ridge?" she asked softly.

Ridge remained squatting in front of the stove, his back to Emma. The silence stretched out until he answered in a voice so soft Emma had to strain to hear him.

"No."

Ridge stared into the stove, at the reddish-orange embers that writhed like a nest of disturbed snakes. His face burned, but the fire wasn't the reason. Memories. All bad. Words he'd buried. Anger he'd swallowed. Pain he'd hidden.

A hand on his shoulder startled him and he barely restrained the instinct to jerk away. Her fingertips made small indents in his skin, each one a gentle brand.

"There's no need to be ashamed," Emma said quietly.

Her words reminded him why she stood so close and why he couldn't stay. He straightened and gazed down at the woman's upturned face. Her eyes were wide, filled with sympathy, and he wished he hadn't looked at her.

"I'm not," he lied.

Emma folded her arms across her waist, her stubbornness revealing itself in her bold stance. "Many men and women are illiterate."

Even though Ridge didn't know how to read, he did understand words and illiterate was one he hated. Ignorant was another. However, they weren't as bad as "simpleton" or "idiot" or "half-wit." He'd heard them all, mostly from his stepfather, but also from his classmates and the teacher who hadn't believed him. It was only his mother who had believed him.

He stalked over to his saddlebags, needing something to occupy his hands and thoughts, but found himself idly playing with a strap as he struggled to escape the memories' harsh blows. He heard Emma come up behind him but didn't turn around.

"Schools were scarce in the Territory," she said.

Ridge kept his neck bowed as his fingers stilled their restless motions. "I grew up in Sunset, same as you."

A frown tugged at her pretty lips and questions flashed in her eyes, but she only asked, "Your parents didn't let you attend?"

He bit the inside of his cheek and tasted blood. "Let it be, Emma."

"I only want to help."

It tore at his gut to hear her wounded tone. But all these

years he'd hidden his failing from everyone but Colt Rivers, who'd helped him hide his condition from the army. "There's nothing you can do," he said, less gruff now. "I could teach you letters and how to read," she offered, then smiled. "I used to dream about being a teacher before—" Her smile faltered.

Ridge gripped his saddlebags to keep from hugging this tenderhearted woman whose cheeks pinkened with uncharacteristic shyness. He could see her as a child, pretending to be at the front of a classroom and calling up imaginary students to read or answer a question.

If only it were as simple as she believed.

He closed his eyes, wondering if he had the strength to confess. He owed it to Emma to try. He guided her to the table and held the chair for her. Although her expression was puzzled, she sat with her hands knotted in her lap and remained silent. That was one of the things Ridge liked about her—she didn't badger him with a passel of questions, but let him speak in his own time.

He perched on the barrel, his hands on his knees. "It wasn't that I didn't go to school," he began. "For three years I did. I learned my letters and numbers. It's just that when they were all together, they didn't make any sense."

A furrow appeared between her eyebrows. "What do you mean?"

Frustrated, Ridge dug his fists into his thighs. "Book pages looked like a jumble of letters. I tried sounding the words out like the teacher said, but I never could get them right. And when I tried writing them, I got the letters all mixed up." He shook his head. "The teacher figured I was either lazy or stupid."

"You aren't either," Emma argued, her eyes blazing with indignation. "From what I've seen you aren't afraid to work and you're one of the smartest men I've met."

Although he was warmed by her belief in him, it was misplaced. His mouth was bone-dry and he tried to work up some moisture. "At first the teacher said I was doing them wrong to be contrary." He ran a trembling hand through his long hair and smiled, although amusement was far from his thoughts. "He broke a lot of rulers on me."

Emma's gaze darted to his fists, and Ridge stilled the impulse to tuck his hands behind his back.

"The scars on your knuckles." Her face paled. "I'm sorry, Ridge."

"It wasn't you who did the deed."

She laid a soft hand on his knee. "I'm sorry you were punished for something that wasn't your fault."

Ridge shrugged aside her concern. "The teacher tried. He'd make me write letters over and over until my hand hurt so bad, I couldn't write anymore, but I still couldn't get it right."

"What about your mother and father?"

"Ma used to read to me and I'd try to follow along. And my stepfather—" He peered out the window beside the bed. Snowflakes dashed by, chasing one another as they raced to the earth. "He thought I was lazy and stupid."

And beat the hell out of me with his leather belt.

"Will you let me try?" she asked softly. "I promise we'll stop whenever you want."

No, Ridge didn't want her witnessing his humiliation. Besides, she'd just think he wasn't trying, just like everybody else.

He stalked to the door and shrugged into his sheepskin coat. "I'm going out to check on the horses and bring in more wood."

He plunged outside before Emma could speak. The wind stole his breath, and he turned his back to it, struggling to breathe against the assault of frigid air. He punched his hands into his pockets and lowered his head against the brittle sheet. He trudged through the drifts, most of which were higher than his knees.

In his haste to escape Emma and the memories she evoked, he'd forgotten his gloves and a scarf to wrap around his face. He wouldn't be able to stay outside long without risking frostbite. He checked the horses and found them huddled together, their backsides to the wind that tore around the corner of the cabin. There was little snow buildup on the lee side so the animals could forage. The horses had drunk the melted snow Ridge had brought earlier, and he picked up the battered tin pan to refill. The metal was so cold it seemed to burn Ridge's fingers and he dropped it, cussing. The horses skittered away.

"Easy," Ridge soothed, running a hand along Paint's neck, then along Clementine's withers. Once the animals were resettled, he tugged his jacket cuff over his hand and picked up the pan, silently cursing his idiocy in leaving his gloves in the cabin.

Idiot.

That was one of those words that had sent him out here like a dog with its tail tucked between its hind legs. Even now, almost twenty-five years later, the remembered jeers made his gut tighten with bottled-up anger and hopelessness. He knew Emma would never taunt him, but if he accepted her offer to try to teach him, she would soon realize the truth.

He was stupid.

NINE

HIS ears began to grow numb and Ridge tramped back to the cabin, pausing by the door to fill the pan with clean snow. With a ball of dread in his belly Ridge entered the cabin, and warmth and peacefulness surrounded him.

Emma was standing by the stove and turned to face him as he set the metal pan on the floor beside the door. He removed his coat, prolonging the moment before he would say no to her generous, but misguided, offer.

"More water for the horses?" she asked, her chin motioning to the pan.

Ridge nodded.

She crossed the floor to pick it up and set it on the stovetop. The snow on the bottom of the pan sizzled and crackled on the hot surface, unusually loud in the cabin's silence.

"I could've done that," Ridge said, unaccountably irritated.

"I know."

She remained by the stove and stared into the pan. Ridge couldn't read her expression, except that she seemed thoughtful. He joined her, standing on the opposite side, and held his chilled hands over the rising heat.

"When I lived with the Indians, my adopted father brought back a horse from a raid," Emma began conversationally.

Ridge lifted his head, but found her gaze aimed at the melting snow.

"The horse tried to bite anyone who came near it. It also had these horrible scars on its back and withers." Emma hugged herself. "Fast Elk said it had been beaten for so long, it had forgotten how to trust. So when anyone came near the poor animal, it expected pain. Fast Elk worked with that horse every day for weeks to get it to trust him."

She paused and worried her lower lip between her teeth.

Ridge knew where she was headed with her story and sighed impatiently. "So your adopted father finally got the horse to trust him and the animal became his favorite pony."

Emma lifted her head and her eyes revealed sadness. "No. The horse never learned to trust and we used him for meat that winter."

Ridge drew back, startled by her blunt words. "So what's your point, Emma?"

She met his gaze unflinchingly. "The point is that the horse refused to trust anyone, and it died because of its stubbornness."

"You can't expect an animal to understand, Emma," Ridge said, not bothering to hide his annoyance. "If it only knows pain from people, it has no reason to let anyone get close."

"That's right. But we're people, not horses."

Ridge saw only sincerity and compassion in her expression. He knew she wanted to help him, but she didn't know that in doing so, she'd only be hurting him.

"Please let me try to teach you," Emma implored.

"You don't know what you're asking, ma'am."

She stepped around the stove and clasped his hands. There was unexpected strength in her grip. "I'm asking you to trust me, Ridge."

He had no defense against her softly spoken words. Although he suspected she was hiding secrets—secrets involving the very Indians they searched for—he trusted her with his. He ignored the tightening in his chest and nodded slowly. "I'm not holding you to any promises," he assured her. "A lot of folks have tried, including my own ma."

"Then I'll be in good company, won't I?"

Her smile thwarted any other arguments he had, and he wished he had the right to take her in his arms and kiss her. "Yes, ma'am."

Emma rubbed her palms together. "First thing is to find something to write on."

"You want to start now?"

Challenging eyes met his. "Do you have something better to do?"

He fumbled around for an excuse to stall his lessons. "I should take the melted snow out to the horses and bring in more wood."

He expected Emma to argue, but she only said, "We'll start whenever you're ready."

"After I do the chores," Ridge felt obligated to add.

This time Ridge took the time to bundle up warmly and, despite himself, found he was growing excited about Emma's offer. What if she could accomplish what no one else had? What if he could actually learn to read and write?

No! He wouldn't let himself hope, only to have that hope crushed yet again. So many times he'd thought he could learn. He'd even come to recognize a few words, like his name and some smaller words. But picking up a book and reading it like Emma did was something beyond his abilities.

Half an hour later, he finished the chores and returned to the cabin with the last armload of wood. Emma sat by the table, biting her lower lip between her teeth as she studied the open book before her. Her braid tumbled over her shoulder and draped her left breast. One of the blankets hung like a sack on her, and his too-large moccasins stuck out from beneath her skirt. But her spine was straight and her slender neck curved enticingly, inviting him to kiss the pale skin. She was a fetching woman, her natural beauty made more evident by her lack of a fancy dress and slippers.

Ridge took a steadying breath and joined her.

"What're you doing?" he asked.

She glanced up, startled. "Trying to figure out how to begin. It's been a few years since I attended school and I don't want to do this wrong."

"It's not like anyone else has done it right," Ridge said with an unexpected swell of bitterness.

"Then we'll both figure out the right way."

His reservations returned twofold, and he knew he should back out now while he still could, but hated to be the one to dim the bright enthusiasm in her eyes. It was a sight better than the unhappiness he'd glimpsed in their depths too many times in the past few days.

He lowered himself onto the barrel.

"Can you read or write at all?" Emma asked.

Her question was cautious, like she was tiptoeing around a family of skunks.

"My name and some words. Not much," he admitted.

She turned the open book so it lay in front of him. "I'd like you to see if you can read the title of this story."

Ridge's heart clamored into his throat, just like when Mr. Porter instructed him to read in front of the class. He cursed himself for being so skittish. He wasn't seven years old anymore and Emma wasn't going to rap his knuckles with a ruler when he got it wrong.

He licked his lips and leaned over the page, which was filled with a terrifying mishmash of letters. Focusing on the largest letters on the page, he began. "The s-stier fo the dab—"

He shoved the book across the table in frustration and Emma caught it before it fell off the edge. He should've known it would be like this—feeling like he was that dumb kid again and standing at the front of the class as the other children laughed at him.

A trickle of sweat rolled down between his shoulder

blades. He squeezed his fists so tightly they began to cramp. "I'm stupid. I told you," he said hoarsely.

She clasped a clenched hand. "It's all right, Ridge." She scooted her chair nearer to the barrel, so her shoulder touched his arm, and dragged the book back into place. She pointed to the first word he'd stumbled over. "Can you read the letters of the word?"

He fought the urge to shove both the book and himself away from the table. For Emma, he'd try. He concentrated on the book and not on Emma's clean scent or her soft hair, which was almost close enough to tickle his nose. "S-T-Y-O-R."

Her brows folded downward. "That's S-T-O-R-Y. Story."

"No, it's not."

Her frown grew, and Ridge recognized that look. It was the same one everyone else had right before they told him to stop making things up. But instead, Emma asked, "What about numbers?"

"What?"

"Can you read numbers?"

He shifted uncomfortably. "I know numbers but it's the same as the words."

"What do you mean?" She was staring at him like he was a bug she'd never seen before.

Ridge gnashed his teeth. It would work better just to show her. "Tell me a number."

"Four."

"A bigger one."

"Four hundred and thirty-two."

Ridge could clearly see the numbers in his mind's eye and he used his forefinger to write them on the table. Four. Two. Three.

"That's four hundred and twenty-three, Ridge," Emma corrected.

He shook his head stubbornly. "It's four hundred and thirty-two."

Emma nibbled her lower lip. "You changed the numbers around."

"It doesn't look that way to me."

Her expression was more puzzled than disbelieving. "What about if I would write a number?"

Another shrug. "Go ahead."

He watched her finger move across the table. Five. Eight. Seven. "Five hundred and eighty-seven."

"Exactly," Emma said, smiling with victory. "You *can* read numbers."

"Only if I watch you make them." Ridge had been through this before, too.

"Stay here." Emma scurried over to the wood and pried a piece of bark from one of the logs, then knelt on the floor and wrote something in the dirt. "All right. Come here."

Wary, Ridge crossed to her side and leaned over, his hands braced on his thighs. He gazed at the number she'd written. "Nine hundred and twenty-four."

She grabbed his hand and tugged him down beside her, then covered the last two numbers in the dirt. "What number is that?" she asked.

"Nine," he replied, barely restraining his exasperation.

"Now put a picture of the nine in your head," Emma instructed.

Ridge did so.

She put her hands over the first and last number. "This number?"

"Four."

She grinned, but only said, "Now place that one beside the nine in your mind."

Ridge narrowed his eyes as comprehension sank in.

Then she covered the first two numbers with her hands.

"Two," he said without prompting. He looked at the three numbers in his mind. "Nine hundred and forty-two."

Emma clapped her dusty hands. "That's right!"

Ridge sat back on his heels and gazed at the number on the floor. He pointed at it. "But that doesn't match the one in my head."

"Can I tell you another story?" she asked.

"As long as there's not a horse involved."

She grinned. "No horses, I promise." She shifted around so her slender legs were folded sideways beneath her and close enough to Ridge that he could feel her dress against his leg.

"I learned much of the Lakota language from the children because the adults were too busy," Emma began. "Thay'd draw pictures in the dirt and give the Lakota name to the thing or animal. Although they didn't have letters or numbers like we do, they used pictures to tell stories."

Ridge nodded, knowing this already from his own association with the Indians.

"There was a little girl named Sweet Blossom who would draw her story pictures out of sequence. But if you asked her to tell her story, she would do so correctly. But if I drew a story for her, she would 'read' it wrong. She actually saw the pictures in a different order than everyone else."

Ridge felt a kinship with the unknown girl, but kept his voice indifferent. "What happened to her?"

Emma smiled. "The Lakota saw her as gifted. She learned to read picture stories by watching others recite theirs; and everyone else learned hers the same way."

"But I can read and draw maps without doing it backward."

"If someone draws picture stories backward, why isn't it possible that another person could see words and numbers turned around?"

Hope, long dead, stirred to life. "So you believe me?"

Emma motioned toward the number drawn on the dirt floor. "The proof is right in front of us."

He studied the individual numbers, trying to separate them mentally as Emma had done physically. It made his head ache. "Knowing that doesn't mean I can learn to read or write," he stated.

"You're right," Emma said honestly. "But I think you *can* learn. It's going to take time and patience to find the right way to do it."

"And someone who understands to teach me," he stated bluntly.

Emma drew lines in the dirt with the piece of bark. "I understand that you see things differently, but I'm not sure how to make sense of what you see."

Ridge locked his hands together. "The number. The way you did that helped me to read it right. Maybe we can try it with words, too."

Emma gazed at him, her expression unrevealing of her thoughts. "For short sentences, maybe, but things like newspapers or books, it would take too much time and you'd lose both interest and patience. You said you can recognize some words?"

He nodded. "Ma used to read things to me over and over again, and after so long I just knew what some of the words looked like."

"So you memorized them." She thought about that a moment, then seemed to come to a decision. "I'd like to try some things this afternoon. That way maybe we can both come up with ideas on what might work."

Although doubts continued to plague Ridge, he suspected that if anybody could come up with a way to help him, it would be Emma. She was determined and intelligent, and too pretty for his peace of mind. Being stranded in the small cabin with her was sweet torture. He was no saint and temptation seemed awfully close in these four walls. He hoped her lessons would steer his thoughts in other directions, even if his body's compass kept swinging back to Emma.

Ridge stood and clasped her hand, tugging her to her feet. He miscalculated his strength and she flew upward, with a little cry of surprise, and into his arms. Her breasts flattened against his chest and his body reacted with all the subtlety of a tomcat in the springtime.

Startled, Ridge looked down into Emma's uptilted face expecting to find shock and disapproval. Instead, he was stunned to see the reflection of his own desire and he instinctively drew her flush against him. His open hands splayed across her lower back, over the rise of her soft buttocks. His masculine pride preened when she moaned ever-so-softly and a flush spread across her cheeks.

Emma was so close he could feel her heart thumping wildly and smell the first tendrils of her passion. Pleasure swirled through his brain, obliterating everything but his need, which had only risen in the hours spent alone with her.

"I want you, Emma," Ridge whispered.

Emma's legs wobbled but Ridge's corded arms kept her upright. She knew intimately what he wanted, as her own body begged for the same, but once they gave in to lust, it would be impossible to undo. The second time would be easier, then a third and fourth even easier. Two lonely people in the middle of nowhere. So easy . . .

But they would both regret it once they returned to civilization. Ridge because of his sense of honor, and Emma, heaven help her, because she would only want him more.

She felt his hardness against her belly and her breath caught in her throat. Long-denied desire surged through her blood, swamping her senses. Ridge's hands caressed her buttocks, cupping and squeezing gently.

Would it be so bad, just this one time, to feel like a woman again? To touch a man's body, to skim her fingers along silky heat and flexing muscles? To smell the heady scent of Ridge's arousal and feel his breath upon her face and breasts?

The choice was hers and her mind knew what she should do, but her heart and body railed against rationality and caution. Ridge wasn't like the others; he never treated her with anything less than respect, despite him knowing she was a "white squaw." And he wanted her.

Just as she wanted him.

It was as simple as that.

Tomorrow she would have to live with her decision, but today she would surrender to the dictates of her heart and body.

She lifted her gaze and shivered at the naked passion that darkened Ridge's eyes. She cupped his cheek and his whiskers rasped against her palm, making her shiver with longing. Drawing closer, she gazed at his lips—lips that had spoken kind, soothing words to her; lips that had defended her; lips she'd fantasized about as she lay in her bed late at night.

He lowered his head, tilting it so their mouths matched perfectly. She'd always imagined his lips would be firm like the rest of him, but they softened beneath hers. Their breaths mingled as the kiss grew deeper. Ridge's tongue swept across her lips and she opened to allow him entry, tasting him for the first time. He caressed her palette and played across her teeth and the inside of her cheeks. He was devouring her as she pressed closer, allowing him everything he wanted.

Ridge drew away and rested his forehead against hers, his breathing swift and shallow. "If you don't want this, Emma, say so now. I can't promise I can stop later."

Emma considered his words for only a second and wrapped her arms around his neck. "I don't want you to stop. Not now, not later," she whispered.

With one fluid motion, Ridge scooped her into his arms and carried her the short distance to the bed. He laid her down and straightened, gazing at her with hot, lust-filled eyes. He slipped his hands under his suspenders and drew them off his well-shaped shoulders. "I wanted you the first time I saw you walking down the road, your shoulders so straight and proud." Passion roughened his voice.

Emma's heart tripped and words abandoned her. Kneeling on the bed, she helped him remove his shirt, leaving him in a wool undershirt. She tugged it out of his waistband and glided her hands beneath the material, losing herself in the sensation of his smooth warm skin. Her mouth grew dry as he lifted the shirt over his head, baring a sleek, well-muscled chest.

Running her hands up his planed torso, Emma felt his nipples pucker beneath her palms. With a little smile, she leaned forward and latched onto one, sucking it to pebble hardness.

Ridge moaned and his hands cupped the back of her head, his fingers wrapping themselves in her silky hair. "Emma."

She kissed a line across his chest and teased the other crest with her tongue and lips. Growing bolder, Emma stroked his back and sides, and felt the goose bumps that arose on his fevered flesh.

Suddenly her shoulders were grasped and she raised her head. Ridge crushed his lips down upon hers, and she met him without flinching, matching his passion with her liberated desire. Clumsy fingers opened her blouse and a work-roughened hand slid under her camisole. He cupped her breast with a tenderness that belied the primal urgency of their bodies. He rolled her nipple between his fingertips and she broke away from his savage kiss, panting heavily as arousal pulsed through her body in unending waves.

With unspoken agreement, they quickly shed the remainder of their clothing. Emma tossed hers onto the floor, uncaring as to where it landed, only wanting to have Ridge's nakedness against her own.

She lay back on the bed and drank in Ridge's virile beauty. He stood at the foot of the bed, solid and self-assured, with his hands on his hips as he stared down at her, his hot gaze caressing every inch of her body. Curious, she brazenly inspected his impressive masculinity, hard and curved against his belly. There was a glimmer of moisture at the tip, and it tantalized her.

She shifted over on the bed and patted the mattress in clear invitation. Ridge immediately settled beside her, his arms coming around her waist as he drew her flush against him. They kissed for lingering moments, then Ridge began to nuzzle her jaw and neck, and lower. He worshiped her body with his hands and mouth, and Emma's breasts tingled beneath his devotion. Her womb felt swollen and damp, and the pressure within rose with each caress.

Ridge cupped the source of her heat and eased a finger into her wetness. He teased the nub, sending a bolt of lightning through Emma's loins. Gasping, she reached down between their bodies to encircle his erection. He throbbed within her fist and she brushed her fingertip across the drop of moisture.

Ridge's muscles bunched and he inhaled sharply. "Emma."

Her heart kicked against her ribs and she tried to calm her stumbling breath. She released him and clutched his rock-solid arms. "Yes. Now Ridge." She hardly recognized the needy voice as her own.

Ridge paused to gaze down at her, as if gauging her readiness. A moment later, he guided himself to her opening and teased her sensitive folds.

Emma pumped her hips upward, straining toward him as her fingers dug into his arms. "Now. Please."

Ridge planted his hands on the mattress on either side of her and raised himself up so they touched only where they were joined. He continued pressing inward at a snail's pace, moving forward with agonizing deliberation.

Emma tensed only for a moment, having forgotten how it felt to be filled by a man. But her body had no trouble welcoming him and opened fully to his breadth. Tears gathered in her eyes and she tried to blink them away.

Ridge froze and a tender finger brushed away one tear that escaped her. "Emma?" he asked with so much concern, she wanted to sob.

She wound her arms and legs around Ridge, drawing him so close not even air could get between them. "I'm fine. It's just so good. Been so long," she whispered.

After a moment's startled hesitation, he began to move. He inched out, then eased back into her moist heat. He had to fight his body's insistence to take her fast and hard, to release the tension gathering in his groin like thunderheads before a storm. But she felt so tight, so hot, and he wanted to bury himself in her, never to come out.

Emma grasped his buttocks, urging him deeper. He could feel her pulsing around him and he groaned.

Capturing her lips with his, he thrust with more force and speed. His urgency boiled hotter and hotter.

He focused on Emma's face—her closed eyes, her arched brow, and her swollen lips. She was so beautiful, so courageous, so giving.

Suddenly, she opened passion-filled eyes and they widened when they met his. She tipped her head back and her body arched upward as a low keen spilled from her parted lips.

Her flesh tightened around him and he thrust into her one final time, spilling his seed deep within her. His heart thundered and he gasped for air as he held his weight on trembling limbs.

Emma peered up at him, her face flushed and damp from her climax. There were no regrets, nor condemnation in her eyes, only warmth and gratitude. She reached up to brush a strand of hair behind his ear. The gesture was so artless, Ridge's throat threatened to close.

He eased out of her and shifted to her side to lie down. Emma immediately curled against him, her arm draped across his waist. Unwilling to surrender their intimacy too quickly, Ridge embraced her. Her breasts flattened against him, tempting him with their plump softness. His groin twitched, but that was all he could manage after his shattering release.

He caressed her thick braid, the motion cozy and soothing. The fire crackled in the stove and the wind rattled icy snow against the windows. Ridge couldn't think of a single place he'd rather be.

"Enapay was my husband," Emma broke the silence some minutes later.

Ridge's fingers stilled. Of course he'd known she wasn't a virgin when he'd entered her, but he hadn't expected her confession. " 'Was'?"

"He died during a raid over two years ago," she replied quietly.

The whispers about her back in Sunset weren't far from

the truth, and Ridge wondered why he wasn't outraged that she'd slept with an Indian. "Was he good to you?"

He felt her nod. "We were married when I was seventeen. He was twenty-one."

Ridge continued to stroke her hair as he digested her words. "Do your parents know?"

"No. You're the first person I've told." She turned onto her side and rested her cheek in her propped-up hand as she gazed down at him. "I thought you would understand."

Her trust in him humbled and touched him. "If he's dead, why do you need to find his people?"

She looked down and stroked his chest with featherlight fingertips. Despite himself, his nipples hardened and renewed desire arrowed to his groin.

"I want to see his family one last time to make sure they're safe and well." She lifted her gaze and sadness shadowed her brown eyes, and Ridge sensed something more in her hesitation. "He was a good man, Ridge."

Jealousy sucker punched him and he forced himself to breathe slowly and evenly. He didn't own Emma and he sure as hell shouldn't care that she'd been married to an Indian. "I reckon that's a good enough reason."

"Thank you." She leaned down and brushed a kiss across his lips.

Lightning arced through Ridge's veins and he rolled Emma on top of him, so he could feel her bare skin from chest to toe. Emma smiled impishly and wriggled against his growing hardness. All thoughts of her past lover disappeared as Ridge growled and, with one smooth motion, had her lying beneath him.

Emma laughed brightly and Ridge suddenly wanted her with a need that bordered on obsession.

$\mathcal{T}$EN

EMMA awoke with a shiver, alone in the bed, and with a driving need that she had to *do* something. But no matter how hard she focused, she couldn't determine what that something was.

She blinked in the dwindling light of the afternoon and spotted Ridge wearing his trousers and untucked undershirt by the stove. He was adding another chunk of wood.

She lay unmoving, not knowing what he expected. After their second joining, both she and Ridge had collapsed from exhaustion and fallen asleep. Her body twinged pleasantly in places she hadn't felt since her husband died. But there was still an unappeased hunger biding within her, a hunger to lie again and again with Ridge. Although Enapay had been a considerate lover, she had always kept a part of herself separate from their lovemaking. But with Ridge, she didn't want to hide any part of her from him, and that frightened her.

Her prediction had been too true. Now that she and Ridge had made love twice, it would be so easy to succumb again. Watching him, his face reflecting the fire and his motions as graceful as a cat's, Emma wasn't certain how she would close her Pandora's box now that it had been unlocked.

Knowing she was only prolonging the inevitable, Emma sat up, hiding her nudity beneath the blanket. "Is the blizzard letting up?" Although she kept the question casual, the urgency she'd awakened with kept prodding at her.

Ridge turned, startled. His gaze slid over her covered breasts then back up to her face. Banked passion flickered in his eyes. "Some. It should quit tonight."

"Which means we can continue on our way tomorrow."

"If the snow ain't too deep for the horses." Ridge gave his attention to the embers. "You'd best get dressed, Emma."

With Ridge's gaze averted, Emma jumped up and tugged on her scattered clothing. The scent of their joining rose around her and embarrassment heated her cheeks. However, she had no regrets for what they'd done.

"I'll make supper," she said.

Ridge straightened and closed the stove. "Good idea." He turned his back to her as he tucked in his undershirt and drew on his wool shirt, then slipped his suspenders back in place. "I'll be back in a few minutes."

Emma nodded and sliced salt pork as Ridge donned his boots and warm outer clothing. He slipped outside without another word and the cabin felt empty without his presence. Emma wondered if he regretted his loss of control. Or perhaps now that he had time to think about it, maybe he was repulsed by her marriage to an Indian.

That thought troubled her as she went about finding something to eat. As she was preparing a batch of biscuits, the door swung open and Ridge entered, his head bowed. Snowflakes peppered his hair and shoulders.

"How're the horses?" she asked, anxious to fill the silence.

"Fine." He removed his coat. "The snow's definitely letting up. We should be able to leave tomorrow."

"That's good."

Now that Ridge knew about Enapay, Emma's conscience nudged her to tell him about Chayton. If he could accept that she'd been married to an Indian, wasn't it a small step for him to accept that she had a child? She opened her mouth to confess, but courage deserted her. She wasn't even certain Ridge *was* comfortable with her marriage to one of the People, and Chayton was tangible proof of that union.

Emma continued to prepare their supper and when Ridge acted as polite as he had before they'd made love, she began to relax. Half an hour later, they sat down to eat fresh biscuits with beans and pork.

Ridge swiped his plate clean with the last biscuit. "Thanks. That hit the spot." He gave her a shy smile reminiscent of the first time she'd met the man.

She smiled back. "You're welcome."

After washing and drying the dishes, Emma donned her coat.

"Where're you going?" Ridge sat by the table where he was working on a bridle by the light of two candles.

"I want to take a sponge bath."

Ridge rose. "I'll fill the pan."

Before she could argue, he was out the door. He returned less than a minute later.

"Thank you, but you don't have to wait on me." Emma took the kettle from him and placed it on the stove.

"We do for each other. You made supper and did the dishes," he simply said, and then returned to his task at the table.

Emma hadn't considered it that way, and suspected few men were as thoughtful as Ridge. Her admiration for him, already considerable, rose another notch.

Knowing it would take some time before the water heated, she joined Ridge by the table and opened her book. But instead of reading, she watched his fingers work the leather with sure, deft motions. Maybe he couldn't read or write, but he had other talents, such as mapmaking, tracking, and mending leather with infinite patience. Where had he learned those skills?

Frowning, she realized how little she knew about him despite the time they'd spent together. "So you fought in the war, Ridge?"

He nodded.

"Union?"

"That's right."

"You don't like to talk about it."

Ridge's gaze turned to something only he could see; something she suspected he wouldn't want her to see. "War isn't pretty, Emma."

She remembered the night the soldiers came to the People's camp—the screams, the blood, the dead and dying. "You're right, it's not," she said, her voice husky. "War. It's such an ugly word—rhetoric used to defend hatred."

"It's man's nature. To fight for what he believes is righteous."

"Who decides what's righteous and what's not?"

"Each person has to make his own decision."

Emma listened to the sizzle of wood in the fire, an oddly comforting sound. "You made the choice to leave the army. Why?"

His gaze dropped and it was a long moment before he answered. "The war changed and I realized I wasn't fighting for a righteous cause anymore."

She touched his sleeve lightly, ignoring the spark between them. "For what it's worth, I think you made the right choice."

"I made the only choice I could," he said quietly in his husky timbre. "Just like you did."

Emma nodded, unable to speak around the lump in her throat. Nobody else could understand that—not her parents, and certainly not the townsfolk.

"Shall we start your lessons?" she asked a few minutes later.

Apprehension flitted across Ridge's face, but he set aside the bridle.

Emma moved her chair next to his and tried to ignore his masculine scent and the curve of long eyelashes framing smoky blue eyes. "Did you say you memorized some words when your mother used to read to you?" she asked.

"That's right. Just smaller words, like 'the' and 'now.'"

"It sounds like memorization might be the best way for you to learn."

Emma wrote twenty-five words on the back of a poster she'd found in the shack. She read them and spelled them aloud twice, then had Ridge do it. He stumbled more than once, but was persistent.

"Now try writing them as you say them," Emma suggested, handing him the pencil.

He stared down at the list of words. "I ain't going to get them right."

Emma cupped her hand over his. "What matters is that you keep trying, Ridge." She smiled tenderly. "You're not a quitter."

Ridge took a deep breath and nodded gamely.

Emma wanted to hug him, like she'd done to Chayton when he needed reassurance, but settled for giving his hand a gentle squeeze. She rose and removed the large kettle from the stove. The water was just right for a sponge bath. She glanced back at Ridge who was concentrating on his task. She took a moment to simply look at him, to admire the strong slope of his forehead and nose, to remember the softness of his hair, which brushed his shoulders when he turned his head, and to recall the lines of muscle beneath his clothing. But right now, it was his intense concentration that she found most compelling. For a little while, that look had been aimed at her as they'd pleasured one another.

Her heart fluttered in her chest even as liquid heat poured into that place beneath her belly. How could she have thought that lying with him twice would slake her desire for him? That she could forget his protective embrace and his body's coiled strength?

She halted the dangerous line of thought and physically turned away. Clearing her mind, she unbuttoned her blouse, then dipped the cloth in the water and squeezed out the excess. She ran the damp cloth around her neck and across her chest, refusing to dwell on why her puckered nipples were so sensitive.

She rebuttoned her blouse and glanced over her shoulder to see Ridge's attention on the words and not her. She chastised herself for feeling a twinge of disappointment. After removing her stockings, she leaned over and trailed the damp cloth up her left leg, then her right. She bunched the front of her skirt in her free hand and held it up as she carefully washed the juncture of her thighs. She closed her eyes at the unintentional pleasure the gentle friction created.

A tingle at the top of her spine caused her to look over her shoulder . . . and her gaze collided with Ridge's. His eyes smoldered and Emma welcomed the heat. Without breaking eye contact, Emma dropped the hem of her skirt.

"How's the studying coming?" she asked huskily.

The corners of his lips quirked upward. "Depends on what kinda studying you're talking about, ma'am."

Ridge stood and ambled over to her. The heat from his body was far more intense than the stove, and Emma swayed toward him. He settled his hands on her hips and she braced herself on his arms.

"Seems to me the student needs some more private tutoring," Ridge said, need underlying his rasping voice.

Emma knew she shouldn't, but knowing and doing weren't always the same. "I happen to know a tutor who'd be more than willing to give you private lessons."

Ridge undid the first button of her blouse.

THE wolf cuffed her cub playfully, and the youngster yipped and raced around his mother. Lying on her side to soak up the sun, the wolf watched her son as his attention was snatched by a hovering butterfly. The cub dashed toward it, but the butterfly fluttered away. The young wolf chased after it, disappearing into the brush.

The female wolf sat up and listened intently for her cub, her nose twitching nervously. She could hear him pad across the fallen leaves and dry twigs. She scented the air and the hair at her nape lifted.

Danger!

She plunged into the brush after her cub.

A lion roared . . .

Emma jerked upright, her heart thumping in her throat. An arm came around her waist. "Easy, Emma."

She blinked and focused on Ridge, who lay beside her in the narrow bed. Caught between her dream and waking, she simply stared at him.

Ridge pushed himself to a sitting position and the moonlight gilded his face and long, thick hair. "Nightmare?" he guessed softly.

She gulped air. "Yes."

"Want to talk about it?"

Emma merely shook her head. Hanging onto one of the blankets, she swung her feet to the floor to stand by the window. She gazed out into the pale night. A three quarter moon hung amidst a sky filled with diamond-like stars, and their light reflected off the fresh white snow. She shuddered at the otherworldly scene, half expecting a mountain lion to charge out from the wavering shadows.

Ridge rose and joined her. He stood quietly, offering silent support. The lump in Emma's throat wasn't all due to her nightmare.

"I dreamt of a mountain lion," she finally confessed.

"We did hear one a couple days back," Ridge said.

Emma shook her head. "That wasn't the first time I've dreamed of a mountain lion."

Ridge turned his head and one side of his face held an ethereal glow from the night's luminescence. "People dream about things that scare them."

Her knuckles whitened as she clenched the blanket between her breasts. "The People say dreams are the spirits talking to you." She studied his steady eyes. "What do you dream about?"

His jaw muscle jumped into his cheek. "I don't dream."

"I envy you."

"Don't." Ridge crossed his arms. "I don't have dreams; I have nightmares."

She leaned against his side, offering him comfort. "I'm sorry."

He wrapped his arm around her shoulders and she rested her head against his chest. Did she dare ignore her visions? To do so might cause death or harm to befall her son, and that she could never live with.

Cold air eddied across her bare feet and she shivered.

"I'd add more wood, but we're running low," Ridge said quietly. "We'll have to make due with our body heat."

Emma stared up at his profile, at the shadows that painted his cheekbones and jaw. She'd never met a man so beautiful both inside and out. She traced his lips with a light fingertip, surprising herself by her audacity.

Ridge's nostrils flared and he caught her hand, then kissed the center of her palm. "Let's go back to bed."

When Ridge slid into her body for the fourth time in less than twenty-four hours, Emma promised herself it would be the last.

A chinook wind had blown down from the mountains overnight, and the snow was already melting when Ridge went out to saddle the horses. He paused on the porch, squinted at the rising sun, and listened to the plink-plink of melting snow dripping off the roof.

He stretched, relishing his body's satisfaction. He went weeks, oftentimes months, without female companionship. Stuck one day in a cabin with Emma Hartwell and he lost the iron control he'd always possessed—and not just once. Even thinking about the things they'd done brought a surge of blood to his groin.

But what of the future? What about when he returned Emma to her father's ranch? Would she tell Hartwell that Ridge Madoc had his way with his daughter?

No, Emma wasn't like that. She wouldn't demand marriage and she would keep their secret, just as she'd kept an even more dangerous secret all this time. A white woman married to a Lakota. Just like a chinook wind, it was unexpected.

He wasn't certain about his own feelings toward her confession. He'd known many Indians, had even lain with a few of the pretty sloe-eyed women, and he'd never disrespected them afterward either. They'd come to him and he'd been encouraged by his newfound friends to accept what was offered. He'd been young and full of wild oats to sow. Hell, hadn't he considered marrying a Sioux maiden years ago? So who was he to judge Emma?

No, he didn't begrudge Emma her marriage. So why did his gut twist up like a mad rattler every time he thought about Emma and her Enapay?

Paint whinnied, snapping Ridge out of his thoughts. Ridge settled his slouch hat on his head more firmly and went to ready the horses. He had a job to do and two hundred dollars waiting at the end of it. One hundred from Hartwell, and one hundred from Emma, whom he'd taken to bed without thinking out the consequences of his actions. But he wasn't a man to waste time worrying about what he'd done. He could, however, ensure he didn't take advantage of her passionate, generous nature again.

Ridge saddled the horses and led them across the damp snow to the front of the line shack, where he loosely tied their reins to a porch post. He took a deep breath and entered the cabin.

Emma was checking the straps on her saddlebags and she glanced up, startled by his entrance. Then she smiled that part shy, part seductive smile and he damned near forgot all his noble intentions.

"I'm ready," she announced. Her gaze traveled around the small cabin, paused a moment on the bed, then continued on, and finally settled on Ridge. The intensity of her soft brown eyes stirred his blood. "I'll remember this place fondly."

Ridge knew he'd never forget this shack and its

cramped bed either. "We'd best move out. The going'll be slow and I want to put in at least thirty-five miles today."

Emma carried her saddlebags in the crook of her arm as she marched to the door, Ridge's oversize moccasins slapping lightly on the dirt floor. "I'm ready."

Ridge tossed his own bag over his shoulder and picked up the cloth sack that held the remains of their foodstuffs. He ushered Emma onto the porch and took one last look at their refuge, then followed her to the horses.

Ridge made a cradle with his hands and gave Emma a boost into the saddle. She smiled her thanks and he tried to squelch the foolish grin that kept creeping across his face.

After mounting Paint, Ridge led the way north, allowing his horse to pick his path across the snow. They wouldn't cover a lot of ground today but they were back on the trail and away from the cabin.

And that damned tempting narrow bed.

BY dusk, Emma was more than ready to call it a day and set up camp. She'd gotten through the initial stiffness of traveling soon after she'd left her father's ranch, but riding after the interlude in the cabin had given her a different kind of ache. Making love with Ridge had been thrilling, but sitting on a horse for ten hours the next day was downright unpleasant.

A few times during the day she'd tried starting a conversation with Ridge to divert her discomfort, but it was obvious he didn't want to talk. Not about reading lessons, not about where they were headed, and definitely not about what had transpired between them in that deserted line shack.

Ridge had been wary all day, his gaze constantly moving from side to side, and dropping to the ground occasionally. But they'd seen nothing but a herd of pronghorns, two mule deer, four squirrels, one waddling skunk they'd steered clear of, and an assortment of birds. However, Emma was well aware of how Indians could seemingly rise out of nowhere. If she and Ridge came across a raiding party or a group of angry braves, she wasn't sure how they would be treated.

It was nearly dark when Ridge finally called a halt for the day. "We'll stay here tonight."

Later, after they'd eaten more beans and biscuits for supper, Emma glanced at Ridge, but he seemed more relaxed than he had been during the day. A twig snapped and her head swung around sharply, her gaze trying to pierce the darkness beyond their circle of light.

"Rabbit, maybe a squirrel," Ridge said quietly.

Emma drew her attention back to the flames, but the hairs at her nape prickled. To take her mind off her unaccountable jumpiness, she asked, "Would you like another lesson?" The dark blue eyes that caught hers flared and her cheeks flamed. "A *reading* lesson?"

The heat in his eyes disappeared and after a moment's hesitation, he answered, "All right."

Emma dug her book out of her saddlebags and motioned for Ridge to join her on the log. Then, with her leg touching his, she began to read as he followed along.

RIDGE swayed to Paint's rocking gait and fought the sun's lure to close his eyes. He'd slept little last night after enduring Emma's proximity as she'd read from her cherished book. He shouldn't have agreed to another lesson, but the temptation had been too powerful. He truly did want to learn, but to be so close to Emma and not touch her was pure torture.

He'd known once they were back on the trail, they couldn't repeat their cabin tryst. But he'd spent too much time thinking about how he wanted to stroke Emma's softness and taste her sweetness. His physical ache had only increased as he'd sat next to her in the evening, listening to her honey-smooth voice and remembering that same voice hoarse with desire as she'd welcomed him into her body.

He shifted uncomfortably in his saddle. It had been hell

lying there last night with Emma little more than an arm's length away. He'd listened to her soft steady breathing, imagining her tucked in his arms like she'd been the night before.

A hawk's cry startled him out of his lusty musings and he sharpened his gaze, searching the panorama. Most of the snow had melted, leaving puddles scattered here and there among the brown scrub and sparse grass. Up ahead lay rocky slopes with canyons tucked into them—perfect camps for a people who didn't want to be found.

"This looks familiar," Emma said quietly, staring at the pockmarked land stretched out before them.

"I got a feeling we're getting close, but whether they're your band or not—" Ridge shrugged. "That's hard to say."

An indistinct movement far ahead caught Ridge's attention, and he narrowed his eyes, but he couldn't see anything amiss. He knew they were being watched, but when he searched the horizon for a plume of smoke or anything that might give away a village or a group's approach, he could spot nothing.

"What is it?" Emma asked.

He tugged his slouch hat lower on his brow, to hide his eyes. "Stay close, Emma. I got a feeling—"

Horses' hooves and bloodcurdling screams suddenly erupted around them. A dozen or so Indians raced toward them from the cover of huge boulders along a hill's slope. Ridge's first reaction was to turn tail and run, but he doubted they'd be able to outrun the expert horsemen.

"Stay where you are and keep your hands in plain view," Ridge ordered Emma.

Although her face paled, she nodded resolutely. She kept Clementine under a tight rein as the mare tugged at the bit. Ridge found Paint just as anxious as the bronzed riders thundered toward them and he focused on keeping calm. Why the hell had he agreed to this fool plan of Emma's? A man couldn't use an extra hundred dollars if he was dead.

Ridge glanced at Emma and was surprised to see her relaxed features. He'd thought she'd be terrified, but then Emma never reacted the way he expected.

Atop their sturdy ponies, the warriors surrounded Emma and Ridge. Their long black hair was divided into two braids with a scalp lock festooned with feathers and quills. Many of them wore necklaces made of animal claws and teeth. Deerhide breechclouts and leggings with moccasins covered their legs and feet, and a few men wore an incongruous gingham shirt. Every warrior carried a bow and arrow; half of them displayed recently obtained scalps.

Ridge's heart hammered in his chest, but he raised his chin. The Indians respected bravery among all peoples. One of the warriors reached out to pluck Ridge's rifle from its scabbard and his revolver from his holster. Ridge didn't argue.

The silence was more harrowing than the earlier war cries. They were definitely Lakota, probably a band of Brules, and they were definitely not pleased to see them.

Ridge easily picked out the leader, a man a few years older than himself with two glossy black braids and a broad face painted with lines and designs of red, black, and yellow. The other warriors, as well as the ponies, were also painted. The leader's piercing brown eyes roamed across Emma, and then Ridge, who met his gaze squarely. The two men parried looks and the horses stamped impatiently as a minute, then two, passed.

"Tuwe?" the leader finally asked.

"I am Winona," Emma replied in Lakota. "Adopted daughter of Fast Elk."

Ridge frowned, irritated by her forthrightness. Within the Sioux society, it was frowned upon for a woman to speak unless directly spoken to.

The leader's eyes narrowed, but he appeared more startled than insulted. He nodded toward Ridge.

"Madoc," Ridge answered the unspoken question. "I lived with your people many winters ago."

The brave scrutinized them, trying to determine if they spoke the truth. Another warrior brought his horse closer to the leader and spoke in a low tone Ridge couldn't distinguish. But when the leader's gaze flickered to Emma, Ridge wondered if maybe she'd been recognized.

"Ihakob." The leader whirled around and a path was made through the other Indians to allow him through.

Ridge and Emma exchanged somber looks, then followed the Lakota. The riders closed in around them as they rode.

"Do you think they're taking us to their camp?" Emma asked Ridge, keeping her voice low.

"I think so. Do you recognize any of them?"

Her brow furrowed as she looked at those warriors she could see without turning in the saddle. "I don't know. Maybe one or two, but it's hard to tell with the war paint. How about you?"

Ridge shook his head.

Emma lapsed into silence as they journeyed. They rode through noon and on into the afternoon, with the Indians keeping a steady pace. There was no break for lunch or to drink from a canteen. Ridge's mouth grew parched and his tongue felt swollen.

The sun wasn't far from the western horizon when Ridge and Emma followed the stoic warriors through a twisting narrow trail between rocks. Ridge scanned the ledges high above them and noticed four boys, not more than eleven or twelve years old watching them closely. They stood with their feet planted apart, a bow in their hands and a quiver of arrows slung across their backs. It was a sure bet the entire village knew they were arriving.

The vista suddenly opened into a valley with a river running through it. Maybe twenty-five buffalo hide lodges were scattered across the greening grass. Dogs raced out from behind the tipis, dancing and barking around the horses' legs. Young and old women wearing deerskin dresses decorated with quills and beads paused in their tasks to gaze at them with impassive features. Groups of children stopped their games and stared at the new arrivals, their dark eyes round with curiosity. Pit fires lent little smoke into the air, but Ridge could smell food cooking and his stomach growled, reminding him it had been a while since they'd eaten a breakfast of cold biscuits and jerky.

Old men with scraggly gray hair and creased faces sat cross-legged in front of lodges and around fires. There were no other men the age of the raiding party warriors around the camp, but Ridge figured another group might be out hunting. Fresh meat would be needed for the celebration of a successful raiding party.

Suddenly the warriors began whooping and racing around the village on their ponies, their horsemanship skills never failing to amaze Ridge. Those few with scalps held them up as evidence of their prowess and success. As if a switch had been thrown, the children joined in the merriment, then the women. The older men remained dispassionate, but Ridge could see the past in their eyes as they relived their own youth through their sons and grandsons.

Situated at the peripheral of the excitement, Emma and Ridge seemed to be forgotten. However, Ridge knew better. If he or Emma tried anything untoward, they'd be surrounded in a matter of seconds.

He glanced at Emma, standing in her stirrups as she scanned the Indian faces. Since her husband was dead, she couldn't be looking for him. She had also talked about adoptive parents—was she searching for them?

"Is this your band?" Ridge asked her.

He could see her frustration in the shake of her head. "I'm not certain. I don't see Talutah or Fast Elk or—" she broke off. "Or anybody else."

Ridge frowned, certain she was going to say another name. But whose? Had she lied about her husband? Was he still alive? That possibility sent jealousy and possessiveness thundering through him. The intensity of his emotions shocked him, and he shoved them aside. There'd been no words exchanged between him and Emma, only mutual pleasure.

Emma suddenly stiffened and he followed her wide-eyed gaze to where an older squaw stood with a young boy who wore miniature deerskin leggings and a tunic. His long dark hair was braided into two plaits and his brown eyes were alive with mischief. But there was something about him, something Ridge couldn't put his finger on. . . .

Emma scrambled off Clementine and scooped up the boy in her arms. Confused, Ridge dismounted and positioned himself in front of the horses with the reins clutched in his hand.

Emma hugged the older woman, who was less demonstrative, although it was obvious she was pleased to see Emma. As they spoke in rapid Sioux, Ridge tried to puzzle out the riddle. It took him only another minute to detect what was odd about the boy—his skin was the color of watered down whiskey instead of the rich bronze of the Lakota.

The boy was half white.

He was Emma's secret.

$\mathcal{E}$LEVEN

EMMA'S vision blurred as tears filled her eyes. She held her son close as she breathed in her little boy's familiar scent. She couldn't tell if Chayton remembered her, but at the moment all that mattered was she'd found him, safe and healthy.

"He's going to be a brave warrior like his father," Talutah said proudly. "Fast Elk says he will make Chayton's first bow and arrows soon."

Although she knew each Lakota boy started training to be a warrior at a very young age, her heart twisted at the thought of her son doing the same. She couldn't even imagine a grown-up Chayton as part of a raiding party like the one that had found her and Ridge.

Ridge.

She'd forgotten all about him when she'd spotted Chayton. Still holding her son, Emma looked over her shoulder. Ridge was standing in front of their horses with one knee slightly bent and his leather-covered shoulders at a relaxed slant. Anybody would've thought he was perfectly at ease, but she knew better. He was observing, noting every tiny nuance, from the way she held Chayton, to the affection between herself and her adopted mother.

Ridge Madoc was a good man. She prayed he wouldn't detest her too much for keeping this truth from him.

Chayton yanked her braid, bringing Emma's attention back. She grasped his fisted hand. "Let go," she said firmly in the Lakota language.

The young boy laughed and the sweet sound traveled clear to the depths of Emma's heart. His fingers, no longer pudgy, remained twined in her hair but she couldn't be angry and smiled at his mischief.

"*Hiya,*" Talutah scolded the boy.

He released Emma's hair. "*Kuta?*"

She lowered him to the ground as he'd asked, and he immediately dashed off to join a group of children his age.

Emma's gaze followed him, and she fought the urge to scoop him back up and never let him go.

"He's grown so much," she said to Talutah.

"*Ha.* Soon he will begin his training with a *leksi.*" Pride was evident in the older woman's tone.

Chayton didn't have an uncle in the white man sense, but according to Lakota definition, every warrior in the village was Uncle. Just as any male elder was Grandfather to everyone in the tribe.

"Who will train him?" Emma asked, trying to keep her voice steady.

"Hotah has offered."

Emma frowned. She remembered him as a bold warrior with a wide streak of cruelty. His bloodthirsty exploits were often told around the fire. He was also one of the few who had disapproved of her living among them.

"Why can't Fast Elk teach him?" Emma asked.

"He is old. He says it is a young man's duty." Talutah shrugged. "I know you do not like Hotah, but he is a skilled warrior. Chayton will learn well under him."

Not if I can help it.

Emma sought Chayton and spotted him dashing around, his legs a blur. She couldn't help but smile at his antics.

"He is always running, and keeps the young girls from becoming lazy in their task," Talutah commented, obviously noting the direction of Emma's gaze.

It appeared Chayton had flourished among his Lakota family. Emma should've been relieved and pleased, but the realization that he'd been fine without her saddened her.

"I saw you fall under a white soldier's blade," Talutah said, her eyes troubled. "Everyone believed you did not live."

Emma dragged her attention away from her son. "I was wounded. They carried me back to my white parents where it took me many moons to heal. Finally, I was able to come look for Chayton. I am grateful you cared for my son."

Talutah shrugged matter-of-factly. It was the way of the People. "Who is this *wasicu* who rides with you?"

"A friend." Emma decided there was no reason to expose the details of their meeting and subsequent journey together.

"He is not like the others?"

"No. He is honorable and brave."

Talutah called over a boy maybe eight years old. "Take care of their horses."

Puffing out his chest, the boy nodded solemnly. He trotted over to Ridge and without a word, took the reins from his hand. Ridge relinquished the horses with a nod at the boy, and strolled toward Emma, his expression unfathomable.

"I take it you found your people," Ridge said.

His drawl caressed Emma's insides. "Some of them. Ridge, I'd like you to meet my adoptive mother, Talutah."

He touched the brim of his hat while the woman bowed her head.

"My husband will be back from the hunt soon," Talutah said.

"I look forward to meeting him," Ridge stated in the native language.

"I will prepare a lodge for you, and find clothing for my daughter." Talutah left them standing there.

"Something you forgot to tell me, Emma?" There was a razor's edge to his casual question.

"Would you have brought me here if you'd have known?" She crossed her arms stubbornly.

"Probably not."

"That's what I thought."

"You have any more surprises?"

"No. At least, none I can think of right now."

"That ain't very comforting," Ridge growled. "We can't stay here long. Even though those scalps were from another tribe, next time they might be white scalps."

"I lived with them. They won't hurt us."

"Those who knew you then might not, but them young bucks that brought us in are itching to count coup. I figure it's only a matter of time until they throw in with Crazy Horse."

A stooped man with straggly gray hair hobbled over to them. A colorful blanket was draped over his thin shoulders and he limped noticeably, but his eyes were penetrating and intelligent.

"Come," the elder merely said.

He led them to an ornately painted lodge and entered, motioning for them to follow. Emma's eyes adjusted quickly to the dim light and she seated herself close to the tipi wall, leaving Ridge and the chief to sit nearer the fire pit in the middle of the floor. Moments later a squaw carried in two bowls of stew. She set them in front of Ridge and the chief.

As the men began to eat with their fingers, Emma surveyed the lodge and noticed Ridge's weapons on a pile of hides behind the leader. She suspected they'd stay there until Ridge left.

Another bowl was brought in and placed in front of Emma. Although her stomach was in knots from wanting to be near Chayton, she couldn't insult their host, especially the leader.

They ate in silence and after they were finished, a pipe was lit and the two men shared puffs for a few minutes before the elder began.

"I am Akecheta, leader of the Wolf band of the Brule

Lakota," the man said. He gazed at Emma shrewdly. "You are Winona of the Elk band, and Chayton is your son."

"Yes," Emma replied, trying to hide her apprehension.

"Your band was attacked by soldiers. Some died; many were taken to the white man's reservation. They escaped and we welcome them." He puffed in silence, the smoke wreathing his lined face and then rising lazily toward the opening at the top of the conical-shaped lodge.

Emma and Ridge exchanged looks, but knew better than to hurry the meeting along. It would be a grave discourtesy to press Akecheta.

"Why do you return?" Akecheta finally asked, his dark eyes pinning Emma.

"To see my son," she stated firmly.

"You have seen him."

Her gaze flickered to Ridge, but he only shrugged. His expression clearly said, *You wanted to find him and you did. Now what?*

"You cannot stay. We want no reason to bring the soldiers to our village. We are a peaceful band and we do not want war," Akecheta said.

Although Emma hadn't planned on staying, she hated to have the option taken away. Still, she was relieved the chief preferred peace to war. "I understand. I would like to visit my family and friends before I return. Is that allowed?"

Akecheta smiled, exposing brown stumps of teeth. "A visit is allowed."

"Thank you." She barely restrained a shout of victory.

The wise elder aimed a piercing look at Ridge. "You wear the face of a white eyes scout."

Suddenly frightened for Ridge's safety, Emma opened her mouth to speak, but Ridge shook his head curtly and she swallowed her words.

"I am no longer a scout for the white eyes," he said to the leader.

Akecheta scrutinized him silently and Ridge held his gaze. Then the chief set the pipe down and nodded. Their meeting was over.

Emma and Ridge rose quietly and slipped out of the lodge. Dusky shadows had fallen while they'd been in the tipi.

"How long, Emma?" Ridge asked.

She pretended not to hear him and continued walking, intent on finding Chayton.

Ridge grasped her wrist. "You made a promise, and I aim to hold you to it."

She jerked out of his grip. "Don't worry, Ridge, you'll get your two hundred dollars."

"I'm not worried about getting it; it's the when I'm thinking of."

"You gave me one week."

Ridge's jaw muscle jumped and his eyes narrowed. "One week. Unless Akecheta tells us to leave sooner."

"If you'll excuse me, I'm going to see my son."

She wove her way between cooking fires and tipis, following the sound of children's laughter. She'd prayed for this day for so long, it was difficult to believe it had arrived.

Now came the second part of her plan—keeping Chayton with her.

RIDGE sat outside, close to the lodge he and Emma had been offered, blending into the deep shadows of the night. He listened to the rhythmic cadence of the drums and the rise and fall of singing voices; he observed the swirling bodies as the Indians—both men and women—danced around the camp. Their skin reflected the firelight, making them appear like night creatures, dipping in and out of the shadows.

He raised a crude cup to his lips and swallowed some of the bittersweet drink. He knew it would make him muddle-headed if he drank too much, so he only sipped small amounts. Being in the Lakota camp he had to remain alert even though the chief had given them his consent to visit.

Ridge patted his belly, which had been more than satisfied. Besides the food he'd eaten in the chief's lodge, he'd also partaken of the fresh venison, which the successful hunters had brought back. Emma had pointed out Fast Elk, her adopted father, a husky man with strands of gray in his long black hair and a stoic face that revealed little. His gaze was direct and although he was wary of Ridge, he didn't appear hostile . . . which was more than he could say for the majority of the young bucks.

Fourteen years ago Ridge had come and gone among the Sioux, counting many of them friends and he'd not worried about his safety. But times had changed.

He leaned back against the stretched buffalo hide wall, but his wariness didn't fade. He and Emma were far too vulnerable in this village, although Emma had some protection from her adopted parents. He hoped she would remain safe.

She sat with her son between Talutah and another woman beside a nearby lodge. The three women were talking and smiling, no doubt trading gossip just like all females, no matter the color of their skin. Emma was wearing a buckskin dress with a hide tossed over her shoulders for extra warmth, and moccasins that fit better than the pair he'd loaned her. Her golden-brown hair was braided into two plaits and if not for the color, and her lighter skin, she could've passed for a Lakota squaw.

Emma turned her head and caught his eye. Heat shot through Ridge's blood at her raw beauty and the memory of what lay beneath the soft deerhide dress. She said something to Talutah then rose gracefully and guided her sleepy son toward Ridge. She sank down beside him, her legs folded to the side beneath her. Chayton immediately curled up with his head on her thighs.

Ridge took the time to study the boy whose droopy eyes had closed the moment he laid down. After leaving Akecheta's lodge, Ridge had checked on their horses, and then strolled around the camp. He hadn't had a chance to really look at Emma's son until now.

"He's a handsome boy, Emma," Ridge said quietly.

"His father was tall and handsome," she said proudly.

Her smile faded. "There were many who thought Enapay should have married one of the Lakota maidens, but he chose me. He was a stubborn man." She paused, her gaze softening. "You remind me of him. He never spoke much either, but he was brave and honorable."

Ridge glanced away, uncomfortable with both the praise and being compared to her husband. "Were you forced to marry him?"

Her eyes widened. "Of course not." Her sight turned inward. "He would play his flute for me in the evenings, then drape a buffalo skin over us." She smiled self-consciously. "It was so different from what I'd grown up with. Mother would've had a fit if I sat outside in the dark with a young man without a chaperone." She laughed, the sound like bells tinkling in the breeze. "Enapay seemed so shy at first and I wasn't certain what I was supposed to do, but together we figured it out."

Ridge remembered how open she'd been during their lovemaking. She'd obviously learned a lot with her husband. "Did you love him?" The question slipped out before he could bridle it.

Emma gazed down at her son and brushed a dark lock from his smooth brow. "He provided well for Chayton and me." She took a deep breath and her troubled eyes met Ridge's. "I remember the first time he came back from a raid carrying a bloody scalp. I thought I was going to be sick. Talutah scolded me, told me that I would embarrass my husband if I didn't celebrate his victory with him. I joined in, but I hated every time he came back with one of his prizes. And then there were the times when he would return with a book or two for me. I tried not to think about how he'd gotten them or who they'd belonged to, but it was getting harder and harder to ignore the killing.

"Enapay was respected and admired in the tribe, and I was proud he was my husband. But love?" She shook her head sadly. "No, I don't think I loved him like a wife should love her husband. He deserved better."

Ridge wrapped his arm around her shoulders, pleased

by her confession yet knowing how much it hurt to admit her shortcoming. Relishing the warmth of her against his side, he said quietly, "But you cared for him and gave him a son. He had more than a lot of men ever get out of life."

"Is that what you're looking for? A woman who'll care for you and give you children?" She seemed to peer straight into his soul.

"I'm looking for a woman who'll work with me to raise our children and build something that'll last," Ridge corrected.

"But what about love?"

He gazed down into her shadowed face, noting the fire reflected in her eyes and her full, glistening lips. "I don't remember much about my real pa, but I do recall how he used to tease Ma and how she used to giggle like a young girl. Then he'd hug and kiss her, and they'd talk in low voices. I didn't understand back then, but I figured out later, a few years after Pa died, that was love. My friend Colt loved his wife, too, but she was killed. Damn near drove him over the edge." He took a deep breath. "I don't ever want to go through the pain they did when they lost their loved ones."

Emma's brow furrowed and Ridge resisted the urge to brush his thumb across the wrinkles.

"But doesn't the joy of loving outweigh the sadness of losing that love?" she asked.

Ridge rested his palm on the boy's head, surprised by his hair's softness, and then gazed at the woman deliberately. "You tell me, Emma."

She looked down at Chayton and her heart did a little roll at the sight of Ridge's large but gentle hand resting atop her son's crown. She forced herself to consider his question. "I wouldn't trade anything for having borne him," she replied firmly. "And loving him."

Emma couldn't see Ridge's eyes, but she suspected he was startled by her vehemence. Chayton was her heart and soul, and during those times she despaired of finding him alive, she wasn't certain she'd survive the torment. But now, with her precious son in her arms, she recognized the depth of her love for him. She took a shaky breath. "I think the higher the reward, the higher the risk. It's like a poker game. The more money that's in the pot, the higher the stakes of winning or losing."

After a moment, he lifted his head. "So how did you learn to play poker?"

She smiled. "How else? From a book."

Ridge laughed, and the rare sound filled Emma with both longing and pleasure.

"You have a beautiful laugh," she said.

His laughter faded, replaced by a man's hunger for a woman. He stroked Emma's cheek with a featherlight touch and shivers coursed through her body to land in a hot pool in her belly. It would be so easy to surrender to passion again, but their talk of love reminded Emma of more important matters, like caring for her son. If she got with child, it would make planning for the future even more difficult. She only hoped she didn't already bear the result of her reckless behavior in the cabin.

Ridge drew back, frowning. "What is it?"

He must've sensed her sudden anxiety.

"I should be getting Chayton settled for the night," she said, hoping he didn't notice the huskiness in her voice.

"I'll carry him," Ridge offered.

Unable to resist, Emma nodded and allowed Ridge to lift him into his arms. He rose carefully with Chayton sleeping openmouthed against his shoulder. Holding Chayton with one arm under his backside, Ridge offered his other hand to Emma to help her to her feet. She released him and opened the flap of their tipi, allowing him with his precious burden to enter first. Emma let the flap fall behind her, muting the drums and chants of the celebration.

She remembered nights like this vividly, except it was Enapay, not Ridge who accompanied her into the lodge. And after Chayton was asleep, Enapay would take Emma, usually gently, but sometimes fiercely, although he was always careful not to hurt her.

But tonight, Emma would sleep with her son, and Ridge would have a separate skin. She couldn't afford to let her body's demands dictate her choices anymore.

"Lay him down over there," Emma said, pointing to a pile of buffalo hides on the far side of the fire pit.

Ridge gently laid the boy down, and remained squatting beside him. With one callused finger, he traced Chayton's cheek. "He looks like you," he whispered.

Despite herself, Emma knelt beside Ridge and gazed down into the beloved boy's round face. "I always thought he looked like Enapay."

"He's got your stubborn chin and cute button nose," Ridge said.

Emma's throat felt thick and she rested her hand on Ridge's forearm, feeling the muscle cord beneath her fingers. He made her feel like a young girl again, giddy and awkward, yet with a woman's knowledge of what could be if she allowed it.

"Emma," Ridge said, his warm breath fanning across her cheek. "We should get some rest, too."

She nodded jerkily and withdrew her hand from his sleeve. "It's been a long day," she managed to say. "I'll sleep with Chayton."

"Good idea."

He crawled over to the other pile of buffalo hides, pulled off his moccasins, and removed his coat. He slid between the thick skins and turned his head toward the tipi wall.

Emma's palms moistened, urging her to glide down beside Ridge's hard body and join with him. They would both enjoy pleasuring the other, and even just after one night together, Emma found she missed sleeping with him spooned behind her with an arm draped around her waist.

She sighed and tugged off her moccasins, then lay beside her son. For the first time in five months, she could sleep knowing Chayton was alive and well.

* * *

RIDGE awoke, instantly alert, but heard nothing but the wind whispering through the budding trees and low snores emanating from nearby lodges. It took him a moment to figure out it was the absence of sound—the drums and chanting—that had awakened him.

The fire in their tipi had burned down and a chill seeped in. Ridge took a deep breath, preparing himself for the cold air, and threw back the heavy hides. He added some wood from the small pile beside the pit and watched a tiny flame flicker to life, only to die and struggle to return. He leaned down and blew gently across the embers, which flared and the added wood burst into flame. This time it remained alive, and Ridge held his cool hands above the growing fire.

A movement from the other bed caught his attention and he spotted Chayton crawling out from between the buffalo hides.

Ridge intercepted the boy before he could slip out of the tipi, and lifted him into his arms. "Where're you going, little fella?"

Chayton pointed down at himself.

Ridge grinned wryly. "I'll go with you, pard," he said quietly, not wanting to wake Emma.

The boy bounced in his arms. *"Wana."*

"Okay, now." Ridge swiftly carried Chayton outside and set him on his feet. The boy lifted his tunic out of the way and aimed toward a bush. While he relieved himself, Ridge shrugged and did the same.

Ridge closed his trousers and adjusted Chayton's tunic, in the pre-dawn's gloom. Another hour or two and the Lakota would be rising.

"Chayton," came Emma's fearful call.

"C'mon, cub, we'd best get back inside before your mama has a fit," Ridge said.

Chayton only yawned and knuckled his sleep-filled eyes.

Ridge took the boy's hand and led him back into the lodge, where Emma was readying to leave, her expression frantic. She gasped and dropped to her knees in front of

Chayton, hugging him close and kissing him.

"You frightened me, Chayton. I didn't know where you were," Emma said hoarsely.

"He had to go outside so I went with him," Ridge explained. "I thought you were asleep."

With her arms still around the boy, she gazed up at him. Fear filled her eyes. "I woke up and he was gone. I thought—" Her voice cracked.

"It's all right, Emma," Ridge reassured her awkwardly, not liking the haunted expression in her eyes. "Chayton's just fine."

She bowed her head, revealing the pale skin at the back of her slender neck. Ridge remembered how sweet her soft skin had tasted there, and her breathy moans of pleasure as she'd begged for more. He dug his fingernails into his palms to keep from reaching for her, to offer her comfort, and anything else she might need. Or want.

"After I was brought back to my parents' ranch, I had nightmares. I couldn't save him no matter how hard I tried." Emma's voice was muffled by Chayton's shoulder. The boy protested her snug grip and she immediately loosened her hold. She drew a hand across her eyes and Ridge could see the effort it took to smile at her son. "Sleep," she said in Lakota to her son.

As Emma resettled Chayton and herself in their bed, Ridge slid back between his own furs and laid on his side, facing them. She sang quietly to her son, and Ridge closed his eyes to listen to her achingly sweet voice. Just as with reading, Emma's singing was easy on his ears and made him recall the only time in his life when he'd felt loved and protected.

Once Chayton's breathing evened out, Emma's song faded away. A hollow yearning filled Ridge, along with bittersweet memories and wishes that were best left locked away.

"I had one of his moccasins in my pocket when the army took me from the village."

Emma's confiding voice startled Ridge out of his musings. He opened his eyes and focused on the dim oval of her face.

"I managed to keep it hidden from my parents," she continued. "But every night when I'd go to bed I'd take it out of its hiding place and hold it against my chest, imagining I was holding my son. It kept me from going crazy."

Merely thinking of Emma's anguish made Ridge's gut ache. He could picture her in her room late at night, the tiny piece of hide clutched to her breast.

"Why didn't you tell your family about him?"

She laughed softly but bitterly. "What do *you* think my father would've said if I had told him?"

Ridge could only imagine, and what he did imagine wasn't fit for a lady's ears.

"I'm fearful about taking Chayton back there," she confessed.

Ridge levered himself up on an elbow. "You're planning on taking him back to your father's ranch?"

"Of course. He's my son."

"He's Lakota."

"He's as much white as he is Lakota."

As much as Ridge understood her dilemma, he also knew how she and her child would be shunned. He had personally seen how white women with half-Indian children were treated. "Have you thought this through, Emma? I mean, folks ain't going to take to him."

"I'll protect him," Emma said and Ridge could almost see her chin jut out stubbornly.

And who'll protect you?

"What about school? No one's going to let a half-breed attend school." Ridge deliberately used the slur others would use as a dirty word.

"I'll teach him myself." He could feel the burn of Emma's glare across the lodge floor. "Why are you saying these things? Once I found my son, did you think I would just abandon him again?"

"He's happy here."

"He's my son! Where I go, he goes." Emma rolled over, turning away from Ridge, and effectively ending their conversation.

Ridge lowered himself back to his bed. Emma was serious about raising Chayton in a world that had little compassion for someone like him. Couldn't she see how much better off he was here with people who loved and cared for him?

Ridge was intimately familiar with how hurtful other children could be to someone who was "different." He wouldn't wish that kind of childhood on anyone, especially an innocent boy like Chayton.

Closing his eyes, Ridge tried to sleep, but found slumber elusive. His eyes flew open as another thought struck—would the People even allow one of their own to be taken away? Even by the boy's own mother? The Lakota treated their children as children of the tribe, and they belonged to everyone, not just the parents who brought them into the world. Children were raised together and women looked after all of them, regardless of blood relationship. Mothers allowed other babies in addition to their own to suckle from their breasts.

Ridge gnashed his teeth. If he'd known Emma's real motive for finding her band, he would never have allowed her to bribe him with one hundred dollars. Chayton was better off here than he would be in a world that would treat him no better—probably even worse—than a stray dog.

$\mathcal{T}$WELVE

EMMA straightened from her task of scraping an antelope hide and stretched her back, hearing a collection of pops along her spine. She'd forgotten how toilsome the day-to-day drudgery could be, but she was determined not to be a burden.

When Fast Elk had handed Emma over to Talutah all those years ago, she had vowed to carry her own weight in spite of being frightened and homesick. The tall, grave Indian had saved Emma's life and she owed him for that. However, as she gained more and more knowledge of the language and their ways, she realized she wasn't a slave, but an adopted daughter. And dutiful daughters were expected to help their mothers with everyday tasks.

However, after spending months away from this life, she ached from her exertions, but being able to look up and see Chayton playing with the other children was more than worth the labor. He and a handful of boys and girls had sticks they used to hit rocks back and forth. Soon, the boys would begin the first stage of their training. Chayton and the others would learn how to trail game, starting with squirrels and rabbits, then they'd begin to practice with their bows to bring down those same small animals they tracked, as well as birds and rodents. By wrestling with his playmates, Chayton would learn how to defend himself and how to defeat an enemy in hand-to-hand combat. All of his fighting skills would be learned under the guise of games, and in a dozen years or less, Chayton would join the ranks of the warriors for his first raid.

Emma used the back of her hand to push aside strands of sweat-dampened hair that stuck to her brow. She would take Chayton away before he even began his training; her son would not die as young as his father had.

"You have become soft like a *wasicu*," Talutah teased.

Emma smiled at her adopted mother who was chopping tubers into the venison stew that would simmer above the fire pit all day. "Yes. It has been a long time since I've prepared a hide."

Talutah knelt beside her to help. "Your world is different than ours."

When Emma understood enough of the Lakota language to follow a conversation, she'd been intrigued and a little shocked by their beliefs. At the time, she'd been too shy and wary to speak of her own world. Now, however, it saddened her to realize how far apart their cultures were. There seemed to be no middle ground and she was fearful the Indians would lose their way of life, which relied heavily upon open range and wild game, especially buffalo.

Emma sighed and continued her backbreaking work. Shimmering Water, whom Emma had known before, joined her after Talutah left. Emma described her return to her parents and subsequent escape to find Chayton.

Then their talk turned to gossip, both serious and amusing, and the work didn't seem quite as difficult.

One time Emma glanced up and saw Ridge playing a game of dice with three men, including Fast Elk. She couldn't help but notice with a note of pride, that Ridge had the most sticks piled in front of him. He caught her eye and winked, and her cheeks bloomed with heat. Her reaction didn't go unnoticed by the other woman.

"He is handsome for a *wasicu*," Shimmering Water commented, elbowing Emma. "I would take him to my skins if my husband asked it of me." She batted her eyes in Ridge's direction.

It wasn't uncommon for a husband to share his wife with a visitor if he wanted to impress him or make him feel welcome. Emma had never been comfortable with that practice and fortunately, Enapay had never asked it of her. She wondered, however, what her reaction would've been if he had. She suspected Enapay wouldn't have liked her response.

She glanced at her friend, who had smooth skin with almond-shaped brown eyes and glossy black hair. Would Ridge accept her company if given a chance? What man wouldn't?

The thought of him lying with Shimmering Water stabbed her heart. She didn't want to imagine him with any other woman, bestowing those same gentle touches as he had given to her with his lips and hands. She didn't want another woman to feel him enter her body as she had rejoiced in feeling him deep within her. She had no right to be possessive, but couldn't deny the jealousy that made her fists clench and her head pound.

Shimmering Water sighed. "His mouth is very nice and I have never seen eyes such as his—the color of a night sky." She ducked her head closer to Emma. "He would look very good in only a breechclout, would he not?"

Emma's gaze traveled to Ridge's backside and pictured him in what Shimmering Water described. She mentally shook herself and returned her attention to her task, refusing to be drawn in. The fact was she didn't want to share Ridge with anyone.

The sun was high when the children and men drifted toward the kettles over the fire pits. Women returned to their tipis to eat stew or soup. Chayton dashed over to Emma's fire and the stew Talutah had made that morning. Emma could almost hear her son's stomach growling. Smiling, she filled a bowl for him and then one for herself. She broke off chunks of flat bread Talutah had made earlier and left on a stone close to the fire. Sitting beside her son, she asked him about his morning as they ate.

When Ridge joined them, Emma was refilling Chayton's bowl. She readied one for Ridge and handed it to him.

"Thank you." He slipped his hat off his head to hang down his back by the drawstring, and sat across the fire from them.

"You're welcome," Emma said, glad he'd come to their fire instead of going to someone else's, like Shimmering Water's. "You seem to have made yourself at home."

He shrugged and swallowed before answering, "In some ways, the Lakota haven't changed at all. They play the same games and brag about victories. But in other ways, they've changed a lot. There's more distrust, and there's more talk of war against the whites."

Emma nodded, having noticed the same changes herself just between the time she lived with them and now. It was sad and frightening, as well as inescapable.

The sun appeared from behind a cloud and caught Ridge's long thick hair, exposing strands of reddish-gold among the maple-brown. Emma tried to imagine him in short hair, like her father's, but couldn't. Before living with the Lakota, she'd daydreamed about beaux with trimmed mustaches and wearing suits and opera hats. Now when she allowed herself to woolgather, she thought of Ridge Madoc with his unfashionably long hair, moccasins, wool trousers, suspenders, buckskin jacket, and slouch hat. Ridge, with his midnight blue eyes, that when turned in her direction, could make her knees feel like honey.

Chayton's empty bowl slipped from his hands, and Emma smiled fondly at his drooped head and closed eyes.

"All that running around tuckered him out," Ridge said quietly. "I'll carry him inside if you'd like."

"Yes, please," Emma replied.

Ridge scooped the child into his arms and ducked into the opening of the tipi. Emma followed but stayed by the entrance with crossed arms as she watched Ridge settle the boy on a pile of skins. He tucked a flung-out thin arm under a hide, then adjusted the blanket under Chayton's chin and smoothed his hand across the boy's hair. Emma wasn't surprised by the man's tenderness—he'd never been anything but gentle with her. Except for the time he'd tied her up, but she didn't blame him for that.

He rose gracefully and Emma backed out of the lodge.

"Most of the children will sleep for an hour or two, then they'll be back at it," Emma commented.

Ridge didn't reply but picked up the bowls they'd used and hunkered down beside a pail of water sitting in front of the tipi. He ducked the dirty dishes into the water to wash them.

"I should do that," Emma said.

He grinned mischievously, making him appear not much older than Chayton. "Worried your friends'll scold you for making your man do a woman's chore?"

Her face warmed. "You're not my man," she responded tartly.

"No, but everyone sees us that way."

His gaze roamed across her, and her body responded as if he'd touched her intimately.

"Does that bother you?" he asked huskily.

"Does it bother *you*?"

"Why should it? You're a beautiful woman, Winona."

His drawl made her Indian name sounded oddly lyrical and Emma's heart tripped in her breast. Here, in the middle of a Lakota village, the white world with all its stuffy rules and harsh prejudices seemed a million miles away. It would be so easy for Emma to ask Ridge to share her furs, but they had to someday return to their own world. They'd already gone beyond civilized boundaries in the cabin; she didn't dare risk it again.

"Thank you," she said stiffly. "But you and I both know it's not that way." She turned away to needlessly stir the remains of the stew. "If you're offered a woman, don't turn her down on account of me."

Strong fingers gripped her shoulders, startling her. She hadn't even heard him approach.

He turned her around to face him. "I don't want any woman but you."

Emma gasped at the heat in his words and the need in his flashing eyes. She stared at his lips, his mouth, and fought the hunger in her own body. One touch, one look— that was all it took for Ridge to set her on fire. She hadn't bargained on her attraction growing after they'd yielded to their passion.

She trembled as she fought the overriding desire, but knew it would be a losing battle if Ridge didn't release her. It would be so easy to remain in his arms and be led into their lodge and join their bodies upon the soft skins. But Emma was under no illusions—if they were back in Sunset, Ridge wouldn't be treating her this way.

"Are you willing to marry me?" she asked, amazed that her voice remained steady.

Ridge released her as if she were scorching hot and growled a curse. "I ain't ready to get hitched."

At least not to me, she added silently with a stab of remorse.

"Then we'll not be lying together again either," she stated.

"Fine," he said curtly. He tugged his hat onto his head. "Fast Elk invited me to race this afternoon. I'd best go ready Paint."

Ridge's stride was fluid, but Emma noticed his clenched jaw and knew she'd made him angry.

She sagged. She'd never force him to marry her for what they'd done or what they might've done again if he had pressed her. But she wasn't strong enough to deny him, and she hated herself for that weakness. If he'd kissed her, she would've been lost, so she'd gambled on his honor. She'd expected his rejection, but it still hurt.

Terribly.

IN the Lakota culture, men were the hunters and warriors, and every activity they engaged in was geared toward being better hunters and better warriors. Emma had seen the men race their ponies countless times in the past and she'd long since lost her fascination with their riding skills. However, knowing Ridge was to participate, Emma made certain she faced the direction of the meadow where the race would take place.

"Is your man good?" Talutah asked.

Emma glanced at the woman sitting beside her who was sewing quills on a shirt for Fast Elk. "Yes," she replied. Although not as certain as she sounded, she knew Ridge possessed a natural grace atop a horse, and suspected he could easily match the other warriors' prowess.

Emma tried to keep her attention on her own sewing task, but her gaze kept shifting to the warriors and horses at the far end of the field. Ponies stamped and snorted as the men lined up in a single row. A boy whooped the signal to start. Horses and men exploded in a blur of motion.

Hoofbeats pounded the hard-packed earth and Emma picked out Ridge near the far end of the group. Her hands fisted and she leaned forward, silently urging him on.

Paint lengthened his stride and began to gain ground, moving forward to overtake the middle of the pack, then passing them. Only four riders were ahead of Ridge, and Paint ate up the ground between them. Finally, there was only one warrior who outdistanced them. Emma shaded her eyes to pick out the brave's features.

Hotah!

Talutah had told her he'd been on a scouting trip, but it appeared he had returned.

"Go Ridge," she murmured, her gaze riveted to the unfolding drama of racing horseflesh and skilled horsemen.

Clods of new grass were thrown back by sharp hooves as Ridge and Hotah leaned low over their horses' manes.

Paint drew neck and neck with Hotah's chestnut horse. Emma could make out flecks of spittle on both animals' muzzles and the faint tremble of the earth from the thundering gait. Just as they crossed the finish line, Ridge and Paint surged ahead to win by less than a head.

Emma clapped and smiled so widely her mouth hurt, but it couldn't lessen her exhilaration at Ridge's victory over Hotah.

A motion caught her eye and she turned to see Chayton standing on a tall boulder some two hundred feet away, jumping up and down as he, too, cheered Ridge's win. Her elation disappeared, replaced by dread at her son's precarious position. If he slipped, the fall could injure him badly, or even kill him. She rose, intent on getting him off the rock before he lost his balance.

Suddenly, Chayton's arms flailed wildly and he stumbled back to disappear behind the boulder. His shrill cry chilled Emma to the bone.

Talutah caught Emma's wrist. "You must allow him to learn on his own," the older woman said sternly. "Do not shame him in front of the others."

Emma's mouth gaped. "He's not even four summers old." She tugged free of the older woman's strong grasp. "How can such a young one be shamed?"

Talutah shook her head in disapproval. "You have changed, Winona. You think more like a *wasicu* than one of the People."

"If being one of the People means I cannot go to my son when he is hurt, then maybe it is better to be a *wasicu*," she said angrily, fear sharpening her words.

"Go then," Talutah said flatly. Her gaze dropped back down to her sewing.

Torn between apologizing to her adopted mother and her need to check on her son, Emma wavered, but her maternal instincts overrode her momentary indecision.

Running, she followed the trail the children had taken

earlier which led to the river's edge. She spotted the group of youngsters with Ridge already in their midst.

"How is—" Emma began, but broke off when she caught a clear view of her son sitting on a rock. He had blood running down the side of his face. She sank to her knees in front of Chayton, her heart jumping into her throat.

"It looks worse than it is," Ridge reassured. "He's a mite dazed, but he wasn't knocked out, and the bleeding's slowed. His head's gonna hurt some, though. And I think his ankle's twisted, but nothing looks broken."

Ridge untied the dark blue bandanna from around his neck and rose to dip it into the edge of the river. When he returned, he handed it to Emma, and spoke to the children. "Chayton will be fine. Go."

The dark-eyed girls ushered their charges away and in a few moments, the children were once again playing and laughing.

"This is one of the reasons I can't leave him here," Emma said hoarsely to Ridge, although her attention was riveted on her task as she wiped the blood from her son's face.

"Don't mollycoddle him. It's not their way."

Emma snapped her gaze to Ridge, her disagreement with Talutah adding fuel to her frustration. "This is *my* way!"

"Look at him, Emma," Ridge ordered. "Go on. Look! He's Lakota."

Reluctantly, Emma scrutinized her son, from his pale complexion to his struggle to remain unmoved by his injuries. There were two tear tracks down his dusky cheeks, but no more were being shed. He reminded Emma too much of Enapay after he'd been injured during a raid—the same withdrawn expression and impassive eyes.

She pressed her lips together and handed Ridge back the bloodied bandanna. "Could you rinse this for me?"

Emma had less than a minute alone with her troubling thoughts before Ridge returned. She continued to wipe away the blood, more than a little shocked that the boy hadn't spoken since she began.

"Does it hurt?" she asked him.

He finally focused on her. "No. I am not a baby."

"I know, Chayton, but I am your mother and I worry about you."

He stared at her, his eyes the same color Emma saw when she looked in a mirror. *"Ina?"*

She nodded solemnly. "Yes. I am your *ina.*" She hadn't tried to explain to him yesterday, hoping that he might remember on his own. "I had to go away for a little while, but I'm back now."

Chayton studied her, almost frightening Emma by his intensity, which was far too profound for a boy his age. "You will stay?"

"I don't know." Emma brushed the gash on his head with the cloth and involuntary tears slid down Chayton's face, his stoic expression giving way to a little boy's pain. He whimpered and Emma drew him into her arms. She was surprised and pleased when his arms wound around her neck.

"If I go, I want to take you with me," she whispered in his ear.

Chayton raised his head. "Where?"

"To see your white grandfather and grandmother."

The boy grasped Emma's hand and stared down at their intertwined fingers. *"Wasicu?"*

She nodded, her throat full.

"Lakota," Chayton exclaimed fiercely, jabbing a thumb into his chest.

"Yes, you are. But you have as much *wasicu* blood as Lakota blood."

The boy raised his gaze to Ridge, as if asking him to deny her words.

Ridge nodded slowly. "Your ma's right, Chayton."

The boy's brow furrowed and for the first time, Emma considered Chayton's feelings about his mixed heritage and leaving his home. There was no doubt he'd heard stories about the whites and their treatment of the Indians, but how much did he understand? The warriors would've embellished atrocities the *wasicu* committed, while celebrating their own victories. Emma's sympathies lay with her adopted family, but she wasn't blind to their fierce tendencies.

"He'll be all right, Emma," Ridge reassured. "It looks like the bleeding's stopped."

Emma eased Chayton back to the rock and raised herself on her knees to tie the cloth around his head. "There. Let's go back to our lodge and you can lie down."

Chayton brushed the back of his hand over his moist cheeks and nodded. Before Emma could help him up, Ridge hoisted him into his arms.

"His ankle's already swelling. When we get back, you need to put a cold cloth around it," he said quietly. "Could you lead Paint back?"

Emma nodded and hurried to gather the horse where he stood with his head lowered. Dark patches on the horse's coat showed where he'd sweat, and his skin rippled occasionally from quivering muscles.

When Emma returned with Paint, she was gratified to see Chayton slumped in Ridge's arms, with his head on the man's shoulder. Leading Paint, she walked behind them on the narrow trail back to the camp, trying not to notice how her son's head rested against Ridge's cheek, or how carefully he walked so he wouldn't jar Chayton.

Ridge abruptly halted and Emma nearly ran into his back. She raised up on her tiptoes to see over his shoulder. A broad, flat-nosed warrior stood in the middle of the path. Her breath caught in her throat and she had the overpowering urge to grab Chayton and run in the opposite direction.

The cruel eyes rested on Ridge a moment and Emma could see he was furious to have lost the horse race to a white man. Hotah's lips thinned and his gaze moved across Chayton to Emma. He reached for Chayton, but Ridge shifted away so the warrior couldn't touch him. Hotah snarled and his shoulders stiffened as his hands fisted at his sides.

Emma stepped forward. "He will carry Chayton. Let us pass," she said firmly, hoping Hotah would listen to a mere squaw.

The warrior remained long enough to prove he could, then stepped to the side. Ridge passed first and Emma retrieved Paint and followed after him.

When they arrived at their lodge, Emma left Paint ground-tied outside the tipi. She removed Chayton's moccasin, nearly crying when the boy whimpered again. She was aware of Ridge building up the fire.

"I need to heat some water," she said quietly.

Ridge nodded and ducked out to retrieve some.

Emma wrapped her son's swollen ankle with a rabbit skin. She brushed her fingers across his cheek. "How are you feeling?"

"Head hurts," he whispered.

Emma swallowed back her tears. "I'll make something that will help."

Chayton bit his lower lip and nodded slightly.

Ridge returned with the water and set the kettle above the fire. He knelt in front of Chayton. "You're a brave warrior," Ridge said to the boy in Lakota.

Emma smiled gratefully at the man and retrieved her saddlebags to pull out her collection of herbs. As she waited for the water to warm, she listened to Ridge speak softly to Chayton.

"I'll bet you've never heard the story of the boy and the wolf, have you?" Ridge asked Chayton.

He shook his head, his amber eyes wide.

Ridge settled into a cross-legged position in front of the boy. "Many winters ago there was a boy who was called Dakota. Even though Dakota was only six summers, he took his bow and arrow and went hunting because his people were starving. He came upon a beautiful gray wolf who growled and snarled and showed his big sharp teeth. Dakota was very frightened, but he was also very brave like you. He did not run but spoke to the wolf. 'Why are you so mean?'

"That wolf stared at him for a long time, trying to decide if he should eat the foolish little boy. But he respected Dakota's courage, so he replied, 'I have a spine in my paw and I cannot get it out.'"

Emma leaned forward as Ridge's low, somewhat husky voice, drew her into the story.

"Dakota, who also had a kind heart, thought for a minute. 'I will help you if you promise not to hurt me.' The wolf nodded and laid down on the ground. Dakota carefully examined the wolf's paw. He found the sharp spine and gently removed it. The wolf was so happy he promised Dakota he would stay with him and protect him always.

"Then the wolf helped Dakota bring down deer and rabbits so Dakota's people wouldn't starve, but the people didn't understand how a little boy and a wolf could be friends. So they threw rocks at the wolf and chased him away. Angry and heartbroken, Dakota went after his new friend and never returned to his village. It is said that Dakota and his gray wolf still run through the woods together and if a person is lucky enough to see them, they will be blessed with a good hunt."

"I want a wolf," Chayton said.

Ridge smiled. "Maybe someday."

Emma stirred some herbs into a cup of warm water and carried it to her son. "Drink."

Chayton took the cup between his small hands and drank over half of it. The boy's eyelids drifted shut and Ridge settled him in the bed. Chayton hadn't napped earlier so Emma was fairly certain his drowsiness was caused by lack of sleep, rather than the bump to his head.

"That was a beautiful story," Emma said softly to Ridge.

He ducked his head. "Ma used to tell me one about a lion and a little boy. I figured Chayton would like a wolf better."

Emma stared at the cup in her hands, knowing it was time to tell Ridge of her dreams. She struggled to find the right words. "Remember when I told you I dreamed of a mountain lion?"

Ridge nodded slowly. "It was our last night in the cabin." His gaze caressed her face, and then flickered down to her breasts and back to her eyes.

The familiar curl of desire unfurled in her belly and she gripped the cup tighter to keep from reaching for Ridge. "The night before I left my parents' ranch, I had a dream about a wolf cub and a mountain lion. The frightened cub was being toyed with by the lion. A full-grown wolf tried to save the cub, and the wolf and the lion fought."

"What happened?"

She shook her head, feeling the urgency rise again. "I don't know. I woke up." She took a deep breath. "I've had the dream more than once since then."

"You think it's some kind of vision?"

Emma met his skeptical gaze without flinching and nodded. "Yes. That's why I had to find Chayton."

"You think he's the cub?"

"Yes."

"But you found him and he's safe."

"For now. In my dream, the moon is always full."

Ridge frowned. "There's a full moon tomorrow night."

Emma's heart leapt into her throat. "I know."

The fire crackled and Chayton snuffled restlessly. Outside the lodge, men and women talked, and children laughed. An occasional bark or whinny added to the peaceful sounds.

"Why didn't you tell me this earlier?" Ridge asked.

She smiled without humor. "Would you have believed me?" His silence gave Emma her answer. "The medicine man said I had a dreaming gift. He used to help me figure out what my dreams meant." She tucked a wayward strand of hair behind her ear as she gathered her courage. "I'm afraid for him, Ridge. I can't let him out of my sight for the next few nights."

"I'll help you watch him."

"I thought you didn't believe me."

"I admit it's kinda hard to swallow, but I've seen a lot of strange things in my time, Emma. I guess this ain't all that different."

Ridge's warm understanding threatened to bring tears to Emma's eyes. It would be so easy to fall in love with Ridge Madoc. No other man—not even Enapay—had been so tender and thoughtful. Among the Lakota, Winona had been Enapay's wife and Chayton's mother. Winona was expected to do her duties with no complaints and be there when her husband or son needed her.

But what about Emma?

She wanted to be Chayton's mother, but Emma wanted more than Winona. She wanted her husband's respect, and she wanted to be involved in decisions affecting her. She wanted—no, needed—to be loved by the man she would share her life with. Winona had accepted less; Emma would not.

She laid her hand on Ridge's and squeezed it. "Thank you."

Ridge merely nodded and then rose. "I'd best take care of Paint. After that race, he needs a good rubdown."

Emma smiled. "By the way, congratulations."

Ridge studied her, his eyes hooded. "Are you glad I won, or glad I beat Hotah?"

"Both."

$\mathcal{T}$HIRTEEN

RIDGE felt the hostile gaze drill his back as he led Paint back to the rope corral. He wasn't surprised someone was watching him. Ever since he and Emma had arrived yesterday, their freedom around the camp had been an illusion. Emma might not see it, but Ridge did. At least one warrior was always guarding him. He didn't think it was the chief's doing, but the men in the village who didn't trust a *wasicu*.

He kept his pace unhurried as he used Paint's saddle blanket to rub the gelding's withers, back, and flanks. He knew he was a fast horse, but hadn't realized how swift until the race. A smile tugged at his lips. The braves had been impressed by the weak white man.

Ridge rested his arms across Paint's back and stared out across the village. Two weeks ago when he'd left Sunset to find Emma Hartwell, he hadn't suspected half of what he'd learned about her since then. Discovering Emma was a widow had been surprising, but even more shocking was her son.

Taking Chayton back to Sunset was only inviting more trouble. Her life would be hell and old man Hartwell would try to cover up Emma's sin as quickly as possible by ridding himself of her and her half breed son. He might even force Emma to give up Chayton and then send her off to live with some far-off relative, like he'd planned before Emma had run away.

Bitter bile rose in Ridge's throat as he imagined the proud woman being forced to bend to her father's will. Emma would break before doing so, but what kind of life would she have? Would she end up in one of the cribs in the part of Sunset that everybody deliberately overlooked, where desperate men went looking for even more desperate women?

Merely imagining Emma lying on a dirty mattress, allowing every kind of man to rut with her made him want to puke. But hadn't he used her? She'd asked him about marriage, but he couldn't offer that to any woman until he had a good start on his ranch.

Would he have asked Emma if he was ready to take a wife?

The near-silent approach of someone made Ridge stiffen and strain to hear who it was. He turned slowly, expecting Hotah, but was pleasantly surprised to see Fast Elk.

"*Hau,*" Ridge greeted.

"*Hau,*" Fast Elk replied, his expression somber. "You raced well."

Ridge inclined his head in acceptance. "My horse is strong and fast."

Fast Elk crossed his arms and stared off into the distance. Ridge waited patiently.

"When I found Winona, she was frightened but she did not give in to tears," Fast Elk began. "Our daughter died when she was fourteen summers. Because she was strong and brave, I chose Winona to become our daughter. She never shamed us, but I knew she missed her white home. After the soldiers came, we thought we would never see her again."

"She wished to return to find her son and see her family," Ridge said.

"We lost many of our people that night and there was

much wailing. Some blamed Winona for their coming."
Fast Elk took a deep breath and exhaled slowly. His dark
eyes overflowed with regrets. "She can no longer live with
us. The young warriors are angry. War will come and we
will have to fight, but we will not win."

Ridge wanted to offer him hope, but Fast Elk would recognize his words as a lie. "What of Winona's son?" he
asked instead.

"He is Lakota."

"Winona wishes to take him to her white home."

Fast Elk's eyes flashed. "No. He will learn the ways of a
warrior as his father did."

"But you said you will not win the war."

"It does not matter. To die honorably in battle is our way."

"She loves him."

"Then she must do what is best for him." Fast Elk
turned and strode away noiselessly.

But who was to say what was best for Chayton? Emma
wouldn't leave her son without a fight.

Ridge patted Paint's neck and headed back to his lodge.
Again, he could sense suspicious eyes on him and knew
someone, maybe even Fast Elk, was observing him.

He passed two young squaws who kept peeking at him
and giggling. He smiled and tipped his hat toward them,
which resulted in more laughter and more heated looks. If
Ridge was ten years younger, he might've fished for an invitation, but there was only one woman who tempted him now.

And she was the one woman he couldn't have.

RIDGE dropped the last armload of wood beside the
lodge and grinned as he listened to Emma give her son,
who'd awakened feeling better, strict orders to stay out of
trouble. From what Ridge could recall, that meant a challenge to see how much trouble the boy could get into without his ma finding out.

"Kids are tougher'n they look," Ridge commented as
Chayton ran off, his limp barely noticeable.

Emma made a face. "Especially that one."

Ridge chuckled and sat down by the fire. Emma bent her head over her task and one honey-brown braid fell across her shoulder and draped down the front of her deerskin tunic. He could see a hint of her bare knee between the top of her moccasins and the bottom of her dress.

"Are you wearing your knife?" Ridge asked.

Emma glanced up. "Yes." She turned her attention back to sewing beads upon a shirt.

Ridge picked up a stick and drew random letters and numbers in the dirt. "I got the impression you and Hotah have a history."

She wrestled with her bone needle, forcing it through a double layer of deerskin. "You're an observant man, Mr. Madoc."

"You're trying to change the subject, Winona." He tossed his stick on the small fire. "Don't you think you've kept enough secrets from me already?"

Her cheeks flushed. "Hotah never liked me. He would taunt me, call me names, when no one was around. I didn't tell anyone." She shrugged. "After I married Enapay, Hotah stopped bothering me, but I could tell he still didn't like me."

"Did he ever hurt you?" Ridge asked, rage simmering in his veins.

"No, but I never felt comfortable around him." She smoothed her hand across the soft deerhide she'd laid in her lap. "Talutah said Hotah wants to be Chayton's teacher."

"But Chayton's part white."

"I know." She shook her head, bewildered. "It doesn't make sense, unless it's his way of hurting me."

"Can't Fast Elk choose someone else?"

"He could, but there may not be anyone else." Emma squared her shoulders. "It doesn't matter. I'm taking Chayton with me when we leave."

Ridge didn't tell her that Fast Elk wouldn't allow it. Besides, the stubborn set of her jaw told him it would do no good to argue.

CAPTAIN Colt Rivers lowered himself to a log beside the campfire, carefully balancing the tin cup of hot coffee. He resisted the urge to stare into the flames and lose himself in their hypnotic flickering. Instead, he pressed his flat-brimmed cavalry hat back and gazed at the stars, picking out Orion, the Big Dipper, and the North Star.

Strange how some things never changed, like the stars, and the rising and setting of the sun. The day-to-day struggles, like birth and death, survival, and the gut-deep pain of losing a loved one didn't so much as make time blink from one moment to the next.

He took a deep breath of the night-fresh air, hoping to blunt the crushing ache in his chest. He'd been married for less than a year, but even after three years, he missed her. He'd gotten drunk for a week after it happened and nobody had dared approach him during that time but Ridge Madoc. He owed the man his life and his sanity.

So why was he following an order he knew his friend would hate? Because, Colt thought bitterly, he was in the army and had to obey his orders no matter how much they rankled him.

Sergeant Gabe Sanders strolled over to join him, easing his considerable frame down beside Colt. "Four guards are set up with changeover every two hours, sir."

Colt nodded at the man who was at least ten years older than himself, and who had experienced most everything a soldier could. "We're in Lakota Territory now."

"Yes, sir," Sanders said neutrally, not meeting Colt's gaze.

Colt sighed. "Spit it out, Gabe."

The sergeant held his big hands up to the fire. "Why the hell are we doing this? So what if a few Indians got away and came up here. Ain't nobody cared before."

Colt stared off into the darkness as he answered in a voice that bordered on sarcasm. "General Mason is coming to visit the fort and Colonel Nyes wants him to think he's got everything under control."

Gabe snorted. "Brown-nosin' son of a bitch."

Colt wasn't surprised by Gabe's contempt. There was no love lost between the seasoned sergeant and the ass-kissing colonel. Bound by military protocol, Colt had to keep his agreement with the sergeant's opinion to himself. "It doesn't change our orders. Bring 'em back, dead or alive."

"Dead, if Cullen's got any say."

Icy apprehension settled between Colt's shoulder blades, and he looked around, searching for the scout. "Cullen's acting too damned sure of himself, like he's got a secret. I have a feeling he and the colonel had a chat before we left."

"Nyes wants another Sand Creek," Gabe stated flatly.

"And I'm his scapegoat if things go south."

"Cullen can't do much by himself and if he starts shootin', I'll kill him myself."

Colt suppressed a smile, but couldn't hide it from his voice. "I'll pretend I didn't hear that, soldier."

"Pretend all you want, Cap'n. I ain't going to have the blood of womenfolk and young 'uns on my hands."

"Nobody will if I can help it."

Another soldier joined them, sitting across the fire on another log.

"Our illustrious scout is missing, sir," Lieutenant Preston Wylie announced softly, his Carolina drawl more apparent than usual.

"Dammit! Any idea *when* he disappeared?" Colt demanded in a low voice.

"His horse was corralled with the others at supper-time. An hour later and it was gone, sir."

"Maybe we're closer than we thought," Gabe commented, his gray eyes glinting silver.

"What can one man do by himself?" Preston asked.

"Not much," Colt replied. "But with a rattlesnake, you never can tell."

"I can try to pick up his trail," Gabe offered.

Colt thought for a moment, then shook his head. "You'll end up stumbling around in the dark and one of the guards might have an itchy trigger finger. No, we'll just let Cullen hang himself."

"If he does," Preston added quietly. "As much as I abhor the degenerate, he always seems to land on his feet. And if you confront him about his departure, he will probably tell you he was merely doing his job and reconnoitering the area."

Although he hated to admit it, Colt recognized the truth in Pres's fancy speech. For a moment, Colt idly wondered anew about the lieutenant's background. Pres never spoke about his past, but it was obvious he had come from a family who could afford an expensive education. It was also clear he was from the South, but had chosen to fight on the Union side.

"Pres is right," Colt said. "There's nothing we can do about him. Yet."

"What if he stumbles upon Ridge?" Pres asked.

"Ridge can take care of himself, son," Gabe reassured.

They were friends of Ridge, and knew of the animosity between him and Cullen. By now, Ridge should've found Emma Hartwell and returned the woman to her father. At least, Colt hoped so. He had no wish to run into Ridge. Although he was a good friend, Colt didn't agree with his friend's views on the Indians. Not that Colt would ever condone a massacre, but sometimes force was required to contain the savages.

Maybe if they'd killed a few more down in Texas, Colt's wife would still be alive.

EMMA awakened early the following morning to cramps in her lower belly. She restrained a groan and carefully extricated herself from the buffalo blankets so she wouldn't wake Chayton. Quietly, she crawled over to a pile of small animal skins and picked out two, as well as some rawhide laces. She stood and walked bent over at the waist to the closed flap.

"Everything all right, Emma?" Ridge asked in a low voice.

"Fine," she reassured quickly, her face warming with embarrassment.

Emma slipped out of the tipi, surprised to see Talutah already up and coaxing the cookfire back to life. She nodded toward her adopted mother and the older woman returned a smile. But Talutah's smile faded when she noticed the skins in Emma's hands.

Emma would've preferred that nobody learned of her condition. In a Lakota village, when a woman had her monthly, she had to stay in a lodge set apart from the rest of the tipis.

However, she wanted to stay near Chayton. How could she do as Lakota beliefs demanded when her son was in danger?

Her hands trembling, Emma merely ducked her head and hurried into the brush. At least her joining with Ridge hadn't resulted in a baby, and for that, she was grateful.

Talutah stood in Emma's path on the way back to her lodge.

"Gather what you will need and go," Talutah said softly.

Emma stiffened her spine. "I cannot. I must stay with Chayton."

"I will watch Chayton."

Emma's heart pounded with fear and she clenched her fists at her sides. "I dreamt of danger for him."

"He will be safe among the People."

She thought of Hotah and wasn't so certain. "Will he? I'm afraid."

Talutah patted her cheek. "Do not worry about that which you cannot control, Winona."

How many times had Talutah given her the same advice

over the years? But just as with all the other times, Emma doubted if she'd be able to heed it.

"Chayton will stay with Ridge, if he agrees," Emma said.

She ducked back into her tipi and found Ridge sitting by the small fire. Keeping her face averted, she gathered her sewing items and placed them in a hide pouch.

"I have to go away for a few days," she finally spoke to Ridge, although she didn't meet his gaze.

"Why?"

If a Lakota had asked her the question, she wouldn't have been so mortified. But Ridge was white, and they'd been raised in the same culture, in a society that didn't speak of such personal matters.

"I have to go to the women's lodge," she said rapidly.

"Oh."

Now she did turn to him and almost smiled at the deep flush on his face that she was certain matched her own. "I should be back in two or three days. Could you—"

"I'll take care of him, Emma," Ridge answered the anticipated question without hesitation.

"Thank you," she whispered past the lump in her throat. It would be impossible not to worry about Chayton, but with her son in Ridge's capable hands, she wouldn't fret nearly as much.

Ridge rose and approached her. When he cupped her jaw and his thumb brushed her cheek, Emma closed her eyes and leaned into his touch. Over the past two weeks, she'd come to trust this man more than any other. He was proud, steadfast, and stubborn, but wasn't afraid to be tender and vulnerable with her. She knew confessing his reading and writing problems had been more than difficult—it had required trust in her and she felt humbled by that trust.

"I'll miss you," Ridge said, his voice husky. Then he kissed her forehead. "You'd best go before you're accused of stealing the medicine man's power."

Emma's eyes widened slightly. He obviously understood as much about Lakota beliefs as she did. Although curious about his past, it was the tender press of his lips on her brow that stayed with her long after she entered the seclusion of the women's lodge.

THROUGHOUT the day Ridge kept his distance from Chayton and the other children, but always ensured he had a clear view of Emma's son. He didn't mind the task, and actually enjoyed the boy's antics. Even though he was half-white, and wasn't the biggest or the oldest, Chayton tended to be a leader among the young children. He excelled at the games they played and often won, but even if he didn't, he never grew short-tempered or angry.

Chayton resembled his mother, from his stubborn chin to his flashing amber eyes. Occasionally, Ridge would catch an expression or a mannerism that reminded him of Emma's, and some unexplainable emotion would tighten his chest.

He found himself debating whether he had the right to convince Emma to leave Chayton behind. How would he feel if Chayton were *his* son? Would anybody be able to convince him that his child was better off with somebody else?

After Chayton ate some of Talutah's stew at noon, Ridge guided him into Emma's lodge to take a short nap. Ridge sat cross-legged on his pile of buffalo skins, a knife and piece of wood in his hand as he carved and kept watch over the boy. He'd promised Emma he would protect him, and he had no intention of breaking that promise.

Chayton slept for an hour, and then was ready to rejoin his young friends in the warm spring day again. Before he could escape, Ridge removed the bandanna from the boy's forehead and examined the injury. The bump was red and angry-looking beneath the gash, but fortunately it looked like it had decreased in size. By the time Emma returned, the swelling should be nearly gone and only a faded bruise and scab remaining. Since the wound would heal better in the open air, Ridge didn't replace the cloth.

"I want you to be careful not to fall on your head again, cub," Ridge warned the boy in Lakota.

Chayton giggled. "I am not a bear or wolf."

Ridge tousled the boy's hair, which was the color and texture of Emma's. "But you are a cub, cub," he teased. Suddenly not looking forward to sitting around the rest of the afternoon, Ridge asked, "Would you like to see if we can track down a wolf or a bear?"

Chayton's eyes widened. "Maybe I will find a wolf like Dakota."

Ridge chuckled and led the boy toward the river. It would be the best place to find tracks and begin Chayton's education in identifying animal's paw prints. Ridge slowed his pace considerably so the small boy could keep up with him.

As they walked, Ridge would stop and show Chayton different plants, giving their names both in Lakota and English, and explain to him how they were used by the People. The boy took the lessons seriously, repeating Ridge's words in both languages and taking the time to study the plants' leaves and flowers.

They passed by Chayton's group of playmates and, although they called out to him to join them, Chayton refused. He told them his *leksi* was teaching him many new things. Although Chayton's voice was smug, there was also pride, which made Ridge wish he truly could be the boy's uncle.

By the river's edge, Ridge squatted down and was immediately joined by the boy, who copied his pose, down to the elbow on the knee and chin in his hand. Ridge focused on the animal track in the mud. "What does this look like, Chayton?"

The boy's lips puckered as he thought. "A dog?"

"Look closer."

He leaned down so his nose was only a scant few inches from the mud. "Not enough toes."

Ridge grinned. "That's right, cub. A dog has only four, this one has five. And there is some webbing, too. And look at the line in the mud behind it—that's where its tail dragged. If you trail it backward, you'll probably find something else, too." Ridge rose and slowly backed up until he found what he sought. He pointed to the small pile of droppings. "See the shiny things in it?"

Chayton gazed at the scat and nodded.

"Those are fish scales. This animal swims in the water and eats fish, but also comes out onto land."

The boy's eyes lit up. *"Pta."*

Ridge's smile broadened. "That's right, Chayton. *Pta*, which means 'otter' in the white man's language."

"Aa-ter," Chayton repeated.

"That's right. Otter. Shall we find more?"

They found numerous signs of spring—prints of mice, porcupines, beavers, and even a blue heron. Nearly a mile upriver from the village, Ridge spotted small hoof indentations in the dirt.

"Tahca," Chayton spoke up.

"Yes. *Tahca.* 'Deer.' "

"Deer," the boy repeated, then scrunched up his face. "Why must I learn the whites' language?"

"Because you carry *wasicu* blood."

Chayton thought about that for a moment, then Ridge could almost see him shrug. The youngster skipped after the trail the deer had left behind. Ridge followed, allowing the boy to find more signs on his own.

A horse's approach caused both Ridge and Chayton to pause as the horse and rider neared them. Ridge squared his stance and hooked his thumbs over his belt.

"Hotah," Ridge greeted with a nod.

The stocky warrior, wearing only a breechclout and moccasins, peered down at him. "You have wandered far from camp."

Ridge shrugged nonchalantly. "I didn't realize I couldn't leave. Me and Chayton here were just doing some tracking."

"I want to find a wolf like the one *Leksi* told me about,"

Chayton announced to Hotah, although his adoring gaze remained on Ridge.

Hotah's jaw clenched and the knuckles of his hand that held his reins whitened. He narrowed his eyes, but the anger shown clearly through the slits. "What does a *wasicu* know about tracking?"

"As much as he knows about horse racing." Ridge smiled darkly.

Hotah's face reddened with rage.

"What are you really doing here, Hotah?" Ridge asked, dispatching of his polite facade.

"It is time I begin to train Chayton." His lips curled into a sneer. "The way a true Lakota trains a warrior."

"Winona asked me to watch over Chayton. I gave her my word."

"Your word." He spat on the ground. "Your word is worth nothing."

Chayton shuffled backward and bumped into Ridge's legs.

Ridge grasped the boy's shoulders. "My word is my bond." He met and held Hotah's hostile glare without blinking. Finally, the warrior glanced at the boy.

"Come with me, Chayton," Hotah ordered.

The boy pressed more firmly against Ridge and shook his head.

"He doesn't want to, Hotah. We will return before the sun sets," Ridge said.

Hotah glared at him over his haughty nose. "One day you and I will fight, *wasicu,* and then we shall learn who has more power."

"Name the time and place and I'll be there."

"It will come," Hotah said, then reined his horse around and galloped away.

Ridge stared at his receding back, knowing he'd made an enemy. But Hotah wasn't the first, and Ridge was still breathing.

$\mathcal{F}$OURTEEN

EMMA paced the tipi, ignoring the glares from the other two women also temporarily residing in it. They hadn't known Emma before, and she explained how she'd been adopted by the Elk Band, but it did little good. Because of her skin color, she was treated with suspicion and resentment, just as she'd been treated in Sunset after her return. It appeared bigotry itself was color-blind.

Unable to endure their cold looks any longer, Emma slipped out into the evening's dusk. The lodge was far enough away from the main village that she couldn't make out individuals, but she could hear the sounds of singing and laughter. Men would be playing the hand game, while women huddled together tossing dice in the air. Songs often accompanied the contests, and Emma could tell the pace of the game simply by the excitement in the singing voices.

She had seen neither Chayton nor Ridge all day, and her frightening dream visions were never far from her thoughts. However, she reassured herself, if something had happened to her son or Ridge, Talutah would've told her.

Emma spotted a shadowy figure walking toward her and

tensed even as she unobtrusively laid a hand on her thigh, beside the hidden knife.

"It's me, Emma," Ridge called out softly in English.

Emma's hand fell away from her weapon as her heart tripped in its chest. She wanted to run to him and throw herself in his arms. Instead, she strolled over to stand in front of him and allowed her gaze to caress him instead of her hands. They'd been apart only twelve hours, yet to Emma it felt like twelve days.

"I'm glad to see you, Ridge." She couldn't keep the pleasure from her voice. "How's Chayton?"

"He's eating with his grandfather and grandmother." His gaze swept over her. "How're you doing?"

Emma crossed her arms beneath her breasts, oddly comforted by speaking English again. "I'm bored and I miss Chayton." She paused, then added softly, "And I miss you."

Ridge looked down and his hair obscured his expression. "We miss you, too."

Emma hugged her sides and wished it was Ridge's arms around her and not her own. "How's Chayton feeling? Is he in any pain?"

Ridge chuckled. "He's so busy, he hardly notices."

"He'll probably be fretting and overtired tonight. If his head hurts, mix some of the herbs I left out with warm water. It'll help him sleep."

"I'll do that."

They stood in awkward silence.

"What did you and Chayton do all day?" Emma asked, wanting to prolong his visit.

"Chayton played in the morning, and after he slept some this afternoon, him and me went looking for wolf tracks." He smiled boyishly, and Emma fought her body's insistence to move closer. "We didn't find any."

"And what would you have done if you had found a wolf?" Emma asked in amusement.

"I suppose we would've brought it back to the village as Chayton's pet."

Emma's mouth dropped open, but Ridge's soft huff of

laughter revealed his teasing. She chuckled. "Heaven help us if he ever finds one." Sobering, she asked, "Did you see Hotah?"

"I saw him."

His short reply told Emma there was more to it than a simple exchange. "What happened?"

He shrugged. "He wanted to begin Chayton's training. I wouldn't let him."

Emma gripped his arm as fear spilled through her veins. "What did he do?"

"Nothing."

Ridge was hiding something from her and she considered his choice of words. "What did he *say?*"

He glanced away and rubbed his clean-cut jaw. "He's got a grudge against me. I figure it'll come down to a fight one of these days."

Emma gasped. "You can't!"

"Fast Elk and some of the others'll make sure it's a fair fight."

"Hotah's bigger than you."

Ridge stiffened. "I can handle him."

She'd insulted his masculinity when all she'd done was express her concern. She forced her muscles to untense and kept her voice calm. "Please, stay away from Hotah. If you don't cross paths, he won't have reason to challenge you."

"I'm not afraid of him."

Emma rolled her eyes at his stubborn male pride. "That's not the issue. This is Hotah's home. If you beat him here, he'll be forced to leave."

"So now you're worried about *him?*" Ridge shook his head, exasperation in his shadowed features. "Make up your mind, Emma. You can't have it both ways."

"You don't understand."

"Damned right I don't." He settled his hat more firmly on his head. "Goodnight." Ridge spun on his heel and strode away.

Emma took a step to follow him, but halted. Ridge was too angry to listen. And what would she say? It was his

safety she was concerned about. If he and Hotah fought and
Ridge won, Hotah would seek revenge against the white
man. Hotah wouldn't care anymore about honor, because if
he lost to Ridge, he'd lose whatever honor he possessed.

Then there was the possibility Hotah would defeat
Ridge, which would be just as disastrous, because Hotah
wouldn't stop at beating him. The cruel warrior would de-
liver a killing blow.

Upset and anxious, Emma was angry with herself for involving Ridge in her personal quest. If only he hadn't found
her, or had let her go on by herself to find Chayton. Now, if
something happened to Ridge, the fault would be hers. And
Emma wasn't certain she could live with the guilt.

*THE black velvety darkness surrounded her, cocooned her,
and she was tempted to sink into it and never emerge. It
would be so easy; she'd been tired for so long now.*

*An owl's hoot startled her and she raised her head. Two
yellow eyes peered down at her, but she could make out nothing else in the pitch blackness. Dread riffled through her, but
the owl's steady gaze held no danger. At least not to her.*

*The sensation of movement made her rise up on four
legs and feral cat scent stung her nose. Moments later, low
growls and higher-pitched mewling sounds filled the air.
Using her nose and ears, the female wolf tried to determine
from where they came.*

*"Lisssten well for the angry one issss near," the owl
spoke in a sibilant whisper from its high perch.*

"Tell me where!"

"Closssse."

*A cloud slid away, revealing a full moon and illuminat-
ing sharp brambles surrounding the female wolf. Blinking,
she focused on movement beyond the thorny bushes and
spotted a mountain lion sitting in regal comfort, a weakly
struggling wolf cub in its mouth.*

*White-hot pain ripped through the female wolf and she
charged through the brambles, but the thorns tangled in*

her coat. She fought to escape, but the needles dug deeper, into her skin, and blood flowed from numerous gashes.

Still, she surged forward, unmindful of the profusely bleeding wounds and the accompanying torment. She had to rescue the cub, her child, her . . .

Emma's eyes flashed open and she lay motionless, her heart pounding and sweat coating her skin.

Where am I?

A long minute later, the answer tumbled back and Emma sat up, throwing off her cover. The other two women were asleep, and Emma tiptoed out of the lodge into the moonlit night.

Raw urgency impelled her to see Chayton, to reassure her he was safe and unharmed, unlike the wolf cub in her dream. Keeping to the shadows, Emma ran in a half-crouch to the lodge she shared with Ridge and her son. She hesitated only a moment, then slipped inside and remained by the opening, allowing her eyes to adjust to the dimness.

Chayton was a lump beneath the buffalo hides and Emma silently passed Ridge's sleeping form. She knelt beside her son and eased the blanket down so she could see his face, which was smooth and peaceful as he slept soundly. Biting back a sob of relief, she stretched out beside him on top of the skins.

"Another dream?"

The low voice startled her and she raised her head to see Ridge sitting with his arms wrapped around his drawn-up knees.

"I didn't mean to wake you," she whispered.

"I wasn't sleeping much anyhow," Ridge admitted. He kept his eyes on the low fire as he stirred it with a twig. "Wanna talk about it?"

She settled back down on the soft buffalo skin and wrapped an arm around her son. "Same dream, but different." She sensed Ridge's confusion. "This time I *was* the female wolf. I couldn't see anything but I could hear the lion and the wolf cub. Then the full moon came out and I was trapped in sharp thorns." Emma paused, then whispered hoarsely, "I couldn't save him."

Ridge didn't speak and Emma closed her eyes. She inhaled the pleasant scent of soapweed on Chayton's skin, and she was soothed by his sleep snuffles.

"If you want to stay here the rest of the night, I'll wake you early enough to get back to the lodge before anyone catches you," Ridge offered.

His understanding filled her eyes with moisture. "Thank you," she said huskily.

She listened to him lie back down and remembered how she'd slept spooned against him with his arms holding her close.

Would she ever feel that safe again?

RIDGE was as good as his word, and Emma was back in the women's lodge before the sun rose the next morning, as well as the following two mornings. The night of the full moon came and went, and the dire dreams didn't return. Immensely relieved, Emma prayed it was because the vision had been averted.

By the afternoon of her fourth day of seclusion, she returned to the lodge she shared with Ridge and Chayton. After seeing her son was safe with the other children, Emma made a pot of stew to hang over the cookfire.

Light footfalls alerted Emma and she turned to see Ridge joining her. Pleasure coursed through her and she smiled warmly.

"Smells good," he said with a boyish grin.

"Are you hungry from playing all day?" she teased.

"I'm always hungry." Ridge winked.

He suddenly tensed and Emma followed his line of sight. Hotah prowled toward them, his lips curled in a sneer.

Uneasiness settled in Emma's belly.

"You will leave now," Hotah announced.

"Akecheta will tell us when it is time to leave," Ridge said coolly.

"He thinks like an old woman."

Emma gasped. To insult a chief was tantamount to treason. She glanced around but found no one near enough to overhear the warrior.

"Does Akecheta know you speak of him that way?" Ridge asked calmly, although Emma could see his lips tighten in anger.

"He knows I do not agree with running like rabbits."

"We do not run!" Akecheta and Fast Elk came out of Fast Elk's tipi, which was close enough for them to overhear Hotah's words.

The chief's words were loud enough to draw the attention of many of the villagers. Hotah flushed, but didn't retreat from Akecheta's glare.

"We do not fight," Hotah shot back. "We run like children if there is word of whites drawing nearer."

"We live! If we die there will be no one to carry our past and our people will disappear," Akecheta argued, his voice strong despite his frail appearance.

"We live like animals, hunting for a burrow when we should fight for what is ours."

Emma sidled closer to Ridge as she listened to the two men. It was obvious this wasn't the first time Hotah and the chief had argued, but it did appear this disagreement was more intense. And this time they had an audience.

"*I* speak for our people," Akecheta stated, his nostrils flaring.

"What of these two?" He pointed to Ridge and Emma. "They are not of the People." Hotah's hand fell to his knife handle. "They are *wasicu*, the enemy."

Emma stiffened with indignation, but Ridge squeezed her arm and she snapped her mouth shut. The People surrounding them shuffled and murmured, but no one interrupted.

"They are guests. You will not harm them." Akecheta lifted his chin. "Perhaps *you* have become the enemy."

Hotah jerked as if slapped. He narrowed his eyes and rage rolled off him in waves. "I will not hide like a coward."

The insult was clear to Akecheta, who stared at Hotah, his black eyes giving away nothing. "Leave this village. You no longer belong."

Gasps and mutterings broke out among the Indians, but Emma could tell it wasn't in protest of the chief's decree. Most of them also wanted to remain at peace.

Hotah straightened his spine and pulled his shoulders back. He glared at the chief, then shifted his fierce look to Ridge and Emma. "I will not forget," he vowed in a tone that sent dread through Emma's veins.

He pivoted and a line opened between the People to allow him through. He swaggered away, leaving shocked silence in his wake.

Akecheta gazed at Ridge and Emma, his lined face impassive. "One more day."

The chief retreated to his lodge, and after a few moments, the crowd dissipated quietly. Fast Elk and Talutah were the last to return to their tipi after a long, lingering look filled with sadness and resignation.

For the first time since she'd been accepted by the tribe years earlier, Emma felt the sting of being an outsider.

She remained standing beside Ridge, fighting tears. "At one time, these were my people, my family." Her voice broke. "Now, it's as if they're strangers."

Ridge cupped her face in his palms. "You can't change your skin color, or the way you were raised. And with the whites pushing the Indians again, lines will be drawn according to those differences."

She knew he spoke the truth, but the realization didn't lessen the pain.

"It's been nearly a week anyhow, Emma. We need to be getting back," Ridge said. "Day after tomorrow, we'll leave early in the morning and get a good start."

Emma nodded. She had one day to prepare her son to leave the only family he'd ever known.

* * *

RIDGE lay awake, his crossed arms pillowing his head as he stared up at the black sky through the smoke hole in the center of the lodge. Restlessness vibrated in his bones. After the confrontation with Hotah, Ridge had wanted to gather Emma and leave immediately. At least Hotah would no longer be a threat to Chayton—some other brave in the village would train the boy.

Chayton snuffled and shifted in his sleep, causing Emma to move also. Ridge closed his eyes against the memories her presence made impossible to forget—the feathery light caress of her hands; her warm, firm lips upon his; and her needy whispers begging him to touch her and fill her.

He shoved the randy thoughts away, but a soft, passionate cry sifted through the stillness from another tipi, bringing unwelcome images. Ridge smothered a groan, not wanting to listen to the amorous coupling, but he couldn't shut the sounds out. Heated blood shot to his groin and it took everything he had to ignore the temptation to bring relief to himself.

"Ridge."

Emma's quiet whisper startled him and he was glad for the darkness that covered his flushed face. "Yeah?"

She remained silent for so long, Ridge thought maybe he'd imagined her voice, confusing it with the breathy murmurs coming from the nearby lodge.

"When we get back home, we can't see each other again or folks will talk even more," she said softly.

Ridge stiffened, angry that she'd think he would further sully her reputation. "I'm not going to give them any more call to gossip, Emma."

He heard her roll over and turned his head to find her peering at him. "That wasn't what I meant."

Even in the dimness, Ridge could see frustration in her pale features.

Across the night air, a loud moan spilled from a man's

lips, echoed by a woman's cry. Emma's head turned in the direction from which the loving sounds had come. When she gave her attention to him once more, tension radiated from her body.

"I won't ever marry again."

Confused, Ridge offered, "You don't know that."

"Yes, I do," she stated firmly. "No man will want me."

"If you move away from Sunset, no one will know. You can say you're a widow."

"With Chayton, everyone will know." Ridge opened his mouth, but she held up a hand. "I don't want to argue with you tonight." She paused and he had the impression something else was on her mind. Something that both frightened and excited him. "I'm a widow, Ridge. I know what I'm giving up when I say I'll never be a wife again, and I most certainly won't be anyone's whore either."

Her use of the vulgar word and the vehemence in her quiet voice surprised him, but before he could speak, she continued.

"Despite what many folks in Sunset believe, I've lain with only two men—my husband and you. Enapay is dead, and you have your own life to return to when we get back to town. But now—" She stuttered to a halt, as if her courage deserted her.

Ridge took a deep breath and hoped he was reading her intentions correctly. His conscience nudged him, but his need for Emma was far too powerful to ignore. He raised one side of the buffalo hide blanket in mute invitation.

After ensuring Chayton was sound asleep, Emma crawled over to join him. She knelt in front of him and lifted the doeskin dress over her head, then tossed it aside. She wore nothing beneath it and her pale skin reflected the orange glow of the embers. Her nipples, surrounded by dusky circles, hardened as he watched. Unable to resist, he reached forward to roll the hard flesh between his thumb and forefinger.

Emma's head fell back, baring her throat and thrusting her breasts toward him. Ridge rose up to embrace her. He nipped and kissed the slender column of her neck as his hands roamed up and down her silky back and sides. Her tiny moans were accompanied by puffs of warm, moist air across his cheek.

How had he thought he could get enough of Emma in just one day? Her rising musky scent teased him and his body responded instinctively to the invitation to mate. But he recognized it as more than mere animalistic urges. He cared for Emma and admired her more than any woman he'd known.

As he gently lowered her to his bed and covered her body with his, something else pierced the lusty fog in his brain.

He was falling in love with her.

EMMA fisted her hands and laid them on her thighs, willing herself to remain calm in the face of Talutah's stubbornness.

"He is my son. He belongs with me," she said, keeping her tone steady.

"He is Lakota. He belongs with his people." Talutah's dark eyes narrowed. "You take him to the *wasicu*'s town and he will be killed."

"No one will hurt him! I will protect him."

"Pah! You will not be able to protect him from words or hate. He will wither and die."

Emma blinked back tears of frustration. "You cannot stop me. He is mine!"

Talutah studied her with a flat gaze that gradually gave way to sympathy. "Think of Chayton. Here he is free to run and play among the other children. Here he will become a respected warrior. But in your world, he will always be a *half-breed*." The term was spat out. "He will wallow in your whiskey and his thoughts will scatter. No longer will he be strong and swift."

"I won't let that happen to him. I will shelter him from the taunts and hatred."

Talutah shook her head sadly. "You are only a woman, Winona, and Chayton needs a *leksi* to teach him what it is to be a man."

Visions of Ridge instructing her son brought a bittersweet swell in her chest. She squared her shoulders and straightened her backbone. "Chayton will leave with me in the morning."

Talutah scowled, but she didn't continue the argument. Emma knew that the older woman could speak to the chief about keeping Chayton here in the village, but doubted her stepmother would. For all her stubbornness, Talutah loved her, just as Emma loved her.

Emma rose gracefully although her body twinged from the night's pleasures in Ridge's arms. Twice they'd joined and she'd flown to the stars each time. Ridge was a skillful lover, who could be gentle or fierce, whichever she wished him to be. She already longed for his touch again.

She slipped out of her adopted parents' lodge and looked around in the afternoon sunshine. Spotting Ridge and Chayton by the river, she smiled and walked toward them.

As she drew nearer, Ridge turned as if sensing her presence. His welcoming smile warmed her and sent a pang of desire through her. He was so handsome, so confident, and so gentle. If she hadn't left Sunset, or if her father hadn't hired Ridge to find her, or if he had given up after she'd escaped him, she would have never known his loving.

"What are you two doing?" she asked in Lakota.

"Searching for frogs," Ridge replied in English.

"Frogs," Chayton repeated exuberantly as he held up a squirming green and black one in his small fist.

Emma gaped at her son. "You know English?"

The slippery frog escaped Chayton and splashed into the water. The boy knelt at the edge of the stream to watch it swim away.

"He knows a few words." Ridge answered her question. "I gave him the English name for plants and animals we came across."

Touched by Ridge's considerateness and generosity, she

couldn't speak. However, knowing he'd be embarrassed if she made too much out of it, she merely said, "Thank you."

"It wasn't any hardship, Emma. He's a good boy."

And she could see the sincerity in his eyes, as well as the fondness he held for her son. Maybe it wouldn't be so difficult to convince him it was best for all involved if Chayton returned to Sunset with them.

With that glimmer of hope, Emma smiled. "Would anyone like to go for a walk?" she asked in Lakota.

Chayton scrambled to his feet and the excitement in his eyes gave Emma her answer.

"Ridge?" she asked quietly as Chayton skipped ahead.

Ridge smiled and guided her down the path after the boy.

Emma focused on Chayton, who squatted down and intently studied something on the ground. She spotted the pile of animal droppings and wrinkled her nose.

Ridge chuckled over her shoulder. "What animal is it, Chayton? Answer in English."

"Rabbit," he replied with an impish grin.

Pride rolled through Emma. Her son was a fast learner.

She followed a few paces behind Ridge and Chayton, listening as Ridge alternated between speaking Lakota and English as he taught the boy more than just a new language. He told Chayton about ice cream and buildings taller than ten men. Maybe Ridge would spend time with Chayton when they returned and continue the informal lessons.

Her good mood vanished as she imagined Ridge being taunted for befriending a half-breed boy. Ridge had endured too much ridicule in his life, and to be seen with Chayton or herself would surely heap more on him. No, it was better if they made a clean break once they arrived back home.

Some time later, she and Ridge sat atop large rocks across from one another while Chayton stretched out on a sun-warmed bed of soft pine needles. He was asleep within moments.

"How did your talk with Talutah go?" Ridge asked neutrally.

Emma drew her knees up and wrapped her arms around them. "Badly. She thinks Chayton is better off staying with the tribe."

"She's right."

Ridge had never been a mother. He couldn't understand the bond a woman developed for the child she carried within her womb for nine months. To abandon her son again would kill her as surely as a bullet to her heart. "What about his mother?" she asked.

"She'll be better off without him, too," Ridge said, his voice gravelly.

Enraged and terrified by his matter-of-fact words, she glared at him. "Have you ever cried yourself to sleep night after night because you missed someone so badly you couldn't *not* cry?" Tears filled her eyes, which she dashed away in embarrassment.

Ridge glanced away, but not before Emma caught a glimpse of soul-deep pain. "Yes. After my ma died. One night my stepfather caught me crying. He whipped me until I passed out, said it wasn't manly to cry. I never cried again."

Emma's fury vanished, replaced by compassion and empathy. She slid off the rock and went to him, placing a hand on his shoulder. "I'm sorry."

He wouldn't—or couldn't—look at her. "It was a long time ago."

"You're still hurting."

"A lot of things hurt, Emma." Ridge finally turned to her and clasped her hand resting on his shoulder. "A person just learns to live with it."

She tried to pull away, but Ridge held firmly to her hand, and she surrendered. "There are some hurts a person can't learn to live with," she said tremulously.

"Can you live with all the hurts Chayton will get from the other children, as well from grown men and women who'll hate him just because his father was a savage redskin?"

Although his words were intentionally cruel, she could hear his concern clearly. "I'll protect him."

"You can't be his shadow every minute of every day, Emma. And as he gets older, he won't want you beside him. He'll have to burden all the narrow-minded insults by himself. Can you do that to him? To your own son?"

She jerked out of his grip, hating what he said and hating him more for being right. "No! I'll take him far away from those kind of people. We'll live off by ourselves if we have to."

Ridge walked up behind her—she could feel the heat radiating from his body.

"And how will you survive? What if one or both of you get sick? What kind of house will you live in?" Ridge pressed.

"I know how to gather food and store it, and I have my herbs if we get sick. We can live in a tipi," Emma replied, her voice rising despite her intention to remain calm.

"And what'll you do when someone stumbles across your place? If it's an Indian, you'll be killed because you're white and he'll take Chayton as a slave. If it's a white man, he'll use you, then probably drag you around for a while until he's tired of you. Then he'll kill you, like he killed Chayton because a half-breed's life is worth less than a dog's."

Rage like she'd never known filled Emma and she whirled around, her arms flailing and her fists striking Ridge's hard chest. "Damn you! Why are you saying such horrible things? Why? Why? Why?"

Each "why" was punctuated by blows against Ridge, blows he didn't fend off or try to stop. He accepted them in stoic silence, which made Emma even angrier. How could he be so calm when she was losing her son?

Emma had no idea how long the blind fury burned, and then suddenly it was gone. And like the aftermath of a fire, only barrenness remained.

Her arms fell to her sides and her head dropped. She turned away from Ridge, but had no strength left for anything more. Numbness spread through her and the sunny afternoon became gray and dark as she stared at nothing.

Ridge's solid hands settled on her shoulders and massaged gently. Part of her wanted to lean back into his touch, but she didn't even have the will to do that.

"You're Chayton's mother and you have to do what's best for him." His mouth was close to her ear, and his voice was raspy, as if he'd been hollering for a long time. "Think long and hard about your decision, Emma, because life doesn't give you second chances."

She closed her eyes, emptying her mind and merely feeling Ridge's fingers kneading the tight muscles in her neck and shoulders. She didn't want to think right now, and didn't want to make a choice that tore Chayton from her forever.

Her son awakened, postponing her decision. He relieved himself before joining Emma and Ridge.

"Walk?" he asked in English.

Despite the sharp ache in her heart, Emma smiled and nodded. "Walk," she confirmed.

Before Chayton could run ahead, she took his hand and followed the narrow game trail. As he walked beside her, he proudly pointed out plants, insects, and objects that he called by their English names.

Even if Chayton remained living with the Lakota he would need to know English in the years ahead. Years that Emma was certain would be filled with more bloodshed and an eventual conquering of many Indian tribes. If Chayton knew English, he could help his people with treaties and ensure they wouldn't be cheated.

She sniffed. Foolish thoughts. She and Ridge would leave tomorrow and nobody would continue Chayton's lessons.

Emma refused to dwell anymore on the future, but focused on the present. Chayton tugged away from her and she followed his every movement with a greedy gaze, storing pictures in her mind to bring out as cherished memories in the days, months, and years down the road.

Chayton making a face over an especially smelly pile of skunk scat. Chayton with wide eyes studying a piece of pink quartz. Chayton giggling as a furry caterpillar marched up and down his knuckles.

In some small part of her mind, she was aware of Ridge walking behind them, allowing her time alone with her son, but close enough he could protect them.

Hours later, after Chayton and Ridge had eaten, and darkness had fallen, Emma guided her sleepy son into their lodge. She settled him on the bed of skins and hugged him until he wriggled in protest. Keeping her expression bright, she tucked him in and sat beside him as he fell asleep, adding more portraits to her memory.

She glanced up when Ridge ducked under the flap and watched as he removed his hat and moccasins. He settled cross-legged on the ground and fed more pieces of wood to the fire. The flames leapt up, illuminating Ridge's handsome, square-jawed face.

"Talutah and Fast Elk will raise him as their own," she finally whispered.

She expected Ridge to smile and nod his agreement. Instead his expression overflowed with compassion and sorrow. He opened his mouth as if to speak, but nothing came out, then he extended a hand toward her.

She crawled over to him and he enveloped her within his arms. Her grief came in ratcheting sobs as Ridge held her close and whispered soft words that could do nothing to soothe her anguish.

$\mathcal{F}$IFTEEN

RIDGE woke before the sun and reluctantly extricated himself from Emma's limbs. She'd cried herself to sleep, and although his grief was only a shadow of hers, he'd felt the sting of tears for the first time in years. Emma was making a sacrifice no mother should ever have to make.

He tugged on his moccasins, then paused beside Emma to study her puffy eyes and pale complexion. Aching for her, he brushed her velvet-soft cheek with his thumb and fought the impulse to kiss her slightly parted lips. "It'll get better, Emma," he whispered.

Ridge grabbed his hat and left the confines of the tipi. Pausing outside, he stretched and his backbone popped. He and Emma wouldn't get far today, not after the restive night. But it was better to make a clean break rather than stay another day and allow the wound to fester.

Talutah dumped an armload of sticks on the ground and knelt to build up her cookfire. Ridge squatted beside her. She kept her gaze averted, but he knew she was aware of him, and probably had been since he'd stepped outside.

"Take care of him for her, Talutah," he said softly in Lakota.

She stilled, then settled a leathery palm on his forearm and met his gaze. "Take care of our daughter."

Ridge grasped the hand that rested on his arm. "I will if she allows it."

Talutah flashed him a gap-toothed smile and returned to her task.

Ridge disappeared into the brush, and after taking care of his personal business, he saddled Paint and Clementine. After nearly a week of lazing around, the two horses were spirited and didn't want to take the bits. But with a little friendly persuasion from Ridge, they finally gave in, then he left them in the rope corral with their reins wrapped around a bush.

He dragged his feet, unsure how Emma would react this morning. After her grief was spent last night, she'd fallen into an exhausted sleep. He'd lain awake long after, savoring her warmth but only wanting to comfort her.

As Ridge rounded a corner, he spotted Emma standing beside Talutah. It was strange to see her wearing a gingham skirt and blouse again with a wool coat over them. Her hair was no longer braided but was pulled back and bound with a leather tie. The only remaining sign of Winona was the moccasins on her feet.

She glanced up at him but quickly averted her gaze. Ridge sighed. Peace would be long in coming for her, and he doubted she'd ever feel whole again. But she'd made the right decision, difficult as it had been.

Ridge nodded at Talutah and Emma, and slipped into their lodge. Chayton lay on his back, his mouth open as he continued to sleep. The familiar soft flutter of his breathing brought an unexpected lump to Ridge's throat. He, too, would miss the boy. Although Chayton was more Lakota than white, he possessed many of his mother's traits.

Blanking his thoughts before he became too maudlin, he quickly shoved his belongings into his saddlebags. After a last look at Chayton, Ridge left the lodge. An old woman with scraggly gray hair hobbled toward him. As she drew closer, he recognized her as the chief's first wife.

"Akecheta wishes to see you before you leave," she said to Ridge, her lively dark eyes belying her age.

Ridge nodded once, and she turned away, satisfied with his answer.

"What did she want?" Emma asked as she joined him.

"The chief wants to see me."

She crossed her arms and watched the elderly woman duck into the tipi in the center of the village. "I'll go with you."

Ridge didn't bother to argue. Emma had more right than he did to visit with the elder one last time.

Talutah handed him some pemmican, which he washed down with water. Emma refused to eat, which earned her a concerned glare from her adopted mother. Instead, Emma returned to their lodge to say her final goodbye to her son.

"Her heart will take time to heal," Ridge said to Talutah.

"*Ha.* But you will help her," Talutah replied firmly.

Ridge doubted Emma would allow him to. What would she do? Bury herself in her father's house and never come out? Or maybe leave Sunset altogether?

The last choice would be the best for Emma, yet Ridge couldn't find it in himself to favor it.

There was a third option, one he'd wrestled with long into the night. He could marry her.

However, his place wasn't big enough for a wife, and all the money he made was to be put into cattle to start his herd, and to buy back the land Hartwell had basically stolen from his stepfather. He couldn't afford a family yet. Would Emma wait for him? Did he want her to?

In all the plans he'd made lying on the hard ground near battlefields and in the wilderness over the last dozen years, he'd never imagined marrying someone like Emma. It had always been someone like Grace Freeman, a gentlewoman whose father was a respected member of the community. Of course, in the eyes of the townsfolk, that applied to Emma's father, too, but Emma herself had lost her respectability the moment she'd been rescued from the Lakota.

Ridge rubbed his aching brow. He had to separate pleasure from practicality. Leaving Sunset would be best for Emma and, despite her claim about never marrying, she'd have no trouble finding a husband.

So why did his gut feel like he'd swallowed glass when he thought of her lying with another man?

Emma ducked out of the tipi and Ridge was relieved to see her eyes were dry. She'd probably cried all her tears last night. She picked up her saddlebags that she'd left lying outside the lodge.

"I'm ready," she announced in a surprisingly strong voice.

But when Ridge looked into her amber eyes, he read the depth of her sorrow. He quickly turned away and nodded to Talutah in farewell. He'd spent an hour talking with Fast Elk last night, and in their own way, had traded unspoken farewells. The Lakota believed all were connected through the earth, and even if they were apart, they were never truly separated. It was a comforting thought, but Ridge wasn't certain he believed it. A belief did little to soothe a mother's loss of her son.

Or a son's loss of his mother.

He led the way to the chief's tipi and paused outside the door. *"Hau."*

"Timá hiyúwo."

Ridge entered the lodge and Emma followed. His eyes took a moment to adjust to the dimness. The tribe's elderly chief sat cross-legged by the fire while the wife who'd summoned Ridge stood a few feet behind him. In her hands was Ridge's gunbelt and knife that had been taken from him when they'd arrived in the village.

Akecheta motioned for them to sit. Emma lowered herself to the ground behind Ridge.

"You will not be welcome here again," the gray-haired man began without preamble.

Ridge heard Emma's sharp intake of breath and his own chest squeezed painfully. He kept his expression emotionless. "We understand." He licked his dry lips. "Winona's son remains."

"He will be cared for and taught our ways."

Ridge nodded. "Thank you."

Akecheta grunted. "Go. It is time."

The stooped woman offered Ridge his weapons. *"Pila-mayaye."*

He nodded his thanks and she merely lowered her head and returned to her previous subservient position. Ridge buckled the gunbelt around his waist, then ushered Emma out of the tipi. The sun was just beginning to inch above the coral-, orange-, and rose-hued horizon. No clouds blotted the lightening sky. It would be a warm spring day, but he and Emma would be hard-pressed to appreciate its beauty.

As they rode, Ridge darted concerned glances at Emma, but she kept her gaze aimed forward and didn't even turn for one last glimpse of her adopted family. However, the strain was plain to see in her pale, drawn face. Knowing he could offer nothing but meaningless words, he merely rode beside her in silence.

THROUGHOUT the long day, every bone and muscle in Emma's body urged her to turn around and return to her son. However, she'd made her decision, though there was little comfort to be found with that choice. The only comfort was Ridge's solid, reassuring presence beside her. Without him, she wouldn't have had the courage to do the right thing. Still, it didn't prevent her from hurting or worrying. Nothing short of having her son with her would fill the hollow anguish.

Emma followed Ridge blindly, her sight focused inward. She was aware that the sun was shining and that birds flitted past, but she took no pleasure in it, as she'd done on their journey to find Chayton.

She'd had hope then, hope that she'd find her son and they wouldn't be parted again. Emma was glad that Chayton was loved, healthy, and safe, but her loss and guilt at leaving him wouldn't let her take satisfaction in that knowledge.

At noon, Ridge stopped so the horses could rest and graze. He offered Emma some jerky, but her stomach lurched at the sight of it and she shook her head. She was relieved he didn't argue but remained by the horses as his hawk-like gaze scoured the craggy bluffs around them.

They traveled throughout the afternoon, stopping only once to water Clementine and Paint. As the sun slid toward the western horizon, Emma finally began to notice their surroundings and the stillness became intrusive.

"How—" Her voice broke after not being used for so long and she cleared her throat. "How far have we traveled?"

Ridge slowed Paint so Emma could ride beside him. "'Bout twenty miles." He shrugged. "I didn't push it."

Emma took a ragged breath. "I appreciate it."

Ridge lifted a shoulder in acknowledgment.

"I didn't think anything could hurt so much," she admitted softly. "Even when I almost drowned and thought I'd never see my family again."

"He's your son, your flesh and blood."

Emma's throat swelled and she glanced away until the lump in her throat wasn't choking her anymore. "You were right. He'll have a better life with the Lakota. He'll be free to grow into a fine man."

"He'd be a fine man no matter where he grew up," Ridge said quietly.

His confident assurance touched her and she reached over to clasp his hand, which rested on the saddle horn. "Thank you."

Ridge's expression seemed to ease and a crooked smile quirked his lips. "You're welcome."

He found a campsite a couple hours before sunset where they could settle for the night. Emma was grateful to stop early and did her share by getting the fire going, and cooking a meal of biscuits and beans. A pot of coffee was boiling over the fire when Ridge returned with a final armload of wood.

They ate in tranquil companionship, listening to the birds in the trees and the scuttle of squirrels in the thatch of shrubs behind them. After the dishes were cleaned and repacked in the saddlebags, Ridge made a last check of the horses and the perimeter of their camp.

Emma watched him circle around, his figure shadowed by the dusk. His steps were stealthy, his limbs loose, and she recognized the tilt of his head as he used all his senses to search for danger. Despite her physical and mental exhaustion, her body tingled and warmed.

When Ridge returned, Emma retrieved her book, which she hadn't touched since they'd arrived at the Lakota camp. She needed something to take her mind off Chayton, at least temporarily.

"Would you like me to read aloud?" she asked Ridge.

He frowned. "I figured you'd be tired."

"I am, but I won't be able to sleep." She glanced away. "Not right away, anyhow."

"Sure." He smiled crookedly. "I could listen to your voice all day and not tire of it."

Despite her embarrassment, she managed an impudent grin. "I never knew you were such a sweet talker."

His face reddened, endearing him even more to her.

"I never had much practice at sweet-talking a gal," he admitted.

She squeezed his work-roughened hand. "You're doing just fine."

He grinned, then glanced deliberately at her book.

She picked up the volume and shifted around to get the best angle of firelight across the pages. As she read, her own tension eased and before long, she reclined against Ridge's side. He curled an arm around her waist and his forearm brushed the underswell of her breasts, causing her words to falter for a moment. She couldn't draw in a full breath and her voice grew husky.

Ridge made tiny circles across her belly with light fingertips, further undoing her faltering concentration. When his thumb grazed her nipple, she gave up the pretense of reading. Allowing the book to fall to her lap, she leaned her head against Ridge's shoulder.

He dropped a gentle kiss to a sensitive spot beneath her ear and she shivered with passion. She tilted her head, allowing him more access to her neck and he trailed a tender line of kisses to her collarbone. He undid the top three buttons of her blouse and slid his hand inside, beneath the camisole and cupped her breast.

Emma wished she was strong enough to stop his seduction, but she couldn't deny the ever-growing attraction. She laid a hand on his thigh and roamed upward, to feel his hard length beneath his trouser buttons. She squeezed him intimately, and he throbbed beneath her palm. He moaned and his warm moist breath wafted across her neck.

He grasped her hand, putting a halt to her teasing touch. "You're going to be the death of me yet, Emma," he said breathlessly.

She kissed his whiskered jaw. "Then we go together," she said, her own voice hoarse with passion.

Ridge groaned and flipped Emma around so she lay on the ground beneath him. With deft fingers, he undid the remaining buttons on her blouse and tried to remove it as Emma struggled to get rid of her confining skirt and heavy stockings.

Emma laughed at their clumsy haste, but they finally had her clothes tossed pell-mell around them. She raised herself up on her elbows and pressed her lips to Ridge's Adam's apple, then licked and nipped it playfully.

Ridge rolled off her and she immediately missed his warm, reassuring weight. But when his fingers moved to his own shirt, Emma rolled onto her side with her head in her hand to watch him.

Firelight created planes and angles across his hewn features and his nostrils flared with desire. Keeping his sultry gaze locked with hers, he stripped. His pants came off last, and Emma allowed herself the luxury of perusing his masculine form at leisure. Little strands of hair graced his chest, but it began to thicken to a line at his waist which trailed down to form a triangle of coarse brown hair. From that nest jutted his erection, which curved toward his belly. Emma licked her suddenly dry lips.

In one graceful motion, he brought his flesh against hers and she ensnared him within her arms. For one brief moment, she thought of Chayton and her heart tripped, but she focused on Ridge's heated skin and his caresses. She kissed the hollow where his neck met his shoulder and dragged her tongue downward until her lips found his nipple. After sucking and licking until Ridge was squirming above her, she switched to the other side.

Suddenly Ridge rolled to his back, tugging Emma with him so she ended up lying on top of him. His hard length dug into her hip and she shifted until she had him poised at the juncture of her thighs. She gripped his biceps and raised her hips until she felt his tip brush her moist flesh.

"Oh God, Emma," Ridge breathed.

He found the tie at the back of her head and released her hair from its confines. She shivered when he buried his fingers in the long tresses and clutched handfuls of it to steer her mouth to his. Their lips met and opened, and his tongue explored her palate in maddeningly slow, delicious flicks.

Emma rocked her hips against him, and he responded by thrusting upward to meet her. Her breasts grazed his chest, and the sweet friction of his chest against her nipples scattered her thoughts. The driving need to join with him brought Emma up on her knees and she reached down to guide him into her.

She lowered her body over the blunt head and closed her eyes as he slowly filled her. She locked her gaze on his lust-filled eyes, which reflected the pleasure she herself experienced as their bodies joined. Once he was buried within her, Emma remained seated upon him, simply feeling his solid body in and around her.

Ridge gripped her hips and she raised herself up inch by inch, then lowered herself equally as deliberately. Emma wanted to prolong the ecstasy, but their needs were too demanding.

She threw back her head and rode him, excited by both the control she wielded and Ridge's obvious enjoyment of it. His fingers tightened on her thighs and Emma's breath gusted in and out as her heart sped out of control.

Ridge thrust upward and stiffened, firing Emma's release that immediately followed his.

"Ridge," she hollered as her body bucked and spasmed around him.

Her strength abandoned her and she fell forward onto him. His arms encircled her and hugged her close.

Sweat-coated and spent, Emma curled against Ridge's side. She laid her arm across his waist and used his shoulder as a pillow. His musky, masculine scent filled her nostrils, stirring her anew, but sleep tugged at her.

She was vaguely aware of Ridge covering them with their blankets. Lips pressed to her forehead just as she drifted into slumber. A small, bittersweet smile claimed her lips.

EMMA bolted upright, coming all the way to her feet. She stared at the darkness around her, but flashes of crimson-red and the echoes of screams surrounded her.

"What's wrong, Emma?"

She blinked, her mind disentangling from her dream, but the feelings caused by the dream remained as powerful, if not more so. "Something's happened."

Ridge stood and she became aware that they were both naked. However, that bothered her little compared to the afterimages that continued to make her stomach roil and her head spin. She clutched his forearms and knew she was digging her fingernails into his skin but couldn't stop.

"What is it?" he demanded.

"Chayton, the village. Something horrible has happened."

Ridge's eyes widened in disbelief. "How do you know?"

"I-I saw it. A vision." She snatched up her clothes and hastily tugged them on. Her limbs trembled, making it difficult to dress quickly.

"We can't go back there. You heard the chief. We're not welcome there anymore."

"I'll go by myself."

Ridge grabbed her wrist, halting her frantic motions. "The hell you will," he swore. "We're going back to Sunset."

She jerked out of his hold. "I can't. Chayton could be dead or hurt."

"Dammit, Emma, you had dreams before and Chayton turned out to be fine. This one's no different."

"Yes, it is." Emma's fingers shook so much she could barely find the holes for her buttons. "I can't explain it. I only know what I know."

Ridge stared at her, his hands on his trim hips. If Emma wasn't so shaken, she might have enjoyed the sight. But she couldn't think of anything but Chayton and the horrific vision that had visited her.

Once dressed, Emma quickly moved to saddle Clementine. She could hear Ridge tugging on his clothes and muttering under his breath, and she was glad she couldn't understand what he was saying.

By the time she had her horse ready to go, Ridge was tightening the girth on Paint's saddle. She mounted her mare and gazed down at Ridge impatiently. "Are you coming or not?"

"Yes, dammit," he growled back. Ridge leapt into the saddle without the use of his stirrups and gathered the reins in one hand.

Ridge didn't look at her, but reined Paint around to go back in the direction from which they'd traveled yesterday. Emma followed, gritting her teeth against the reminder of the previous night's loving as her mare shifted into a trot.

If she hadn't been so busy with her selfish needs, maybe she would have experienced the vision earlier. What if they were too late because she'd allowed her body to lead her mind?

Her temples pounded with the rhythm of the horses' hooves, and she chanted as they rode.

Let him live. Let him live. Let him live.

IT was nearly noon when Emma spied the first signs of the village's fate. Ridge had forced her to stop, insisting the horses needed a rest. He was right, but Emma chafed at the delay. She held the mare's reins as Clementine drank from a narrow, but swiftly running stream. Searching the horizon ahead, Emma spotted a curl of smoke rising into the blue sky. Fear clogged her throat until she thought she'd suffocate.

Ridge joined her, his gaze locked on the same sight. "It could be anything."

Emma shook her head, her heart thumping a harsh cadence. "It's happened again. Another massacre."

"You don't know that."

"Yes, I do," she whispered.

Feeling as if her sore, travel-abused body was separate from her mind, Emma mounted her mare and kicked Clementine into a gallop. She was aware of Ridge calling her name, but she simply ignored him.

Ridge caught up with her just as she came to the entrance to the camp. No Indian boys stood guard in the rocks and that chilled Emma to the bone.

Ridge tugged on Emma's reins and moved ahead to take the lead. Although irritated, she didn't have time to argue. She followed closely even though she dreaded what they would find.

They rounded the last corner and froze at the scene in front of them. Half the tipis had been destroyed and soldiers dressed in the blue uniform of the cavalry milled around, keeping guard on a circle of braves, some of whom appeared to be dazed and wounded. Another group watched over a collection of women and children.

The only sounds were voices speaking English and horses snorting occasionally. The Lakota were mute, and even the children were silent.

Rusty splotches on the earth were evidence of spilled blood. Emma's vision tunneled and she swayed in the saddle. A strong hand caught her arm and held her upright.

Had Chayton survived one massacre only to die in this one?

$\mathcal{S}$IXTEEN

RIDGE'S nostrils filled with the nauseating stench of blood and burnt flesh. His stomach heaved, but he managed to choke back the nausea. He glanced at Emma, whose face was the color of ash. She pressed a hand to her mouth as she gagged uncontrollably.

Ridge looked away, afraid he'd lose the bit of control he'd managed to gain. Then he thought of Chayton, and guilt and fear sliced his chest. If he was dead, it was Ridge's fault. He was the one who'd talked Emma into leaving him behind.

He frantically searched for Emma's son among the women and children, but they were clumped together so closely he couldn't make out individuals. He swore under his breath and urged Paint forward.

"Ridge!"

The sound of his name caused him to pull back on the reins. Preston Wylie's uniform was usually spotless and flawlessly creased, but now it was splotched with brown and his left sleeve was cut off, exposing a makeshift bandage around his upper arm.

Ridge glared down at him. "What the hell's going on?"

Pres's jaw muscle clenched, exposing his own anger. But before he could speak, Emma launched herself out of her saddle and ran toward the circle of captives. Chayton tottered at the edge of the group. He appeared unhurt, but groggy and shaken.

Light-headed with relief, Ridge watched her fall to her knees and hug her son. The boy only stood there, his arms limp at his sides, and Ridge recognized shock in his features.

Renewed anger flooded through him and he turned back to the lieutenant. "What the hell happened?"

"Captain Rivers led the patrol," Pres began, his voice weary. "He—"

Before Pres could finish, Ridge caught sight of Colt, the commanding officer whom he'd counted as a friend. He dismounted and strode toward Colt.

The captain's eyes widened. "Ridge, what're you doing—"

Ridge's fist connected with Colt's jaw and he felt the impact all the way from his knuckles to his shoulder. Colt stumbled back and his hat fell to the ground, but the officer remained on his feet. Two soldiers grabbed Ridge's arms and bent them behind his back. Pain shot through his shoulder blades but he only glared at Colt.

The captain raised his head and glared back at Ridge as he used the back of his wrist to wipe away the trickle of blood at the corner of his mouth. "Why the hell did you do that?" Colt demanded, fury reddening his face.

Ridge motioned with his chin toward the captive Indians. "Did Nyes promise you a nice promotion? Or did it depend on how many savages you killed?"

Colt's mouth closed, his lips forming a thin slash across his face. His pulse throbbed in his neck and it was a long moment before he asked in a flat tone, "What're you doing here?"

"We figured something had happened," Ridge replied, unwilling to share Emma's vision with a man who'd become a stranger.

"We?"

"Emma—Miss Hartwell and me."

"You found her?"

"Yeah, I found her. Mind calling off your guard dogs?" Ridge deliberately looked at the men imprisoning him.

After a moment's hesitation, Colt waved the two soldiers away. Ridge flexed his arms and shoulders gingerly.

Gabe Sanders joined them, his face made grimmer by a streak of dried blood across his brow. "I got him trussed up tight, sir," he said to Colt, then turned to Ridge. "You're a long way from home."

"Who do you got trussed up?" Ridge asked.

"Pony Cullen. Son of a bitch tried turning this into a massacre. If Cap'n Rivers hadn't winged him, it might've happened."

Ridge stared at Colt, who met his gaze without flinching. "Why didn't you say so?"

Colt's eyes glittered ice blue. "You didn't give me a chance."

"When I saw—" Ridge broke off. "Me and Emma lived in this village for a week. They're not part of a war party."

Gabe and Colt's gazes flickered to the side and Ridge turned to see Emma walking toward them. She carried Chayton, who had his head tucked against her shoulder and his legs wrapped around her waist. The boy didn't even look up when Emma stopped in front of the men.

"Miss Emma Hartwell," Ridge said, reverting back to formality. "This is Captain Colt Rivers and Sergeant Gabe Sanders."

Colt and Gabe tipped their hats politely.

Despite the paleness of her complexion, her eyes blazed with rage. "These people were no threat to you. All they wanted was to be left in peace."

"Yes, ma'am," Colt replied. "But we were ordered to find those who left the reservation. We followed them here."

"So you decided just to kill them instead of going

through the trouble of taking them back?" Her voice trembled with derision.

"We were attacked," Colt explained. "We defended ourselves."

"You'd attack people who invaded your home, wouldn't you, Captain?"

Ridge squelched a smile of admiration. "She's right. These folks were only defending their home."

"Cullen reported that some of the warriors here had ridden with Crazy Horse," Gabe added.

"And you believed him?" Emma asked.

Gabe shook his leonine head. "If we believed everything he said, ma'am, everyone in this here village would've been killed."

Colt held up a hand. "Cullen tried to incite the men to a massacre. We stopped him, but there were casualties."

"Fast Elk was one of them," Emma said, her anger replaced by grief.

Ridge snapped his gaze back to Emma, whose eyes filled with tears. Without thought, he hugged her and Chayton. Emma leaned heavily against him and the boy roused enough to wrap a thin arm around his neck.

"I'm sorry, Emma," Ridge whispered, massaging her back soothingly.

Chayton began to whimper and Ridge cupped the back of his head. "You're safe, cub," he said in Lakota.

Chayton quieted and laid his head back down on Emma's shoulder.

"Who's Fast Elk?" Colt demanded.

"My adopted father." Emma raised her chin defiantly.

"We're taking them back," Colt replied stiffly.

"Why? They're not hurting anybody."

"We have our orders, ma'am."

"Orders ain't always right," Ridge interjected. "They're mostly women and kids."

"I can't leave them here," Colt stated.

Clenching his jaw, Ridge steered Emma toward what remained of the lodge they'd used and lowered her to the ground. He knelt beside her, unsure of what to say.

He lifted his head and took in the carnage. A dog's carcass, barely recognizable, had been trampled into the ground, and two dead horses lay at the edge of the village. The chief's tipi, along with another half-dozen were completely destroyed with only ashes and tufts of buffalo hide marking where they had been. The pit fires were cold and the embers scattered. Kettles were upended and their contents spilt across the ground. Skinny dogs were lapping up the food, growling at anyone who came near them.

Naked children around Chayton's age were held tight in women's arms. Tears stained both young and old ruddy cheeks, and shoulders hitched with sobs that were eerily silent. There were two dozen men and boys being guarded, and many of them were bloodstained. It appeared their wounds had gone untended.

"How's Talutah?" Ridge asked Emma.

"Grieving." Her red-rimmed eyes stared past him.

Ridge restrained a sigh. "I'm sorry."

"Tell them." She made a wide arcing motion toward the People.

"I'm going to see what else I can find out," Ridge said. "You stay here."

"No, I'm going to help."

"You'll be safe here."

Emma's laugh was brittle. "From who?"

Ridge gritted his teeth. He'd noticed the soldiers' disrespectful gazes at Emma and he knew it was only the beginning. Once the cavalry unit returned to their post, word would spread fast about Emma and her son. She would be accosted like a whore and her son taunted with cruel barbs.

"Could you get my saddlebags? I need my herbs," she said.

He muttered an oath and helped her to her feet. "What about Chayton?"

She hesitated only a moment. "I'll leave him with the women."

Emma was arguing with one of the men guarding the warriors when he returned with her saddlebags.

"I'm only going to take care of their wounds," she snapped at the soldier.

"Nobody's allowed near them," the guard repeated.

"Who said that?"

"Captain Rivers."

Emma turned her glare on Ridge. "He's your friend."

The way she said "friend" made Ridge cringe inwardly.

"What does she want?" Colt Rivers's voice startled Ridge.

" 'She' wants to treat their injuries since you don't seem to care whether they live or die," Emma replied curtly.

Colt fixed his frigid gaze on Emma. "If you're willing to risk your life, go ahead."

"They won't hurt me," she argued.

"You don't know that, ma'am. But like I said, it's your neck."

Emma wavered only a moment. "I'll take that chance."

"I'll help," Ridge offered.

"Leave your weapons out here," Colt ordered.

Ridge reluctantly did as he said. Irritated, he followed Emma, aware of Colt's stare burning a hole between his shoulder blades.

Despite Colt's dire warnings, the warriors allowed Emma to examine their wounds. Four had been shot, while another had been slashed with a knife across his chest, and most all of them had minor cuts and bruises.

Akecheta, the old chief, had the most serious wound—a bullet in the chest. He'd been propped up with a rolled-up buffalo skin and his weathered face was washed-out and slack.

Emma examined the wound carefully, but even Ridge could see there was no hope. She sat back on her heels and her eyes welled with tears.

"My time has come. I will join those who have gone before me," the chief said, his voice so weak Ridge had to strain to hear it.

Ridge didn't bother with pointless platitudes. "You ruled your people well."

Akecheta coughed and blood flecked his bluish lips. "Help them," he wheezed. "Honor the dead."

Ridge had seen an Indian burial or two and knew of the ceremony, but he wasn't certain he could convince Colt to allow them time to take care of their dead.

"We will," Emma promised.

Ridge flashed her a dark look, but her gaze was locked with Akecheta's. Then the chief closed his eyes and his breathing grew labored, until it stopped altogether.

Ridge removed his hat and bowed his head as Emma touched his forehead, as if in a benediction.

"Good journey," she said in a husky whisper.

The guard closest to them called for two other soldiers to take Akecheta's body to lie with the others.

Although the sun was warm, a chill swept through Ridge. He raised his head and settled his hat back on his head. He followed Emma and assisted her as she diligently took care of the others' injuries.

Just as they finished, a woman's wail broke the silence, followed by another and another until the air seemed to vibrate with the unnatural laments. The mourning had begun.

He felt Emma shudder beside him.

"I hate that sound," she confessed. "When Enapay died, I mourned until I was so hoarse no more sound would come. I had nightmares every night for a week." She swallowed hard. "I expect the nightmares will last longer this time."

Ridge guided Emma past the guards, some of whom appeared irritated by the anguished cries. Most of the soldiers, however, kept their gazes averted from the Lakota. Ridge escorted Emma to the women and children, where Chayton was more than ready to return to her arms.

"I have to go talk to Co—the captain," Ridge said. "Will you be all right?"

She nodded but didn't meet his gaze.

Ridge went in search of Colt and found him by Pony

Cullen, along with Gabe and Pres. At one time, Ridge had called the three men friends. Now, he wasn't certain.

Cullen glared at Ridge. "If it ain't the Injun lover himself."

Gabe kicked the scout's outstretched legs. "Shut up, Cullen."

"What do you want?" Colt asked Ridge, his expression stony.

"Akecheta, the chief, just died. He asked me if his people could have proper burials."

Cullen snorted, but one look from Gabe ensured that the scout kept the rest of his comments to himself.

"How long is it going to take?" Colt asked.

"Probably a day, maybe two."

Colt scowled and swore under his breath.

"It's the right thing to do, Captain," Pres Wylie said in his soft Southern drawl. "I'll help them, sir."

Colt nodded sharply. "All right. Get them started."

"Yes, sir," Gabe replied without hesitation.

Pres and Gabe headed toward the survivors.

After a curt command to Cullen's two guards, Colt walked away in the opposite direction and Ridge followed. Once they were out of Cullen's hearing, Colt stopped.

"I didn't want this to happen, Ridge. In fact, I was hoping Cullen wouldn't find them," Colt admitted in a low voice.

"But he did, and you weren't able to maintain control of your men," Ridge said.

Two red splotches colored Colt's cheeks. "Dammit, Ridge, I did what I could."

"You could've done more."

"Do you actually think I wanted this to turn into a massacre?"

"Maybe it was payback for what the Indians did to your wife down in Texas."

Colt's face whitened and his eyes glittered with rage. "No!"

Ridge took a step toward him. "These Indians saved

Emma Hartwell's life and gave her a home. In fact, the Lakota who found her and adopted her was killed by *your* men." He punctuated his words with a forefinger to Colt's chest.

The captain grabbed his wrist in a bruising grip. "If you actually believe I could order the murder of innocent lives—Indian or otherwise—you don't know me at all."

Ridge stared into Colt's piercing blue eyes. "Maybe I don't," he finally said.

Colt released him with a flicker of disappointment, which he masked immediately. "Did you know about the Hartwell woman's son?"

"Not until we got here."

"Bastard?"

Ridge stifled his impatience. "She was married to the boy's father."

Colt's lips turned downward. "Once word gets out, her past few months in Sunset will have been a cakewalk compared to what's ahead."

"We left the boy here and were headed back to Sunset when—" he broke off, unable to explain Emma's gift. "When we had a feeling something was wrong."

"And now?"

"Now there's no way in hell she'll leave her boy behind to be raised on a reservation."

"Old man Hartwell's going to have a fit."

Ridge snorted, not giving a tinker's damn about Hartwell. "Good for the son of a bitch."

"What about Miss Hartwell and her son?"

Ridge only shook his head, unwilling to think about Emma's upcoming trials. "Me and Emma'll stay through the burials; then we'll be heading back. Emma will want to see Fast Elk laid to rest." Ridge turned to leave, but Colt's hand fastened on his sleeve.

"She's a squaw woman, Ridge," Colt stated. "With a half-breed son. She'll only bring you trouble."

Ridge's muscles bunched, but he managed not to take

another swing at Colt. Besides, Colt was only repeating the same thoughts Ridge had already had.

"I know." And with that, Ridge trudged back to Emma.

EMMA moved in a daze, helping prepare the bodies for burial by dressing them in their finest clothing and painting their faces. A little girl whom Chayton had often played with, was the only child casualty. However, four of the nine warriors killed were younger than Emma.

Smudges of pungent smoke that purified the living and dead surrounded the women as they silently performed the final preparations for the burials. Two of the soldiers, those whom Emma had seen Ridge speaking to, helped the Indians build the wooden platforms for the bodies. She was grateful for their help but it still took the rest of the day and into the evening to complete them.

Once she'd walked within ten yards of Pony Cullen, outwardly ignoring his taunts but barely controlling the impulse to take a knife to his heart. She'd never felt such overwhelming hatred for another person, and it frightened her to know she could.

As she worked, Chayton slept with the other children on a buffalo skin pallet in the middle of the camp. Four young girls watched them closely. Every few minutes Emma would glance at him to reassure herself he was alive.

Emma was concerned with Talutah's stoic silence as the older woman prepared Fast Elk for his final journey. She didn't even seem to know Emma was there, nor did she search out Chayton. Talutah focused entirely on her husband of many years.

A long shadow fell across Emma and she looked up.

"How's Talutah doing?" Ridge asked softly.

Emma followed the woman's deliberate motions with growing trepidation. "Not very well."

"Once the shock wears off, she'll be able to grieve and move on."

Emma shook her head. "She was only able to give Fast Elk a daughter, and she died. I remember her telling me how she urged him to take another wife to bear him a son, but he wouldn't." Emma absently wiped away a tear rolling down her cheek.

Ridge shifted uncomfortably. "Indians don't show their feelings much, but I know Fast Elk loved you like you were his flesh and blood."

More tears coursed down her cheeks, but she wasn't crying. "I know."

Ridge took Emma's arm and helped her to her feet. He remained standing close and cupped her face to wipe away the tear tracks with his thumbs. She grasped his wrists and lowered his hands.

"Would you mind staying close to Chayton tonight?" Emma asked. "I'll be sitting with Talutah."

"I'll watch him," Ridge reassured. He lowered his hands to his sides and opened his mouth as if to say something more. Instead he spun around and strode away.

Too tired to look away, Emma followed his progress across the camp. He didn't pause until he joined Captain Rivers.

She didn't know who to trust. Although she'd treated their wounds and helped them with the burial preparations, the Lakota avoided her like the plague, and Talutah was lost in misery. Most of the soldiers were eyeing her like she was a bottle of whiskey in a dry town.

Emma rubbed her throbbing brow and pulled her hand away, only to notice dried blood across her knuckles. She wondered whose it was.

She lifted her gaze to Chayton and a tiny shimmer of light broke through the black sorrow. Her resolve strengthened. No matter what anyone said, she wouldn't leave him behind again.

THE long night passed, underscored by the survivors' grieving for their dead. Moans rose and fell, interspersed with an occasional wail which ululated through the camp. Fires flickered brightly, but smoke hazed the air and the cloying scent of cedar infiltrated everything.

Ridge lay on his side facing Chayton who slept restlessly beside him. Every time Ridge closed his eyes, he saw blood being lapped up by the earth beneath still bodies. He couldn't distinguish between memory, reality, and nightmare. The massacre he'd unwittingly been involved in last fall blurred with the one that had occurred twenty-four hours ago. Unknown victims took on the faces of those killed here.

As an army scout, Ridge had believed in what he was doing—making the wilderness safer for the incoming tide of settlers. However, on his last scouting mission, he'd been ordered to find a band of renegade Indians who'd attacked a wagon train. Ridge tracked them to a village. Instead of culling out the guilty, the army unit had ridden into the camp with guns blazing and swords flashing. Ridge had tried to stop the bloodlust, but he'd only been able to watch in horror as women and children were cut down, screams dying in their throats as their bodies fell under bullets and blades. He would never forgive himself for his part in the bloody massacre.

Ridge sat up, careful not to wake Chayton. As exhausted as he was, Ridge knew he wouldn't be able to go back to sleep any time soon. He added some wood to the fire and settled beside its warmth.

A figure emerged out of the shadows and Ridge tensed until he recognized Emma's slumped figure. She sank to the ground beside Chayton, her legs folded to the side. Gazing down at her son, she brushed her hand across his long, straight hair.

Ridge didn't break the companionable silence, leaving that to Emma if she was inclined to talk.

"Sergeant Sanders ordered me to get some sleep," she said, minutes later.

Ridge smiled. "He's hard to ignore."

Her lips curved upward, but the smile was fleeting. "I like him."

Ridge felt a stirring of jealousy. "He doesn't judge folks by the color of their skin."

Emma continued to stroke her son's hair. "What'll happen to them?"

"They'll be taken to the reservation."

"Will your friend let them take their belongings?"

"He's a fair man. He'll give them time to get their things together."

"If he's so fair, he'd let them stay here."

"He's only doing his job, Emma." Ridge felt compelled to defend him.

"He should find another job," she shot back.

After the somber task of preparing bodies for burial, Ridge was glad to see some of her spirit returned. "Colt's got his reasons for what he does."

"Maybe so, but it doesn't make it right."

Ridge sighed and lifted his gaze to the star-filled sky. "I didn't say it did."

Low voices crawled through the night and a muffled snore or two came from the soldiers who slept some forty yards away. The Lakota's wrenching moans continued unabated.

"Get some sleep, Emma. After the dead are put to rest, we're leaving for Sunset," Ridge said.

"With Chayton."

"With Chayton," Ridge repeated.

Emma was too tired for little more than a nod. She curled up beside Chayton and was asleep in moments.

Ridge rose and covered mother and child with his blanket, then watched over them until morning.

SEVENTEEN

FROM atop his horse, Ridge watched the Lakota prepare to leave the camp at noon the next day. Despite the resentment of some of the soldiers, Colt had given the Indians time to dismantle the remaining tipis and pack their things. The dogs were put into harness to pull the travois loaded with the Lakota's sparse belongings.

Emma had helped Talutah with her preparations. Any other time the older woman wouldn't have accepted her assistance, but since they'd left Fast Elk on his burial platform early that morning, Talutah had become distant and unresponsive. Ridge saw the fear in Emma's face, as well as Chayton's confusion, at Talutah's uncharacteristic behavior.

A horse trotted up and he turned to see Colt draw up alongside him.

"When are you and Miss Hartwell leaving?" he asked without preamble.

Ridge fingered the reins of Emma's horse, which stood docilely beside Paint. "As soon as Talutah has her belongings ready to go."

Colt shifted in his saddle. "I'm sorry things turned out this way, Ridge."

"It only takes one man to rouse up the bloodlust. We've seen it before," Ridge allowed. Violent memories stirred and he mentally shook his head to rid his mind of the images.

Colt cursed under his breath. "I should've shot him as soon as we left the fort."

Ridge's gaze traveled to Cullen, who watched the activity with contempt from his bound position atop a horse. "You ain't a cold-blooded murderer like him."

"You thought I was."

Ridge's gaze flickered across his friend's swollen and discolored jaw. "Hell, Colt, I wasn't thinking straight."

"Yeah, I noticed," Colt said dryly. "When it comes to Miss Hartwell you got the same problem. She's got you where you don't know up from down, and you don't even know it."

Ridge stiffened. "What's between me and her is none of your concern."

"The hell it isn't. I don't want to see you lose all you've been working for because of her and her kid."

At least he hadn't said *half-breed*.

"Leave it alone, Colt," Ridge warned.

The captain narrowed his eyes and pursed his lips. He looked away. "We'll be behind you, but I won't be pushing them. There's too many wounded and old folks."

"That'll ease Emma's mind," Ridge said stiffly.

"It'll ease *my* mind when you two head out. But watch yourselves."

"Are you going to be all right without a scout?"

"Sarge is pretty good about picking up sign." Colt scanned their surroundings. "I know you and Nyes don't see eye-to-eye, but if we don't make it back tell him what happened."

Guilt nudged Ridge's conscience. "We could ride with you and I could scout."

"No. You need to get Miss Hartwell back to her father's ranch and give her some time before the rest of the town hears about her situation. And you can bet when we get back the gossip's going to start flying."

Colt was right. The townspeople would ravenously devour the newest tidbit about the fallen Miss Hartwell. If they made it back before the cavalry, that gave Emma's family time to overcome their shock and decide what to do. No matter what Ridge thought of old man Hartwell, he did seem to care for his daughters.

"All right," Ridge agreed reluctantly. "Keep your powder dry, pard."

"You, too."

Each placing a hand on the other's forearm, the two men said goodbye, but it lacked the warmth of past farewells.

Colt wheeled away to see if the caravan was ready to move out. Ridge watched him until his attention was drawn by Emma's approach. If possible, she looked more tense than yesterday. Her wan face and lank hair gave the impression she was ill, but it was a sickness of the heart, not body.

Ridge dismounted and went to her side. He helped her onto Clementine while Chayton leaned against his leg. Then Ridge lifted the boy onto the saddle in front of Emma. His little hands wrapped around the pommel and his hollow eyes lit with delight. Ridge's heart missed a beat at the boy's obvious pleasure. He patted Chayton's knee before climbing into his own saddle.

"Is Talutah any better?" Ridge asked.

Emma shrugged listlessly. "She does what she's told, but doesn't seem to know what's going on."

It was hard for Ridge to imagine the tough woman so beaten, but losing Fast Elk had been a terrible blow. "Is someone with her?"

"Shimmering Water said she would stay close to her."

"Good. Colt said he wouldn't push them."

Emma snorted in disbelief. "Just like he didn't lead the charge on the village."

Caught between loyalties, Ridge didn't comment. "We'll go on ahead of them."

"No. I want to make sure Talutah is all right."

"You said Shimmering Water will take care of her. We

need to get you back before the soldiers arrive." Ridge took a deep breath. "The truth of the matter is as soon as Colt's unit gets back, word's going to spread like wildfire about you and Chayton. If we can get to your folks beforehand, that'll give them some time to get used to the idea before tongues start wagging."

If possible, Emma's face paled further. "I hadn't thought of that."

"It's no wonder. You're exhausted and grieving." He glanced around to see the last of the caravan winding out of the camp. "We'd best head out."

Ridge felt the hostile looks from both sides—Lakota and white—as he and Emma trotted past them. He glanced at Emma and noticed the stern set of her chin. If he hadn't been looking so closely, he wouldn't have noticed the accompanying quiver.

Chayton fell asleep not long after they began their journey. Ridge and Emma didn't speak, but not because of the sleeping boy. Talking about what had happened would be pointless.

At dusk, they made camp. Chayton roused long enough to eat some food, then dropped off again. Drained emotionally and physically, Ridge and Emma fell asleep soon after the boy.

The following morning was brisk and they ate quickly. While readying their horses, Ridge noticed Emma pause and stare back in the direction from which they'd come. Guilt creased her brow and Ridge could do nothing more than give her shoulders a sympathetic squeeze.

They traveled steadily through the day despite the dreary gray clouds and occasional light showers that felt more like a cool mist. During the midday break, the sun burst through for a few minutes of relief from the dampness. Chayton regained much of his energy and spent the respite chasing bugs and searching for odd-shaped rocks. Ridge challenged him to a foot race and let the boy win, which delighted Chayton and brought a smile to Emma's haggard face.

They crossed rolling brown hills broken by massive gray jagged rocks thrusting up from the earth, and plodded through temporary ponds formed from the spring melt. Knowing their destination, they made better time traveling back. It had taken nearly two weeks to find the Lakota, but by Ridge's reckoning, it would take only five days to return to Sunset.

Chayton grew more animated and excited, probably thinking of it all as a big adventure. He buoyed Emma and Ridge's spirits with his childish questions and enthusiasm, but he also exhausted them. By the third night, Emma and Ridge were both relieved when Chayton went to sleep.

Sipping coffee, Ridge glanced across the fire at the boy's dark head, which peeped above his blanket. "You're going to have your hands full with him."

Emma, leaning against her saddle with her legs outstretched in front of her, nodded. "He's going to miss playing with other children."

Ridge looked at the woman and saw sadness lingering in her eyes. "I s'pect he will. Have you thought about what you're going to do when we get back?"

"It depends on my father." She rubbed her suspiciously bright eyes. "If he can accept Chayton, things won't be easy, but they won't be impossible either."

"And if he doesn't?"

She granted him a small smile. "I'm hoping my aunt in St. Paul will be willing to take us in. Maybe I could find a job in the city."

Ridge considered the jobs Emma might be able to get. He didn't think much of any of them. "Do you think your father will throw you out?"

"I don't know."

He barely heard her soft words. Ridge's stepfather had beaten him, but he hadn't cast him out. Could John Hartwell actually disown his daughter?

"I don't want your money for finding the village," Ridge finally spoke.

Emma snapped her head up to meet his gaze. "We made a deal."

Ridge shifted on the unforgiving ground. "You can use that hundred dollars to make a new start."

"I always keep my word," she said stubbornly.

"And I'm releasing you from it."

"You can't do that."

"It's my hundred dollars. I can do anything I want with it."

"Buy some cattle, or better yet, buy back some of your land from my father. It would serve him right."

Ever since he returned to Sunset and claimed his inheritance, Ridge had wanted nothing else. But now, he couldn't bring himself to take money from a woman and her son whom he'd come to care about far too much.

He held his tongue, but the argument wasn't over. Besides, even if her pride demanded he accept it, he'd find a way to give the money back.

"We'd best turn in," he said. "We'll be covering a lot of miles tomorrow."

Emma lay down beside her son, just as she'd done since they'd started back. Ridge stretched out on the other side of the fire and tried to ignore the cold emptiness beside him. And inside him.

He had a feeling it'd be a long time before he stopped missing Emma's warmth.

IT was the afternoon of the fifth day when Emma caught sight of her father's imposing home. They'd passed cattle with the Hartwell brand in the morning, but they had to ride some distance before arriving at the ranch house itself.

They paused on a rise a quarter of a mile from the buildings. Emma saw three men around the corral, working with unbroken horses. She heard the whoops and hollers, but couldn't understand the words. She could imagine them, though.

Chayton shifted in front of her. "What is that?" he asked in Lakota as he pointed toward the ranch house.

"That's where your white grandfather and grandmother live," Emma replied in the same language. "Remember how to say their names in English?"

"Gran-fa-ter and gran-ma-ter," Chayton said after a moment.

Emma patted his small shoulder. "Good. Do you remember your aunt's name?"

Another pause as the boy's face scrunched in thought. "Sarah."

Emma had been teaching him English throughout the trek, giving the boy's lively mind something to focus on during the long hours in the saddle. She wanted him to greet her family in their own language, hoping to make a good impression. Not that it would help if her parents were bound and determined to despise their own grandson.

Emma sighed heavily.

"Are you ready for this?" Ridge asked quietly.

"No," she said huskily. Ridge's long, cool fingers brushed hers and she clutched his hand. "Thank you. For finding Chayton and for—" She glanced away. "Everything."

Ridge's eyes burned with passion, as if remembering those nights filled with "everything." Attraction blazed and flared to settle as an ache in her chest.

Emma released his hand and asked with forced brightness, "Shall we?"

"Follow me," Ridge said.

Puzzled, she waited for him to go ahead. He led her down a circuitous route to the kitchen door at the back of the house. Realizing he did it so the ranch hands wouldn't see Chayton or herself, she wasn't certain if she should be grateful or upset. She wasn't ashamed of Chayton. He was her son. But she understood his reasoning—it was the same one used for going ahead of Captain Rivers and his unit.

Ridge dismounted and walked around the horses to lift

Chayton from Emma's saddle. Once Chayton was safely on the ground, Ridge wrapped his hands around Emma's waist and eased her down, drawing her body along his as he lowered her. His thumbs brushed the sensitive skin beneath her breasts and she gasped at the bolt of desire.

Quickly stepping away from Ridge, she took Chayton's hand in her sweat-dampened one and pushed open the door. She was relieved when Ridge followed them inside. Since it was too early to begin supper, no one was in the kitchen. Chayton tried to see everything at once as he pressed closer to Emma.

She took a deep breath and looked back at the man who'd unintentionally claimed her heart. She took strength and comfort in his solid presence, and walked through the swinging doorway into the dining room. Footsteps on the stairs made her turn to the wide staircase to see Sarah descending.

"Sarah?" she called softly when her sister reached the bottom of the stairs.

Sarah turned and froze, her eyes huge and her mouth agape. "Emma?" she whispered hoarsely.

"I'm home." Emma's voice trembled with anxiety.

Sarah raced across the floor and flung her arms around Emma, who hugged her sister with equal enthusiasm. Sarah stepped back, but clung to Emma's hands. "Are you all right? Where have you been? Everyone's been sick with worry."

"I'm sorry. Ridge—Mr. Madoc found me and brought me home," Emma said. Her heart pounding like a smithy's hammer, she released her sister and put a hand on Chayton's small shoulder. "He's why I had to leave."

Sarah's shocked expression would've been comical if Emma hadn't been on pins and needles. "An Indian boy?"

"This is Chayton, my son." Emma paused. "Your nephew."

Sarah's face paled and she swayed. Ridge caught her arm to steady her.

"Sarah, are you all right?" Emma asked with concern.

"Sarah?" Chayton piped up.

Emma looked down at her son's curious and excited expression. "Yes, Chayton. This is your aunt," she said in Lakota. "Sarah."

"Oh my," Sarah whispered. "Oh my."

"Do you need to sit down, ma'am?" Ridge asked.

"I think that might be a good idea," Sarah replied weakly.

Ridge led her to a heavy oak dining room chair and eased her into it. Emma and Chayton followed and stood in front of Sarah.

The younger girl stared at Chayton, lifted her gaze to Emma, then returned to study Chayton. "He has your chin and nose," she finally said.

"That's what Talutah, my adopted mother, always said, too." Emma fought the lump in her throat. "My husband Enapay said our son had my eyes, too."

"Your husband?" Sarah squeaked out the question.

"Yes. He's dead. I'm a widow," Emma said, trying to hold a tremulous smile.

"Sarah," Chayton said again with a wide grin. He tugged on her hands and raised his arms.

"I think he wants you to pick him up," Emma translated.

For a long, heart-pounding moment, Sarah stared at the boy. Then, with a radiant smile, she lifted Chayton onto her lap. Sarah's eyes sparkled with unshed tears. "I'm an aunt."

Emma stepped closer to Ridge, wanting to share her relief and happiness at Sarah's acceptance. Ridge smiled back, understanding without words like he so often did.

"How old is he? What does his name mean? Are you both going to live here now?" Sarah started throwing out questions as Chayton stared in fascination at her blond hair.

Sharp footsteps sounded on the polished wood floor and Emma turned to see her father and mother enter the dining room.

"Emma!" Martha Hartwell cried and hugged her daughter.

Dazed, Emma wrapped her arms around her mother. The familiar scent of rose water wafted around her, reminding her of long-ago days. "I've missed you, Mother."

Emma glanced over her mother's shoulder at her father to find his gaze locked on Chayton. She drew away from the older woman and moved to Sarah and Chayton's side. Trembling, Emma announced, "Mother, Father, I want to introduce Chayton. My son."

Her mother's eyes rolled upward and she collapsed. Ridge lunged toward her and managed to partially catch her, saving her from a bump on the head.

"Get some water," her father ordered. He shoved Ridge away from her, as if he thought Ridge intended to murder her.

Emma lifted Chayton into her arms and Sarah bustled into the kitchen for the water. She returned carrying a glass and a damp cloth. Glowering, Ridge kept his distance, turning the brim of his hat around and around in his hands.

Her mother roused and glanced around in confusion, but when her gaze settled on Emma and Chayton she let out a moan. Sarah and their father helped her into the chair Sarah had vacated.

Her father's lips thinned and his eyes were stormy. "Explain yourself, Emma."

Although she bristled at the command, Emma knew they deserved an explanation. "I'd been living with the Lakota for two years when Enapay began courting me. I had given up on ever being found and brought back home. I cared for him and we married three months later. Chayton was born a year after our marriage. My husband was killed during a raid when Chayton was less than two years old."

"You married a—a savage?" her mother asked, shock evident in her lined features.

"Yes, Mother, I married a 'savage' who loved me and treated me well. He even spoiled me." She smiled tenderly, remembering the times Enapay would return, bearing some gift for her.

Her father's face deepened to scarlet and a vein pulsed in his brow. "He was an Indian, for God's sake."

"He was a decent, honorable man." Emma lifted her chin and met her father's gaze head-on. No longer was she a girl, and no longer would she cower under John Hartwell's dictates.

He cursed loudly and fluently, drawing shocked looks from Sarah and their mother. Chayton buried his face in the curve of Emma's neck. "And now you want to raise your half-breed bast—"

"Hold on, Hartwell," Ridge broke in, stepping forward. Every taut line in his muscular body radiated furious indignation. "Chayton's parents were married so he's no—" He crushed the brim of his hat in his fists. "He's an innocent little boy who don't deserve your narrow-minded insults."

Emma's throat tightened and her eyes smarted. If she didn't love Ridge already, she would've fallen for him at that moment.

Timidly Sarah stepped forward, her hands twisting together in front of her. "Mr. Madoc is right," she stated, shocking Emma with her mettle. "Emma and Chayton have had a long journey and would probably like to clean up and rest before dinner. Isn't that right, Emma?"

"Yes, thank you, Sarah," Emma managed to say past her shock at her sister's newfound assertiveness.

Sarah smiled, but when she laid an ice-cold hand on Emma's arm, Emma knew how terrified she was defying their father.

"Could you take Chayton upstairs?" Emma asked her sister. "I'll be up shortly."

Sarah's smile wavered for only a moment. Emma spoke some soothing words to Chayton and passed him to his aunt. Once Sarah and Chayton were out-of-sight, Emma faced her parents. Never before had she felt so many mixed emotions—anger, disappointment, resentment, and fear. But it was anguish which prevailed and enveloped her heart.

"When do you want us gone?" Emma asked her parents bluntly.

Her father's jaw muscle clenched. "Why didn't you tell us?"

Emma laughed bitterly. "After your reaction to Chayton you have to ask?" Out of the corner of her eye, she saw Ridge shift uncomfortably. "Maybe you should pay Mr. Madoc so he can leave and not be witness to any more of our family squabbles. Oh, and you owe him another hundred dollars."

"Why?"

"I promised him a bonus for bringing Chayton back," Emma said. She figured Ridge would accept the hundred from her father more readily than from herself, and she would pay her father back. Someday.

"Did you come through town?" her father asked with a scowl.

Emma shook her head, immediately guessing the reason for his question. "No. And Mr. Madoc brought us around to the back door so none of the hired men saw us either."

"Emma, go upstairs. Madoc, come with me into my study," her father commanded. He gave his wife's shoulder a reassuring squeeze. "Keep the cool cloth on your brow, Martha, and don't try to rise until I return."

"What are you—" Emma began.

"I'll pay him. Go upstairs."

Emma didn't like being ordered about like a child, but the long journey had exhausted her. A bath and clean clothes were also enticing. It seemed like she'd been living in the same skirt and blouse for months rather than days.

Realizing she might not see Ridge again, her heart skipped a beat. For three weeks they'd not been far from one another. Thinking of the nights they'd lain together, Emma shivered with longing. But she reminded herself she'd known it couldn't last. Ridge had his own life to attend to, and she had a son whose needs came before her own.

"Thank you for everything, Mr. Madoc," Emma said

formally, refusing to give her father another reason to hate Ridge Madoc.

His warm blue eyes caressed her but he kept his expression bland. "You're welcome, Miss Hartwell. You take care of yourself and that fine boy of yours."

"I will," Emma whispered, her emotions overcoming her.

Before she did something she'd regret, she hurried up the wide staircase. Suddenly weary beyond words, Emma wanted to ensure Chayton was all right, then sleep for a week.

She only wished it would be in Ridge's bed.

$\mathcal{E}$IGHTEEN

RIDGE'S gaze followed Emma until she disappeared from view and a sharp ache arrowed through him. Already he could feel unfamiliar loneliness, the kind he hadn't felt since his ma had died. But Emma didn't need him anymore. Her sister would stand beside her, and hopefully her parents would come around to accept her son.

Suddenly weary, Ridge followed John Hartwell into his fancy office. Books lined the bookshelves that covered two of the walls, and Ridge had this vision of a young Emma sneaking in here to search for one to read. A fireplace encompassed much of the third wall, and the fourth was dominated by large windows.

Hartwell sat behind his desk, looking like some king presiding over his kingdom. He didn't invite Ridge to sit, but Ridge did so anyhow, and earned a scowl from Hartwell. After dropping into a brown leather chair, he eyed Hartwell's cool mask.

"The boy wasn't part of the deal," Hartwell said.

Ridge shrugged. "I didn't even know about him until we found the village."

" 'We?' You were only supposed to find Emma and bring her home immediately."

Cursing his unintentional slip, Ridge propped his elbows on the chair arms and steepled his fingers, effecting a nonchalance at odds with the tight coil in his gut. "You didn't say *when* you wanted her home. I signed on to find her and bring her back. I fulfilled my end of the bargain." He inwardly flinched at the inference that Emma was merely a business matter—the subject of a black-and-white contract. She'd long ago ceased being a means to an end.

Hartwell slumped back in his chair and his face sagged, as if he'd aged twenty years. "Do you realize what kind of life she'll have raising a half-breed child?"

Ridge felt a fleeting sympathy for the man. "Yes, sir. For what it's worth, I tried to talk her out of bringing him back."

The rancher blinked in surprise, but quickly covered it with a scowl. "When people find out, she's going to be turned away from businesses and respectable folks won't want anything to do with her. Her son won't be allowed to attend school and the children will tease him, and worse."

"She knows." Ridge narrowed his eyes. "What about you? You gonna turn her away, too?"

Irritation sharpened Hartwell's features. "She's my daughter."

"And Chayton's your grandson."

Hartwell flinched. "I can send them away someplace where no one will know about her unfortunate past."

"You might be able to hide her past, but Chayton can't be hidden away and Emma won't be parted from him. He's her flesh and blood." Ridge paused. "Unless you're only getting rid of them because you're embarrassed by her."

"Emma's my daughter!" Hartwell spun his chair around to stare outside, hiding his face from Ridge. "I'll do what's best for her."

"She's not your little girl anymore, Hartwell, and she won't take kindly to you making her decisions."

Silence filled the room.

Finally, Hartwell opened a desk drawer and counted some bills. He held them out to Ridge. "Two hundred dollars. The one hundred we agreed on, and another hundred to keep your mouth shut. It'll get out soon enough but as long as her bast—her boy stays inside, nobody will find out."

"You can't hide him away forever."

"No, but the longer I can keep him out-of-sight, the longer I can protect Emma."

Ridge debated whether to tell him about the soldiers who had seen Emma and Chayton together in the village, but decided that was Emma's business. If Hartwell wanted to pay him an extra hundred, he wasn't going to argue. In fact, he even felt a measure of satisfaction. Hell, the man owed him that and more for cheating Ridge out of his rightful legacy.

"I won't tell anyone," Ridge promised. He stood and pocketed his money, then walked to the door. Halting, he looked at Hartwell over his shoulder. "Instead of being ashamed of her, you ought to be proud of her."

With that quiet remark, Ridge strode out by way of the kitchen to gather Paint and lead Clementine over to the hostler. As he rode away from Hartwell's ranch, loneliness settled like an iron mantle across his shoulders.

THE following days dragged for Ridge. With the needed money in his pocket, he sent a telegram to the seller of the bull in Cheyenne and told him he'd be down to purchase the animal soon. The only reason Ridge didn't leave Sunset right away was because he'd promised Colt he'd pay a visit to Colonel Nyes if the captain didn't show up.

Five days after returning to Sunset, Ridge dropped by the hardware store to talk with Howard Freeman and ended up taking his daughter Grace to lunch at the café. By the time their meals were served, Ridge was certain he'd go crazy with Grace's prattling on about this person's dress and that person's hair. When Grace clumsily turned the subject to Emma Hartwell, Ridge recognized the baited hook.

"I just can't imagine living among the savages like she did," Grace said, round-eyed and a little too innocent. "Why on earth did she want to go back to them?"

Ridge wiped his mouth with his napkin as his appetite fled. "You'll have to ask Miss Hartwell."

"Oh, I could never. Some things just aren't discussed in polite conversation."

Ridge bit the inside of his cheek to refrain from biting off the girl's feather-brained head. To his way of thinking, bustles and coiffures weren't polite conversation either.

"Nobody's seen Emma since she's been home," Grace said.

"She probably needed to rest up," Ridge replied. He'd kept his word and told nobody about Emma's son, but it wasn't Hartwell's money that bought his silence. It was his sense of protectiveness toward Emma and Chayton. "I'd best be getting back to my place."

Grace deliberately looked down at her nearly full plate. "I haven't finished yet."

You would've if you hadn't been running off at the mouth, Ridge thought peevishly. He forced a smile that barely made it past a grimace. "Don't hurry. I'll pay the bill on my way out." He stood and grabbed his hat before she could argue. "Good day, Grace."

He paid for the two meals and escaped outside. Why had Grace's chattering bothered him so much today? He'd spent some time with her before, and had managed to nod and utter the right comments at the right moment. But this time, her high-pitched voice and endless claptrap had nearly driven him crazy.

His gaze strayed up the road, to where Emma Hartwell and Chayton were hidden from prying eyes at her father's ranch. At least a dozen times a day he had to talk himself out of riding over to see how they were faring.

Be honest. You want to see Emma.

He thought the pang of missing her would fade, but it

only gnawed at him, like the hollow left by a pulled tooth. If Colt would just return, Ridge could take off to Cheyenne and pick up the bull. Time and distance would help him get past his pining for Emma.

Disgusted with his weakness, he stepped off the board-walk onto the main street. Puffs of dust arose around his moccasins. While he'd been chasing after Emma in the wilderness, the snow had melted and the ground had dried, leaving the town coated with a fine layer of grime.

He climbed into his saddle and, without making a con-scious decision, headed toward the fort, which lay seven miles east. Maybe Colt had made it back last night, thus freeing Ridge from his obligation. Forty-five minutes later he could tell by the signs that no unit with a passel of Indi-ans had come near the fort. He veered Paint away from the military post and rode in the direction from where they'd be coming. If they weren't far off, Ridge could leave for Cheyenne with a clear conscience.

After an hour of steady travel, he spotted a plume of ris-ing dust. Another hour and he called out to Colt who rode at the front of the column. Dust coated the captain's face and uniform, but his smile was welcoming when Ridge ap-proached him.

"You never were much on waiting," Colt said.

Ridge ignored the familiar jibe. "Any trouble?"

Colt shook his head. "Quiet as a horse thief after a hanging. How about you and Miss Hartwell?"

"No problems unless you count her ma fainting when she saw her grandson."

"How was old man Hartwell?"

"Just what you'd expect. He's only worried about how it'll reflect on him." Ridge stood in his stirrups to study the column. "I see you still got Cullen tied up."

"Gagged him, too. Son of a bitch wouldn't stop cussing. Every time we took the gag off, he'd start in on how the colonel's going to have my bars."

Ridge studied his friend who had dark crescents be-neath his eyes. "Any truth to it?"

Colt looked away. "It isn't a secret that me and the old man don't see eye to eye. That was one of the reasons I was surprised he assigned me this mission. Nyes also knows I have no respect for Cullen."

"And Nyes and Cullen are thick as thieves," Ridge interjected.

"Yep. The problem is I don't have any proof Cullen was intending to kill every man, woman, and child in that village. All I got is my gut, and Nyes isn't going to accept that."

"But Sarge and Pres—they'll stand behind you."

Colt dragged his bleak gaze to Ridge. "Nyes also knows they're loyal to me."

Ridge shook his head slowly, pondering something that had been stuck in his craw since he and Emma arrived at the destroyed camp. "How'd you get past the sentries? They had a natural defense with that narrow trail into the valley and guards always watching it."

Colt shrugged. "We didn't run into anybody until we almost stumbled into the camp. The lookouts must've been sleeping, or maybe they thought they were safe enough without them."

"Maybe." Ridge didn't think it likely but he couldn't come up with a better excuse. "You're close enough to the post now that you shouldn't have any problems."

"You in a hurry to get somewhere?"

"Cheyenne. I'm going to pick up my bull."

Colt grinned. "Congratulations. It won't be long until you're an honest to God rancher."

Ridge chuckled. "I need more than a bull for that, but it's a good start."

"Good luck to you."

"Thanks." Ridge paused and fixed a serious gaze on his friend. "I know you and me don't agree about Miss Hartwell, but could you keep an eye on her? With the soldiers back, things might get ugly."

Colt narrowed his eyes. "She really got under your skin."

Ridge scowled and shifted his backside on the saddle. "Would you do it?"

"Yeah, but I doubt old man Hartwell will be letting her out of her cage."

That's probably what the ranch felt like to Emma—a gilded cage with everything but the one thing she truly wanted—her and her son's freedom.

"Thanks. I'll stop at my place, then head out. I should be back in a week, maybe ten days," Ridge said. "Good luck with Nyes."

Colt grimaced. "I'll need it."

Ridge glimpsed Talutah in the line of Indians, and he gnashed his teeth at her weary shuffle and slumped figure. "You mind if I talk to her a minute?"

Colt shook his head, his face somber. "You're welcome to try. She doesn't speak to anyone. I'm not even sure she knows where she's going."

"She knows," Ridge said softly.

He nodded to Colt and trotted closer to the Lakota woman. Dismounting, he fell in step with her. Her hair, which she'd hacked off during her mourning for Fast Elk, lay uneven and straggly across her shoulders.

"Winona and Chayton are safe and well," Ridge said to Talutah in her language.

A slight stumble in her plodding shuffle was Ridge's only sign that she heard him. He continued walking beside her, leading Paint. Finally, Talutah raised her head. Ridge was shocked by the grayness of her pallor and the lifelessness in her eyes.

"It is good," she said, her voice hoarse from disuse. "Chayton will grow strong, like his grandfather Fast Elk."

"*Ha.* You taught Winona well the ways of the People. She will honor you and Fast Elk, as will her son."

Talutah grasped his hand with cold, bony fingers. "Be well and live with honor."

Ridge gently squeezed her painfully thin hand. "I'll do my best," he whispered.

She released him and her gaze dropped to the ground

once more. Ridge stepped out of line and watched the rag-tag Indians pass by in silence. A group of soldiers brought up the rear. They glanced at Ridge curiously, but they, too, seemed to understand the sad injustice done to their Lakota captives.

Once everyone had passed, Ridge reined Paint around to ride back to his home.

THE slant of the sun told Emma she could wait only five more minutes. She'd been pacing outside Ridge's small cabin for the last twenty minutes, hoping to speak to him one more time. When she'd arrived, she'd called out his name but he wasn't around. Neither was Paint. He might have already left for Cheyenne to pick up the bull he'd proudly told her about some nights ago. It was the reason he'd come to find her—he needed the money to buy the animal. After everything that happened on their journey, she wondered if he regretted taking the job, and shuddered at the thought of someone like Pony Cullen coming after her instead.

Emma spied a rider coming down the road, and the black-and-white horse was easily recognizable as Ridge's. Relief made her shoulders slump, and awakened awareness made her heart race. Although she thought of him often, it couldn't compare to seeing him in the flesh, his lean, muscular body flowing smoothly with his horse's gait. Awareness of the man brought flutters to her belly, and her breasts became heavy and more sensitive. Glancing down, she could see her hard nipples clearly outlined by her dress.

Scolding her body's wanton response, she smoothed back her hair and attempted to gather her composure as she watched him approach.

He kicked Paint into a ground-eating canter and jumped out of the saddle before the horse came to a complete stop. "Is something wrong? Is it Chayton? Are you all right? What happened?" he asked in alarm.

Emma shook her head and almost put her palm to his mouth to halt his questions, but doubted she could withstand the temptation of his lips against her skin. "Chayton's fine. I'm fine. Nothing's wrong." That wasn't exactly true, but she couldn't afford to weaken.

"Where's Chayton?" Ridge looked around.

"Sarah's watching him."

He removed his hat, wiping his brow with his forearm. A hat mark flattened his hair in a circle around his head, giving him a boyish look, which made Emma smile with affection.

"Do you want to come inside? I can warm up a pot of coffee," Ridge said.

"I can't stay long," she said with genuine remorse. "I just wanted to be certain Father paid you."

"He did. All two hundred dollars."

"I'm glad. He may be a stubborn man, but he does pay his debts."

Ridge rested a gentle hand on her shoulder and she nearly wept with the tender feeling that swept through her. "Has he been able to accept Chayton?"

"Yes and no," she replied.

"Let's go inside and sit down."

Emma should have argued with him, but after being apart for so long, she craved his company—the sight and sound of him. He guided her into his tiny cabin and she perched on a straight-back chair. After slipping his hat off his head, Ridge placed the other chair in front of her and sat down, their knees brushing.

"Tell me," he commanded gently.

His compassionate eyes invited her to lay out all her troubles, but she steeled herself against the seduction of his kindness. "He doesn't talk to Chayton directly, but doesn't ignore him either. He had Sarah buy some clothes for Chayton, and I cut his hair." She smiled wryly. "It's a good thing all the hands were out working when I did, or they would've come running in to see who was getting killed.

I'm still trying to convince him that since we live with the *wasicu* now, we have to act and dress like them."

"I'll bet he doesn't like that one bit." Ridge sent her a crooked grin.

"You'd win that bet. Getting him used to wearing so many pieces of clothing has been even harder. The first time he took them off faster than I could put them on him. The second time they stayed on for all of ten minutes. I followed the trail of clothes to find him naked in the dining room. Mother had a fit." Emma laughed, remembering her prudish mother's expression when she'd caught sight of Chayton running atop the oak table without a lick of clothing.

Ridge chuckled. "That must've been quite a sight."

"Oh, it was." She sobered. "Until Father showed up to see what all the commotion was about. He had Chayton in tears by the time he was done, and Chayton didn't even know what he was saying."

Ridge's strong hand covered Emma's clutched ones. "I'm sorry."

Emma embraced his concern and acceptance, fighting the yearning to unload all her fears and worries upon his broad shoulders. "Don't be. It's not your doing."

"Have things gotten better?" Ridge asked.

"They haven't gotten worse," she answered evasively, and then forced a smile. "What I came over for was to give you something." She rose and went back outside.

Ridge followed her to her horse, where she opened one side of her saddlebags and tugged out a cloth bag. She handed it to him. "I want you to use this to practice reading and making your letters."

He took the bag from her and, with a puzzled expression, withdrew the book. She'd put the papers he'd practiced writing the alphabet, between the pages. "It's the same one you read from."

She nodded, ignoring the lump threatening to clog her throat. "It's my favorite."

He thrust the book back in the bag and held it out to her. "I can't take it."

"I want you to have it," she argued, pressing it back to him. "If nothing else, keep it as a remembrance of our time together."

"I don't need anything to remember you, Emma," Ridge said huskily. He cupped her face with his free hand, and slid his fingers into her hair as his thumb stroked her cheek. "I don't think I could forget you if I tried."

Emma's heart threatened to gallop out of her chest and she didn't know where she gained the strength to step away from him. She even managed light laughter. "You'll forget me easily enough once you find the right woman. Then you'll have a whole wagonload of beautiful children with dark blue eyes, who'll do you proud and carry on your name."

She quickly mounted Clementine, overtly aware of Ridge's hand above her elbow as he helped her. Intending to leave before he suspected her feelings, she reined her mare around. But Ridge caught the horse's bridle.

"I saw Talutah. They should be at the reservation tomorrow," he said quietly.

Emma's stomach dropped. "How was she?"

Ridge glanced down and shook his head. "Not good. Sounds like she's willing herself to die."

Emma squeezed her eyes shut and her breath stammered in her chest. It didn't come as a complete surprise, but she'd been hoping and praying that Talutah would overcome her sorrow and grief. "I'll go see her after they're settled."

"That wouldn't be a good idea."

She glared down at him. "I don't care what people think."

"What about Chayton? Do you care about him?"

Bitterness welled in her throat. "Nothing I say or do will change anyone's mind about a half-Indian, half-white child."

Ridge dropped his forehead to her thigh for just a moment, but it was long enough to inflame the smoldering spark between them. She ignored the bittersweet ache.

"Think about it before you go, Emma," he said quietly. "Just promise me that."

The reins cut into her palms. She nodded. "I'll think about it."

The furrows in Ridge's brow eased. "I'm headed to Cheyenne to pick up the bull. I should be back in a week."

Emma's heart clenched. A full week with no chance of seeing him, even from a distance. "Have a good trip," she said. "Goodbye."

She kicked Clementine's flanks, urging the mare into a trot. Although she felt Ridge watching her, she didn't dare turn around for one last look, afraid he'd see in her face what she had to keep hidden.

"TAKE him to the stockade, Sarge," Captain Rivers ordered.

"With pleasure, sir," Gabe Sanders replied with a jaunty salute.

"Not too much pleasure, Sergeant."

Gabe merely smiled crookedly.

Colt watched Sarge escort Cullen to the stockade, then turned to his men in formation behind him. "Dismissed," he commanded in a strong voice.

The exhausted soldiers headed to the corrals to take care of their equally tired horses.

Colt smiled at Pres, who remained beside him. "That order was for you, too."

"Would you like a corroborating witness when you beard the lion in his own den?" Pres asked.

"If Nyes won't listen to me, he won't listen to you either." Colt held up his hand before Pres could argue. "Go on, clean up, get something to eat at the mess, and then get some sleep. Something tells me we're going to be busy with the general showing up later this week."

Pres snorted. "Busy polishing our boots."

"Whatever needs to be done," Colt said. "Go on."

Reluctantly, he left. Colt remained sitting atop his horse in the middle of the parade ground for a moment longer.

Five minutes later he took a steadying breath before knocking on Colonel Nyes's door.

"Enter," the colonel barked.

Colt marched in, stood at attention, and saluted his commanding officer. He held the position until Nyes saluted back.

"Our mission was successful, sir. The Indians have been returned to the reservation."

Nyes smiled widely. "Good, good. I knew I could count on you, Captain. How many of the savages were eliminated?"

Colt stiffened. "I believe our mission was to return the Indians to the reservation, not kill them, sir."

The colonel's smile vanished. "The more we're rid of, the less to make trouble. How many, Captain?"

His muscles taut with anger, Colt replied tersely, "Ten killed, including the chief of the village."

"Well done, Captain Rivers. Obviously, Cullen was able to track them to their lair."

"He's in the stockade, sir."

Nyes rose and leaned forward, flattening his palms on his desktop. "Why in blue blazes is he there?"

"He incited the men to murder everyone, including the women and children, in the camp, Colonel."

"Can you prove this?"

"I know what I saw and heard, sir," Colt stated curtly.

"Perhaps you misinterpreted."

"I don't believe so, Colonel."

"You don't *believe* so?" Nyes roared. "Cullen has done an exemplary job as a scout. You can't have him arrested for something you can neither corroborate nor quantify, Captain."

Colt remained silent, his hands clasped at the base of his spine. Too angry to look directly at the colonel, Colt gazed out the window, over Nyes' shoulder.

"Corporal," Nyes boomed out.

The clerk in the outer office scurried in and saluted. "Sir?"

"Have Pony Cullen released from the stockade immediately."

The enlisted soldier bobbed his head. "Yes, sir."

Colt clenched his jaw, fighting the urge to countermand his commanding officer.

Nyes sank back into his chair. "Perhaps you should take some time off, Captain," he suggested coolly. "Maybe think about what you want to accomplish in the military."

"Yes, sir." Taut with suppressed anger, Colt barely managed a civil tone.

"You're dismissed, Captain."

Colt saluted sharply and marched out of the office. Back on the parade grounds, he paused to watch Cullen swagger out of the stockade. The scout spotted him and made a bee-line toward him.

"You better sleep with one eye open, Rivers, 'cause I ain't gonna forget what you done," Cullen threatened.

"That's *Captain* Rivers," Colt said, his tone low and warning. "And you're not the only one who won't forget."

Colt pivoted on his heel and strode to his quarters. He'd take the time off and keep his word to Ridge by checking on Miss Hartwell.

And maybe make some long overdue decisions in the process.

NINETEEN

RIDGE made thirty miles before nightfall and set up his sparse camp like he'd done uncountable times in the past. Only the memory of those times he shared with Emma remained the sharpest in his thoughts.

Sitting cross-legged by the fire, he sipped a cup of coffee. A faint sense of unease made Ridge's gaze survey the surrounding shadows. He had the impression someone was watching him from the darkness, but Paint would've made a fuss if something or someone was out there, and he was placidly foraging at the edge of the camp.

Unable to find any reason for his disquiet, Ridge set aside his empty tin cup and reverently opened the bag containing the book Emma had given him. He drew it out and something dropped onto his leg. He picked it up, recognizing it as Chayton's moccasin that Emma had held close for months. It must have gotten into the sack by accident.

He fingered the soft, supple deerskin, noting the intricate bead design across the top. Emma had obviously spent a fair amount of time sewing it.

As he reluctantly placed the small boot back in the sack, he felt something within the moccasin. Pulling the small shoe back out, he peered inside to find a folded piece of paper. Staring at the confusing mix of words, Ridge struggled to read the note. He recognized his name at the top, but then had to focus, using the tricks Emma had taught him to figure out the remainder.

Finally, after long frustrating minutes, he was able to piece the words together.

Ridge. Remember Chayton and me with fondness, and may his moccasin bring you the good fortune it brought me. Yours, Emma.

He clutched the moccasin in one hand, rereading the message over and over until he had it memorized. That Emma had given him something that meant so much to her humbled him. Nobody had given him a gift since he was Chayton's age, but it was nothing like this one—a gift that couldn't be bought.

The book and his lessons forgotten, Ridge stared into the fire's flames, the moccasin cupped within his palm.

IT didn't take long for the news about Emma's son to circulate once the soldiers returned. Her father was furious she hadn't told him about meeting them at the Indian village. She refused to explain the circumstances, but John Hartwell wasn't stupid. He'd figured it out through her non-answers.

Sitting on the porch one warm spring afternoon a week after she'd arrived home, Emma watched Chayton play with a litter of kittens. His trousers were already dirt-stained, but at least he had stopped removing them. His dark hair, once covering his back, was trimmed above the collar of his blue plaid shirt. It had taken Emma more time than Chayton to get accustomed to his short hair.

Only old Rory the hostler was left in the ranch yard, which was why she and Chayton were allowed outside. When the ranch hands started returning, she and Chayton would be relegated to the house again, which was growing increasingly frustrating.

What did it matter if they saw Chayton? Everybody knew. Cullen made sure of that, spreading the rumor with, according to Sarah, sadistic enthusiasm.

What Emma wanted to know was why the murderer had been set free. The last time she'd seen Pony Cullen he was a prisoner, arrested for inciting a massacre. She'd taken solace in the fact the captain was Ridge's friend and hoped he would see justice done. But it seemed Captain Rivers wasn't any better than many others who believed the only good Indian was a dead Indian. So why had he gone through the trouble of pretending to restrain the scout? The most painful question, however: Was Ridge part of the deception?

Movement on the road caught her eye and her pulse quickened. Had Ridge returned early? She shaded her eyes against the glaring sun and her excitement died. It was only one of the ranch hands coming in.

Disappointment weighed heavily upon her although she knew she had no right to feel that way. She had no claim on Ridge Madoc despite her heart's insistence.

Already accustomed to staying out of sight, Chayton joined her on the porch. "Go in?" he asked.

Emma stopped herself before nodding. "No, not this time." She was tired of acting like a wanted outlaw around her own home. "You can stay outside if you'd like."

Chayton grinned impishly and ran over to the corral to watch the man ride in. Emma recognized the ranch hand but didn't know his name. She stood and leaned against the porch post to watch closely and to ensure that the man didn't get ugly toward her son.

Although she couldn't hear the words, Emma saw Chayton's mouth moving and the startled man replying. When the hired hand smiled, Emma relaxed. And when he lifted Chayton onto his horse to give him a ride around the yard, tears filled her eyes with gratitude. She'd thank him later for his kindness.

"Are you all right, Emma?"

She turned to see her sister standing behind her, and

dashed the moisture from her eyes. "I'm fine, Sarah. Better than fine, actually."

Sarah's gaze found Chayton and his new friend. She smiled. "Father won't be very happy."

"Not happy at all," Emma agreed with mock severity.

Emma and Sarah looked at each other and broke into laughter.

"It's nice to hear you laugh, Emma. I've missed that," Sarah said after their mirth faded.

"I haven't had much to laugh about. I've been so worried about Chayton, but I was afraid to tell anyone about him," Emma admitted. "Ridge didn't even know about him until we rode into the village where Chayton was."

"Mr. Madoc?"

Emma warmed under Sarah's scrutiny. "Yes."

"Was he angry?"

"Not that I had a child. He was upset that I hadn't told him."

"Father doesn't like Mr. Madoc, but I always thought he was nice and kind of shy."

Emma chuckled. "He's not really shy—just quiet. He and Chayton got on like two peas in a pod when we were at the village. It was Ridge who started teaching him English. He has a way with children."

"Why, Emma Louise Hartwell, I do believe you're sweet on him," Sarah teased.

Much to her chagrin, Emma's cheeks burned with embarrassment. "Like you said, he's a nice man. He treated me like a lady, even after I knifed him."

Sarah gasped. "What?"

Emma reluctantly told her about the night Ridge found her, and how she used herbs to put him to sleep. Then she kept on talking, telling Sarah about him finding her again, tying her up, how she fell in the river, and finally locating the Lakota. She left out their nocturnal activities in the cabin, and the other nights she'd willingly crawled into his arms.

"You love him," Sarah said softly.

"I've only known him a month," Emma argued, keeping her gaze on Chayton who was now petting the hired man's horse through the corral poles.

"Did you tell him?"

Emma sighed, wishing Sarah wasn't quite so perceptive. "He doesn't love me."

"How do you know? Did you ask him?"

"He brought me back and hasn't tried to see me since we returned. That isn't what a man in love does."

"Did Mr. Madoc kiss you?"

"Sarah! You're impossible." Emma descended the porch steps. "I'd best get Chayton inside. The rest of the men will be coming in soon."

Emma ignored her sister's speculative gaze as she gathered her son and returned to the house. The coolness of the interior made her shiver, or maybe it was the occupants who chilled her.

Her mother walked into the front room. "Sarah, is that—Oh, it's you, Emma."

"Yes, Mother, it's only Emma," she said churlishly. "And don't forget her son Chayton. Oh, that's right. You *are* trying to forget him."

"Emma Louise Hartwell," her mother rebuked.

Twice in less than half an hour she'd been called by her full name. She was either being especially peevish today or her family was growing increasingly impatient with her. Perhaps both.

She sighed. "Did you want something, Mother?"

"Would you like a cookie, Chayton?" the older woman asked her grandson.

Chayton nodded eagerly. Cookie was one of those words he'd quickly learned. After a moment, Martha Hartwell extended her hand to Chayton. He took it eagerly with a shy smile.

Emma followed them into the kitchen, unable to believe her eyes. Although Emma had caught her mother watching Chayton numerous times, she hadn't gone out of her way to get to know him.

The older woman had Chayton wash up first, then sat him down beside the small table in the corner. Emma's mother placed two molasses cookies on a plate and poured him a glass of milk. She placed the snack in front of Chayton and tentatively laid a hand on his head.

"I'm sure you're hungry after playing with the kittens," she said with a smile. "When your mother was your age, she enjoyed playing with the animals, too." She smiled wryly. "Of course, I tried breaking her of the nasty habit, but her father only laughed and said I should leave her be."

"I didn't know that," Emma said quietly.

"You don't know a lot of things, Emma." Her mother busied herself with punching down the rising bread dough. The scent of yeast wafted through the kitchen. "You don't know how I prayed day and night for your safe return after you disappeared. You don't know that I never gave up, even when your father insisted you were dead. You don't know the nights I had to wake your father from a nightmare as he called out your name." She wiped her floury hands on a sackcloth. "When you were returned to us, we called it a miracle. But your father couldn't bear people talking about you after what you'd been through. He's the one who decided to keep you away from town after you recovered from your wounds. He didn't want you hurt by those who'd once been your friends."

She walked over to Emma and laid her hands on her shoulders. "When you left to find the Indians, your father was devastated. He swallowed his pride and asked Ridge Madoc to find you—that's how worried he was. Then you came back with a child and told us you were married to one of those people who kept our daughter from us for seven years." Her voice faltered and she cleared her throat. "How do you expect your father and me to feel?"

Had she been that selfish to not even notice her parents' grief? She'd learned of Sarah's the night before she'd run away to find Chayton, but she hadn't even considered her father and mother's feelings. She'd only seen their unbending strictness and assumed they were ashamed of her.

"I'm sorry," Emma whispered. "I didn't know."

She embraced her mother, who hugged her back, and something inside Emma fractured and broke. All the lost years; years she'd matured while her parents prayed they'd find their little girl. Only the Emma who came back to them had evolved into a widow with a child of her own. The adolescent her mother and father prayed for no longer existed. It was no wonder they seemed like strangers to her, too.

"More cookie?"

Emma glanced down to see Chayton standing beside them. She smiled. "What do you think, Mother? Would another cookie spoil his appetite?"

Martha Hartwell, her eyes shimmering with moisture, but with a smile much like her daughter's, thought for a moment. She stepped over to the tin and handed him a cookie. "This is the last one for now, Chayton."

The boy's face lit up. "Thank you, Grandmother."

"You're welcome—" She glanced at Emma then back at her grandson. "Chayton."

"Thank you," Emma mouthed.

Her mother turned away to surreptitiously wipe her eyes. "I don't feel like a grandmother. I used to call my grandmother Nana." She faced her daughter once more. "Do you think Chayton would mind calling me Nana?"

"I think he'd like that." Emma looped her arm around her mother's. "I know I would."

ALTHOUGH Emma was tired, her mind raced. She rolled onto her back and placed her hands behind her head to stare at the whitewashed ceiling. From the trundle bed beside her, Chayton murmured in his sleep. She thought she heard the word "Nana" and smiled.

Only her father remained to be won over by his grandson. Emma suspected that would be a near-impossible task, despite what her mother had confessed earlier. While eating dinner, she'd tried to see behind her father's stoicism. However, when he'd scolded Chayton for using his fingers to eat a piece of chicken, she decided her mother was simply making excuses for his callous nature. Emma had argued with her father, pointing out that Chayton was doing extremely well with a spoon and fork considering he'd never used either until the previous week. She'd ended up getting the cold shoulder the rest of the meal.

The clock downstairs struck twelve.

Emma sighed. Although she hadn't had one of her dream visions since the night Chayton's village was attacked, her sleep had been restless. Waking often, she found herself reaching for a hard, warm body, but found only cool sheets. She missed Ridge, especially during the long nights. She missed the tickle of his hair against her nose while she lay on his shoulder, and the deep vibrations in his chest when he laughed quietly. But mostly she missed how he made her feel when they joined.

Desire encircled her, heated her blood, and made her body ache. She pressed her thighs together, determined to overcome the need.

She wondered if Ridge missed her even a little bit.

ALTHOUGH it was late, Ridge remained awake. The bull he'd bought that morning stood tethered to a twenty-foot rope far enough away that he wouldn't bother Ridge, but close enough that he could hear the animal if something bothered it. Ridge also trusted Paint to let him know if a dangerous predator—two- or four-legged—came close. The bull was foraging, and alternated between contented snorts and chewing the tender sprouts of spring grass.

Ridge had traveled longer that day than he planned, but he'd felt a sense of urgency that had only increased as the hours passed. It wasn't anything he could pin down, but a general feeling of unease. He didn't think it involved his home, but suspected it was more Emma who drew him.

During his long hours in the saddle, she was never far

from his thoughts. What was she doing now? Was she being shunned in town?

He had no doubt everyone now knew about Chayton, which meant they probably knew his part in finding her son and bringing them back to Sunset. Surprisingly, it didn't bother him. What troubled him the most was the fact Emma was facing the gossipmongers alone.

He ate a piece of jerky and washed it down with water. His stomach protested even that small amount of food.

After scouting around his camp and checking on Paint and the bull one last time, he settled into his bedroll. As if of its own accord, his hand found the leather moccasin beneath his saddle that he used as a pillow. He fingered the child's soft boot, as well as the scrap of paper within it.

Yours, Emma.

He savored the entire note, but especially those two words. He rolled them around, over and over in his head, and had even spoken them aloud where only Paint and the bull could hear him.

He was acting like a lovesick fool. Emma had no intention of marrying again, and even if she did, her father would never allow her to wed him.

Ridge crushed the moccasin and the note in his fist, and shoved them back under his saddle.

"I don't think this is a good idea."

The trepidation in Sarah's voice made Emma wish she hadn't asked her sister if she wanted to accompany them to the reservation.

"Nobody will know," Emma reassured. "With Father and Mother gone all day, and Rory thinking we went on another picnic, we won't even be missed."

"But what if someone sees us? Or Father and Mother return early? Or—"

"You can stay here if you want, but Chayton and I are going," Emma said firmly.

Sarah stood beside the buggy for a long moment, her expression undecided.

Chayton grinned down at her and clapped his hands. "Go for ride, Aunt Sarah."

Emma smiled as Sarah surrendered to her nephew. When it came to Chayton, Sarah had no defense against his innocent charms. Their mother, too, was fast becoming a willing subject of her grandson. It seemed all Chayton had to do was smile and gaze at them with his big brown eyes and they'd do his bidding.

For Emma, her mother and sister's acceptance was a miracle. The only stumbling stone was her father, who spoke to Chayton only when necessary and not a word more. His hardheadedness aggravated Emma and confused Chayton.

Emma slapped the reins against the horse's rump and the sturdy sorrel headed down the road. As Sarah answered Chayton's endless questions and added to his rapidly expanding English vocabulary, Emma allowed her thoughts to wander.

She'd been home ten days and this was only the second time she was leaving the ranch. The first had been to give Ridge the book and that had only been a short foray. Her father had forbade her to set foot off Hartwell land and her mother agreed with him, although her reasons were bound with affection rather than censure. The smidgen of guilt Emma felt for disobeying now was inspired by her mother's loving concern rather than her father's strictness.

Emma was worried about Talutah. She'd had a dream last night for the first time in over two weeks. A spotted owl had come to her with a tiny mouse in its talons. The mouse moved feebly within the owl's grasp. When Emma had awakened and the dream vision faded, Talutah was heavy in her thoughts.

The drive to the reservation took two hours and by that time, even Chayton was tired of riding. The boy brightened at the sight of the tipis, but Sarah's pinched features revealed anxiety and fear. "I've never seen so many Indians," she whispered.

"It's all right, Sarah. They won't hurt us," Emma reassured.

"How can you be so sure?"

"Because many of them are friends," Emma replied with more confidence than she felt.

Emma spied Shimmering Water and stopped the buggy. She hopped down and turned to help Chayton, only to find him on the ground, already beside Sarah and holding his aunt's hand. Emma smiled at her son's protectiveness.

"*Ha*, Shimmering Water. We have come to visit." Emma greeted her friend, the Lakota words sounding awkward across her tongue. In addition, Emma's clothing—a brown calico skirt and white muslin blouse with a twilled silk shawl and a matching bonnet—made her feel out of place among those she'd lived and worked with. She introduced Sarah to her friend.

The sparkle in Shimmering Water's eyes was gone, and her dark hair lay dull and lifeless across her shoulders. "Winona. I did not expect to see you again."

Emma heard the flat censure in her voice and, although she wasn't surprised, it still hurt. She glanced at Sarah who was staring at her like she was a stranger.

Chayton suddenly pointed at two children his own age and Emma recognized them as former playmates of her son's. "Play? Please?"

Emma smiled. "Yes, but don't stray far."

He released Sarah's hand and scampered away to join the children. When they began to play together, Emma gave her attention back to Shimmering Water. "How is Talutah?"

Shimmering Water's eyes were blank. "Gone."

Emma's heart skipped a beat. "Gone?"

"Her spirit has joined her husband's."

Moisture filled Emma's eyes and a tear rolled down her cheek in a maddeningly slow trickle. Images of her adopted mother teaching her, scolding her, laughing with her flooded Emma's mind. Fast Elk and Talutah had saved her life and she'd come to love them. Now they were gone. Just as Enapay and Ohanzee, the shaman who'd helped her understand her gift of dream visions, were gone. Only Chayton remained.

"What is it?" Sarah asked, unable to follow the conversation.

"Talutah, my adopted mother, died," Emma replied, her throat thick with tears.

"Oh, Emma, I'm so sorry." Sarah hugged her and Emma was glad her sister had accompanied them.

After a few moments, Emma turned back to the Indian woman. "Was her death mourned?"

"Yes." Shimmering Water's eyes softened. "She spoke of you and Chayton at the end."

Emma closed her eyes, willing her tears away. Talutah was with her husband. Neither of them would have to live caged on a reservation, but would now roam the plains with their ancestors.

She drew a hand across her face and surveyed the Lakota's new home. Lodges of various sizes and quality were scattered like scabs across the flat, greening earth. In some ways it didn't look that much different from the village in the wilderness where she'd lived with them. Women continued to stir stews and soups over small fire pits, and sew beside their tipis. Children still ran around, chasing the dogs and one another. The men played dice in the shade of the lodges.

However, where there would've been chanting and singing, there was only silence and subdued tones. The Lakota's heart no longer beat in this place.

She glanced up to see Shimmering Water gone and the truth struck Emma. No longer would Winona be welcome here.

"She didn't even say goodbye," Sarah commented with a frown.

"It's the Lakota way," Emma said absently. "Our visit is over."

"Don't you want to see her grave?"

"They don't bury their dead. They place them on plat-forms." Emma swallowed back her grief. "I don't think I could handle seeing her that way."

Her chest tight, Emma gathered Chayton and climbed into the buggy. Sarah kept a hand around her nephew's shoulders as she gazed out across the quiet camp.

"I never imagined Indian villages were this—this sad," Sarah said.

"This is a reservation, Sarah. It's different. The village I lived in, the People were content—they were always laugh-ing and singing." Emma motioned to the disarray. "Here they're prisoners, so they have nothing to laugh or sing about."

"It's not fair."

Emma squeezed her hand. "I know, but there's nothing we can do."

"There should be."

"Maybe you'll think of something."

Sarah met her gaze squarely, her chin raised. "Maybe I will."

Pride flared in Emma at her younger sister's new matu-rity. Sarah had even begun questioning their father's dic-tates.

After one last look at the somber camp, Emma flicked the reins over the horse's rump. She thought of Talutah and Fast Elk, but the images were from seven years ago. They had no children left to repeat their stories nor remember them, except Emma and Chayton.

"Do you remember the story Grandmother used to tell you of White Buffalo Woman, Chayton?" she asked her son.

His dark eyes lit with excitement and nodded. "Tell again?"

"Many, many summers ago, two young warriors went hunting because the People were starving. A beautiful woman dressed in white buckskin approached them. Now one of those men thought bad thoughts about her, but the other one thought she was holy," Emma began.

Both Chayton and Sarah listened intently to the story of how the holy woman brought the Lakota the sacred Buffalo Calf Pipe and instructed the People in the ways to pray to Wakan Tanka. Emma described how the holy woman rolled four times as she walked away from the village, and how she turned into a black buffalo, then a brown one and a red one, and finally a white female buffalo calf. And after she was gone, great buffalo herds appeared to give the People food and clothing and everything they needed to live.

"That's beautiful," Sarah said when Emma was done.

"It is, isn't it?" Emma swept her hand across her eyes. "It's part of Chayton's legacy and I want to make sure he knows the Lakota teachings, and learns how to read and write in my world."

Sarah brushed a strand of hair from Chayton's forehead. "I'd like to learn more about the Indians, too."

Emma smiled and opened her mouth to speak, but a rider in the distance caught her attention. She watched as the horse drew nearer, until she could make out an Indian mounted on the pony. Frowning, she eased back on the reins and halted the buggy.

"Do you know him?" Sarah asked.

The brave's face grew clearer and Emma worried her lower lip. "It's Hotah. He's from the village Ridge and I stayed at."

"Why isn't he on the reservation?"

"He was banished the day before it happened."

Hotah stopped his horse close to the buggy, his dark face impassive but his gaze raking up and down both Emma and Sarah.

"What are you doing here?" Emma asked in Lakota, hoping he couldn't hear the frantic beating of her heart.

Hotah narrowed his eyes. "I have come for Chayton."

Emma instinctively shifted to shield Chayton from Hotah's possessive gaze. "He is my son."

"I will teach him to be a warrior so he may ride with his people."

"No. He stays with me. With *my* people."

Although Sarah didn't understand the words, she comprehended the tone and wrapped an arm around Chayton's waist, holding him snugly against her side.

"He is one of the People," Hotah said, his nostrils flaring.

"He is also white." Although trembling on the inside, Emma met his gaze. "Leave us, Hotah."

His lips curled in a sneer and he pressed his horse closer to Emma. He grabbed her wrist. "Chayton is Lakota. I will take him and join Crazy Horse."

"No!" Emma twisted to escape his grip, but his fingers dug into her skin cruelly.

"Let her go!" Sarah shouted.

Hotah glared at Sarah.

The sound of galloping hooves startled Emma and Hotah released her. He leaned close. "He is not yours. I will have him." Then he kicked his horse's flanks, escaping as the other rider neared.

Emma's heart pounded against her ribs and her breath came in stuttered gasps. She didn't know if she was more angry or frightened. Blinking, she focused on the arrival who was dressed in black trousers and a gray shirt, with a wool vest.

"Miss Hartwell, are you and your son all right?" the blond man asked.

Emma nodded, recognizing him as Ridge's cavalry captain friend out of uniform. "Yes, thank you, Captain Rivers," she said stiffly. She couldn't forget nor forgive what he'd done to her Lakota friends.

Captain Rivers looked at Sarah. "How about you, ma'am?"

"I'm fine, thank you," she murmured.

"Who was that?" Rivers asked Emma.

"He lived in the village you attacked," Emma answered tartly.

The man's jaw muscle clenched. "What did he want?"

"Chayton."

"Your son?"

Emma nodded, the fear expanding once more. Her fingernails dug into her palms. "What're you doing here?"

Rivers placed his crossed wrists on his saddle horn and grinned. "I was just out for a ride."

Emma narrowed her eyes. "Why don't I believe you?"

He shrugged indolently. "Believe what you want, Miss Hartwell." His gaze flickered over Sarah and back to Emma. "What're you doing out here?"

"We were visiting friends."

"Talutah?"

The name brought a rush of fresh grief. "She's—" Emma glanced at Chayton "—passed away."

Rivers shifted uncomfortably. "I'm sorry, ma'am. Ridge told me how much she meant to you."

"Maybe it's better this way," Emma said quietly, then had to ask, "Why did you release Pony Cullen?"

"I didn't. Colonel Nyes wouldn't hold him on my word and released him."

"He's a murderer!"

"You don't have to convince me, but it wasn't up to me." Captain Rivers's face became as hard as granite.

Emma searched his features for a sign of deception, but there was only cool anger. It was obvious Rivers didn't agree with the colonel, which meant he and Ridge hadn't deceived her. The captain had planned on prosecuting Cullen.

"Thank you for your assistance, Captain Rivers," Emma said with more warmth.

"My pleasure. If you don't mind, I'd like to ride alongside for a little while."

Although Emma wasn't certain about his motives, she did see the wisdom in his suggestion. "We don't mind."

Rivers touched the brim of his hat and moved to Sarah's side of the buggy. As they traveled down the rutted road, Rivers made small talk with Sarah and Chayton, allowing Emma to ponder her own thoughts.

$\mathcal{T}$WENTY

IT was early afternoon when Emma caught sight of Sunset. She halted the buggy and Chayton, who'd fallen asleep against Sarah's side, awakened. He rubbed his eyes and yawned. At that moment, he looked no different than any other sleepy child, white or Indian.

"Would you like to see a town?" Emma suddenly asked.

"Emma," Sarah spoke up. "We can't."

"Why not?" Although Emma's suggestion had been impulsive, she found herself wanting to defy all those people who felt it was their right to judge. What did they know of her experience with the Lakota? For that matter, what did any of them know about Indians, besides what they'd read in dime novels and newspaper articles that were meant to shock and titillate?

"Your sister's right," Captain Rivers said seriously. "Folks here won't like having a half-breed boy shoved in their faces."

"We're hardly shoving anybody in anyone's face," Emma retorted coldly. "Women bring their children into town all the time."

Sarah folded her hands in her lap and remained silent.

"What's a town?" Chayton asked, oblivious to the adults' undercurrents.

She pointed to the gathering of buildings half a mile away. "That's a town, where the whites—we—gather to buy food and supplies, and attend dances and socials."

Chayton's blank expression made Emma smile. She gave him a one-armed hug as she looked at Sarah and Captain Rivers. "Gertrude has known us ever since we were children. We could eat lunch there."

"I still don't think it's a good idea," Rivers said skeptically.

Sarah's gaze jumped from Emma to the captain and back to her sister. Her backbone straightened. "I'll do whatever you decide."

Emma's stomach fluttered. Now that she actually thought about it, she was uncertain. She peered at Chayton, noticing the excitement in his expression as he stared at the town.

Taking a deep breath, she hiyahed the sorrel and steered it around the edge of the town to enter on the side closest to Gertrude's restaurant. She wished Ridge were with her instead of Captain Rivers. Ridge's presence calmed her, made her feel as if nothing could harm her, including words.

People paused on the boardwalk and stared at her and Chayton. Fortunately, the boy was too busy oohing and aahing the unfamiliar sights, but Emma noticed. So did Sarah and Captain Rivers.

She drew the buggy to a stop in front of the restaurant. She'd been coming here with her family since she was Chayton's age. Surely Gertrude would treat her decently.

The cavalry captain dismounted and assisted Sarah down from the buggy, then Chayton. Rivers walked around to her side since no one offered to help her. It wasn't because there was a shortage of men. Most of them were gaping at her—some with disgust, others with curiosity, and a small number of them with something akin to lust.

Bees buzzed in her belly, but Emma pasted a smile on

her face. She thanked Captain Rivers and joined Chayton and Sarah on the boardwalk.

One woman standing in front of the restaurant swept her skirts aside so they wouldn't touch Emma or Chayton. Lifting her chin, Emma eyed her coolly until the woman looked away and whispered something to her companion.

The moment they stepped inside Emma realized she'd made a mistake. The interior grew silent and everyone stared at them as if they were part of a circus.

Gertrude met them at the door.

"I can't serve you in here, Emma," she said furtively.

"You've known me since I was a child," Emma argued.

Gertrude wrung her hands. "If it were up to me, I would do it, but if I serve you and your son, I'll lose business. Folks don't want his kind in here," she whispered as she deliberately looked down at Chayton.

"Thank you for your honesty, Gertrude," Emma said, her throat thick.

Emma, Sarah, and Chayton returned to their buggy, where Captain Rivers helped them into it. He placed Emma and Chayton in the backseat, then tied his horse's reins to the end of the buggy and joined Sarah in the front.

"Hungry," Chayton complained.

Relieved he hadn't noticed the disgust aimed at him, Emma wrapped her arm around his shoulders. "We'll eat when we get home."

Chayton pouted, but didn't fuss.

As Captain Rivers drove the buggy out of Sunset Emma stared down at her hands, which were the same hands she'd always had, and then looked at her laced-up shoes, skirt, blouse, and shawl. From the outside, she was the same as everyone else in town, yet a chasm of experience separated her from the others—experiences that made her different and alien. A stranger. She'd experienced the same sense of dispossession the second time she'd been among the Lakota, and even more so at the reservation.

With startling clarity, she realized it was only with Ridge that she felt like she belonged.

* * *

RIDGE made it back to his place in six days. The bull had shed some weight with the rushed journey, but the animal could spend the rest of the spring and summer grazing and growing fat.

Once home, Ridge got the bull settled in its pen and the lean-to he'd built while waiting for Colt to return. He planned to comb the government-owned broken hills to the west for unbranded cattle to start his herd. Ridge hoped to use the open range since he didn't own enough land to graze them. If Hartwell hadn't bilked Ridge's stepfather out of his land, Ridge wouldn't need the open range.

By evening, Ridge was restless. Although it'd been a long day, he saddled Paint and rode into Sunset. He claimed a table in the saloon, ordered a thick steak, and a shot of whiskey with a glass of beer. As he waited for his supper, he sipped his beer, and it eased the burn of the stronger liquor. He listened to the muted conversations around him, ignoring most until he heard Emma Hartwell's name.

"I heard she came into town today with her half-breed boy. Gertrude threw her and her nit out of the restaurant."

Ridge recognized the man who spoke as the foreman from the Circle C, where he'd worked before taking off to find Emma. Sam Pesant was a fair man, treating all the hired hands, including Ridge, equally. It surprised Ridge that he was bandying around Emma Hartwell's name in a saloon like she was less than a lady.

Unable to stop himself, Ridge leaned his chair back and said to Pesant, "Miss Hartwell know you're spreading rumors about her?"

The foreman turned toward Ridge and his ruddy face was flushed. "I'm not saying anything that ain't already been said. That scout, Cullen, has been pretty free with his words."

"Cullen? I thought he was in the stockade."

Another man playing poker with Pesant barked a humorless laugh. "Cullen? Word is he's got Colonel Nyes wrapped around his finger."

Nyes. Ridge should have known. Nyes was going to protect his ass, which meant he had to protect Cullen.

"Damn shame about Miss Hartwell, though," the foreman added. "Too bad the Indians weren't taken care of years ago before one of the sons of bitches got her with child. Nobody wants a squaw woman with a half-breed bastard. She would've been better off if she'd died instead."

"Hell, maybe she enjoyed it," a man with a missing front tooth said with a crude gesture.

"That's enough, Harley," Pesant warned.

"I don't know what Cullen's been saying, but Miss Hartwell wasn't used like that. The Lakota adopted her, treated her like their own," Ridge refuted sharply.

"If that's so, what about the kid?" the foreman asked with more curiosity than meanness.

"That ain't for me to say," Ridge replied, afraid he already let too much slip. "I was with her in the village for almost a week before the soldiers came. They treated Emma respectfully, which is more than I can say for anyone in this town."

Ridge thumped his chair back around to his table. Josey, the waitress, set a plate covered by a thick steak in front of him.

"Anything else I can get you?" she asked with a deep-throated purr.

Ridge shook his head at her obvious invitation. "No thanks, ma'am."

Josey's practiced smile was replaced by the girl beneath the face powder. She patted his arm. "You enjoy your steak, Ridge. I made Floyd give you the biggest one he had."

"Thank him for me, Miss Josey."

"I will. You need anything else, just holler."

Ridge cut into his steak.

"You know, you oughta take her up on her offer sometime. Might make you less ornery."

Ridge smiled as Colt joined him.

"Maybe you oughta take your own advice," Ridge bantered.

The two men shook hands over the table.

"You just get back?" Colt asked, slumping in his chair.

"This afternoon."

"Pushed pretty hard."

"The bull's in good shape." Ridge forced himself to chew a piece of steak. "What's this I hear about Emma Hartwell?"

Colt propped his elbows on the chair arms and clasped his hands. "What'd you hear?"

"That she and her son were in town today."

"You heard right. Her sister was with her." Colt described the short, but disastrous visit.

"I s'pected that'd happen, but it doesn't make it go down any easier." Ridge stared at his steak, his appetite gone. "I heard about Cullen, too."

"Hell, I'm lucky Nyes didn't throw me in the stockade when he let Cullen walk out."

Josey brought two beers to their table and took away the empty one in front of Ridge.

"You know an Indian named Hotah?" Colt asked.

"Yeah. How'd you hear about him?"

"He was bothering the Hartwell sisters and the boy on their way back from the reservation."

Ridge swore. "I told her not to go there."

"That old squaw you talked to died."

Ridge scrubbed his face with his palms. "Dammit. How did Emma take it?"

"'Bout how you'd expect. Good thing her sister was with her. She seems to be a levelheaded gal. Pretty, too." Colt finished his beer and called for another. "It'd be better all around if Emma and her son left town."

"Where the hell would they go?"

"Any place has to be better than here. No one wants anything to do with her."

"That's not true," Ridge said quietly.

Colt took a sip from his second beer that Josey brought. "I hope you're not thinking what I think you're thinking." Ridge angled a scowl at his friend. "What if I am?"

"First off, old man Hartwell won't allow it. Second, if you manage to get past Hartwell, folks around here won't be forgiving. Third, that boy's going to be running into even bigger problems as he grows up."

"She started helping me figure out words and numbers."

"I thought—"

Ridge angled a look at him. "I just see things different than other people."

Colt shook his head, obviously catching the double meaning. "You always have." He sighed. "If you're hell-bent on doing this, I'd be wasting my breath trying to talk you out of it."

Ridge grinned. "That's what I like about you, Colt. You never did like wasting time."

"Except when I'm in a saloon with a beer."

Ridge chuckled and found his appetite had made a rebound.

"I'm gonna take a walk out back," Colt said. He wended his way to the door that led to the outhouse.

Ridge continued eating the steak, washing it down with warm beer. He finished the entire slab and pushed his plate away with a quiet burp.

Just as he began to wonder what was taking Colt so long, Josey scurried over to him, her face pale and eyes wide.

"Captain Rivers is hurt," she whispered hoarsely.

Ridge grabbed his hat and followed the woman out the back door into the alley. A dark figure lay on the ground and Ridge could smell the coppery scent of blood. He dropped to his knees beside Colt as Josey hovered anxiously.

"Go get the doc, Josey. Hurry!" Ridge hissed.

The girl dashed away.

Dark liquid pooled on the ground beside Colt and Ridge frantically searched for the wound. He found a stab wound above the heart, which continued to beat slowly.

Someone had tried to kill him, and might very well have succeeded.

WINGS *fluttered almost soundlessly in the darkness. Only the sigh of air across feathers gave away the owl's presence. It swooped onto a tree branch, its talons curling around wood with innate grace.*

The female wolf peered upward, into the crown of the tree where the owl perched. "I've come."

"The lion is gone."

"The pup?"

"Gone."

"Where?"

"Must find."

The wolf growled. "How?"

"The search must be yours alone."

The wolf lifted its muzzle to the full moon and howled.

Emma lurched up, struggling to breathe past the crushing weight on her chest. She crossed her arms as she bent at the waist, her forehead touching her drawn-up knees.

It was happening again.

The same messenger animals, the same full moon, the same breath-robbing fear.

Her heart gradually slowed its frantic pace and the sweat began to cool, causing her to shiver. She leaned back against her pillows and tugged the blankets up to her chin.

The last time she'd dreamt of the wolf and the owl, the full moon came and went without a ripple of trouble. The trouble had come three nights later when the soldiers found the village.

She mentally calculated the number of days before the next full moon. Would her dreams become increasingly vivid over the next week? Or was this only a remaining fragment of the former vision, meaning nothing?

A horse galloped into the yard, startling Emma. She jumped out of bed and pressed aside her curtain. Blinking against the morning sunlight, she focused on the horse and rider. She recognized the black-and-white horse immediately.

Ridge.

Why was he here? And why at such an early hour?

She donned her dressing gown and tied the sash snugly around her waist. She heard the pounding on the door as she flew down the stairs. Her father, who'd been eating breakfast, made it to the door seconds before Emma and swung it open. His scowl deepened.

"What do you want?" her father demanded.

"Captain Rivers has been hurt," Ridge replied coolly. "I need to talk to your two daughters."

"Why? They don't even know him."

"Yes, we do," Emma said as Sarah, also dressed in her robe, joined them. "What happened, Ridge?"

"Girls, return to your rooms and put on decent clothing," their father ordered.

Martha Hartwell glided in from the dining room wearing her morning wrapper. "Don't be silly, John. Mr. Madoc wouldn't have come calling so early if it weren't important. Come in, Mr. Madoc."

Despite the situation, Emma had to restrain a smile at her mother's graceful maneuvering.

Ridge stepped across the threshold and removed his hat. Sooty smudges lay beneath his eyes and whiskers shadowed his lower cheeks and jaw. Rust-colored stains on his buckskin jacket and tan trousers appeared to be bloodstains.

Concerned, Emma grasped his hand, which was shockingly cool. "What happened?"

"Colt was stabbed in the alley behind the saloon. I think someone was waiting for him," Ridge explained grimly. His shoulders slumped. "I was talking to him right before it happened. He told me he'd spent time with you and your sister and Chayton yesterday."

Her father's lips thinned as he brought his glare of disapproval to bear on Emma. "What was he doing here while we were away?"

Emma didn't hesitate to correct him. "He didn't come

to the ranch. I took Chayton and Sarah to the reservation, then we stopped in town. Captain Rivers escorted us from the reservation to Sunset and then home." She was more worried about Ridge and his friend than her father's pique.

"He said Hotah was bothering you," Ridge pressed.

Emma tightened her grip on his hand as anxiety washed through her. "Hotah showed up out of nowhere. He wanted Chayton. He wants to train Chayton to be a warrior in Crazy Horse's camp."

Her father was staring at her as if she'd sprouted a third eye.

"When we were at the village, I heard talk among some of the young bucks that they were going to join up with Crazy Horse," Ridge said. "Hotah might've had a hand in stirring them up. It would explain why there was already bad blood between him and the chief."

"Yet it was Akecheta's village that was attacked by Cullen and the soldiers." Emma felt sick to her stomach.

"One Indian's the same as another to most white folks," Ridge said quietly. "Did Colt have words with Hotah?"

Emma focused on the dilemma at hand. "No. Hotah rode away when he saw Captain Rivers riding toward us."

"How is he, Mr. Madoc?" Sarah asked, her doll-like face marred with worry.

"Doc says he was lucky. He was stabbed in the back. An inch lower and it would've gotten his heart," Ridge answered, his jaw taut.

"Have you been with him all night?" Emma asked.

Ridge gazed down at her and Emma floundered in the eyes she'd seen filled with impatience, exasperation, shame, humor, affection, and desire. And she realized she knew this man better than she'd known her own husband.

"Yeah. It was close," he finally replied with a raspy voice.

"You're going to keel over if you don't rest and have something to eat," Emma scolded gently.

"Emma," her father growled in warning.

"Emma's right. Join us in the dining room," her mother

insisted, overruling her husband without a flicker of hesitancy.

John Hartwell balked, his fists clenched at his sides.

"Father, are you coming?" Sarah asked innocently as she wrapped her arm around his.

Their father glared at Ridge, and Emma stepped between them defiantly. Her father deflated before her, and allowed Sarah to lead him into the dining room. Emma and Ridge followed.

"When did you get home?" she asked Ridge.

"Yesterday afternoon. You and Chayton should come by and see the bull," Ridge said, attempting a smile, but too tired to complete it.

"We'll do that. Will Captain Rivers be all right?"

"Doc thinks he will. He lost a lot of blood." Ridge took a shaky breath.

Emma considered Ridge's suspicions about the Lakota warrior. "As much as I'd like to blame Hotah, it doesn't sound like something he'd do—stabbing a man in an alley. Hotah might use a knife on him, but not in the back. He has his own sense of honor and I don't think he'd kill a man without facing him. Besides, he wouldn't come into Sunset. He would've ambushed Captain Rivers between the post and town."

"Yeah, I thought about that, too," Ridge admitted reluctantly. "Did you see Cullen yesterday?"

Emma shook her head, recalling too well her hatred of the scout, which far surpassed her dislike of Hotah. "That doesn't mean *he* didn't do it. Stabbing someone in the back sounds more like his style," she said bitterly.

"I think I'll have a talk with him."

"Be careful, Ridge. Cullen reminds me of a mad dog."

She guided him to a chair by the table then went to retrieve a plate of food from the sideboard for him and herself. As she returned, Chayton with his hair tousled and wearing a nightshirt, joined them.

"*Leksi*," the boy shouted. He threw himself at Ridge, who caught him and plopped him on his lap.

"What did he call you?" Emma's father demanded.

"*Uncle*," Emma replied. "It's a term Indian children use for a man who teaches them. Ridge taught Chayton his first English words." She didn't think her father needed to know those were learned over animal tracks and piles of scat.

Father studied Ridge, his expression blank but his gaze oddly speculative.

"You going to live here, too?" Chayton asked Ridge.

Emma choked on her coffee. Ridge leaned toward her and patted her back. After a minute, she nodded that she was fine.

"This isn't my home," Ridge answered Chayton after he settled back in his chair. "Maybe someday you'll see my place."

Chayton bounced on Ridge's lap. "Today?"

"I don't think so, cub. Maybe next week."

Emma leaned over Ridge's arm. "You should eat breakfast, Chayton. I'm sure Mrs. Wright would make up a special plate for you if you ask nicely."

The boy scrambled off Ridge's lap and scampered toward the kitchen.

"I'll go with him and make sure she doesn't spoil him." Sarah rolled her eyes. "He could charm the spots off a cat."

Ridge, Emma, and her mother laughed, and Emma was surprised to see a flicker of amusement in her father's face.

Ridge leaned close to Emma and whispered in her ear, "I think your father might be warming toward Chayton."

Emma nodded, oddly pleased that Ridge had noticed, too. It was like sharing a secret—another secret—with him.

Sarah and Chayton returned from the kitchen, bearing a plate piled high with hotcakes and syrup—Chayton's favorite, which the cook had obviously made special for him.

"It's a good thing you went with him, Sarah," Emma teased her sister.

Sarah's cheeks flushed and she shrugged helplessly.

Emma glanced at Ridge, who grinned and winked, sharing the good-natured jest.

The family ate in companionable silence and Emma's

father even stopped glaring at Ridge. Far too soon, empty dishes were pushed aside. Emma was glad, however, that Ridge ate everything on his plate. His haggard expression had lessened and his face had more color to it.

"Thank you, ma'am," Ridge said to her mother. "I guess I was hungrier than I thought."

"You're welcome, Mr. Madoc. Besides, it's the least we could do considering what you've given us—our daughter and grandson," the older woman said.

Over the past few days, Emma's mother had become more spirited and didn't blindly agree with John Hartwell anymore. Emma found it oddly disconcerting, although she approved wholeheartedly. Maybe her mother had just needed a reason to stand up to him.

"I'd best get going," Ridge said, pushing back his chair and standing. "I want to check on Captain Rivers before heading home."

"Emma, why don't you escort him to the door?" her mother suggested.

Emma smiled. "I'll do that, Mother."

She walked Ridge to the door and picked up his hat from the table where he'd left it. She handed it to him and their fingers brushed.

"Tell Captain Rivers we're thinking of him and praying for his swift recovery," Emma said.

Ridge's shy smile made Emma's heart quicken. "Thanks. I will." He fiddled with the brim of his hat. "Colt told me what happened yesterday in town. I'm sorry, Emma."

The sour tang of humiliation rose in her throat. "You warned me. So did my parents and Captain Rivers, but I'd hoped . . ." She shrugged, although she hardly felt indifferent. "I'm not sure what to do. I don't want to leave Sunset, but I don't have a choice. Father's contacted Aunt Alice, but we haven't heard back from her. Maybe she doesn't want anything to do with me anymore." Unwelcome tears stung her eyes and she savagely ignored them.

Ridge lightly stroked her cheek with his knuckles. "It's

not you, Emma. It's them and you can't make folks change their minds. It's something they got to do themselves." He took a deep breath. "You have another choice, Emma."

"I'm not Catholic so I don't think a convent would take me," she joked weakly.

A slow, sweet smile curved Ridge's lips. "You could marry me."

Emma's heart tripped and stumbled, then pounded with joy and hope. She hadn't even allowed herself to think about being Ridge's wife—it hurt too much. But now he was offering . . . and she couldn't accept. "No. If you marry me, you'll be treated the same or worse than Chayton and me. You don't deserve that, Ridge."

"That doesn't matter—"

"Yes, it does," Emma argued. "You won't be able to buy your supplies in town anymore."

"I'll get them in Redfield."

"Until they find out about your squaw wife and her half-breed boy." Emma kept her tone caustic.

"Not everybody is like that." He grabbed her shoulders. "Dammit, Emma, I want to protect you."

"I can protect myself," she snapped. "Besides, it's too big a sacrifice for you to make."

"I'm a grown man and I can make my own decisions. I'd be honored to have you as my wife."

Ridge didn't say he loved her, but he seemed sincere in wanting to marry her.

"If I say yes, Chayton and I get a home and your name. But what do you get, Ridge?" she asked softly.

"I get a son to raise like he was my own, and I get Emma Hartwell in my bed every night."

Lightning arced through her veins and settled beneath her belly. Suddenly too aware of her thin nightclothes and Ridge's masculinity, she took a step back. She smiled through her misery. "Sounds like you're getting the short end of the deal."

His heated gaze traveled down her body, pausing at her

breasts, and then moved back up to her face. "I don't see it that way."

She peered at him, at the crow's feet at the corner of his eyes, his generous lips, and thick tawny hair. What lay beneath his handsome exterior, however, was infinitely more attractive—his honesty, integrity, honor, and shy tenderness. There was no doubt he'd honor their marriage vows and treat her and Chayton well. But what of love? Where did that figure? Or was she asking too much?

"Madoc has a point, Emma."

She swung around to see her father coming around the corner. It was obvious he'd been listening to their conversation.

Ridge straightened and met her father's gaze. "I'd like your permission to marry your daughter, Mr. Hartwell."

Emma's mouth gaped as John Hartwell seriously considered Ridge's request. "No, I won't let him do it, Father," she said.

"I'd say you don't have a lot of choice in the matter, Emma," her father said.

"He's right," Ridge added, although she could tell he didn't like her father's cutting bluntness.

Emma glared at one man, then the other. "I can't believe you two are actually agreeing on something."

Her father scowled. "I'm only stating the obvious. Madoc isn't the man I would've chosen for you, but considering the circumstances, he's probably the best you can do."

Furious indignation clouded Emma's thoughts. "How dare you! Ridge Madoc is a decent and honorable man. He doesn't cheat men out of their land or treat people like dirt just because they weren't as fortunate."

Father's eyes glittered with anger, but his voice was steady, almost calm, when he spoke. "It sounds to me like you wouldn't mind becoming Mrs. Ridge Madoc."

Emma's mouth fluttered open, then snapped shut, and her face burned with embarrassment. Her father struck too close to the truth.

"I only asked your permission, Hartwell," Ridge said. "It's up to Emma whether she agrees or not. I won't marry her because you order her to."

Emma found her voice. "Don't worry, Ridge, he can't force me. I'll make my own decision." She crossed her arms, suddenly chilled. "I have to think about it."

"How long?" Ridge asked.

"Two days."

"That's fair enough. I'll come calling Wednesday afternoon."

"Come at five. You can have dinner with us," Emma said. She sent her father a pointed look. "Isn't that right, Father?"

His lips pressed together, he nodded once.

Emma turned back to Ridge. "Is Captain Rivers at the doctor's office?"

"Yeah," he replied somberly. "I'm hoping he woke up so I can talk to him. I want to find out if he saw who did it."

"Be careful," Emma said.

He lent her a wan smile. "I will. Goodbye."

"Bye." It was difficult to ignore the passion that sparked between them, but Emma did so, ensuring they didn't touch as he walked out.

She closed the door behind him and peered up at her father. "He didn't have to offer marriage," she stated.

He glanced away. "I know."

"It's not fair to him."

Her father's gaze shot back to her. "What about you? You didn't ask to be in this position."

Emma stiffened her backbone. "I made the decision to marry an Indian and I willingly had his child. If that's a sin, it's mine to bear, not Ridge's."

She marched up the stairs, needing to be alone to think and make a decision that would directly impact two lives other than her own. It was a responsibility she feared almost as much as she loved Ridge.

$\mathcal{T}$WENTY-ONE

THE doctor had closed the curtains so the corner room was dim and gloomy. Colt lay still and pale in the single bed, but the rise and fall of his chest assured Ridge he was alive.

"Any change?" Ridge asked Dr. Harold Winters.

"He's breathin' easier," the gray-haired doctor replied. "And the wound's stopped bleedin' completely. I've been tryin' to get him to drink some water, but more comes out than goes in. Once he wakes up, we gotta get some in him to replace that blood he lost."

"So he'll make it?"

"I reckon. He's young and strong."

Ridge breathed a sigh of relief and leaned one shoulder against the wall. Crossing his arms and ankles, he asked, "Has anybody else checked on him?"

"The sheriff stopped by 'bout an hour ago. Said he didn't have much hope in findin' whoever did it."

Ridge sighed. "Doesn't surprise me. Nobody saw anything and the bastard didn't leave anything behind."

"You got any idea who might've done this?" Dr. Winters asked.

"One or two," Ridge answered coolly.

"Don't you be doin' somethin' stupid, Ridge Madoc. I only got one bed."

"Don't worry, Doc."

"Goes along with the job, Ridge." Winters removed his glasses and wiped the lenses with his handkerchief. "Pony Cullen is a poor excuse for a human being," he suddenly commented. "And it's no secret that he and Rivers don't see eye to eye."

Ridge smiled darkly. "Nope."

Colt shifted and moaned. Ridge straightened as he watched his friend fight his way to consciousness. A low groan accompanied his opening eyes.

"Lie still, Captain," the doctor ordered.

Colt focused on Winters. "Wha—"

"You were stabbed, Colt," Ridge said, stepping up to the side of the bed.

Colt peered blearily up at Ridge. "Stabbed?"

"We were in the saloon having a drink. You went out to use the privy and someone put a knife in your back," Ridge explained.

"Remember goin' out . . . then heard something." He frowned. "Turned, but—" Confusion clouded Colt's eyes.

"Did you see who it was?"

His eyelids drooped. "Smelled—"

Ridge leaned nearer. "Smelled what?"

"Dirty. Sweat, stink."

"That would describe Pony Cullen," Dr. Winters said dryly.

"Do you remember anything else, Colt?" Ridge asked. "Anything at all?"

"Hurt. Blood."

Ridge touched his arm. "It's okay. I'll find him."

"You need to drink somethin', Captain," Dr. Winters said, holding a glass of water to Colt's lips. The officer drank it all, then closed his eyes and his breathing evened out.

"Best thing for him now is rest," the doctor said quietly.

"I'll be back tomorrow," Ridge said.

"See that you are, and in one piece."

Grinning, Ridge waved and strode out. Once he stood on the boardwalk, his smile turned feral.

CLOUDS slid across the night sky, obliterating the nearly three-quarter moon and casting a pall over the shantytown. Nearly every post had a nearby shantytown where laundresses and others whose main trade was with the soldiers lived. Some of the women who took in laundry also took in men at night, making more money on their backs than sweating over the washtubs during the day. But the washing kept them reputable and out of trouble with the post commander.

Ridge had paid a laundress once for more than cleaning his uniform, but even as his body had gained its release, his conscience hadn't let him enjoy it. It was a sad life for the women, many of whom were widows of soldiers who'd been killed doing their duty, and they had children to feed and clothe. Doing what they did was the only way to keep their babies from starving.

Emma might very well have ended up as one of those women if her parents had disowned her. Ridge's gut churned at the thought of Emma lying on her back to make enough money to keep her and Chayton alive.

Shaking the morbid thoughts away, Ridge focused on one specific shanty, a small lean-to with just enough room inside for a bed and little else. From what he'd gleaned from talking to people, Cullen's current squaw lived there. She was like Chayton, part Indian and part white. Cullen had bought her from her father with a jug of whiskey and put her in the dilapidated building so he could visit her whenever the urge took him. Word was the urge took him pretty much every night, so Ridge figured he'd be showing up soon.

A nearing horse caught Ridge's attention and he squinted to make out the rider in the dim light. It wasn't a soldier this time. Cullen. Finally. The scout reined his horse in front of the shack and dismounted. He rubbed his crotch as he wound the reins around a crooked post. Ridge would give Cullen time to get down to business, then make his appearance.

After a few minutes, he heard a loud steady thumping and a woman's muffled cries. Swallowing the bile in his throat, Ridge darted across the open ground and to the shanty's door. He kicked it open with a thunderous crash.

Before Cullen could recover, Ridge grabbed his greasy ponytail and jerked him off the woman. Her eyes widened and she quickly covered her bruised and emaciated body with a thin, dirty blanket.

The fully clothed Cullen struggled to escape, but Ridge tightened his grasp and forced Cullen's head back as he caught the scout's left arm, bending it behind him.

"What the fu—" Cullen growled, awkwardly tucking himself into his grimy trousers with his free hand.

"Sorry to bother you at such a delicate time," Ridge said with sarcastic apology. "But I wanted to have a little talk with you and this just seemed the most private place to do it."

"What the hell are you doin' here, Madoc?"

"Didn't you listen? I said I wanted to chat," Ridge scolded.

"About what?"

"Where were you two nights ago, about nine o'clock?"

"Here. Just ask her." He motioned to the terrified girl who didn't appear more than fifteen or sixteen years old.

Ridge pressed Cullen's pinned arm upward, and the scout cursed. "She's so scared of you, she'll say anything you want her to, you son of a bitch." He slowly eased his grip on Cullen's arm. "Let's try this again, where were you two nights ago around nine o'clock?"

"I don't know," Cullen replied sulkily.

"Let me help you remember. You were behind the saloon where you waited until Captain Rivers came out, then you stabbed him in the back like the craven coward you are." Ridge's anger climbed and he fought the impulse to break Cullen's arm. It would be so easy, a bit more pressure and . . .

"You're gonna break my arm," Cullen said through thinned lips.

"That's the idea," Ridge stated coldly.

Cullen hissed and Ridge reluctantly loosened his grip.

"Tell me where you were," Ridge reiterated.

"I was in town, yeah, but I didn't stab Rivers. But I wouldn't mind shakin' the hand of the man who did."

Ridge shoved Cullen away, afraid he'd kill the man. "You're lying."

Cullen flexed his twisted arm as he glared at Ridge. "You can't prove it."

"I *know* you are, and I'm going to keep digging until I find the proof." Ridge paused, fighting for control. "Or I get a confession out of you."

"Don't hold your breath, Madoc."

"Be damned glad Captain Rivers didn't die or I'd just be shooting you down instead of trying to put you in jail."

"Yeah, I hear you're good at shootin' down men," Cullen baited. "Got enough practice when you were bounty huntin'."

Ridge clenched and unclenched his hands at his sides. He hadn't broken the law bringing in outlaws dead when they were wanted dead or alive, but he wasn't proud of what he'd done either. He'd been a kid back then, not much older than Cullen's squaw.

"I'm gonna be keeping an eye on you, Cullen." Ridge pivoted on his heel and stalked out of the filthy hovel.

He wended his way back to Paint and stood for a moment, leaning against the gelding's side. Ridge had no doubt that it was Cullen who'd stabbed Colt, but to prove it would be damned near impossible. If only Colt could identify Cullen as his attacker, but the captain hadn't seen anything.

Cullen may not be bright, but he was smart enough to

hide his tracks. If Ridge was the same person he'd been fifteen years ago, he would take justice in his own hands, but he couldn't do that anymore. It was simple—he'd have to get Cullen to confess.

Simple. Right.

EMMA rocked gently on the porch, the chair making soothing creaks with every forward motion. Her gaze followed Chayton who was "helping" Rory take care of the horses. Although she hadn't seen Hotah since the confrontation on the way back from the reservation, he was never far from her thoughts. She made certain Chayton was either in her sight, or in her sister or mother's. Hotah might be desperate enough to come into the yard to steal him away, and Emma couldn't bear the thought of losing her son ever again.

Rory had taken a shine to Chayton, and didn't hold his Lakota blood against him. More surprising since it was Indians who had been the cause of the hostler's crippled leg. A half-dozen of the other hired hands, including the foreman Bob Tucker, had warmed toward her son, too, but the majority of the men ignored him. Only one or two were openly antagonistic, but Tucker had given them fair warning and the cruel jibes had stopped.

Although pleased with Chayton's well-being, Emma had worried herself sick the past two days as she wrestled with Ridge's marriage proposal. With the growing acceptance of Chayton, her fears had lessened about their future. Her father wouldn't force her to leave the ranch, especially since Emma's mother was firmly in her and Chayton's camp. But living with her parents for the next twenty or more years didn't set right with Emma, either. She wanted her own life and, if truth be told, she wanted to share it with a man she loved.

And that man would be arriving in less than five minutes expecting her answer. But how could she allow Ridge to sacrifice so much for her and Chayton? She couldn't deny his sincerity in wanting to marry her, but was it only because he'd enjoyed their lovemaking as much as she had? Or did he have deeper feelings?

She shook her head at her own foolishness. There was no doubt Ridge cared for her and Chayton. There would be fondness and passion in their marriage, of that Emma was certain. And on her side, there would be love. But would that be enough to withstand the criticism and hostility of the townsfolk? Or would tolerance come with time just as it had at the ranch?

A movement down the road caught her attention. It was Ridge and he would arrive at the house in a matter of minutes. Her stomach lurched, knowing her time for making a decision was rapidly approaching.

Gathering her composure, she stood and called for Chayton. He scampered across the ranch yard to join her on the porch. When he caught sight of Ridge, Emma had to restrain him from running out to greet him. Only after Ridge dismounted did she allow her son to race over to his *leksi.*

Emma's pace was much more controlled as she joined them, and her gaze drank in the sight of the man. Dressed in a dark suit with a white shirt and black tie, Ridge didn't resemble the buckskin-clad man with whom she'd spent so much time. But she couldn't find fault in his appearance— no matter what he wore; the sight of him always left her feeling like her corset was too tight.

Holding Chayton, Ridge swept off his black broad-brimmed hat and smiled at Emma. "Good afternoon, Miss Hartwell. I do believe we have a dinner engagement."

Emma laughed, enjoying this playful side she'd never seen before. "I do believe you're correct, Mr. Madoc. Won't you come inside?"

"After you." He motioned for her to precede him, and scooped Chayton into his arms.

Emma smiled as she listened to Chayton tell Ridge all about the kitties and the horses, as well as his new friends. His words came jumbling out as he mixed English and

Lakota, but Ridge didn't have any trouble interpreting the constant stream.

Once in the house, she took Ridge's hat and placed it on the foyer's receiving table. Ridge lowered Chayton to the floor and the boy finally paused to take a breath.

"Hello, Mr. Madoc," Sarah said as she came down the wide staircase.

"Miss Hartwell," he greeted.

"How's Captain Rivers?"

Ridge grinned. "The doc is threatening to tie him down."

Sarah laughed. "I have to go into town tomorrow. Maybe I'll stop by to see him."

"He'd like that."

"So would Sarah," Emma whispered loud enough for Ridge to hear.

"Dinner will be ready in half an hour," Sarah announced. She held out her hand to her nephew. "Come on, Chay. I'll help you change for dinner."

With a wave to Ridge and Emma, Chayton took Sarah's hand and they ascended the stairs.

"He's settling in well," Ridge commented.

"Better than I expected. Sarah and Mother have made a big difference." Suddenly alone with him, Emma's mouth grew dry. "Uh, would you like to go into the parlor?"

"Sure."

Ridge offered her his arm, and she threaded her trembling hand through the crook and rested her palm on his forearm. Even through the wool suit, she could feel his planed muscles.

"Have you found out anything more about the attack on Captain Rivers?" she asked in an attempt to postpone the marriage proposal conversation. She felt his muscles bunch beneath her touch.

"I paid a visit to Cullen. He admitted to being in town the night Colt was stabbed, but said he didn't do it," Ridge said disgustedly.

"You don't believe him?"

"No. That sorry excuse for a human being did it, but I can't prove it."

"Captain Rivers didn't remember anything?"

Ridge shook his head. "He remembers going out to the alley, and the stink of dirt and sweat, but that's it." He sighed and raked his fingers through his thick, wavy hair.

Emma caught a whiff of soapweed scented with sage, reminding her of happier, more carefree times spent with the Lakota. "So what can you do?"

"If it was anyone but Colonel Nyes, I'd go to the post commander."

They entered the parlor, where flames flickered invitingly in the fireplace. Emma motioned to the loveseat. He waited until she sat down, then perched on the stiff cushion at the other end.

"Father was telling me that a general is coming to visit the fort," Emma said.

"General Mason. He showed up this morning."

"Would he listen to you?"

"I doubt it. I don't know him."

"I do," John Hartwell said as he entered the room.

Emma curbed her irritation at his intrusion. By all rights, she and Ridge should have a chaperone, although after all they'd gone through together, it seemed a ridiculous issue.

Her father sank into the high-backed, floral chair across from them. "He's a fair man, intelligent, not like that idiot Nyes."

Emma couldn't help but smile. "That makes two things you're both in agreement on."

Ridge scowled, but it was halfhearted. "What's his stand on the Indians?" he asked her father.

"He'll do what he's ordered to do, but doesn't condone killing for the sake of killing, unlike Nyes."

"And Cullen."

"The one you think backstabbed the captain?"

Ridge nodded grimly.

"Talk to General Mason," the older man suggested. "Maybe he can help."

Emma leaned back, amazed that her father was having a civil conversation with Ridge, as well as offering assistance. But, then, Ridge had offered to take responsibility for her and Chayton, a burden John Hartwell would be glad to be rid of.

Ridge scowled, but it was directed at himself rather than her father. "I don't see how. It's my gut feeling against Cullen, and he's backed by Nyes."

"How about setting a trap?" Emma suggested.

"What're you talking about, Emma?" her father asked.

She leaned forward and her hands flowed with her words. "Ridge said Captain Rivers didn't remember anything, but what if his memory miraculously returned? What if the rumor was started that the captain knew who did it, but would only speak to General Mason? What do you think Cullen would do?"

"He'd try to finish the job he started," Ridge murmured.

"But what if he doesn't?" her father asked.

Emma shrugged. "We're in the same place we are now—nothing gained, nothing lost."

Ridge's eyes glittered. "It just might work. Do you think General Mason would agree to help?" he asked her father.

"If I'm with you when you talk to him, he might." He stroked his chin. "I might even mention to him how Colonel Nyes refused to send out a search party for Emma."

Ridge smiled with reluctant admiration.

"I'll set up an appointment with him and let you know when it is," her father said. "I'm looking forward to bringing Nyes down a notch or two."

Emma's mother stepped into the parlor. "Dinner is served."

The meal passed in lively conversation, with her father and Ridge even managing to discuss ranching without raising their voices. Emma's father seemed sincerely interested in Ridge's plans, and although Ridge was cautious, he answered his questions honestly. Emma wondered how much of it was because he might very well become Ridge's father-in-law.

After everyone was done eating, Ridge asked Emma to accompany him on a stroll outside. Emma's pulse skittered out of control. The moment of truth had arrived.

Emma wrapped a heavy shawl around her shoulders since the evening had cooled considerably. Ridge guided her out the door with his fingertips resting lightly at her waist. They walked in silence to the corral and stopped to watch the yearlings prance around. The sun still peeped through the mountain range in the distance, but it wouldn't be long before it disappeared completely.

"Your father surprised me," Ridge said.

"Me, too," Emma admitted. "I wonder what his ulterior motive is."

Ridge shrugged. "Maybe he just wants to help."

"Maybe." Emma shivered.

Ridge stepped behind her, his chest to her back, and wrapped his arms around her waist. Almost against her will, she leaned into his strong embrace and covered his clasped hands with hers.

"What's your decision, Emma?" he whispered, his lips caressing her ear.

She couldn't think, couldn't do anything but feel his hard body flush against hers and his breath wafting warmly across her neck. All sensation shifted to her breasts and between her thighs as longing flowed through her like thick molasses. Ridge's groin pressed against her backside, and even through all the layers of clothing, she felt his desire.

"I-I don't know," she said huskily.

He kissed the underside of her jaw. "What's your answer, Emma?"

Her knees wobbled like a newborn foal and the temptation to press her lips to his freshly shaven cheek was almost overwhelming. "Why-why do you want to marry me?"

"I told you. I want you in my bed and I want to raise Chayton as my own. In exchange, you'll have my name and protection. Not to mention—" He licked a path from beneath her ear down to where her shoulder met her neck. *Me* in *your* bed every night."

Emma trembled, wishing she could deny his body's claim over hers, but that was the only thing she was absolutely certain of. Ridge Madoc knew her body better than she knew her own, and she knew his—every delicious nook, cranny, and hard muscle.

Physical love was better than no love at all.

She nodded. "Yes. Yes, Ridge, I'll marry you."

Without releasing her, Ridge shifted around until she faced him. His eyes glowed and his smile brought creases to the corner of his eyes. "Thank you, Emma. I promise I'll make you happy."

They weren't the words she wanted to hear, but they were close enough.

"You already have," she whispered, then wrapped her arms around his neck and brought his head down so she could taste his lips.

After long minutes of kissing and fondling, Emma drew away. Panting, she laid her forehead against Ridge's chest. "When do you want the wedding?"

Ridge pressed his lips to her hair and rubbed his groin against her belly. "The sooner the better."

Emma laughed. "I have this feeling we'll be spending an awful lot of time in bed."

He cupped her buttocks. "Or in the grass or beside the river or in the barn."

Emma smacked his chest playfully. "Let's start with a bed—a bed wide enough for both of us," she said, recalling the narrow bed in the cabin where they'd first made love.

Ridge kissed the tip of her nose. "I can do that."

They remained standing with arms around one another, drinking in the quiet of the evening before returning to the house to share their news.

THE meeting with General Mason and John Hartwell went amazingly well. Between Hartwell's criticism of Nyes and Ridge's own experiences with the colonel, the general's eyes had burned with angry indignation. He'd even promised to sow some seeds of gossip with Nyes and around the post. If Cullen was responsible for the attack on Colt, the scout was bound to get nervous. Hopefully, nervous enough to make another attempt on Colt's life.

As Ridge and Hartwell rode away from the post, silence surrounded the two men, but it wasn't uncomfortable. Emma had provided a bridge between them, and although Ridge doubted Hartwell would ever be a good friend, they could now be in the same room together without wanting to kill one another.

"Why did you offer marriage to my daughter, Madoc?" Hartwell asked after they'd traveled a mile or two.

"Why wouldn't I?"

Hartwell's face flushed and he tugged his hat brim lower on his brow. "You know why."

"I lived with the Indians off and on before I joined the cavalry. I got nothing against them."

"But—" Hartwell cleared his throat. "Emma laid with one."

"She was his wife." Ridge grinned with wry amusement. "Seems to me when a man and a woman are married, they're going to lie together. It doesn't matter what color they are."

Hartwell studied him. "You really don't care that she was married to an Indian and has a half-br—half Indian child?"

"Do you love her less than before she disappeared for seven years?"

"No, of course not. She's still my daughter."

"That's right, she is." Ridge took a deep breath and let it out slowly. "Emma braved the weather, the rivers and mountains, the Indians, and her own family to find her child. No man could ask for a stronger, more loyal and courageous daughter. And I want that woman to be my wife."

Hartwell swallowed and quickly turned his gaze away.

Ridge allowed the man his semblance of privacy and rode in contemplative silence.

*   *   *

"YOU think he'll come tonight?" Colt whispered from his bed in the doctor's office.

Ridge restrained a yawn. "It's been two days—the word's been spread. It'll happen soon."

"*If* it was Cullen."

Ridge, hidden in a corner filled with dark shadows, leaned forward in his chair. "Now you don't think it was?"

Colt muttered under his breath. "I don't know anymore. Maybe it was Hotah or one of a few dozen other men who have a grudge against me."

"You said Cullen threatened you when he was let out of the stockade. Do you think he meant it?"

"Yeah," Colt admitted. "I just hate laying around and waiting."

Ridge grinned, knowing full well how his friend hated inactivity. "You can thank Emma later. She's the one who came up with the plan."

"Emma Hartwell?"

"Yep."

"Oh." Colt grew silent, but Ridge could tell he remained awake. "I heard a rumor about you and Miss Hartwell."

Ridge flinched. "It's true. The wedding's next Sunday out at Hartwell's ranch."

"So when were you going to tell me?"

Ridge shifted on the hard chair, trying to relieve the soreness of his backside. "I didn't figure you wanted to know."

"You figured wrong. Do you love her?"

"I care for her."

"Do you love her?" Colt demanded in a low tone.

"Hell, I don't know. I've never been in love before."

Colt's deep chuckle startled Ridge. "Damn, you've got it bad, pard."

"Shut up," Ridge said without force.

Colt was quiet for so long Ridge thought the healing man had finally fallen asleep.

"Don't I get to be your best man?" Colt suddenly asked.

"You want to be?"

"Hell, yes."

"All right, as long as you don't pass out during the vows." Ridge smiled. "Get some sleep. Sarge and Pres are outside. If Cullen can get through them, he's still gonna have to go through me."

Midnight came and went. Colt snored softly from the bed across the room. Ridge's eyes closed and his chin dropped to his chest, startling him awake. He raised his arms above his head, stretching to relieve the kinks in his back and shoulders.

Surely if Cullen was going to make his move, he would've done so by now. Maybe he'd been wrong about the scout being behind the attack.

He sensed movement and scanned the room, but there was nothing to see. His nape tingled. There. By the window. A shadowy figure reaching out to raise the pane. Only a small screek betrayed the intruder's presence.

Keeping close to the wall, Ridge padded around to the window. The man lifted one leg over the ledge, then swung his upper body through and stood up in the room, a knife held in his right hand. The intruder stunk—like old sweat and dirty buckskins.

Ridge eased back the trigger of his revolver and held the barrel to the man's head. "Drop it."

The man froze, but held onto the knife.

Ridge nudged him with the barrel. "I said drop it."

The knife clattered to the floor, awakening Colt.

"What's going on?" the captain asked sleepily.

"Light the lamp, Colt. We got him," Ridge replied with smug satisfaction.

A match flared and Colt lit the lamp's wick.

Pony Cullen glared at Colt. "You shoulda died the first time, you son of a bitch."

"I would say that's a confession, wouldn't you, Captain?" General Mason entered the room, followed by Sarge and Pres.

"Yes, sir," Colt said with a grin.

"Lieutenant, place the manacles on Cullen and escort him to the stockade," the general ordered.

"Yes, sir," Pres said with a sharp salute.

"And don't let Colonel Nyes release him this time," the general added with a satisfied smirk. "You can also tell the colonel I'll be speaking with him in the morning about a new assignment."

"Yes, sir."

Ridge allowed Pres and Sarge to bind Cullen and take him away. As they left, Dr. Winters slipped inside to check on his patient.

General Mason shook hands with Ridge. "It's been a pleasure working with you, Madoc. If you ever want your old job back, just let me know. The army can always use some honest scouts."

"Thank you, sir, but after Sunday, I'll be a married man," Ridge said.

"That's right. It's been a long time since I've attended a wedding. I'm looking forward to it." Mason turned to Colt. "And you, Captain, hurry up and heal. I'd like to present you with your gold leaves personally."

General Mason pivoted sharply and left the two men alone with the doctor.

"I'll be damned. Congratulations, Colt," Ridge said with a wide grin. "Or should I say *Major* Rivers?"

Colt appeared dazed by the rapidity of the events. "What the hell just happened?"

"Cullen's gettin' his due and you just got promoted," Dr. Winters replied curtly. His old face creased with a smile. "And I didn't even have to sew anyone back together again."

Ridge grinned and met Colt's gaze. Things were finally looking up.

$\mathcal{T}$WENTY-TWO

"GOODNESS gracious, the dress will never be ready on time. Why on earth couldn't the wedding have waited one more week?" Martha Hartwell chirped in agitation.

"Because Ridge couldn't wait that long," Sarah replied, her eyes twinkling with mischief.

Emma managed to smile despite the headache that had plagued her since the early morning when her dreams awakened her. She patted her mother's shoulder. "Don't worry. Everything will work out."

"Easy for you to say. You just have to state your vows and look beautiful," her mother chided with an affectionate smile. She sighed from her place at the dining room table where they'd been finalizing the wedding details. "I have to talk to Mrs. Wright about the food and make sure she has everything she needs." Still muttering to herself, her mother and her list disappeared into the kitchen.

Emma propped her elbows on the table and buried her face in her hands. But closing her eyes only made her remember the dream visions with more clarity.

A hand settled between her shoulder blades. "What's

wrong, Emma?" Sarah asked with quiet concern. "Are you having nightmares again?"

Emma raised her head and peered blearily at her sister. "How did you know?"

"I've heard you cry out, but every time I go to your room, you get quiet again." Sarah's eyes clouded with worry. "What are your nightmares about?"

Emma waved a hand. "Just nightmares."

Sarah leaned closer. "I don't believe you. There's something you're not telling me."

"There might be a good reason I'm not telling you."

"You're scaring me, Emma. What's wrong?"

Emma slumped back in her chair and stretched out her arms on the table. She stared at a framed picture of the mountains on the wall, although her vision was directed inward.

The dreams always began the same way, with the owl flying out of the night to land in an oak tree. The wolf cub played innocently below on the ground until the mountain lion pounced, batting around the cub with malicious amusement. Sometimes Emma thought the lion's face changed shape to something more human, but she could never see the details clearly. And always, when the female wolf arrived, the lion attacked her. The fight would be brutal, but the cat would gain the advantage. That's when the eagle would swoop down and Emma woke.

Over the last two nights the dreams had changed subtly. Emma now had a sense of another creature in the shadows, but its intentions were unclear, which worried her even more.

She blinked back to the present and found Sarah's troubled countenance in front of her. Emma smiled and patted her sister's hand. "It's probably just wedding collywobbles. I'm sure all brides have them."

The furrows in Sarah's normally smooth brow remained. "Do you love him?" she asked.

Emma considered lying, but found she couldn't do that to her sister who'd been nothing but supportive since Emma had returned with Chayton. "Yes, but it's not returned."

Sarah's mouth gaped. "Any fool can see he's head over heels in love with you."

"I'm not a fool, Sarah," Emma said with a pained smile. "He has feelings for me, but not those kind."

Sarah clucked her tongue. "Think what you will, but the only fool here is you, Emma Hartwell." She stood and shook the wrinkles from her skirt. "I'm going to see if Rory is tired of Chay following him around."

Folding her arms on the tabletop, Emma laid her cheek on them and closed her eyes. She didn't want to think about weddings or love or the future. She just wanted to sleep without dreams.

The sound of her father's office door opening and closing brought Emma's head up from her uncomfortable position. She hoped he was only going outside, or to talk to her mother. Although he'd been more civil toward her and Chayton lately, she wasn't ready to lower her guard.

He entered the dining room and appeared surprised to see her. "Emma, I'd like to have a word with you."

"What about?" she asked suspiciously.

He joined her at the table. "I think it's time your son started learning how to ride."

Her wariness didn't fade. "He's been riding since he was old enough to stay on a horse by himself."

Her father's eyes widened. "Why didn't you tell me?"

"You never asked." She failed to keep the bitterness from her voice.

He dropped his gaze and twined his fingers together. Emma stared at his hands. She'd always assumed they were smooth, but there were numerous small scars and his fingers had obviously done more than hold a pen.

"I'd like to give him one of the new foals after it's weaned," he said. "I know you'll be living with Madoc, but I wouldn't mind coming by to help the boy work with it."

"The boy's name is Chayton, or Chay, whichever you prefer to call him," Emma said sharply.

He stood and glared at his daughter. "If you don't want *Chayton* to have a horse, that's fine. He's your son."

Emma's anger died as quickly as it flared, and she said quietly, "He's also your grandson." She thought about what he'd said. "Are you serious about helping him train the foal?"

"I wouldn't have offered if I wasn't."

Emma noticed the flush in his cheeks and the uncertainty in his face. *This* was the man who'd embraced her and shed tears when he'd seen his daughter for the first time in seven years after she was believed dead.

Emma rose and walked up to him. "I think Chayton would like his own pony, and he'd like his grandfather to teach him."

Her father's eyes glimmered suspiciously, and Emma reached out and hugged him. "Thank you," she said, her throat tight.

He returned the hug, enfolding her within his arms. "You're welcome, Emma."

His voice was as husky as hers.

THE day before the wedding Emma awakened with a scream trapped in her throat. She gasped and panted as her heart beat a harsh tattoo against her breast. The dream had been so real—she could almost smell the lingering feral scent of the mountain lion and the wolf.

The dim light in the room told her it wasn't even dawn, and she could sleep another hour or two, but the dream's memory was too vivid. She leaned over to glance down at Chayton, assuring he was safe. His mouth was open as he snored softly in his trundle bed. Smiling, Emma rose quietly and peeked out her curtain. The fat moon hung high in the sky—tonight it would be full.

Just as in her dreams.

Her smile disappeared and her stomach clenched. She had to talk to Ridge. He was the only one who would believe her.

After donning a split riding skirt and plain tan blouse, Emma tiptoed out of her bedroom, carrying her boots. She wrote a short note telling her family where she'd gone, then pulled on the boots and a jacket in the foyer. Tightening the chinstrap of her wide-brimmed hat, Emma stepped out into the morning's tranquillity, a sharp contrast to the dream visions which continued to haunt her.

Even Rory was still asleep when Emma saddled Clementine. By the time she led the mare out of the barn and mounted her, a rose tinge was dusting the eastern sky. As she rode to Ridge's, she watched the mountains transform from dark blue to coral and pink, and by the time she arrived at his place, the sun peeped above the horizon.

The cabin's door opened and Ridge stepped out wearing brown trousers, moccasins, and an unbuttoned undershirt, with a pair of suspenders hanging down the side of his lean legs. For a moment, she could only stare as her mouth grew dry at the tempting sight.

"Emma, what're you doing here?" Ridge demanded, hurrying over to grab Clementine's bridle.

She smiled, already feeling the crushing weight of her nightmare easing. "I know it's early, but I need to talk to you."

Ridge's hands spanned her waist as he helped her to the ground. "I just put some coffee on. It should be ready in a minute or two."

He took her hand and she curved her fingers around his. Despite her exhaustion and fear, the intimacy warmed her and reassured her that she'd made the right decision in agreeing to marry him, even if he didn't love her. Once inside the cabin, Ridge urged her into a chair and she thankfully sank down onto it.

As Ridge retrieved two cups and poured the coffee, Emma took the time to examine the one-room cabin that would be her home after tomorrow. A ladder led up to the loft, and she envisioned Chayton climbing up to his bed every evening. It was a cozy, homey picture.

An Atlantic Box stove, used for heating and cooking, sat in the center of the cabin. A table and four chairs had obviously been made by Ridge's meticulous hands, and smoothed by his sensitive fingers. They were solid and steady, much like the man who'd created them.

Her attention wandered to the bed. The cot that had been there was replaced by a store-bought four poster bed, large enough for two to sleep—and make love—comfortably.

"Coffee?" Ridge's voice broke into her musings.

Startled, she jerked her attention back to him and accepted the cup with a murmured "thank you."

"I know this place ain't much, but I already have plans to make it bigger," Ridge said awkwardly.

"No, it's fine, truly," Emma assured, then grinned mischievously. "It's bigger than a tipi, and the bed's not on the ground."

An endearing blush stained his cheeks and he sipped coffee to cover his embarrassment.

"You bought a new bed," she commented.

A roguish grin stole across his lips. "I thought you'd like it."

"I do," she said softly. "But you didn't have to do it."

"I wanted to." He shrugged. "I had some money left after buying the bull."

"But you were going to start buying your land back from my father."

"I will someday."

Emma blinked back tears and wished she dared confess how much she loved him. "Thank you," she whispered, clasping his hand across the table.

Ridge brushed his thumb across her knuckles. "Tell me why you rode over here so early."

Emma gathered her thoughts, reluctantly setting aside

the infinitely more pleasant ones involving Ridge and the new bed in the corner. "Remember when I had the dreams?"

"You were worried about Chayton. You thought something would happen the night of the full moon."

"I-I'm having those same dreams again, but this time they're even more frightening." She went on to describe them and was relieved when Ridge listened without comment, his expression somber.

"What do you think it means?" he asked as he continued to caress Emma's hand.

"That something will happen to Chayton tonight," she replied unhesitantly.

Ridge frowned. "And maybe you, too. But who's the mountain lion?"

"I don't know." Frustration laced her voice. "I don't know who the eagle is either."

"Easy, Emma. Last time, nothing happened. Maybe it'll be the same this time."

She shook her head vehemently. "No. This feels different, more real and more menacing."

Before Ridge could say anything, the sound of an approaching horseman broke the morning's quiet. Emma exchanged a puzzled glance with Ridge, and they rose together and went out to face the visitor.

Preston Wylie galloped into the yard and reined sharply in front of the shack. The usually fastidious officer's uniform shirt was misbuttoned and untucked. He spotted Emma and his eyes widened slightly in his dirt-streaked face.

"Where's the fire, Pres?" Ridge asked.

The lieutenant dragged his gaze away from Emma and replied, "Cullen's escaped. Whoever helped him killed the guard."

Emma inhaled sharply.

"Is someone watching Colt?" Ridge demanded.

"Sarge."

"Where's Nyes?"

"Back at the post. General Mason's questioning him now. The general wants you to track down Cullen."

"Cullen and whoever got him out of the stockade," Ridge said grimly. "I'll grab some supplies and ride over."

Pres touched the brim of his hat and said to Emma, "Ma'am."

Emma managed a nod and the officer rode away.

Ridge grasped her shoulders. "I have to go, Emma."

Again she nodded, unable to speak past the irrational fear lodged in her throat.

"Are you all right?" Ridge asked, ducking to peer into her face.

"Yes."

Ridge didn't appear convinced, but he drew back, his reluctance obvious. "I have to see if I can track down Cullen before his trail gets cold, but I'll come back to the ranch before nightfall so we can figure out your dreams."

"All right."

Although Ridge was anxious, he remained with Emma. "I'll escort you back to your place before I ride over to the post."

Emma mentally shook herself. "No. That'll add eight miles. You need to find Cullen and lock him up again before he hurts someone else."

She could see the fiery determination in his expression, but his eyes were uncertain. She gave him a little shove. "Go! I'll be fine."

After another moment of indecision, Ridge kissed her. It was brief but fierce—a promise he'd return to her as soon as he could.

He walked her to Clementine and gave her a boost into the saddle. He laid his hand on her leg and gazed up at her anxiously. "Are you sure?"

She leaned down and feathered a touch across his whisker-roughened jaw. "Yes. Now go."

He grinned, a crooked, wry grin that never failed to

arouse Emma's passion. Stifling a moan, she tapped her heels to the mare's flanks and the animal sprinted away.

RIDGE hunkered down, tipping his head from one side to the other as he tried to make out the footprints in the dirt. He had no trouble distinguishing Cullen's from the soldiers' since the scout wore moccasins. Except there was a second set of moccasin prints, slightly smaller than Cullen's. Ridge's first thought was Cullen's squaw had broken him out, but the prints were too big for a slip of a gal like her.

"Anything?" Pres Wylie asked, standing a couple yards away from the tracker so he wouldn't mess up the ground with his own boot prints.

"I'm not sure," Ridge replied. "It looks like whoever killed the guard and busted him out was wearing moccasins."

"There aren't many so-called civilized folks who wear them," Pres remarked.

Ridge glanced at his own comfortable, knee-high moccasins. "Yeah. Me, Cullen—" he broke off as a stray thought struck him. "Did you have any trouble getting into that village a couple weeks ago?"

Pres blinked owlishly at the change of subjects. "No, not that I can recall. Cullen led us through a serpentine trail that cut through rock. I remember thinking it was an opportune place for an ambush."

Ridge pushed himself upright. "While Emma and I were in the village they always had sentries stationed up there."

"So where were the sentries?"

"That's a damned good question." He strode back to Paint, his mind racing with possibilities. "Who's coming with me?"

"General Mason's authorized ten men for the search. I'm the ranking officer."

"Is someone guarding Colt?"

"Sarge is in charge of the guard detail."

Despite the gravity of the situation, Ridge smiled. "Betcha Colt's having a fit. Being out of the action is going to do what Cullen didn't—kill him."

Pres laughed. "I don't know about that, but Sarge is threatening to bind and gag him."

Ridge shook his head in amusement, but the moment passed and he sobered. "I'll meet you and your contingent outside the gate."

By late afternoon, Ridge was using every trick he knew to find the trail. At first the stolen horses' tracks were easy to follow. But as Cullen and his accomplice moved into rockier terrain, the prints disappeared. Ridge had to search for darker soil spots, which were exposed when a stone was disturbed; or a metal-gray slash on a rock from the graze of a horseshoe; or the fresh break of a twig. It was time-consuming and laborious.

Ridge gripped his saddle horn and shifted his stiff backside on the unforgiving leather saddle. He rubbed his eyes, which were sore from intently studying the ground for hours on end.

"Any ideas?" Pres Wylie asked, setting his horse beside Ridge.

"Yeah, but I don't like any of 'em."

Pres pushed his hat off his forehead. "If it wasn't another white man wearing moccasins, it was an Indian."

Although it wasn't a question, Ridge replied, "Yep. And I've got a bad feeling I know who it was."

"Who?"

"Hotah. He was from the village you attacked." He couldn't hide his simmering resentment.

Pres's gaze hardened. "We were under orders to recapture the natives and return them to the reservation. It wasn't our intention to do battle."

Ridge took a deep breath to dispel his anger. "It was Cullen, who somehow got Hotah to help him get the detachment into the camp without being seen."

"Why would this Hotah assist Cullen in murdering his people?"

"Revenge, maybe. The chief banished him from the village the day before the attack. Hotah didn't like that the chief wanted peace, not war." A lead ball settled in Ridge's stomach. "I could be wrong. I ain't never heard of an Indian turning on his own before, but if Hotah is hell-bent on stirring things up, this is a good way to help it along."

"Maybe Cullen offered him some incentive."

"What kind?"

"Half a dozen repeating rifles and boxes of shells were stolen from the armory the night before Colt was stabbed."

"Shit," Ridge swore. "Those would kill a lot of soldiers and settlers." He stiffened his backbone. "Let's get back to it. If Hotah and Cullen have those rifles, we need to stop them."

Determination driving him, Ridge led the small group of soldiers and hoped he was on the right trail.

EMMA trudged downstairs after trying on her wedding dress for the umpteenth time. This time, however, it fit perfectly, much to her mother's relief. Mrs. Wright was frying chicken and Emma's stomach growled, reminding her she'd eaten little during the day. Between her nightmares and her fear for Ridge with Cullen on the loose, she'd simply been unable to force food into her rebelling stomach.

She entered the front room and found her mother and Sarah with their heads bent over something as they sat on the comfortable sofa.

"What're you doing?" Emma asked.

The two women jumped in guilty surprise and Sarah moved to block her mother from Emma.

"Doing?" Sarah repeated too brightly.

Emma crossed her arms. "What's going on?"

"We have no idea what you mean, dear," her mother said innocently.

Emma suspected it was some surprise for the wedding

tomorrow, and didn't have the heart to spoil it for them. "Where's Chayton?"

"He went out to help Rory," Sarah replied.

"How long ago?"

"A half an hour or so."

"I think I'll go find him and let you two get back to doing nothing." Emma smiled sweetly.

She refrained from laughing at Sarah's loud sigh of relief as she left them to their scheming. Outside, the sun was dropping toward the mountains. It wouldn't be long before twilight came and went, which meant the rising of the full moon. She shivered uncontrollably and wrapped her arms around herself.

Where are you, Ridge? You said you'd be here.

Emma spotted Rory leading a bay gelding that had cut his front right fetlock two days earlier. She was pleased to see the horse's limp was barely noticeable now.

"Rory, have you seen Chayton?" she called out.

The old hostler shook his head. "Ain't seen him since early this afternoon."

"Sarah said he came out here half an hour ago."

"Ain't seen him," he repeated with a frown, a deep crease between his eyebrows. "Check the barn. Maybe he's just playin' with them kittens."

Emma was panting by the time she arrived at the barn and threw open the door. The kittens were nowhere to be seen. Neither was Chayton. Emma's anxiety turned to dread and her heart pounded so hard it made her dizzy.

"He ain't there?" Rory asked, limping up behind her.

"No. Where would he go?" she asked, her voice climbing.

"I'll start lookin' around and as soon as the boys start comin' in, I'll have them help." Rory patted her shoulder awkwardly. "Don't you worry, Miss Emma. He probably just found a new place to play."

Emma managed a nod and raced back to the house. Her cry brought her father out of his office, as well as Sarah and her mother from the parlor.

"Chayton's missing," Emma announced, her voice thready. "Rory hasn't seen him and he's not in the barn. When he's not with Rory and the horses, he likes to play in the barn with the kittens, so I thought he'd be there, but he wasn't." She knew she was rambling, but it was either that or fall apart completely.

"I'll get the men out looking immediately," her father assured, his mouth set in a grim line. "We'll find him, Emma."

He grabbed his hat on the way out the door, his stride purposeful.

"I'm sorry, Emma," Sarah cried. "I should've gone with him and made sure he made it over to Rory."

"I'm sure he'll be fine, Emma," her mother reassured, although her face was wan. "Why, I'll bet they'll find him curled up someplace taking a nap."

"I'm going to change clothes and help look for him," Emma said, her voice stronger.

Without waiting for a reply, Emma flew upstairs and changed into the same split riding skirt and blouse she'd worn that morning to Ridge's. Within ten minutes, she was searching the ground for a sign of a scuffle. Although she wasn't a tracker like Ridge, she'd learned a few things from him and Fast Elk.

Behind the barn Emma found what she was seeking. She called to her father, who joined her. She showed him the marks in the dirt—small boots and a larger set of footprints that weren't boots. Rather, they were moccasins.

Hotah.

Emma swayed and her father caught her arm.

"Emma, are you all right?" he asked, wrapping a steadying arm around her shoulders.

"It was Hotah, the Indian I told you about that Captain Rivers chased away."

"You said he wanted Chayton. Why?"

"He thinks Chayton should grow up to be a Lakota warrior. Hotah never liked me and when I took Chayton away, he must've followed me back here."

Her father scowled. "I'll have one of the men ride to the fort and tell General Mason what happened. He should be able to assign some soldiers to help us search."

Emma nodded absently, wishing with all her heart that Ridge were here. He would be able to make sense of the tracks. Besides, his confident presence would be a balm to her hysteria threatening to escape.

Her father led her back to the barn and joined some of the hired hands who had just returned from the range. Emma waited until his attention was on them and then slipped into the barn to saddle Clementine. A rifle leaned up against a stall and she slid it into the scabbard on the saddle.

She led the mare out the back door of the barn, hidden from the men, and began to follow the faint moccasin prints left behind. It would be night soon and she'd lose the trail in the darkness . . . except there was a full moon. More light. More danger.

Tonight her vision would come to life.

$\mathscr{T}$WENTY-THREE

RIDGE cursed the bad luck that had him arriving at the Hartwell ranch after sunset. As he rode closer, he noticed the activity around the outbuildings and corrals. Lanterns bobbed about, carried by men who appeared to be looking for something.

Looking for what?

He dismounted in front of the house and his blood grew cold when he saw the door standing open. He took the steps with one leap and strode into the foyer.

"Emma! Emma, where are you?" he shouted in the house.

Sarah scurried around the corner, her eyes red-rimmed. "Ridge, I'm so glad you're here."

He grasped her cold hands. "What is it, Sarah? Where's Emma?"

Sarah shook her head, strands of blond hair falling around her face. "We don't know. First it was Chayton, and now Emma's missing, too."

The air in Ridge's lungs whooshed out as if he'd been gut-punched. He led Sarah to the front room and set her down in a chair. "Tell me everything."

Sarah described how Chayton disappeared, then Emma an hour later.

"Who saw Emma last?" Ridge asked, trying to keep his impatience reined in.

"Father, I think."

Ridge turned to leave, but Sarah latched onto his wrist. "Find her and Chayton. Just like you did before," the girl pleaded.

Ridge gave her hand a squeeze and managed a shaky smile. "I will. I promise."

Outside, Ridge found Hartwell saddling up with a dozen hired hands.

"Madoc, I'm glad you're here," Hartwell said with sincere relief. "Emma and Chayton are missing."

"Sarah told me. Were there any tracks?"

"Emma found some. I was getting the men organized to follow them and the next thing I know, she's gone." Hartwell's eyes couldn't hide his grief.

"Show me the tracks."

Two minutes later, Ridge knew. "It was Hotah or Cullen—both of them wear moccasins."

"Emma said it was Hotah," Hartwell said.

Ridge gazed down at the track, noticing it was the smaller of the two moccasin prints he'd been following all day. He nodded. "I think she's right." He pointed to the shod horse's tracks beside it. "And that's Emma's horse. I recognize the chipped shoe on the left rear foot."

"She must be following them herself."

Ridge curled his trembling fingers into his palms. Hotah wouldn't hesitate to take Emma if he knew she was behind them, alone.

Struggling to curb his rage and foreboding, Ridge led the search party through the increasing darkness. He glanced up to catch an eyeful of the full moon, which would give him enough light to follow the trail. It also reminded him of Emma's dream, which was starting to make sense. Hotah was the mountain lion, intent on stealing the cub Chayton.

But who was the eagle? Cullen?

* * *

THE only thing Emma could hear was the pounding of her heart. The nocturnal creatures had gone silent, even the nighthawks that usually began to skirl as soon as it darkened. Emma had managed to keep on the trail, although it was nonexistent in some places. But she'd been able to pick it up again each time, and knew deep down inside that she was on the right track.

An owl hooted and Emma froze, her gaze flitting across the branches of the scrub oak around her. There. Twin orbs reflected golden light.

"Whooo-whoooo."

The owl from her vision. Which meant Chayton was near. She peered through the brush and spotted a dim light—a small campfire. Her pulse doubled and Clementine shied, sensing her nervousness.

"Easy girl," Emma soothed, running a calming hand along the horse's withers.

Emma dismounted and let the reins drop to the ground. Cold fire licked through her veins. She should go back and get her father and the others, but what if Chayton and his kidnapper left? Or she couldn't find her way back?

She would get closer, but not try anything herself. Hotah could easily overpower her, just as the mountain lion overpowered the wolf.

Grabbing the rifle from the boot, Emma crept nearer to the fire, keeping low on the ground and ignoring the scratches from twigs and branches. As she approached, she could see a small bundle lying on the ground. She paused to look more closely and recognized Chayton curled up, his upper body moving up and down with his even breaths. He was probably exhausted.

Biting her lower lip against tears of relief, Emma shimmied closer until she was lying behind a growth of brush and could see Chayton's kidnapper.

Only it wasn't Hotah. It was Cullen's greasy buckskins and long stringy hair.

"Come on out, Emma," Cullen suddenly hollered out. "I know you're there."

Emma's breath caught and her heart skipped a beat, then another. She remained motionless.

"Don't play games. You don't come out, I hurt your bastard." He grabbed Chayton's arm, jerking the boy up and against his chest.

Emma's hands closed on the rifle and she lifted it to her shoulder. Sighting down the barrel, she found Chayton too close to Cullen to risk taking a shot. Her hands shaking, she closed her eyes briefly, her chest squeezing and her mouth desert-dry. She set the rifle on the ground and pushed herself to her feet slowly. "I'm coming. Don't hurt him."

On legs that felt like they belonged to someone else, Emma staggered into the fire's circle of light. She stopped shy of Cullen's reach.

His lecherous gaze roamed over her, making her feel soiled. "Get over here, Emma. I been locked up for four days and I'm hornier'n a toady frog."

Emma felt like throwing up. One glance at his crotch confirmed his words. She stepped back reflexively.

"*Ina?*"

Chayton's frightened voice grabbed her attention and her heart thudded at the lost look on his face. "Yes, Chay, I'm here."

"Home?" he murmured.

"Soon," she promised.

"Don't bet on it." Cullen wrapped his arm around Chayton's small neck.

Emma started toward them. "No! Leave him alone!"

"You don't do as I say, and I'm gonna have to hurt him again."

In the fire's flickering light, she spotted a bruise forming on her son's right cheekbone and a swollen lower lip.

Rage buried her fear. "What did you do to him?"

"Bastard tried to run off after I got rid of Hotah." Cullen laughed, the sound like glass on a blackboard. "Stupid Injun said he had to have the kid before we left the territory.

Threatened to slice my neck iffen I interfered. He's the one who ended up with a knife in the back."

"You murdered Hotah? Just like you tried to kill Captain Rivers."

Cullen shrugged. "The Injun wasn't useful no more. And now I got me six repeatin' rifles to sell. Figure it's a good deal all around."

"Except for Hotah."

"Why're you cryin' over him? He's the one who stole your kid from the ranch. I told him not to bother, but the stubborn redskin didn't listen. And now I got me a kid to sell, too. Too young to bring much, but I'll get somethin' for my time."

Emma's eyes widened and her insides twisted into a knot. What Cullen planned to do was so appalling, so horrible that she was robbed of speech.

"Get over here, Emma. Now!" Cullen tightened his hold around Chayton's neck and the young boy's mouth gaped as he clawed at Cullen's arm. The brute didn't even notice his struggles.

Emma obeyed immediately, falling to her knees beside the foul-smelling Cullen. "I'll do anything you want! Just stop hurting him."

Cullen released Chayton, who dropped to the ground and Emma swooped him into her arms. He was trembling and she could feel his heart pounding in his chest. "Shhhh, it's all right, Chayton. You're safe now."

"Not for long if you don't do like I tell you," Cullen growled.

More terrified for Chayton than herself, she leaned as far away from Cullen as she could and eased her arms away from her son. "Run away," she whispered in his ear. "Find *Leksi*."

As she turned back to Cullen, she heard Chayton scramble to his feet and into the brush.

Cullen roared and jumped up to chase the boy. Emma grabbed one of his legs, unable to trip him, but stopping him from his pursuit. Cruel fingers twisted in her hair and tugged her to her feet. Tears filled Emma's eyes, but as long as Cullen was busy with her, the more time Chayton had to escape.

"You'll pay for that, squaw woman." He backhanded her and the world spun crazily, nearly driving her to unconsciousness. She struggled to clear her muddled thoughts as her cheek throbbed from the blow.

She had no illusions about what he planned for her, and she knew without a doubt the mountain lion would beat the wolf. But what of the eagle?

RIDGE cursed as he rolled the body over. Hotah. He'd been killed by a knife to the back—same method Cullen had tried with Colt. But this time he'd succeeded.

"Who is it?" Hartwell asked from atop his horse.

"Hotah."

"The one Emma thought kidnapped Chayton?"

"The same."

"Who—?"

"Probably Cullen. Double-crossed Hotah." Ridge rubbed his brow, wishing he could press the ache away. It robbed him of his usual alertness and made him impatient, tense, and he needed his wits if he was to find Emma and Chayton. "Have one of your men take the body back."

Hartwell's frown was evident in the moon's glow. "I'm not going to send a man back who can help search."

"Look, Hartwell, the trail pretty much ends here. Between what little light we got and the rocks, we ain't going to be picking up a trail until morning." Although Ridge fully intended to remain searching for Emma and Chayton, he figured a dozen men bumping into each other in the dark would only hinder him.

"I'm not leaving my daughter and grandson out there with a murderer."

Ridge's irritation was diminished by Hartwell's concern for both Emma and Chayton. "I don't want to do it anymore than you do, but we don't have a choice unless we just want to stumble around blind."

"We can split up, each man taking a section. If someone finds Emma, it'll be two shots; Chayton, three."

Although Hartwell's suggestion was like shooting fish in an ocean, Ridge reckoned it was better than doing nothing and he wouldn't be saddled with a crowd trailing after him. He nodded. "We'll do it your way. Just make sure your men go slow and easy."

Hartwell seemed surprised by Ridge's acquiescence. "All right."

After giving the orders to his men and having one of them take Hotah's body back, Hartwell turned back to Ridge. "Good luck, Madoc."

Ridge nodded once. He listened to the men move away, keeping their horses to a walk. He climbed back into Paint's saddle and patted the horse's neck. "Let's go find 'em, fella."

Paint snorted and they continued the search. Half an hour later, Ridge removed his hat and raked his hand through his hair in frustration. He might as well be riding in circles for all the good he was doing. He hadn't caught a glimpse of anything remotely resembling a trail.

With Hotah dead, why had Cullen kept Chayton? The scout had wanted Emma at one time, but not her boy. Unless he had some use for him.

What if Cullen had both Emma and Chayton? After seeing how Cullen treated his squaw, Ridge knew what awaited Emma. Loathing surged up from his belly. He couldn't stop. He had to find them.

The rustle of an owl's wings caused Ridge to swivel in his saddle. He spied the large bird flying between a patch of scrub oak to land on a high branch. A chill settled down Ridge's spine and he urged Paint forward, toward the tree where the owl perched. As soon as Ridge neared it, the owl leapt from the branch, opened its wings and dipped past Ridge to fly ahead.

Without hesitation, Ridge urged Paint after the owl. He wasn't certain he believed Emma's dream visions, but he did believe in his gut, and it told him to follow the owl. Twice Ridge thought he lost the bird of prey, but the owl reappeared in front of him both times. Afraid to think about it too much, Ridge just concentrated on keeping it in sight.

Finally, the owl landed on another scrub oak and began to preen itself. Ridge stood in his stirrups and looked around the silver-gilded wilderness. A light flickered in the distance. Ridge urged Paint on once more, until he came to another horse, saddled and ground-reined. He dismounted and examined the mare closer. Clementine.

A woman's cry broke the silence. Cold fire froze Ridge's blood and he shoved through the underbrush toward the camp. One look told him everything: Emma, trying to kick and claw Cullen as the son of a bitch ripped at her clothes.

Ridge charged toward them.

AN eagle's scream froze Emma. For a split second, Emma stared into the black eyes of a sharp-taloned eagle as it dove toward them. Then the eagle was gone and in its stead was Ridge, colliding with Cullen. The villain released her as he tried to defend himself and Emma rolled away. Terror pumped blood through her veins as she scuttled backward on her hands and knees.

Her breath came in fast, jerky gasps as she watched Ridge and Cullen roll around on the ground. Ridge landed a fist in Cullen's face. The taller man barely flinched and brought up his knee between Ridge's legs. Ridge rolled away, grimacing and panting. Cullen jumped up and attacked Ridge with a roar of fury. Ridge bounced to his feet and spun away, causing the other man to pause.

Ridge delivered a right punch, then a left. The first snapped Cullen's head back and the second sent him staggering backward. Ridge followed him, pressing his advantage with a blow to Cullen's belly. The murderer doubled over and Ridge moved in again, but pulled up sharply when Cullen straightened, holding a knife in his right hand. Emma was certain it was the same one used to wound Colt and kill Hotah.

Cullen swung the blade at him and Ridge sucked in his gut as he jumped back. The knife's tip barely missed him. Cullen tried again, but Ridge grabbed the wrist of Cullen's hand holding the knife. His face reddened as he struggled to force Cullen to drop the weapon. Cullen brought up his other hand and slugged Ridge in the face, but Ridge managed to hold onto Cullen's wrist.

Ridge hooked a leg behind Cullen's and shoved, tumbling the two men to the ground. The knife disappeared between their bodies and Emma struggled to her feet, her lungs fighting for air. She had to do something. Cullen could kill Ridge.

Suddenly the two men froze in a tableau of shock, then they both collapsed, Ridge on top of Cullen. They lay still and silent.

A scream crawled up Emma's throat and she swallowed once, twice to stifle it. She staggered over to them and fell to her knees, her hand hovering an inch above Ridge's back.

"Ridge?" she whispered.

A movement, then a groan and Ridge rolled off Cullen. There was a circle of scarlet blood on Ridge's shirtfront and Emma trembled with horror.

"It's not mine, Emma," he reassured her.

She stared at him, trying to comprehend his words.

Ridge sat up, but didn't touch her. "It's not my blood. It's Cullen's."

Emma's gaze shifted to Cullen's motionless body. "H-he's dead?"

"Yeah."

Emma tugged her ripped blouse tight across her breasts and satisfaction brought her chin up. "Good. I'm glad."

Ridge helped her to her feet and led her away from the

body, ensuring her back was to the grisly sight. "Are you all right? Did he—"

Emma shook her head, her own shock dissipating as the shakes settled in. "No. He wanted to. Tried to. But you got here before—"

Her shoulders shuddered as the sobs she'd been restraining broke free. Ridge enfolded her in his arms, smoothing a hand up and down her back. "It's all over now, Emma. He can't hurt you or Chayton anymore."

She jerked up. "Chayton. Did you find him?"

"No. Where is he?"

"I t-told him to run . . . I d-distracted Cullen. I told him to find you," she stammered out. "He's out there all alone."

As if in reply, three gunshots sounded, breaking the night's stillness. Ridge's smile was brilliant in the moonlight. "Someone just found Chayton. Three shots was the signal for him."

Hope flooded through Emma, replacing her despair. "Who?"

"Your father has most of his men out looking for you and Chayton. I lost Cullen's trail about an hour ago and we split up. The signals were three shots when Chayton was found, and two for you." Ridge brushed her cheek with his fingertips. "I suppose I'd better signal them."

With the danger gone and Chayton safe, Emma slumped against Ridge in exhaustion. "Could we maybe wait a few minutes? I'd like to be able to stand on my own when they get here."

"Anything you want, Emma. Anything you want," Ridge whispered, holding her close.

Emma wrapped her arms around Ridge's waist, reveling in the scent and feel of him. After Cullen's obscene pawings, Ridge's gentleness was seductive yet calming.

"An owl brought me to you," Ridge said after some moments of companionable silence.

Emma drew away from him, but stayed close enough to remain in his embrace. "My dream." She smiled gently. "You were the fearless eagle."

"I don't know about fearless," Ridge said with a wry chuckle. "I was plenty scared for you." He framed her face in his palms. "You could've been killed."

"But I wasn't." Emma took a deep breath and smiled, giddy with relief. "And I still have a chance to make you fall in love with me."

Ridge swallowed hard. "Colt asked me the other night if I loved you. I told him I didn't know, that I'd never been in love before so didn't know what it felt like." Naked devotion shown in his deep, dark blue eyes. "I think I figured it out."

Emma's heart soared and her voice trembled as she spoke the words she'd hidden away for so long. "I love you."

"And I love you, Emma Louise Hartwell." Ridge lowered his mouth to hers, teasing her lips open with the tip of his tongue.

Joy bubbled through her until she could no longer contain it and she broke away from Ridge's too-tempting lips, smiling. "If we don't signal them, we may not get to it until morning and my mother will have a fit. All her wedding plans would be totally ruined."

Ridge laughed. "Your family's going to take some getting used to."

"But it's going to be all right."

Ridge's amusement faded. "Things will be far from perfect, Emma, but we'll have each other and your family, plus some good friends. We'll carve out a home for us."

"I'm not worried. As long as I have you and Chayton, I'll be home."

ALTHOUGH the ranch yard was far from overflowing with guests, those who attended were genuinely happy for Emma and Ridge. Among them were most of the ranch hands; General Mason; the hardware store owner Howard Freeman, his wife and daughter; Gertrude Manning, who couldn't stop apologizing and promised a free meal the next time they were in town; Lieutenant Pres Wylie,

Sergeant Gabe Sanders, and the newly promoted Major Rivers, who managed not to pass out during the ceremony; and a handful of other townsfolk who went out of their way to tell Ridge and Emma they were more than welcome in their homes and businesses. The banker and his son were even there, although Emma suspected it was more her father's threat to take all his money elsewhere than well wishes toward the bride and groom that had them in attendance.

Smiling, Emma adjusted the wildflower garland perched on her head—a surprise from Sarah and her mother—and watched Chayton play with George and Sally Orton's children. Emma knew there would be hard times ahead, but she was also confident the good would outweigh them.

Arms came around her waist from behind and lips pressed against her ear. "A penny for your thoughts," Ridge whispered.

Emma leaned back and clasped his hands. "They're not worth nearly that much." He huffed a laugh and warm air wafted across her neck. She shivered and told her body to behave. She watched Sarah, her cheeks pink and her eyes glowing, lean close to Colt Rivers. "Did you notice how Sarah is hovering around Colt?"

"And that Colt doesn't mind her hovering?"

Emma laughed. "It's too bad he's not resigning his commission."

"He would've if General Mason hadn't talked him into accepting a staff position."

"The promotion was an added incentive, too."

Ridge nodded. "The army needs more officers like him."

Someone cleared his throat behind them and they turned as one to face John Hartwell, who had an amused glint in his eyes. Ridge kept his arm around Emma's waist as he nodded at his new father-in-law. "Hartwell."

The older man flinched slightly. "Since we're related now, you could call me John."

Ridge smiled wryly. "That'll take some getting used to."

Her father chuckled. "I imagine it will . . . Ridge." He withdrew an envelope from his suitcoat pocket and handed it to his son-in-law.

"What's this?"

"A wedding present."

Frowning, Emma watched Ridge open the envelope flap and withdraw an official looking piece of paper that read *Certificate of Deed* at the top. Ridge glanced at her, a question in his eyes. Although he was learning to read, the progress was slow and vexing. She skimmed the form and her eyes widened.

"He's deeded back all the acres he bought from your stepfather," Emma announced. "And a hundred more, for a total of five hundred acres."

Ridge caught his breath and his gaze shot to the older man. "Why?"

Her father straightened his shoulders and met Ridge's gaze. "I was wrong to cheat him out of that land and I apologize." He held out his hand.

Emma held her breath as Ridge stared at it for a long moment. Then he reached out and clasped her father's hand in a firm grip.

"Thank you, Hart—John," Ridge said with a genuine smile.

The older man turned an affectionate gaze to Emma. "Thank your wife. She's an extraordinary woman."

Emma's eyes filled with tears, and she kissed her father's cheek and hugged him. "Thank you," she whispered.

She released him and stepped back into Ridge's waiting arms.

"I'd best go ask your mother to dance or I'll never hear the end of it," her father said with a wink.

Emma followed his progress through the small throng and smiled as he whisked her mother into his arms.

"Did I tell you about my dream last night?" Emma asked, watching her parents dance.

Ridge's eyes widened slightly as he shook his head.

"There was a female wolf and four young cubs curled

up beside her, with an eagle perched above them, guarding them while they slept."

Ridge appeared dazed. "Four?"

"Too many?"

He gazed down at her affectionately. "Not nearly enough, Emma Madoc."

She grinned. "Then we'll have to work on that."

He wrapped her in his strong arms and kissed her tenderly.